WE KNOW YOU REMEMBER

A NOVEL

TOVE ALSTERDAL

ENGLISH TRANSLATION BY ALICE MENZIES

faber

First published in the UK in 2022
by Faber & Faber Ltd
Bloomsbury House
74–77 Great Russell Street,
London WC1B 3DA

This export edition first published in 2022

First published in the USA in 2021
by HarperCollins Publishers
195 Broadway
New York NY10007

Originally published as *Rotvälta* in Sweden in 2020 by Lind & Co.

Printed and bound by CPI Group (UK) Ltd, Croydon CR0 4YY

A CIP record for this book
is available from the British Library

ISBN 978–0–571–36891–4

10 9 8 7 6 5 4 3 2 1

WE KNOW YOU REMEMBER

Tove Alsterdal is one of Sweden's most renowned suspense writers. She has written five critically acclaimed stand-alone thrillers and has won literary prizes in Sweden and France. *We Know You Remember* was named Best Swedish Crime Novel of the Year in 2020 and was awarded the Glass Key Award for the Best Nordic Crime Novel in 2021.

WE KNOW YOU REMEMBER

There it was, the looming shadow of the mountains. A petrol station flashed by out of the corner of his eye, followed by yet more trees. He'd needed to pee for over two hundred kilometers by then.

He pulled off onto a side road and stumbled out of the car, through the wildflowers on the verge. Turned towards the forest and relieved himself.

There was something about the scents. The flowers along the edge of the ditch. The dew in the grass and the haze in the evening air, the buttercups and fireweed and cow parsley, standing a meter tall. Or maybe it was timothy grass, what did he know. He just recognized the smell.

The tarmac was bumpy with frost damage, and soon gave over to gravel. He could take a left in twenty or so kilometers and be back on the highway; it wasn't a big detour. The landscape opened out in front of him, green hills and low valleys. There was something comforting about it, like the gentle curves of a soft, warm woman's body.

He drove past sleepy farms and abandoned houses, a small lake so calm that the reflection of the forest looked just like the forest itself. Each tree identical to the next. He had once climbed a mountain and looked down at the endless forests of the Ådalen Valley, realized they went on forever.

There were no other cars around when he reached the fork in the road. He recognized the yellow wooden building straight ahead. These days all he could see through its dusty display window were piles of construction waste, but the sign was still there; the shop had once sold food. Olof remembered sweets on a Saturday, the taste of jelly frogs and salty licorice fish. He turned the wrong way, heading farther inland. He would still be able to reach the northern fringes of Stockholm before morning. Besides, the boss would be asleep; no one would check the mileage or the exact amount of petrol he'd used. Another five kilometers was no big deal. Olof could always blame the caravans and roadworks; everyone knew what the Swedish roads were like during the summer.

At this time of year. Late June.

The scents, the light, they made his mouth turn dry and his legs go numb. Every fiber of his being knew it was that time of year. After term had ended and the boredom took over, the longest days, when he was thrown out of sync. Olof remembered it as a grayish half-darkness, though it must have been just as bright as now, an endless summer night, pale midnight hours when the sun simply dipped below the horizon.

He drove past things he had long forgotten or simply never thought about. Yet they had been there all along. The yellow house that always had guests in the summer, their children forbidden from cycling on the main road. The old schoolhouse, closed down before he could remember; the fields where the trotter horses huddled together, staring at the road. The white plastic bales of hay, you could climb on top of those and pretend to be king of the hill; and there was the weeping birch on the left, where he slowed down and turned off. It had grown so big. Branches bowed low, clouds of vivid green leaves hiding the letter boxes.

He knew exactly which one it was: gray plastic, the third along. There was a newspaper sticking out of it. Olof hauled himself out of the car and walked over to check the name.

Hagström.

He swatted at the mosquitoes and pulled out the local newspaper. There were another two beneath it, hence why it didn't quite fit. Ads for fiber broadband, a bill from Kramfors Council. Someone still lived there, received post and newspapers; someone was still paying for the water and to have the bins emptied, or whatever else the bill might be for. Olof felt a shiver pass through him as he read the name on the envelope.

Sven Hagström.

He shoved everything back into the letter box and returned to the car. Grabbed a chocolate biscuit from the bag on the floor, just for something to chew on. He knocked back a can of energy drink and killed the mosquitoes that had followed him in. One had already drunk its fill, and a fleck of red spread across the leather seat. He rubbed it away with some spit and toilet paper, then continued slowly along the old tractor road. The grass in the middle brushed against the bumper, and the car bounced through one pothole after another. Past the Strinneviks' place, their gray barn visible among the greenery. Down one hill and then up again, he reached the top, where the dark pines ended and nature seemed to open out onto the river and beyond. Olof didn't dare look. The red house flashed by at the edge of his field of vision. He turned at the end of the road and slowly drove back.

The paint around the windows was peeling. He couldn't see a car, but it could easily be in the garage. The grass was tall around the woodshed, dotted with small saplings that would soon turn to brush.

Olof didn't know why he had expected it to be any different: abandoned and dilapidated, or sold to strangers who had since moved in.

And yet, it wasn't.

He pulled over behind the bin and switched off the engine. Golden dandelions studded the lawn. He remembered how hard they were to pull up. You had to get rid of them before they went to seed, otherwise they would spread in the wind. Use a hoe to dig down to the roots so they wouldn't come back. In his memory, his hands were so small. He looked down at the broad hand that should have been turning the ignition key now.

The sun rose above the tops of the spruce trees, its rays hitting the rearview mirror and blinding him. He closed his eyes and pictured her in front of him, or inside him, he couldn't quite tell where she was, but that was how he had seen her over and over again, night after night through all these years, whenever he didn't doze off immediately, blind drunk or exhausted, half-dead, that was how he always saw her, walking into the forest. She wandered in and out of him. So close, not far from there, down towards the river.

That look as she turns onto the trail. Is she smiling at him? Did she just wave? Come on then, Olof! Come on! Was that really to him?

Then their voices are all around him, the tang of petrol from their souped-up mopeds, cigarette smoke keeping the mosquitoes at bay.

Seriously, Olof, you're practically in already. Go after her. Lina's no tease. Come on, man, you can see she wants it. Maybe he's a fag? Are you a fag, Olof? Have you ever even kissed a girl, or just your mum?

Come on, Olof! You've never done it, have you? Just get your hand under her top, do it all quick, that's what you need to do, get them horny before they have time to think too much.

Their voices are still in his head as he walks along the trail. Her skirt flutters up ahead, her yellow cardigan between the tree trunks.

Lina.

Velvety smooth arms, laughing, nettle scented, burning tangles around his calves, clouds of mosquitoes and bastard horseflies, blood on her arm where he squashed a horsefly, pow, just like that, and her laughter, Thanks Olof, my hero. There are her lips, right up close. He imagines how soft they must be, like moss, damp, sinking, sucking him in. Tongue in before she has time to speak, he hears them say. Some just want to talk all night, but watch out for that, you'll end up in the friend zone. Nope, get your hands on her boobs, squeeze 'em and play with 'em, they like it when you suck on their tits, you do that and you're home free, I swear, just don't fucking hesitate, girls learn all that shit about saying no and keeping their legs together even though they're wet and horny and dream about it too, but you can't just pound away at them; you've got to do it their way. Fingers in, poke her pussy, then go full throttle, pedal to the metal, yeah?

Suddenly Olof is falling headlong into the nettles and he feels her all around him.

There was no air in the car, just humidity and heat. He had to get out.

Thin veils of mist swept over the bay down below. On the other side of the river, the eternal mountains loomed in the distance, columns of steam rising from the paper mill. It was so quiet he could hear the leaves of the aspen trees rustling in a breeze so soft he couldn't feel it, the buzz of the bees toiling away on the lupins and mayweed. Then he heard the whimpering. Pitiful, as though it was being made by something that was injured, unhappy.

It was coming from inside the house. Olof tried to cover the short distance back to the car without making a sound, before the dog noticed him, but that was impossible with a body like his; the grass and twigs broke under his weight. He could hear his own heavy breathing over the buzzing of the insects, and the dog could too. It started barking like crazy. Howling and scratching, throwing itself against the wall or the door. The sound made him think of the wild barks of the hunting dogs, the way they leapt at the mesh in their cages when you cycled by. The police dogs. When they were brought down to the river to track Lina's scent, their distant barks when they found her things.

He knew he should get back in the car and drive away, fast, before the old man woke up and saw someone outside. Would he grab his hunting rifle, the one Olof had been allowed to hold, the one he was never old enough to fire? Colors and furniture tumbled around in his memory. The painted green stairs, the floral pattern on the wallpaper, his old bed beneath the sloping roof.

Then he saw the water, trickling slowly down the side of the house. Had one of the pipes sprung a leak? And why was the dog shut in? Olof could hear that it wasn't in the hall by the front door, the natural place for a hunting dog, for any dog; the sound was farther back. Possibly in the kitchen, at the far end of the hallway. Olof pictured pale blue panels, white-painted cabinets, something cooking slowly on the hob.

The dog must be home alone. Surely no one could sleep that deeply.

His thoughts turned to the rock, the round one, by the corner of the house. A couple of wood lice scuttled away as he picked it up. The key was still there.

His hand was shaking so much that pushing it into the lock proved difficult. Olof had no right to unlock the door. *You should know that they have declined all contact.*

The particular scent of the house hit him, a sense of being a child again. The painting of the old man with a big mustache that used to look down at him from the wall, some prime minister from a hundred years ago, was now at eye level. And there was the bench with the cushion where they took off their shoes, the rag rugs his grandmother had weaved. They were barely visible beneath the things dumped all over the place, tools and equipment leaving only a narrow passageway down the hall, bags of empty cans and bottles. His mother never would have allowed the place to get into this state.

He heard claws scrabbling against wood. Olof had been right: the dog was shut in the kitchen, a broom wedged against the door. No one should be allowed to do that to a dog, he knew that much, despite the tangle of thoughts swirling through his mind.

He yanked the broom away and took cover behind the door as he turned the handle. Broom still in hand, in case he needed to ward off the dog's jaws. But it shot straight past him, a black blur, darting outside. The stench of urine and shit followed it out, awful, the poor bastard had made a real mess in there.

That was when he noticed the water coming from the bathroom. It was seeping out beneath the door, washing over the rag rugs in the living room and forming small rivers and lakes on the brown linoleum floor.

The little indicator on the lock was white, not red, as it was when someone was in the bathroom. Olof had learned to lock himself in there with his comics. That was what you had to do when you had an annoying older sister screaming to let her in.

He opened the door and the water surged out over his shoes.

There was a sponge floating inside, dirt and loose hair, dead flies. The striped shower curtain was closed, and Olof felt the cold water seep through his socks as he stepped into the room. He could do that, if nothing else: try to turn off the water before he left, so the house wouldn't be completely ruined. He pulled back the curtain.

There was someone sitting behind it. A crooked body slumped in an unfamiliar chair. Olof knew what he was looking at, but he couldn't quite process it. The old man was hunched over, completely white. In the sunlight filtering through the window, his skin seemed to glisten like the scales of a fish. Tendrils of wet hair were plastered across his scalp. Olof managed to take another step forward to reach the knob, and the water finally stopped flowing.

Other than his own hoarse breathing and the flies buzzing against the windowpane, he couldn't hear a sound. The last few drops of water. The naked body seemed to draw his gaze, holding it firmly. The man's skin seemed loose somehow, with greenish patches across his back. Gripping the handbasin, Olof leaned in. He couldn't see the man's eyes, but his prominent nose had a bump in the middle, an old bandy injury from his youth. He saw the man's penis, crooked as a worm between his legs.

Then the handbasin came loose from the wall. A deafening crash, as though the house itself were falling down, and he lost his balance. Splashed around, hitting his head on the washing machine, slipping when he tried to get up.

Crawling on all fours, he managed to leave the bathroom and struggle to his feet.

Out of there.

He slammed the door behind him and locked up. Put the key back where he had found it and walked towards the car as quickly and as normally as he could. He started the engine and put it into reverse, ramming into the bin.

Plenty of old people died like that, he thought as he pulled away, his heart still beating so hard he could hear it thundering in his ears. They had a heart attack or a stroke and then just keeled over and died. The police wouldn't care. A lot of them live alone, some aren't found until years later.

But why had he shut the dog in?

Olof slammed on the brakes. There it was, right in front of him, standing in the middle of the road. Another ten meters and he would have flattened the stupid thing. Mouth open, tongue lolling out, shaggy and excited and jet black. It looked like the product of some kind of wild dalliance in the woods, with the head of a Labrador and the coat of an overgrown terrier, ears standing to attention.

Olof revved the engine. He had to deliver the car, a beautiful Pontiac, a real find; it needed to be parked outside the boss's garage by morning, the key hidden in the usual place.

But the dog wasn't moving.

If he blasted the horn, the neighbors might have heard it and put two and two together, so instead he got out and shooed it. The dog glared at him.

"Get out of the way, you stupid bastard," he hissed, throwing a stick at it. The dog caught it midair and bounded forward, dropping it by his feet and wagging its entire rear end as though it thought life were some kind of damn game. Olof hurled the stick as far as he could into the woods, and the dog charged after it through the bilberry bushes. He was just about to climb back into the car when he heard footsteps on the gravel behind him.

"Nice ride," a voice called out. "Not exactly what you expect to see out here in the sticks."

Olof saw a man approaching with fast, light steps. He was wearing a pair of long shorts and a polo shirt, white canvas shoes. He patted the black lid of the boot as though it were a horse.

"Trans Am third generation, right?"

Olof had frozen with one foot in the car, the other on the road.

"Mmm, an eighty-eight," he mumbled into the paintwork. "It's heading to Stockholm, Upplands Bro." He wanted to say that he was in a hurry, that he had to get going before the summer traffic built up; it was Midsummer's Eve, a Friday, meaning there would be queues in every direction, and on top of that there were warnings about roadworks and lane closures between Hudiksvall and Gävle. But he couldn't get the words to come out. The dog had also returned with the stick, nudging him with its nose.

"So it's not for sale?"

"It's not mine. I'm just driving it."

"And you ended up here?"

The man was smiling, but Olof could hear what lay behind his voice, behind his smile. There was always something else there.

"Just needed to take a leak."

"And you chose this road? Sorry for asking, but we've had a bit of trouble in the past—gangs of thieves scoping out the cabins. The neighbor down there had his lawn mower stolen. We all try to keep an eye out. For strange cars, that kind of thing."

The dog had sniffed out his food, and was attempting to get into the car between his legs. The dirt in the kitchen flashed through his mind, the cartons scattered across the floor. It must have fought its way into the cupboards trying to find something to eat.

Olof grabbed it by the scruff of its neck, making it growl and squirm.

"Is it yours?"

"No, I . . . It was in the middle of the road."

"Hang on, isn't that Sven Hagström's dog?" The man turned around and peered up towards the house, still visible among the trees. "Is he home?"

Olof struggled with the words. The truth. The shower running and running, the pale skin dissolving before his eyes. The key beneath the rock. He cleared his throat and gripped the car door.

"Sven's dead." Something inside him shifted, contracting his throat as he spoke, like tying a knot and pulling it tight. He knew he had to say something else, because the man was now backing away from him, staring at the number plate. Olof saw he had a phone in his hand.

"The key was under the rock," he managed to blurt out. "I wanted to let the dog out . . . I was just driving by."

"And who are you?" The man was holding his phone out in front of him. Olof heard a click, then another. Was he taking photos of the car, of him?

"I'm calling," he said. "I'm calling the police right now."

"He's my dad. Sven Hagström."

The man glanced down at the dog and then up at Olof. His eyes seemed to bore beneath the layers of the person he had become.

"Olof? You're Olof Hagström?"

"I was going to call, but . . ."

"My name's Patrik Nydalen," the man told him, backing away again. "You might not remember me, I'm Tryggve and Mejan's son, from up there." He pointed along the road, towards a house farther back among the trees. Olof couldn't see it, but he knew it appeared in a clearing when you walked along the snowmobile trail. "I can't say I remember you, but I was only five or six when . . ."

In the silence that followed, Olof could see the cogs turning in his blond head, the flicker in his eyes as the memories returned. Everything he had been told over the years.

"Maybe you should tell them what happened yourself," he continued. "I'll dial the number and pass the phone to you, OK?" The man held out the phone to him, stretching his arm as far as he could. "It's my personal phone. But I have my work phone on me too, I always do."

The dog was now in the car, nose deep in his bag of food, rooting around in it.

"Or I can call them myself," said Patrik Nydalen, backing up again.

Olof slumped into the driver's seat. He remembered a couple of little kids up at the Nydalen homestead. Didn't they have rabbits, in a cage behind the house? Olof had snuck over and opened it one summer night, luring them out with dandelion leaves. Maybe the fox had caught them.

Or maybe they were finally free.

With its beautiful traditions of leaf-clad maypoles, nonstop drinking, violence, and abuse, Midsummer's Eve was possibly the worst day of the year to be at work.

Eira Sjödin had volunteered to take the shift on the brightest of Swedish nights. Her colleagues needed the time off more than she did, people with kids and that kind of thing.

"Are you leaving already?" Her mother followed her out into the hallway, hands wandering, picking up whatever happened to be lying on top of the chest of drawers.

"I have to go to work, Mum, I told you. Have you seen the car keys?"

"When are you coming back?"

Shoehorn in one hand, a glove in the other.

"Tonight, but late."

"You don't have to come running over here all the time, you know. I'm sure you have better things to be doing."

"I live here now, Mum, remember?"

The conversation was followed by a frantic search for the keys Kerstin Sjödin insisted she hadn't moved—"You can't claim I've forgotten when I know I haven't touched them"—until Eira eventually found them in her own back pocket, where she had left them the night before.

A pat on the cheek.

"We can celebrate tomorrow, Mum. With herring and strawberries."

"And a nice glass of schnapps."

"And some schnapps."

Fourteen degrees, a thin layer of cloud overhead. The radio forecast was promising sun across the whole of central Norrland; it would be glorious drinking weather by the afternoon. The aquavit would already be chilling in every house she passed, in Lunde and Frånö and Gudmunrå, in the summerhouses people returned to for generation after generation, in coolers at the campsites.

The car park outside the police station in Kramfors was half-empty. Most of the force had been concentrated onto the evening shift.

One of Eira's young colleagues met her in the entrance.

"We've been called out," he said. "Suspicious death, an elderly man in Kungsgården."

Eira glanced down at the name badge on his chest. She had said hello to him the previous day, but they had never worked the same shift before.

"The old man must've collapsed in the shower," he continued, eyes on the report from the control center in Umeå. "It was his son who found him, a neighbor called it in."

"Sounds like something for the care system," said Eira. "Why have we been called out?"

"Ambiguities. Apparently the son was about to clear off."

Eira ran inside to get changed. August Engelhardt, that was it. Yet another newly qualified rookie with a short back and sides, a sweeping fringe at the front. Barely a day over twenty-seven, and looked like he worked out. The kind of police officers you saw on TV, who worked together year after year, seemed more like a fantasy than anything else, a relic of a bygone era.

In reality people graduated from the police academy in Umeå and then fought for the jobs there. They applied to unappealing districts like Kramfors in an attempt to gain experience, staying for a maximum of six months. Drove the 250 kilometers home each weekend until something better turned up in the regional capital, with its cafés and vegan restaurants. This particular kid was different in that he had studied down south. They rarely ever got anyone from Stockholm.

"I've got a girlfriend down there, too," he explained as they turned off through Nyland. Eira saw the clocks on the tower above the former courthouse which had stopped at different times, each one facing a different direction. At least it was right four times a day.

"We bought a flat, but I want to work in the inner city," August continued. "So I can cycle to work and that kind of thing. And avoid having someone slam a rock into my head when I get out of the car. I thought I might as well come out here to work for a while, until a position opens up."

"And take it easy, you mean?"

"Yeah, why not?"

He hadn't noticed the sarcasm in her voice. Eira had worked in Stockholm for four years after graduation, and had a rose-tinted memory of constantly being surrounded by colleagues. If you called for backup, they were there within minutes.

She took the Hammar Bridge over the river, turning downstream towards Kungsgården. This side of the river was home to the Ådalen river valley's farmland. Eira unconsciously found herself searching for the hill with the stick rising from the top of it.

Her father had once pointed it out, the site of the most northerly royal estate in the fourteenth century, back when the sea levels were six meters higher and the hills all around them were small islands. She occasionally managed to catch a glimpse of the stick before it merged with the rest of the landscape. This was how far Swedish royal power had stretched back then, no farther.

But to the north, wilderness and freedom reigned.

The story was on the tip of Eira's tongue, but she managed to stop herself in time. It was bad enough that she was always the older officer at the age of just thirty-two; she didn't need to become the person who told stories about every stick and rock they passed, too.

The letter boxes appeared on the side of the road, and Eira turned abruptly, braking in the gravel.

There was something about this place, an immediate feeling of familiarity. A forest road like hundreds of others, with weeds poking up in the middle. Rough tire tracks in the compressed clay, studded with gravel laid years earlier, flattened pine cones, and last year's leaves. An unremarkable house hidden from the road, the remains of an old barn at the edge of the trees.

Eira had a strong sense of having cycled here with one of her friends, probably Stina. She hadn't thought about her in years, but suddenly it felt like she was right by her side. The tense silence as they pedaled up to the tangled forest, the breathlessness, something forbidden.

"I don't think I caught the name," she said. "What's he called?"

"Patrik Nydalen." August peered down at his phone, searching the report. "That's who called it in. The dead man is Sven Hagström."

Right there, behind those first few trees: that was where they had hidden their bikes. Tall, powerful spruces, an area of forest that had never been cleared. A suspense she almost couldn't bear, heart in her throat.

"And the son?" she asked, breathless. "The one who was trying to leave?"

"Yeah, what was his name? It's here somewhere . . . actually, no it's not."

Eira hit the wheel. Once, twice.

"Why didn't anyone notice? Doesn't anyone bloody remember anything?"

"Sorry, you've lost me. What am I supposed to have noticed?"

"Not you. I know you don't know anything." Eira let the car roll forward again, unbearably slowly, the forest creeping closer, a deep and ancient darkness. The kid beside her had probably been crawling around in nappies when it happened. Every blue-light case in Norrland went through the regional control center in Umeå these days, and had done so for the past few years. She couldn't expect them to remember a twenty-year-old case from Ångermanland at the drop of a hat.

Particularly not since his name had never been made public.

"It might not be anything," she said.

"What? What might?"

Eira glanced among the trees. Rocks covered in moss, bilberry bushes, they had crept through here, she and Stina, bent double, along the game trails leading up to the house. Ducking beneath branches to get a glimpse of it. To see where someone like that could live.

The years rattled through her head, quick calculations. Twenty-three years had passed. Olof Hagström was now thirty-seven, and waiting somewhere at the top of this hill—assuming the report was correct.

Eira swerved to avoid a pothole, hit a rock instead.

"Olof Hagström committed a serious crime a long time ago," she said. "He confessed to rape and murder."

"Oh wow," said August Engelhardt. "So has he served his sentence now? I agree, they should've picked up on that at control."

"It's not on his record, he was never convicted. It didn't even go to trial. His name was never published anywhere; the press didn't do that kind of thing back then."

"And when was this, the Stone Age?"

"He was a minor," Eira explained. "He was only fourteen."

The case had been closed and the record sealed, but everyone knew whose boy it was—right across Ådalen, from the High Coast to a good way up to Sollefteå, in all likelihood. "The fourteen-year-old," as the press had called him. It had been investigated and solved; it was over. The kids were allowed to play outside on their own again. He had been sent away, which meant they were free to duck beneath branches and spy on the house where he had once lived. See his sister sunbathing in the garden, the bike with the crossbar that must have been his, a killer's bedroom window. Everything that could have gone on inside.

I can't believe it looks like any other house.

Eira drove up onto the property and came to a halt.

One of thousands of simple timber houses slowly worn down by the elements, by a lack of the attention and care needed in the forest, red wood turning gray, flaking white paint at the corners.

"It might not be relevant," she said. "The cause of death could be perfectly natural."

A small group of people had gathered by a cairn on the other side of the gravel track. A youngish couple, somewhere around thirty. Dressed like summer visitors—a little too much white, a little too expensive. The woman was sitting on a boulder, and the man was standing so close that their relationship couldn't be anything other than intimate. A few meters away from them was a stocky older man in a fleece and a pair of trousers that had slipped low on his hips. He seemed uncomfortable to be standing still. Definitely a permanent resident.

Up ahead, on the driveway by the garage: a flashy black American car. There was a large man slumped back in the driver's seat. He looked like he was sleeping.

"You took your time."

The man in white peeled away from the group and came forward to meet them, shaking their hands and introducing himself. Patrik Nydalen, he was the one who had made the call. Eira didn't need to ask him to take her through what had happened in detail; he did it voluntarily.

They were staying next door for the summer—Patrik pointed up the road—he was born and raised there but didn't know Hagström particularly well. Neither did his wife. Sofi Nydalen got up from the rock. Slender hand, anxious smile.

The older neighbor shook his head. He didn't know Sven Hagström well either, not really, no. They spoke whenever their paths crossed at the letter boxes; both helped keep the road clear in the winter.

As neighbors do.

Eira made a few notes and saw that August was doing the same.

"I think he's in shock," said Patrik Nydalen, nodding to the man in the American car. "Who wouldn't be—if what he says is true."

He hadn't recognized Olof Hagström at first, barely even remembered him. It was just lucky he'd gone out for a run so early, before the roads got too busy. And to bring in the daily paper too, they'd had their subscription redirected over the summer. Otherwise God knew what might have happened.

He had asked Olof Hagström to reverse up the road and wait until the police arrived.

"It felt pretty unpleasant standing here, I have to say, but the operator asked me to wait, so I did. Even if it did take forever." Patrik glanced at his watch, leaving no doubt what he thought about the speed of the police.

Eira could have told him that there were just two patrol cars covering an area stretching from the coast to the mountains, from south of Härnösand to the border with Jämtland; she could have talked about the many kilometers of road and the fact that it was Midsummer, which meant the staffing focus was on that evening, the one night of the year when they also had a helicopter stationed in Härnösand, because it was geographically impossible for them to attend call outs in both Junsele and Norrfällsviken at the same time.

"So none of you have been into the house?" she asked instead.

They hadn't.

His wife, Sofi, had come out later in her billowy summer dress, bringing Patrik a coffee and a sandwich—he never ate breakfast before he went running, she explained. Her voice lacked the occasional note of Ångermanland melody that her husband still possessed. She was from Stockholm, she said, but she loved the countryside. Didn't want to be afraid of the silence and the remoteness up here, both of which she loved. They spent almost all summer here, on the small farmstead where Patrik grew up; the house wasn't anything special, but it was authentic. Her parents-in-law were still fit and healthy and moved into the old bakehouse during the summer months, to make space for them. They were down at the beach with the kids now, thank God. Sofi felt for her husband's hand.

The older man, Kjell Strinnevik, lived in the house closest to the main road. He'd noticed that Hagström hadn't taken in his paper the day before, he said. That was virtually all he had to say. Hadn't seen the old man all week, as far as he could remember, but then again he wasn't the curtain-twitching type. He had plenty of his own things to worry about.

"You're Veine Sjödin's girl, from Lunde, aren't you? Mmm, heard she'd joined the police." Kjell Strinnevik's eyes narrowed disapprovingly, though he may also have been impressed.

Eira asked her younger colleague to take down their details. Not because it was necessarily his job, but because speaking to Olof Hagström was more important, and it made sense for the more experienced officer to take care of that.

The nine-year-old in her agreed.

She walked over to the car. A Pontiac Firebird Trans Am, 1988 model, according to Patrik Nydalen, his voice ringing out as she crossed the lawn.

"Bit strange that he was talking about cars when he'd just found his father dead, but who knows how you'd react in his shoes. We've got a good relationship, me and my parents; my dad would never just be left there like . . ."

The garden was neglected but not overgrown, the grass yellow from the early-summer heat. Someone had been looking after it until relatively recently. Given up over the last year or so.

A black dog appeared, paws on the car window, and let out a bark. The man looked up.

"Olof Hagström?"

She held her ID at eye level. EIRA SJÖDIN, POLICE ASSISTANT. KRAMFORS, SOUTHERN ÅNGERMANLAND DISTRICT.

His arm seemed heavy as he wound down the window.

"Could you tell me what happened?" she said.

"He was just sitting there."

"In the shower?"

"Mmm." Olof Hagström looked down at the dog, which was rooting around in a torn burger bag on the floor. Eira had to make a real effort to hear what he mumbled. That he had wanted to call an ambulance. Poor signal. He wasn't trying to run away, he just wanted to go down to the road.

"Did your father live alone?"

"I don't know. He had the dog."

Maybe it was the smell that made her feel nauseated, the odor of someone who hadn't showered in a long time, the filthy dog nosing around in the leftover food on the floor. Or maybe it was the thought that beneath all the years and the rolls of fat was a man who had raped a sixteen-year-old girl, strangling her with a sallow branch before throwing her body into the river.

To be carried by the current, out into the expanse and the oblivion of the Bothnian Sea.

Eira straightened up, made a few notes.

"When did you last see him?"

"It's been a while."

"Was he ill in any way?"

"We haven't spoken . . . I don't know anything."

His eyes were small and deep set in his round face. When he looked up at her, his gaze seemed to hover somewhere below her chin. It bothered her that she suddenly became aware of her breasts.

"We need to go into the house," she said. "Is the door unlocked?"

She took a quick step back as the car door swung open. Her colleague noticed the movement and was by her side in an instant, but Olof Hagström didn't climb out of the car. He just leaned out slightly, so that he could point.

A round stone by the porch, distinct from all the others. Eira pulled on a pair of gloves. That was about as bad as a flowerpot on the porch, or hiding it in a broken clog. People must think that thieves were complete idiots, which was also often the case.

"What do you think?" her colleague asked quietly.

"I don't think anything yet," Eira replied, unlocking the door.

"Jesus Christ." August covered his mouth with his hand as they stepped inside. The air stunk of dog shit. No abnormal amount of flies, just an awful lot of junk in the hallway, continuing through to the kitchen. Bags of newspapers and empty bottles, brush cutters and weed whackers and metal tubs and other rubbish. Eira breathed through her mouth. She had seen worse. Once, a body had been lying for six months.

The violence was something she had expected when she became a police officer, but not the loneliness. It cut deep. Homes like this, where life ended and no one came.

She took a few steps into the kitchen, taking care where she put her feet. The dog had been running around in its own excrement. Torn packs of food, full of teeth marks.

Eira wished she were the type of police officer who instinctively knew what had happened with a single glance, but she wasn't. She got by on being thorough. Observing, documenting, putting the pieces together one by one.

The dregs of his coffee had dried in the bottom of his mug. An empty plate, crumbs from a sandwich. The newspaper lying open on the table was from Monday. Four days earlier. The last thing Sven Hagström had read was an article about burglaries in the area. The thieves were likely a couple of local addicts who were out after a brief spell inside, she knew that, just as she knew the stolen goods were likely being stashed in a barn in Lo, but the press continued to speculate about criminal gangs from the other side of the Baltic.

August Engelhardt followed her as they continued through to the bathroom. *You get used to it*, Eira thought. *It happens quicker than you might think.*

A small lake had formed in front of the open door.

There was something unbearably sad about the sight that met them. The man looked so defenseless, hunched over and naked. His white skin reminded her of marble.

Before Eira moved back to Ådalen the previous winter, she had seen a body that had been lying in the bathtub for two weeks, in an apartment in Blackeberg. The skin had come loose when the technicians touched it.

"Aren't we going to wait for forensics?" August asked behind her.

She didn't bother to answer. *What do you think? If we were going to wait, if it wasn't our job to be taking in whatever happened here, why would I be standing with my nose right up close to someone who died four days ago? Feeling the steam that has started to rise, the rot that set in as soon as the water stopped running.*

Eira carefully turned the chair. It was the kind used in hospital showers, for those at risk of falling, made from plastic and steel. The man's backside had pushed through the open seat.

She half-crouched in front of the body so that his abdomen and chest were visible. There was no blood, but the wound was deep. A horizontal gash across the top of his belly. She could make out the edges of the wound and some of the tissue within.

A pang of dizziness as she stood up.

"What do you reckon?" her colleague asked.

"A single wound," said Eira. "As far as I could see."

"So it's professional, you mean?"

"Possibly."

Eira studied the door. There was no sign of forced entry.

"Do you think it was someone he knew?" August continued, backing over to the window and looking out onto the driveway, where the American car was still parked. "Someone who could just walk straight in. It doesn't look like anyone broke in, but they might have known where he kept the key."

"If it happened on Monday," said Eira, "then he'd been out to get the paper. He might've left the front door unlocked after he came back in. And the kind of lock on the bathroom door is easy enough to turn with a knife or a screwdriver—assuming he even locked it. Why would he bother if he lived alone?"

"Shit."

August raced out. Eira caught up with him by the porch. Olof Hagström was no longer sitting in the car. The driver's side door was wide open.

"I couldn't see him through the window," her colleague panted. "Just that the car was empty. He can't have made it very far, not in the shape he's in."

Hadn't they told the neighbors to go home? Kjell Strinnevik

certainly hadn't listened, in any case, which was fortunate for them. He was standing slightly farther up the road, pointing into the woods. Towards the river.

"Where did he go?"

"Said he was going to take a leak."

They each rounded one side of the house, but there was no sign of Olof Hagström. The rocks sloped sharply downwards, the forest dense and pale, young trees that had grown since a clearing some twenty or so years earlier, raspberries and fireweed. Eira called for backup as they took the first path down the slope, running as hard as they could through the piles of rocks and brush.

"My mistake," said Eira. "I didn't have him down as a flight risk."

"Why did he wait for us, if he is?"

Eira swore as the branches of a fallen tree tore at her shins. "Welcome to reality," she said. "Not everything makes sense here."

They spotted the dog first, through the birches, standing a few meters into the water. Then the man. He was sitting on a log by the edge of the river, completely motionless. Her colleague waded through the meter-high stinging nettles ahead of her. A few gulls lifted off into the air, screeching.

"We need to ask you to come with us," said August Engelhardt.

Olof Hagström peered blankly across the river. A gust of wind crept over the surface of the water, shattering the mirrored sky.

"The boat used to be pulled up here," he said. "But I guess it's gone now."

No, Mum, Midsummer's Eve was yesterday," Eira explained for the third time as she opened the jars of herring. "I told you we'd celebrate today instead."

"Yes, yes, it doesn't make any difference."

Eira tore back the plastic from the salmon fillets and set the table, cut the chives. She had managed to get her mother to sit down and scrub the potatoes. Participation. Familiarity. The kind of thing it was important to cling to.

"Are the other potatoes really not ready yet?" Kerstin Sjödin muttered. "I don't know how these will be enough for everyone."

"It's just the two of us today," said Eira. Through the window, she saw the weeds in the potato patch, the drooping tops. She didn't tell her mother that the potatoes she was cleaning were from the supermarket.

"But what about Magnus? And the boys?"

Wrapping her up in cotton wool and bending the truth was hardly the right way to deal with worsening dementia, was it?

"I invited him," said Eira. "But he's not coming. Magnus isn't in great shape at the moment."

The first part was a lie. She hadn't called her brother. The rest was true, however. She had spotted him in the main square in Kramfors a few weeks earlier.

"So he doesn't have the kids this weekend?" Kerstin stopped her stubborn scrubbing and her eyes became hazy, heavy. Her hands limp in the muddy water.

"Not this weekend," said Eira.

Their shadows fell over the table set for two. The bouquet of Midsummer flowers and buttercups looked so childish. *I'm here*, Eira wanted to say, though she knew it wouldn't help.

"Do you remember Lina Stavred?" she asked instead, as the potatoes boiled and they nibbled on strawberries. She opened a couple of beers—lager for her mother, an IPA for herself, from the new microbrewery in Nässom. You had to do whatever you could to support anyone brave enough to start a business in the area. "You know, the girl who went missing?"

"No, I don't know . . ."

"Come on, Mum, you remember. The summer of 1996, she was only sixteen. It happened up in Marieberg, on the path along the river there, by the woodyard belonging to the sawmill, near the old workers' bathing hut."

She was careful to name specific locations. The significant and the concrete, things her mother had once known and could cling to. Her maternal grandfather had worked at the sawmill in the sixties, before it closed down; her mother's first childhood home was nearby. It struck Eira that almost every part of the area could be described as old, former. Memories of what used to be.

"You had a friend over there, Unni. She rented a flat in one of the old workers' barracks, Paradise they called it. I remember she came here—she lived alone, so she stayed with us while all that stuff was happening."

"Yes, yes, I'm not completely senile, even if you seem to think I am. She moved away, when was it? Met a jazz musician in Sundsvall. Some women just can't handle being on their own."

Kerstin tested one of the potatoes with a skewer. It was perfect, soft but not yet falling apart, as though she had an inbuilt timer. *There are still moments like this*, Eira thought, *still so much of her left*.

"The fourteen-year-old," she continued. "You know, the boy who did it, he's back in Kungsgården. I met him yesterday."

"Uff." Her mother mashed butter into a potato and mixed it with the soured cream, taking far too big a mouthful. Eating the herring and salmon together, wolfing down everything much too quickly. It was part of her illness, this desire for food. Maybe she had forgotten that she ate just a few hours earlier, or maybe she was afraid she might not be given any more food, afraid of losing control of her own survival. "I can't understand how they can let someone like that out."

"Do you know Sven Hagström?"

A moment of silence followed. Chewing.

"Who did you say?"

"Olof Hagström's dad. The father of Lina's killer. Seems like he stayed put in Kungsgården all these years."

Her mother pushed back her chair and got to her feet, searching for something in the fridge.

"I know I put a bottle in here, but now I can't find it."

"Mum." Eira waved the bottle that had been standing on the counter, a wormwood schnapps. They had already had a small glass each, but she poured another.

"*Hej tomtegubbar*," Kerstin quoted an old Christmas song, knocking back her glass.

It was as though the color of her eyes had changed with the progression of her illness. The more she lost her grip of time, the paler they became, flashing brightly whenever she managed to find a foothold. In that moment, they seemed deep blue.

"Sven Hagström was found dead yesterday," said Eira. "I want to know what kind of person he was. What something like that does to a man. When your son . . ."

"Was he related to Emil Hagström?"

"I don't know, who's that?"

"The poet!" Her eyes showed a flash of brilliant blue again, and for a moment Kerstin Sjödin was as gruff and confident as ever. "Surely even you must have heard of him—not that you ever read anything."

She reached for the bottle and poured herself another schnapps. Eira covered her own glass and was tempted to say that of course she read, or that she listened to books at the very least, sometimes while she was out running, and ideally at a slightly faster pace, to stop them from being so damned boring.

"Sven Hagström," she repeated instead, reminding herself of the basic facts they had established the day before, while they were waiting for the on-duty commanding officer to arrive. "He was born in nineteen forty-five, just like Dad. Moved to Kungsgården with his parents in the fifties, so it seems pretty likely that your paths must have crossed at some point. He worked at the sorting yard in Sandslån before they stopped the log driving, and he actually played on the bandy team for a season or two . . ."

"No, I don't know the man." Kerstin knocked back her entire glass again, coughing and dabbing her mouth with her napkin. A wandering look of anxiety in her eye. "And your dad didn't either. Neither of us did."

"I was in his house," Eira continued without any real idea of why she was pushing such a hopeless and, professionally speaking, dubious line of inquiry. Maybe it was irritation, over the fact that she wasn't being given any answers yet again. Or maybe it was revenge for everything they had kept quiet, whispered about, when she was younger. Besides, if she slipped up in her duty of confidentiality here, it would soon be forgotten.

"I saw he had a lot of books, almost an entire wall full. Maybe he used to borrow from the book bus? You could always remember everyone, you knew exactly what they liked reading—you found books for them and brought what they were looking for when you loaded the bus. Or maybe you knew Gunnel Hagström, his wife? They got divorced. After Lina was killed, after Olof was sent away . . ."

The shrill sound of the phone interrupted her. It was work calling, finally. She picked up her mobile and went out through the kitchen door. Eira had fought the urge to check in while she was preparing lunch. The first twenty-four hours had passed, the limit for detaining someone. Olof Hagström could be a free man now. Or not.

"Hey," said August Engelhardt. "I thought you might want an update. Assuming you don't value your free time too highly."

"Is he being held?"

"Yup, I just heard. So we've got seventy-two hours."

"We?" she blurted out. Murder investigations never stayed in their laps for long; they had a tendency to blow straight down to Sundsvall and the Violent Crimes Unit there. They always called in all the resources they could at first: the on-duty investigator, local officers, civilian investigators—even trainees could be assigned overtime shifts to secure the most pressing evidence. But the vast majority of the important work would be done one hundred kilometers to the south, in the city by the coast. She had hesitated for a moment too long that morning, phone in hand. Was just about to volunteer for overtime when a timer went off in the kitchen, and she had to drop her phone to take the Västerbotten cheese pie out of the oven. Then she had seen the bouquet of flowers her mother had picked, and hadn't been able to bring herself to push back their Midsummer celebrations again.

"Have they found anything else?" she asked, slumping into the hammock. It creaked, and she lowered her feet to the ground to stop it swinging.

"Not much more than yesterday," said August. "They're still waiting for the phone provider and the train company and the traffic cameras, all that stuff, but they had more than enough to hold him. Risk of hindering the investigation, flight risk."

"Is he talking?"

"Still denies it. They're taking him to Sundsvall tomorrow morning so they can keep questioning him there."

And so the lead interviewer can get home in time for dinner with the family, Eira thought.

She pictured Olof Hagström in the cramped interrogation room, the way he'd seemed to completely fill it during the first interview she had conducted the day before.

The strain stemming from the knowledge of what he had done. A killer could act in rage or panic, but rape was something else entirely. She had been determined not to let him get to her when he did eventually look up. His breathing. His huge hands, resting on the table. Eira had fixed her eyes on his enormous wristwatch, an analog thing with a compass and various other features built in—you rarely saw anything like that these days—watching the second hand complete rotation after rotation as she waited for him to speak.

All interviews followed a strict pattern. If a suspect started talking freely, she was supposed to interrupt him to prevent him from saying too much before his lawyer arrived. But with Olof Hagström, that hadn't been a problem. He kept quiet as Eira read him his rights, explaining why he was there, what he was suspected of. She had just one question for him: How did he plead?

She had found his silence obstinate, almost aggressive, and had to repeat the question. The mumble that followed was faint, reeled off like a prayer.

I didn't do it.

I didn't do it.

How many times had he repeated those words?

"Thanks for calling," said Eira, crushing a mosquito that was feasting on her ankle.

She spent a while in the hammock, heard the creaking and the wind, noise from a porch somewhere nearby. Her mother's voice inside, anxious and weak.

"Hello? Is there someone out there?"

Their words seemed to follow him. Voices seeping into his cell, penetrating his skull, the woman's in particular. Hot-tempered and pushy, the kind of person who wanted to root around in him.

Poking about in things she should leave the fuck alone.

How do you plead to that?

Blah, blah, blah.

Olof paced around his cell, five steps forward, five steps back: he was nothing but a caged animal. It was as though he were back in the past, even though it was all so long ago. He'd had a more normal room then, in the place where kids like him were sent, but it still felt the same. He was locked up. Served lunch and dinner on a tray. Not that there was anything wrong with the food—beef and potatoes with sauce. It was the lack of air, the heat, making him sweat more than usual. The hole they had told him he could drink from stunk of piss. They wanted to make him drink piss. Claimed he killed his own father.

As though he'd had a father.

It almost felt easier to keep quiet in front of the male officer, from Sundsvall. Men understood something about silence. They knew it was a strength not to blabber unnecessarily. A battle to see who would cave first. Power, being measured out. Who was bigger, what you were capable of.

Olof lay down on the floor again. It wasn't comfortable, but he would rather lie there than on the bed. It was too small for him. He glared up at the ceiling. Saw a chink of sky through the window.

If he closed his eyes, he could see his father's aged body and was reminded of all the years that had passed.

His father, getting up from the shower and coming towards him.

In this family, we don't lie. Haven't I taught you that? A man takes responsibility for the things he's done.

Then he had hit him.

You tell the truth now, you little shit.

In his head, his father's voice didn't sound old, there was nothing pathetic or weak about it.

They're waiting. Are you going to walk out there like a man or do I have to carry you? Well? Just how ashamed does your mother have to be of you? Don't you have legs? Get out there now, for God's bloody sake . . .

He didn't remember his mother's voice at all. A memory of being in the back seat of a car, turning around to see his home disappear through the rear window. No one standing outside.

Olof kept his eyes open for as long as he could.

The clouds raced by overhead. One looked like a spaceship, and there was a dragon, or possibly a dog. What had they done with the pooch? Shot it, sent it to a kennel somewhere? He wondered about the car, too. Was it still parked by the house, or had they taken it too—like they had taken his phone and his driving license and the clothes off his back? He didn't want to think about what the boss would say. How many times he must have screamed into his voice-mail by now, asking where the fuck the Pontiac was. Or maybe he was celebrating Midsummer, telling himself it would show up when it showed up. Olof had always done a good job on the drives, that was why he got a decent cut. And he hadn't actually said a word to the police about where the car was going, just that he'd bought it from a private individual in Harads. That was technically true, though the money wasn't his.

This was probably the end of the driving for him. It was the best job he'd ever had—on the road all by himself, better than both the lumberyard and the warehouse. There was always someone checking up on him there, bossing him about and giving him orders in a way that made him make mistakes.

In the end he closed his eyes. The door rattled and the guard strode in. Olof rolled over and propped himself up on his elbows.

"What now?"

The guard was the pumped-up type, with a shaved head and Schwarzeneggeresque muscles. It looked like he was smiling. Probably laughing at him. Olof was used to people staring.

"You can keep the clothes," said the guard.

"What else would I do? Go to the pisser naked?" Olof tugged at the sleeve of his sweater, which was a little too short, the tracksuit bottoms they'd pulled from a box when they booked him in. His own had probably been sent off for analysis. To be scrutinized, studied under a microscope. He wondered whether they would find any blood they could use to send him down. He hadn't seen any blood. If there had been any, it must have washed away.

The guard was still standing in the doorway, may have said something else.

"What?"

"I said you're free to go."

A suspected drunk driver in Bollstabruk, a car that had left the road on the bend. A number of different calls, the same vehicle. The driver had destroyed the barriers but missed the rock face, a wrecked Saab smoking by the side of the road.

"Oh, shit, you're Mange Sjödin's sister," the man groaned as they pulled him out.

Eira vaguely recognized him from high school, one of the handsome kids a year or two ahead of her. She grabbed the fire extinguisher and sprayed the smoke as she racked her brain trying to remember whether they had ever made out.

"I was on my way home," he slurred. "My girl broke up with me on Saturday, you know what it's like. I thought the boys were giving me low-alcohol beer, I swear, I just swerved to avoid some idiot driver, swerved on the curve, ha-ha."

The Breathalyser gave a reading of 2.0 per mill.

"How's Mange doing these days? Been ages since I saw him. Come on, Eva, you know me."

His rant continued from the back seat as they drove him to Kramfors. All deceitful buddies and feminists and closures, everything that could happen to an innocent man. The dimensions of the bend in the road were all wrong; they should take it up with the authorities, not him.

"Can't be easy to lock up your old friends," August Engelhardt said once they had dumped him in custody.

"He's not my friend."

"But it must happen all the time in places like this."

"You just deal with it," Eira muttered, sounding more irritated than intended. "It's not a problem so long as you're professional."

She asked August to write up the report and took her coffee over to her desk. He wouldn't be around for long. Three months, that was Eira's guess. He wouldn't last six.

She had two messages. Someone called Ingela Berg Haider had tried to get in touch, and Georg Georgsson, the murder detective from Violent Crimes, wanted a chat. Eira had caught a glimpse of him down the corridor, just before the call came in from Boll-stabruk. Six foot five and slightly scruffy, in a tailored jacket that showed he came from the city.

"Ah, good, we meet at last. Eva Sjöberg, right?"

Georg Georgsson put his newspaper to one side as she stepped into the room. His handshake was strong, eager. They had met at least three times before, while investigating an arson the previous winter, and at a conference where he gave a talk.

"Eira," she said. "Sjödin."

"Right, right, me and names. Great you could come by."

He sat down on the edge of the desk. The room was sterile, with two hardy potted plants in the window. No family photographs or children's drawings on the walls; it was an anonymous space for visiting detectives to work. She had heard that in Sundsvall, they called him GG.

"Good work on Friday. That was no small guy you took on."

"Thanks, but there were two of us."

"So if it wasn't the son going all Oedipus and killing his father, what have we got?" GG drummed his pen against his palm, as though to raise the tempo. *He probably wants to get home within the next few days*, thought Eira, *to escape the mute loneliness of a room at the Hotel Kramm*. Assuming he wasn't commuting back and forth, of course. "Some people want to believe that we don't prioritize this kind of thing," he continued. "That we're far too willing to release suspected criminals, that the old folks who live out in the sticks aren't our priority."

"As far as I know, he wasn't even in the area at the time."

Though Eira wasn't involved in the investigation, she had heard the prosecutor's justification for releasing Olof Hagström. They weren't talking about a perfectly doable detour of a few miles—it was a distance of five hundred kilometers. And his claims had been carefully verified by the technicians.

According to the preliminary report, Sven Hagström had died at some point on Monday. Olof had been at home at the time, in Upplands Bro, a suburb of Stockholm. He hadn't taken the train north until Wednesday, traveling to Harads to buy a car. The journey took him eighteen hours, with various changes along the way, and the digital ticketing system had tracked his movements on each leg of the journey.

Being a detective today was child's play: that was what one of her older colleagues would have said if he hadn't already retired. In the past, when the conductors clipped the tickets by hand, you just had to hope they could remember a particular face in the crowd.

The widow who'd sold the Pontiac online had also identified Olof Hagström. She described it as a day of relief; the car was useless in the winter and took up all the space in the garage. Her husband was dead, and you couldn't take anything with you—not even a Firebird.

Using traffic cameras, they had been able to follow his journey south along the E4 motorway, all the way to Docksta. His phone had then pinged off the only telephone mast in the Kramfors area as Olof Hagström approached his childhood home at around midnight on Thursday, almost four days after his father died.

"You were there, what impression did you get of him? Did he do it?"

"There doesn't seem to be anything to support that idea." Eira chose her words carefully.

"You're young," said GG, "but you've been here a while, and you and I both know that it's almost always someone close to the victim. Families are bloody dangerous."

Eira weighed up the possible answers: agree or disagree, speculate or not, come to much too speedy a conclusion, not particularly professional, a suspect she herself had arrested, watch out for personal prestige.

"Nothing," she said.

"Sorry?"

"You asked what we've got—if it wasn't Olof Hagström. Next to nothing, as far as I know. The shower washed away any evidence. There are a few unidentified fingerprints in various places around the house. No murder weapon, but according to the pathologist we're looking at a big knife with a blade measuring around 110 millimeters. That could be the type of hunting knife practically everyone around here has."

"Including Sven Hagström," GG agreed. "But his was safely locked away in the gun cabinet under the stairs."

There was something restless about the lead investigator, a tendency to constantly glance out through the window or into the corridor.

"And no witnesses," Eira continued. "But this is Ådalen. People don't always come forward to talk to the police, especially not if the detectives aren't local."

GG frowned slightly. That was probably a smile passing over his face, though his mouth remained straight. He was at least twenty years older than Eira, but attractive in a confident and fairly irritating way.

"Could've been a kitchen knife, too," he said. "A decent one, sharpened."

"I want to assist on the case," said Eira.

No one could take the sunset away from her. Her evening swim down by their secret beach, as the kids called it.

Sofi Nydalen fetched her towel and toilet bag, as she did every night once the kids had settled down in front of a cartoon and her parents-in-law had gone back to the bakehouse. She kissed Patrik, who was hunched over his computer, and didn't say a word about her fears.

"You don't want me to go with you?"

"Honey," she said with a laugh. "Do you really want to swim? In seventeen-degree water?"

They had to keep the laughter alive, though it wasn't easy. Her husband, who was so brave but preferred to keep his feet on dry land. He put a hand on her waist, trying to make her stay.

"Given everything that's happened, I mean."

"It's fine; it's all over now."

Sofi decided to take her usual shortcut straight through the forest. She wouldn't give in. Her fear of the dark was irrational, all nonsense and childish ghosts, figments of her imagination lurking in the shadows. Besides, it never really got dark. The light simply faded and took on different tones, shimmering in the evening.

She could barely hear her own footsteps in the soft undergrowth.

The forest is a safe space for me: that was what Patrik had said during their first summer there, when he was so eager to share everything that made him who he was.

The nature. The river. The open expanses.

And the forest, above all the forest. The huge, occasionally impenetrable forest, trails she would never manage to find but that were engrained in him, graying trunks that made her think of old age.

The forest doesn't want to hurt you. It protects. And if there was ever a bear or anything out there, the forest would warn you. You can hear it in the leaves if there's a threat, in the dry branches on the ground, in the birds and the tiny creatures; if you listen carefully, the forest will speak to you.

Were there bears?

For a long time, she had thought she could see them whenever she went outside, lurking in the darkness beyond the trees.

Statistically speaking, Patrik had told her, it's a hundred times more dangerous to walk through town on your own.

Or to be married to a man, said Sofi.

Then they had made love. In the forest, with the trees arching overhead, the moss rising and falling. She wanted to believe that that was when Lukas was conceived.

She scanned her surroundings more carefully now, of course, before dropping her dress to the sand. Gliding out into the water. The only thing that existed was her body breaking the surface, the depths beneath her. A few black birds soaring high above, possibly crows, or ravens. The sound of a motorboat in the distance, lonely houses on the other side of the bay.

She swam in a small circle, quickly returning to the shallows, where she could feel the clay and the sand beneath her feet. She stood at the edge of the beach, washing her hair, trying to capture the sense of purity and peace. Ordinarily she swam a lap around the entire bay, but today she simply ducked under the water once more, rinsing her hair and drying herself off faster than planned.

The forest felt darker as she walked back. A twig broke, a bird rustled among the leaves. The fear was all around her, the presence of evil. More trees had uprooted, as though the earth itself was screaming. She felt a rage inside her, at the fact that she had allowed it to get to her.

Sofi didn't like herself when she was anxious and weak. That was why she stopped, as she always did, in her special place, to take a picture of the sunset. The sky beyond the rocks seemed to be burning, the river disappearing to the northwest. The same small segment of the world, night after night all summer long, yet no two pictures were the same. The landscape was constantly changing. The light, the clouds, the time. There was something so fluid yet comforting in that.

Her special place wasn't far from Sven Hagström's house. The police tape was gone now, and Sofi could see the shabby cottage from above and the side. The tin roof, with an old-fashioned TV antenna still sprouting out of it. The porch to the rear, and what she assumed had been his bedroom window. She pictured the old man who had lived there, so lonely and humdrum, behind the half-drawn curtains.

The absolute silence of death. A never again, a lingering beyond. Thoughts of what could have been.

Imagine if, imagine if.

Imagine if Patrik hadn't been so quick to act, if Hagström's sick son had walked free. That it had happened here, so close to them.

The sun dipped behind the trees.

Let's not think about it anymore, they had said to each other. *It all worked out in the end.*

It's over now.

A curtain fluttered, or was she imagining things? *One of the windows must be open down there.* Sofi thought that was sloppy of the police, if they had left it that way. The curtain seemed to move again, and a fear she was powerless to defend herself against took hold. *His spirit*, Sofi thought, though she would never say anything like that to her husband; *the incomprehensible, the thing we leave behind after death.*

A light inside, a shadow, a movement.

Then something more: a darkness filling the entire window. Sofi raised her phone. It was hard to get it to focus, and the image became blurry as she zoomed in, in the soft evening light, but later, once she had shuffled down the rocks and half-run the last few meters home, she would keep studying it.

She really had seen what she thought she had: there was someone there. In the midst of everything, that felt slightly reassuring. Sofi wasn't imagining things; she wasn't the one who was confused and crazy.

Her husband agreed, once she showed him the photograph and they talked about how disgusting it was that the police had let that man go, once she was lying in Patrik's arms and he was stroking her hair, kissing her as she grew ever colder inside. No, she wasn't the one who was crazy; it was the world they lived in.

The countryside," Georg Georgsson said with a sweeping hand gesture, the smoke of his cigarette swirling across fields and farms. "People get up when the rooster crows round here. They have coffee at six in the morning, they look out, they notice anything unusual."

"Not many people have chickens anymore," Eira told him.

"Still. Habits, duties. That kind of thing is deep rooted. So why the hell didn't anyone see or hear anything?"

They had just been to see the third of Sven Hagström's neighbors, Kjell Strinnevik, who lived in the house closest to the road. All those living nearby had already been interviewed, of course, but there was a chance they might have remembered something else.

Now that they had a clearer idea about the timeframe.

Sven Hagström had turned on his shower at twenty past seven in the morning. The computerized system the water company had installed measured his usage exactly. The victim typically used around sixty liters every morning, which corresponded to a five-minute shower. On the Monday in question, however, and over the three days that followed, his usage had gone through the roof.

Kjell Strinnevik maintained that his neighbor had gone out to fetch the paper at the usual time that morning, around six.

Yes, he always woke before six himself. It was probably 1972 when he last had a decent lie-in.

But had he heard anything unusual? Seen a car he didn't recognize around seven o'clock?

No, he hadn't.

"It could well be the ideal time," said Eira once the conversation was over and they were standing outside, looking down to the letter boxes and the turnoff onto the main road. "People tend to pay more attention to strange cars at night. There are local volunteers patrolling the area, reporting that kind of thing to us. But in the mornings, no one cares."

"So you think it was planned?" asked GG.

"I've been thinking about the dog," said Eira. "He or she must have had something edible with them, to distract it, otherwise Hagström would've heard it barking. Then there's the front door. Obviously it could have been left unlocked after the victim brought the paper in, but it was locked when his son arrived. The question is whether he or she knew about the hiding place beneath the rock."

"They," said GG.

"Sorry?"

"You don't need to say 'he or she' all the time."

"No, sorry," said Eira, getting lost in her notes, her thoughts, the pattern she was trying to discern.

GG peered up the forest track, which disappeared around the bend.

"A son who's killed before, returning home. It's all a bit too much of a coincidence if you ask me."

"Do you want to go and talk to him?"

They had been circling around the area all morning, out of sight, sticking to the edges. Olof Hagström had returned to his father's house. He had been spotted at the supermarket in Nyland, seen washing down by the beach one evening, in the window as people walked by—and they were the ones who had let him go. Several of the neighbors had pointed out as much, with vocal disapproval, fear, even anger.

"Not yet," said GG. "We need to close in on him, crack his alibi; we'll check the traffic cameras on some of the other roads and call in on the other houses until we find someone who saw him here on Monday, someone who'll testify that the father felt threatened, anything."

GG even had people out and about in Stockholm, talking to Hagström's neighbors there. They might have seen him leave, noticed he was gone. Someone had always seen something.

"We can talk to him once we've got more," said Georgsson.

"If he's still here then."

"If not, we'll track him down wherever he is."

There was one possible explanation. One of the other members of the investigation team had brought it up at the morning meeting, in which several people had joined by video link from Sundsvall.

Olof Hagström could have left his phone at home.

Traveled up on the Sunday night, killed his father and then driven home, only to take the train north again two days later with his phone switched on this time, making it look like he had found his old man by chance.

Circumstantial, yes, but it would explain why the house—after twenty-three years' absence—was full of Olof Hagström's fingerprints.

GG stubbed out his cigarette on his heel. He was trying to quit, that was what he'd said when he lit his first one several hours earlier. That was what he had promised his new girlfriend.

"Is there anywhere to get a decent lunch round here?"

They had just sat down in the restaurant at the High Coast Whisky distillery, with beautiful views out over the river and the distant blue mountains, when Eira's phone rang. She went out onto the terrace to answer. Strictly speaking, the new whisky distillery wasn't anywhere near the coast, but the name High Coast conjured up images of dramatic nature and world heritage. The Ådalen river valley was often associated with strikes in the past; Communists, and soldiers shooting at workers more than anything, and that was far less appealing.

Even the airport was called High Coast, though again, you couldn't see the coast from it.

There was a woman's voice on the other end of the line, deep yet slightly hesitant. She introduced herself as Ingela Berg Haider.

"I'm glad you called again," said Eira. She had tried to reach her several times the day before.

"I need to know what happens with the funeral in a case like this." The woman sounded absent. In shock, Eira thought, speaking slowly. She knew what it was like to lose a father. The weightlessness, the sense of falling.

Ingela Berg Haider was Sven Hagström's daughter, Olof's sister, three years his senior. She was the girl who had been sunbathing on the lawn, back when she still went by the name Ingela Hagström and Eira still crept through bushes. Ingela had been in her late teens at the time, with breasts and headphones and a leopard-print bikini; she had short hair, she was tough—everything a nine-year-old girl wanted to be. Minus the part about being a killer's sister.

Eira explained that her father's body was still with the forensic examiner in Umeå, that it would perhaps take another few days, possibly even weeks.

"I just want to do things right," said Ingela Berg Haider.

"How much do you know about what happened?"

"An officer called to say that my dad was dead, and I read the papers. Someone else called me at work, but I lost their number, and when I looked on the website I thought I recognized your name. Didn't you have a brother?"

The new terrace smelled like linseed oil, rising above the ground below like the sundeck on a boat. The old brick power station nearby now housed the distillery.

According to her records, Ingela Berg Haider was forty years old and worked as a director at Sveriges Television, the national broadcaster. Married, with a twelve-year-old daughter, living on Swedenborgsgatan in Södermalm. Eira associated that part of Stockholm with stone buildings from the turn of the last century, a sought-after neighborhood close to Mariatorget. She pictured a front door with two surnames on it, Berg and Haider. Neither was Hagström.

"When did you last speak to your father?"

"I haven't seen him in years."

"Have you had any contact with your brother?"

"Would you have? If he was your brother?"

Eira felt a few drops of rain. The river had turned pale, shifting to silvery-gray. She stepped beneath the overhanging roof.

"We need to get a clearer picture of your father's life lately," she said. "Do you know anyone he might have been close to?"

"No."

"Could be a childhood friend, old colleagues . . ."

"No idea. I left home when I was seventeen, three months after everything with Olof. My dad wasn't an easy man to be around, even before all that, and it just got worse. With his drinking and his anger and everything else. I've always felt guilty about abandoning Mum there. It took her two years to break free. Still, at least she doesn't have to go through all this now; she died of cancer last year."

GG had finished his salmon and was half-engrossed in the list of whiskies by the time Eira got back to the table.

"Too early in the day for a taster, or what do you think?"

She recapped the phone call, which hadn't given her anything but an indistinct sense of unease. She had detected a hint of aggression in much of what Ingela Berg Haider had said, something icy cool, as though the things they were talking about didn't concern her in any way.

"Would be nice to avoid the angry neighbors for now," GG said as they headed back to the car. "At least while we're digesting lunch."

"The old workmate from Sandslån?" Eira suggested.

"Do we even have a name for him?"

The list of people who may or may not have known Sven Hagström was short. Irritatingly vague. Still, it was a list of sorts.

Eira brought up the recording from their interview with Kjell Strinnevik, fast-forwarding to the end, where they had tried to get him to remember anything else, anyone who may have known Sven Hagström, anything at all, even if it was from the past.

"*. . . an old workmate from the log-sorting yard came knocking a few years ago, but Hagström didn't answer. The bloke knocked on my* *door instead, wanted to know if I knew anything. If Sven was ill. His car was there, you see. They'd been trying to reach him for some anniversary, but Sven never replied to the invite.*

"Ah, what was his name? He said he lived in Sandslån. That's the kind of thing you remember, but names . . . there are so many names . . .

Rolle!"

Eira reversed out of the parking bay.

"Rolle from Sandslån," she said. "That's as good as an address."

GG laughed. "Have I told you I love it out here in the sticks?"

Sandslån was a sleepy little idyll stretched out along the bank of the river. A narrow channel of water divided the community from the island where the timber sorting once took place. During the golden years of the log-driving industry, some seven hundred men had worked in the yard, and the river practically simmered with logs sent downstream for sorting before being sold on to sawmills or paper factories. Sandslån was once home to three different supermarkets and a bandy team in the national league, but that was then.

A lone robotic lawn mower moved slowly over a lawn like an overgrown beetle. On the river, two canoeists drifted by. A cartoonist who had grown up in Bollstabruk and recently returned from Stockholm answered the door in the first house. He didn't know anyone called Rolle, but the widow in the yellow place over there, he said, pointing, had been living in Sandslån since the dawn of time.

Eira moved on to the next house while GG made a few calls. She tried to keep it as brief as she could without seeming impolite. The woman was eighty-three and had to sit down while they spoke. Something about her back, but it would pass.

Oh, Rolle, yes. Of course she knew Rolle Mattsson.

They had worked together at the timber-sorting yard. She'd joined after they mechanized the work, once they discovered that young women were best suited to the job. She could have "swift" written on her gravestone—that was the nickname they gave the quick-fingered girls working out in the control tower. Thanks to the latest technology, the job was all about precision and maintaining an overview, and it meant they could avoid having to dash over the floating logs, which were absolutely lethal; you could be sucked in between them in the blink of an eye, and that would be thank you and goodnight. She had an uncle who had gone that way.

Sven Hagström?

Oh yes, she knew the name, she'd heard all about that terrible business, but she didn't remember him. It was easy to forget people you'd never had any fondness for, the outlines of their faces seemed to seep away like watercolors, and names were even worse. But Rolle Mattsson, he lived three doors down, "in the log house behind the trampoline over there."

Eira caught up with GG by the car. He had enjoyed yet another last cigarette and called some of the other members of the team in Sundsvall for an update. So much of the job involved sitting indoors, going through call lists and databases, analyzing forensic reports. The detectives were able to eat dinner with their families and keep their overtime to a minimum, but they could still be on the scene within a few hours, if needed.

"Olof Hagström got in touch," he said as they walked over to the log cabin. The sudden rain shower hadn't come this way, and the tarmac in front of them was bone dry.

"What did he want?"

"To know what we'd done with the dog. Seems like father and son hadn't been in touch after all. Sven Hagström only used his landline to complain about the road maintenance in the area. That and to make a few calls to the library and your station, actually."

"Why did he phone us?"

"No record," said GG. "The calls lasted less than a minute each. Maybe he wanted to report something and changed his mind."

"And he didn't have a mobile phone?"

"Not that we've found."

Rolle Mattsson was busy cutting his lawn, pushing an old-fashioned reel mower in front of him. Bare chest, wiry arms.

Beads of sweat trickled down him as he took a seat on the garden bench.

He asked Eira to go inside and fetch a pilsner or three—assuming they were allowed to drink on the job. Otherwise she would find some squash in the pantry.

There was nothing depressing about his house, nothing sad and old; it was meticulously clean and tidy, and smelled good. The same lush peonies on the kitchen table as in the flower beds outside. She had heard that they used to be known as the poor man's rose.

"Who would do something like that to an old bloke?" Rolle Mattsson muttered after a few swigs of beer. "It's a damn shame a man's not even safe in his own home these days."

He had known Sven Hagström since the sixties, through work and the union and the bandy team. Sven had even helped him lug the timber he'd used to build the house on a corner of his parents' land—the lower-quality wood you could buy for next to nothing, not that you could tell. The house was still solid as a rock. It had housed four kids, the wife too. Though she was now in a home.

A flicker of grief passed over his face, but he smiled. "Forty-seven good years. That's more than most people get."

He had ended up at the sawmill in Bollstabruk when the log driving dried up and the last float took place. Sven Hagström kept working in the forest. The former workmates hadn't had much contact over the last few years. Not since all that terrible business with Lina and his son, in fact. In the years that followed, Sven had lost the rest of his family and was left all alone.

"Something breaks in a man when that happens. It's the point of all this." Rolle Mattsson used his bottle to gesture towards the garden and the forests.

"Did Sven talk about his son?"

"Never. It was like he didn't exist. I knew Olof as a lad, he used to play with my boys. It makes you question yourself—how did I miss it? He was awkward and could get angry, the way boys do, never really looked you straight in the eye, but I always thought he was an ordinary kid."

Rolle Mattsson knocked back the rest of his beer. A few stubborn wasps were circling them, and one crawled into the neck of the empty bottle.

"So was it the son who did it?" he asked. "Or what?"

"We don't know what happened," said GG. "That's what we're trying to work out."

"Who else could've wanted to hurt Sven?"

"Did Olof want to hurt his father?"

"Sven never mentioned anything . . . But it does make you wonder. Being sent away like that. He was just a lad, that's what I've thought sometimes, though I never brought it up with Sven. You can't ever escape being your son's father. I don't know how you do things in Sundsvall, whether it's reached there yet, whether men go around talking about their feelings?"

"It happens," said GG.

Rolle Mattsson opened another pilsner. "All this keeping quiet, bottling everything up inside. Watch out if you ever see anyone raise an eyebrow; he might be bloody furious."

They took turns asking more questions, about who else Sven Hagström used to spend time with, what Rolle Mattsson was doing that morning.

He'd had the grandchildren over, they could ask the kids themselves—if they were willing to trust the words of a three- and five-year-old. As far as he could remember, they had watched a cartoon and eaten some chocolate cereal. He knew that Sven Hagström had become someone's odd-job lover in Sörviken seven or eight years back, a widow who ran a bric-a-brac sale over there.

"Maybe she got him to open up a bit, would probably take a woman to do that."

"Odd-job suitor?"

Rolle laughed. "Nice little arrangement between two lonely people, you know? The bloke goes over to the woman's place, she makes him dinner and he helps out with all the man's jobs about the house, then they have a nice time together before he goes home. No staying overnight, no obligations. No putting your eggs in the same basket, mixing everything up."

Eira thought she noticed a brief glance over to the house she had visited just before his. The widow who likened people to watercolors, a hint of a smile in his voice.

"Sounds like a dream," said GG.

"It strikes me now," said Rolle Mattsson, "that Sven never talked about his daughter either, not once she moved away. A tough little girl, if I remember. Rebellious. Don't know what happened to her. Most people are always boasting about whatever their children get up to."

"Everyone's kids are geniuses," GG agreed.

"She works in TV, lives in Stockholm," said Eira. "She has a child."

Rolle caught a wasp in one hand and hurled it away. It buzzed off, confused.

"Then why didn't he mention that?"

You got kids?" GG asked as they drove slowly out of Sandslån.
"Not yet," said Eira.

"And you're what, thirtysomething?"

"Mmh."

"Not in any rush, then?"

"Seriously, do they have to cycle on the road?" Eira braked to avoid a young girl teetering on a bicycle, giving her a wide berth as she passed. "No," she said. "No rush."

"I'm just wondering," GG continued, "because my girlfriend's about your age . . . When we first met I was clear that I didn't want any more kids, but then we got together and it turned out she hadn't closed that door after all, which really leaves you with a dilemma."

Eira came to a halt at the end of the Hammar Bridge, at the crossroads. If she had been in the car with a twentysomething police assistant, she would have told him to leave his private life at home and focus on the job.

"Shall we continue with the neighbors?" she asked instead.

GG checked his list. "Nydalen," he said. "Patrik, the son, came in to give a statement, but the parents were only spoken to at the first stage. Saw nothing, heard nothing."

He sighed.

"And this Patrik guy has been in touch asking what we're doing to protect his family now that Olof Hagström has been released."

Eira pulled up at the stop sign and allowed a German caravan to pass, heading down towards the coast from Sollefteå. She made a mental note to contact the Jämtland district, assuming it hadn't been done already. To check whether they had seen any aggravated break-ins, whether any known violent offenders had been released or let out on day leave. They had checked their own area, but the county line was only one hundred kilometers inland, where the mountains and the reindeer pastures took over. Beyond that: the border with Norway. That couldn't be ruled out either. If Hagström had emerged from the shower and startled him, or if he wasn't your typical kind of intruder. She remembered the forensic report, what she herself had noticed: there was nothing obvious missing from the house. The TV was still there, a worthless old lump. The radio, too. There were several beautiful antique barometers and compasses, china and paintings. All the kind of thing the local thieves liked to load into their cars and sell at less scrupulous flea markets.

"I really didn't plan to do it all again," said GG, still lost in thought. "My kids are already grown up—I'm actually going to be a grandfather this autumn . . . But then you realize it's a second chance, and those are pretty rare."

Eira held back behind a timber lorry and tried to think of something to say. About how people changed their minds all the time, said one thing and meant another, and how we just had to count on being dragged into something other than what we had planned. Perhaps that was one of the very foundations of love.

She didn't manage a single word.

"Last time I was far too busy with work and my career," GG continued, "but now I could be present in a completely different way . . ."

He trailed off and swore as a car overtook them, swinging into a side road. The bright red logo on its side revealed it was from a radio station.

GG hit the car door.

"What are they after now, making the sex offender speak out? Can we take a different route? There's a chance they might recognize me."

Eira did a U-turn, aiming for a gravel track a kilometer or so back. Nydalen's house wasn't particularly far from it, so they should be able to get pretty close. If nothing else, it would give GG a chance to test out his dress shoes on the rough terrain.

They had managed to keep the name Hagström out of the press so far. Everyone in the area knew, of course, but on TV and in the newspapers, the reports were still talking about "the elderly man who was killed . . ." They hadn't yet made the connection to "the fourteen-year-old" whose name had never been made public and didn't appear in the archives. They weren't under too much pressure. It was too long ago, the area too sparsely populated. The national media had combed through earlier cases involving older men who were killed in their own homes, in Rosvik and Kalamark, an elderly skier in Kivikangas. They had started asking questions about just how dangerous it was to live alone in the more rural parts of the country, and concluded that it was worse to leave the pub in town, or to be involved in organized crime.

With any luck the reporters were simply heading to Hagström's house in order to say a few words about the area, possibly even record a segment from the place where the crime occurred. *Standing here, with views of the Ångerman River glittering in the sunlight, it is hard to imagine such evil. And yet an old man was murdered in his home here a little more than a week ago. Fear is now spreading among the elderly in the area. What are the police doing, they ask; has society abandoned us?*

Something like that.

The homestead occupied a magnificent position at the top of the hill. If it hadn't been for the forest around it, the Nydalen family would have had views in every direction, but as things stood they could see only a thin sliver of the river at its widest point and the mountains on the horizon, created by the remarkable postglacial uplift along the High Coast.

A well-tended main building, a paddling pool on the lawn, pots of geraniums outside the old bakehouse.

Tryggve Nydalen was almost as tall as Georgsson, with a slightly heavier build and a handshake that showed no hesitation whatsoever.

"I don't know that we have anything else to add," he said. "But it feels reassuring to see you working. My son is very upset, I'm sure you can understand. He's just thinking of the kids."

"Of course."

"I've tried to tell Patrik that we have to have faith that the police are doing their job, to hope for the best."

"We're doing everything we can," said GG.

Eira took in the movements across the yard, Sofi Nydalen coaxing the kids into the house with promises of a film, her husband shouting something from inside, a glimpse of a woman in her sixties in the doorway of the bakehouse.

"But are you getting anywhere?" asked Tryggve Nydalen, glancing through the trees, towards Hagström's house. "So the grandkids can have their freedom back. You don't want to have to watch them constantly, you know?"

Patrik Nydalen came storming out into the yard, repeating much of what he had already vented over the phone.

That he had practically done the police's job for them, preventing Olof Hagström from leaving the scene of the crime. That their incompetence was now coming back to bite him and his family, that this was precisely the kind of thing that made people lose faith in the police and the justice system, democracy as a whole.

"I want to know what you're doing, in concrete terms, to protect my wife and children and everyone else living around here."

"Has Olof Hagström threatened you in any way?" asked GG.

"Isn't it enough that we've got a sex offender hunkering down a hundred meters from here? Does he have to threaten us too? I can't even let my wife go swimming alone anymore, on our own beach. I saw him down there this morning, with the dog. Do you know how that feels?"

"Without a specific threat, I'm afraid we can't offer you any protection," GG said calmly. "The best we can do is sit down and have a chat. If you answer our questions, we can solve this."

Sofi had taken a seat on the porch. The older woman, Marianne Nydalen, came out with a tray of coffee and cinnamon buns.

"Sit down," she said, "and we can get this over and done with."

From the house, they heard the theme tune to a popular children's movie: *The Children of Noisy Village*. It depicted an idyll of Swedish security: a childhood in red wooden cottages in the country, where the worst that could happen was . . . what? A lamb having to be bottle-fed?

Patrik Nydalen continued to question their work.

"Where were they between seven and eight? Do you seriously need my parents to answer that again? What the hell difference does it make if they were in the bakehouse or chopping wood in the yard?"

"It's all part of the process, they have to ask," Tryggve Nydalen reassured his son, placing a fatherly hand on his. Patrik pulled away.

"As though you could be suspects when they know perfectly well who did it. This is all a bloody charade."

"Let's just get this over with so the children can come out and play."

"We weren't even here," Sofi Nydalen spoke up. "We've told you already. Our holiday started last week, and we drove up on Monday afternoon, to avoid the weekend traffic. Stopped for something to eat and to let the kids stretch their legs. We didn't get here until nine in the evening."

"Ask how it feels to live here," Patrik muttered. "Ask how it feels when you lose sight of your two-year-old daughter for even a split second."

His mother Marianne—"Everyone calls me Mejan"—gave the officers an apologetic glance and a smile that seemed strained. "It's just a few questions, Patrik. They have to ask." There was something sturdy and robust about her that not even the murder of her neighbor could shake. "More coffee?"

Tryggve and Mejan had both been home that morning, pottering about in the two buildings, getting ready for the grandkids' arrival. He had chopped wood and fixed one of the legs on the master bed, probably a few other chores too, while she got the bakehouse ready for them to sleep in. Both busy with their own little tasks, so who would have noticed a car or anyone moving about outside Hagström's place? They didn't even have a clear line of sight over there. And there was a constant roar from the traffic on the motorway, too—though they barely even noticed it anymore.

When GG moved on to their relationship with Sven Hagström, Patrik lost his temper again. Stood up so abruptly that his chair tipped over.

"No one here has any kind of *relationship* with him. Can't you leave us in peace? It's bad enough just being here."

He stormed across the yard and disappeared behind the barn.

"You'll have to excuse him," said Sofi. "He gets like this sometimes. Blurts things out, as though it'll help. He doesn't mean much by it."

"It's just who he is," said Mejan. "Patrik has always been a bit of a whirlwind."

"You make it sound like he's unpredictable," said Tryggve.

"Well, that's not what I mean at all."

Mejan's husband patted her hand, the same gesture he had attempted on his son. She gripped his hand.

"I was over at Sven's house a couple of months ago," said Tryggve. "But I wouldn't exactly say we were friends."

Sofi Nydalen excused herself, said she wanted to check on the children. Besides, she barely knew who Sven Hagström was.

"Did you spend much time together?" GG asked once she had disappeared into the house. "As neighbors, I mean."

"He wasn't the kind of man you'd want to sit and make small talk with."

"Things were better before," said Mejan. "When he still had Gunnel."

"But she left," Tryggve filled in. "Couldn't bear it any longer. When was it . . . ?"

"Mmm, must've been a year or two after . . ."

". . . everything with their son."

They both nodded and continued to finish each other's sentences.

"Sven Hagström mostly kept himself to himself . . ." said Mejan.

"And you can understand why," said Tryggve. "People talk. They have their theories."

"About what?" GG asked.

"What makes a person who they are. If it's the parents." Tryggve Nydalen glanced over to the barn. Patrik was no longer visible.

"How long have you lived here?" asked Eira.

"Thirty years," said Mejan. "We met while we were working in Norway. We managed to save up enough money to buy the house the same year we got married. You know what the prices are like round here; it's the most beautiful place, but you couldn't find a cheaper house anywhere in the country." A flicker seemed to pass across her face. "We never thought it would end up like this."

"We used to talk about the road," said Tryggve. "The maintenance. That's why I went over to Hagström's recently. You can see what a state it's in."

"How did it go?"

"We agreed, for the most part. But getting the council to do anything is a long process, and I say that as someone who works there."

"In the finance department, but that's by the by." Mejan got up and began collecting the plates, brushing crumbs into the palm of her hand. "So we don't attract any wasps, they're such a bother this year."

"Let me help," said Eira.

"No need."

Eira grabbed a couple of mugs and followed her inside. The bakehouse consisted of a kitchen and a small bedroom, charmingly renovated with the original features intact. There was a calmness inside, an opportunity to speak one-on-one. The Nydalens' long marriage almost seemed to have forged them together to the point that they said practically the same things.

"This is more than enough for us during the summer; the kids need more space." Mejan carefully rinsed out the mugs. They had a daughter too, she explained. Jenny, who had gone traveling to Sydney and never come back. She didn't have any children, so it was Patrik's kids they got to treasure.

"You have a lovely home," said Eira.

"We wanted to create our own little place on earth," said Mejan. "I was born and raised in the area, but Tryggve has loved this place from the very beginning. Nydalen is actually my family name. I come from a small village twenty or so kilometers from here."

"It's generous of the two of you to squeeze in here all summer."

"So long as they want to come to stay. That means everything."

From the window to the side of the kitchen worktop, a small sliver of the roof on Hagström's house was visible. Mejan's eyes kept drifting over to it.

"Did you used to chat with Sven Hagström?" asked Eira.

"I said hello if I saw him, of course, as you do. Took him some jam sometimes, but we rarely said much. More about the weather than anything. I've thought about that from time to time, about how lonely he seemed. I don't even think his daughter came to see him."

"Have you ever heard about him having any disagreements, being angry with anyone . . . ?" Eira continued. "I'm from round here myself, and I know how people talk about that kind of thing— sometimes for generations."

Mejan thought as the water ran into the sink, peering outside for what felt like a long time.

"It'd be about the forest if anything. That's what people fall out over—someone taking wood from someone else's land, cutting up trees brought down by storms, that kind of thing. Or selling the felling rights to some big company, so that the neighbors wake up one morning with a clearing outside their window."

The thought made the woman shudder. Either that or she had seen something outside.

"Are you really sure it wasn't him, the son? Who else could it have been?"

Olof slammed on the brakes at the crown of the hill. There was another car parked by his house. A slim woman dressed in black standing outside, talking into a microphone. He could see another head in the driver's seat; there were two of them.

He didn't have time to work out whether they were from the TV or the radio before he put the car into reverse and rolled back down the gravel track.

He remembered their type from before. The questions that whizzed around him, like they had been fired from an air rifle, as he walked alongside his mother and father on the way out of the station; the cars with letters on their sides clustered down by the road. His mother had pulled his jacket over his head, held him close. His father had told them to go to hell.

He had once seen that very thing on TV, seen himself in their old car, jacket covering his face, heard the echo of his father's swearing. Then someone switched off the TV.

They had a red Passat back then, and there was something about the smell of this car that reminded him of it. Olof had left the Pontiac at the house when he went to pick up the dog, taking his father's car from the garage instead.

It was like he was invisible as he drove to the kennels in Frånö. No one paid any notice to a 2007 Toyota Corolla. The dog had licked his face when it saw him, and Olof had left with a sense of having liberated it from captivity—which, of course, he had.

He reached out and scratched its head. The dog was sitting in the passenger seat, ears pricked. It barked at a cow, jumped excitedly as a couple of horses bounded across a field. It didn't feel right to give it a name when it must already have had one, so he simply called it Dog.

"You probably want to get out and run around, don't you?" he said, turning off towards Marieberg.

He didn't think about where he was heading. There were the little wooden houses lining the bay, the beachside meadows thick with fireweed. If he turned around, he would have been able to see his childhood home up on the hill. He wondered how long it would be before they gave up and left him in peace. Twice earlier he had heard the sound of an engine, someone knocking on the door, but he had hidden and kept quiet.

They couldn't call him, at the very least. His phone was switched off. He had listened to the messages from his boss once he got it back from the police, heard him ranting and raving about having a buyer lined up for the Pontiac, how Olof would pay for this.

He reached for the fifth of the ten burgers he had bought in Kramfors. It was stone cold by then, but that didn't matter. The food served as a blanket over his anxiety. He gave the sixth to the dog, not caring that it slobbered mayonnaise all over the seat. It wasn't like his father was going to need the car again.

The road sloped upwards, one of the longest and toughest hills to cycle in the entire universe. The old co-op was at the top. He pulled over to the edge of the road and came to a halt. He opened the door for the dog, which raced off among the trees.

"See you by the old co-op," they used to say, though no one could actually remember it ever having been a shop. The building had stood empty for a long time, which was why his gang used to hang out there sometimes. Someone had got hold of some hash, that was probably why. Or did the others know? That Lina would walk by, bag slung over one shoulder, the skirt of her dress fluttering around her legs, just a thin cardigan on top, the fabric as yellow as a dandelion, like the sun, dazzling.

Why did she go straight into the forest, along that narrow track, if she didn't want someone to follow her?

That was what Olof thought as he saw it all happen again: that she wasn't dressed for the forest. He felt himself break out in a sweat. Maybe he needed to throw up. If he went a little deeper among the trees, no one would be able to see him. The dog darted around him, immediately sniffing out his vomit among the ferns and rocks.

Olof shooed it away. He found what he thought was wood sorrel, and chewed on the leaf to get rid of the disgusting taste in his mouth.

The trail snaked away, upwards at first, before turning sharply down towards the old sawmill. It was over there somewhere, beyond the grand old house that loomed like a manor over the area, in among the trees where no one could see them. That was where she had stopped, waited for him.

What do you want? Are you following me?

Her laugh, reserved for him.

Olof had the sense that no one had walked along the trail since. The police had, of course; they had scoured the entire forest and the area round about, sent out dogs to look for her. And later, the reconstruction. When they brought him out there and told him to point. There was a glade, a fallen tree. He couldn't see either now. The birches were so much taller, the trail so much narrower, eventually disappearing completely. Overgrown, of course, hidden beneath the bilberry bushes and nettles. He could taste soil.

What did you do to her, Olof?

And then, down by the river, behind the brick shed known as Meken. At the edge of the beach where the remains of the old timber quay still rose up out of the water like rotten piles. That was where they had found her things.

Was this where you threw her in? Or was it farther down?

Past the huge metal warehouse that had started to rust, between the concrete pillars in the deepwater harbor.

Sometimes we don't want to remember, they had told him; the brain represses awful things.

That was why they had returned to the place, to help him remember.

You want to remember, don't you, Olof?

It's right there inside you, everything you've ever done and experienced.

Was it here? Was she still alive when you threw her in? Did you toss her over the edge, did you know that the water is thirty meters deep here?

You remember, Olof. We know you remember.

Out of sheer habit, Eira took a detour on her way to the library. It meant she could avoid the blustery open square where everything was visible, the benches around the fountain where she might run into her brother.

She wasn't in uniform, which was good because it made her less noticeable, but it was also bad. It increased the risk of him being overly familiar. Wanting to borrow money. Asking how their mother was.

It was worth the longer walk around the block.

GG had gone back to Sundsvall, and she had spent a few hours making routine calls to addiction treatment centers in neighboring districts, trying to find out who might have been released recently.

"Hello, Eira, lovely to see you." The librarian's name was Susanne, and she had worked there for the best part of twenty years. "You must tell me how your mother is."

"Good, but not so good."

"It's an awful disease. I know all too well, my dad . . ."

"She still has lucid moments."

"Are you getting any help?"

"You know Kerstin, she wants to manage on her own."

"This part is the worst, the transition. When you have to respect everything they think they can manage, knowing they can't. Is she still reading?"

"Every day," said Eira. "But it's often the same book."

"Then let's hope it's a good one."

They laughed, but in a way that was dangerously close to tears.

"I'm actually here on duty," said Eira. "I'm sure you've heard about Sven Hagström in Kungsgården."

"Of course, what an awful thing. But how can I help?"

"Did he ever borrow books from here?"

Susanne thought for a moment, then shook her head. She could certainly check the records, but she knew her customers, particularly the older ones. He may have used the library at some point, but not over the last few years. That corroborated the picture Eira had of him. She hadn't seen any library books lying around his house, and she had checked the photographs. Surely no one kept their library books on their shelves; they were guaranteed to forget about them.

"He called the library in mid-May," said Eira. "Several times. Do you remember whether you spoke to him?"

"Oh, of course, why didn't I think of that?" Susanne slumped into her chair. "He was looking for a couple of articles, of course that was him!"

Eira felt a pang of grief. The librarian possessed that special kind of memory, almost like a living catalog. Her mother had been the same until very recently; she always knew what every borrower wanted, the books they didn't yet know they would enjoy. Just the previous year Kerstin would have been able to remember a specific phone call among hundreds of others, too. Assuming they actually got that many—perhaps people didn't borrow so many books anymore. During the fifteen minutes she had been there, Eira had seen only three other people come into the building, and one of them was to use the toilet.

"But we don't have access to the newspaper archives here," Susanne continued. "And the papers were from up in Norrbotten, or maybe it was Västerbotten, from back before everything was online. I told him he was welcome to come in and use one of our computers if he didn't have his own, and I could help him make contact."

"Did he?"

"He might've been in when one of my colleagues was working, but he never came to see me. I would have remembered if he did."

"I'm sure you would," said Eira.

"Say hello to your mum, if she remembers me. No, say hello any-way."

August Engelhardt was sitting at her desk when she got back to the station. Strictly speaking, they didn't have fixed seats in the office, and Eira was technically on loan to another department, but she still thought of it as hers.

"I think you're going to want to see this," he said, rolling back slightly in his chair.

As Eira leaned in, she found herself extremely close to him. A sensation she didn't want to acknowledge raced through her.

"My girlfriend saw it in her feed," said August.

It was a page from social media, comments filling the entire screen.

The name Olof Hagström flickered by in post after post.

They should castrate him and everyone else like him and it's a fucking outrage that people like that get to walk free and the police are protecting rapists because they're rapists themselves and that's why all these sick bastards should be named and shamed and all power to anyone brave enough to do it, and so on, and so on.

Eira swore to herself.

They had tried to keep his name out of the news, though natu-rally everyone on the force knew it. There were a thousand possible sources for this leak, on top of which everyone in the area also knew who he was.

August reached out, his arm brushing against her hip.

"It's been shared over a hundred times," he said, scrolling down. "Seven times just while I've been sitting here."

We should tell everyone where they live, read one of the posts. **We have to warn one another. The media is keeping us in the dark. It's our right to know.**

"And your girlfriend," said Eira. "Has she written anything?"

"She just shared it."

"Maybe you should ask her to stop."

The lucid moments often occurred in the morning, at some time between five and six, when Kerstin Sjödin got up and put the coffee on.

At times it was strong, occasionally much too strong, but Eira never said a word. The mornings were a refuge, before all the sights and sounds of the day complicated things. When the meadow down by the old dock in Lunde lay still and silent. It had once been so busy down there, with ships arriving from all over the world. The dock was also where the demonstrators had been brought to a halt almost ninety years earlier. Their society had frozen in that moment, as the army's bullets whizzed through the air, as friends hit the ground. Five fatalities within the space of just a few seconds.

"Here lies a Swedish worker": that was the inscription on their common grave. Their crime was hunger, never forget him.

Those shots in the Ådalen Valley forever echoed through Lunde. The Events in Ådalen, as many preferred to call them—it sounded more neutral, as though the sharp edges of reality could be ground down by words. The state, protecting the strikebreakers, shooting its own workers. The blood that day. The trumpeter blowing cease-fire. It was a story too powerful to escape. It never ceased to matter who had taken part in the demonstration and who had not, whose parents, grandparents. People preferred not to talk about it, yet couldn't bear for it to be forgotten.

"A flea market in Sörviken?" Kerstin looked up from the newspaper. She read it from cover to cover, but would soon forget the majority of it. "Yes, of course I know. It's in the white house when you reach the bend. I used to go there to buy fabric. But what was her name . . ."

Eira knew she could pull over anywhere in Sörviken and find out the name of the woman who ran the flea market, Hagström's odd-job lover, but it was something to talk about, a way to make Kerstin remember. Over the past year it had often struck her just how much revolved around that: Do you remember him or her, do you remember that song, that film, that book; do you remember what we did, which year was it again?

"Karin Backe," Kerstin called out just as Eira was about to leave. "That's her name! Maybe I could come along to see if she has anything new in?"

"I have to go there for work," said Eira. "It's to do with Sven Hagström's death. Do you remember we talked about that? You read about it in the paper."

The news was no longer news, it had slipped off the front page and the coverage was now largely focused on the fact that the police were keeping quiet, that they didn't have any new leads. Online, she had read that they had ignored a tip about a foreign gang of thieves.

"The thought of you doing that stuff," said Kerstin. Eyes anxious again. Worry constantly lurking beneath the surface, fingers searching for something to fiddle with. "You're careful, aren't you?"

She passed Eira a scarf, as though she were still a child.

As though it were winter.

Eira tossed the scarf into the car and called the station. GG was waiting for one of the other investigators; they were going to track down a couple of Lithuanian construction workers living in a campsite seven kilometers from the scene of the crime.

"Public tips," he said, "can never be ignored."

He had full confidence in letting her deal with Karin Backe.

The house in Sörviken was small and cluttered, but in a different sort of way. It wasn't like Sven Hagström's place, where the junk was piled up in layer after layer. Eira could see several overarching themes: floral vases, blue ceramic, countless glass birds.

"I've stopped selling," Karin Backe explained, "but I keep buying anyway. People talk about having a clearout so that whoever's left behind doesn't have to deal with it after they die, but I can't stop myself going around and looking for things. What else would I do?"

She was white-haired, with a graceful way of speaking and moving, a little like the kind of delicate coffee service people used to bring out for guests.

"Do you know what's happening with the funeral?" she asked, making a slight gesture towards the newspaper on the kitchen table. "I haven't seen an announcement yet. It would be so awful if the church was empty. Will it be at the church?"

There was the bubbling of the percolator, the view across the water, an audiobook paused on her phone. Pictures of children and grandchildren on the sideboard, a late husband, a black-and-white wedding photograph and faces from several earlier generations, the people who had once surrounded this woman, but still. All the kitchen tables across the country, in houses someone had departed, where another was left behind.

Eira explained that Sven Hagström couldn't be buried yet, that it might still be a while before his body was released.

"He used to come out here to the barn nine or ten years ago," the woman told her as they sat down. "Looking for specific objects I helped him to find. An old barometer, a compass from the war years—he was really interested in that kind of thing. And then I suppose we sort of knocked about together for a while. It was always him who came here, always at dinnertime. I cooked for him, and he helped me with various jobs about the house. Changed the washers in the tap. There's always something breaking. We used to watch a bit of TV together too, mostly documentaries. But then it just didn't work anymore. He was too gloomy. You don't want that kind of gloominess in your house. I do sometimes miss it, though. Having someone else breathing beside you."

"Did you ever talk about what happened, with his son?"

"No, no, that was off limits. What do they call it—a no-go zone. I asked once, but he got angry. You don't want that either, not after a long life."

Eira ticked off the usual questions. When did you last see him, did he have any enemies . . . Though did normal people really have enemies?

Was he on bad terms with anyone? she asked instead.

"Most of Ådalen," said Karin Backe. "That's probably how he saw it, anyway. Like everyone was against him. Thought it was all down to him, that he'd raised his son to do all that stuff. But I doubt even Sven thought he'd be killed for it. How did he die?"

"I'm afraid I can't say."

Karin Backe dug out a photograph of her old odd-job lover, from the racetrack five years earlier. Sven Hagström had a dogged look on his face, yet he seemed more alive than in his seven-year-old driver's license picture.

She had taken the photo one day when she joined him at the race-track, thinking they could have a nice dinner together.

"But he was only interested in the races. Wanted to stand down by the track with all the other old blokes; you get a better view from there, and you can really feel the speed, the thud of the hooves."

They hadn't stayed in touch, though of course they ran into each other from time to time. She saw him not long before, in fact, in late spring, once the last few stubborn ice floes had finally drifted off towards the sea. Sven Hagström was walking Rabble, and Karin spotted him through the window, decided to go out.

"Is that its name, the dog?"

She laughed. "Sven thought it suited it. He got it from the pound, it had a terrible background, but he was good with dogs. They don't ask you to spill your heart and all that."

The strange thing about that final meeting had been that he had cried. They stood out on the jetty, down by the water's edge. From there, you could see right up to Hagström's house, clinging to the slope on the other side of the bay like a lonely nesting box in the middle of the forest. Maybe it was the distance, or the fact that, for a brief moment, he had really understood his place on earth. What it had become.

It wasn't just that the earth was turning, he said; that wasn't the only reason they had brought him before the Inquisition.

Karin had realized he was talking about Galileo. They had watched a documentary about him together. Sven was interested in the history of science and often said that everything we really know is ancient knowledge, that most of what has come since is a false doctrine. Not that Karin agreed, but she knew what he was talking about.

"It was the whole idea that two truths can exist in parallel," she remembered he went on. "That was what they couldn't tolerate, the church and the Inquisition. When Galileo discovered that the earth wasn't the center of the universe, the thing the sun and the stars revolved around, they finally reached their limit. They could only handle one truth: the Bible's. They couldn't allow him to nudge them into uncertainty. It was the confusion that terrified them."

"Did he say anything else?"

"I asked if he was OK, of course."

"And?"

Karin Backe shook her head. A lock of silver hair came loose, falling over her forehead, and she pushed it back into the clip. It was decorated with a small feather.

"He just called for the dog."

He waited until as late in the day as possible to go down to the river and wash, once the sun took its own dip below the treetops and the chatter of the birds was the only sound he could hear. The dog swam in circles, paddling frantically as though it were afraid of drowning.

Beads of water flew from its coat as it shook itself off. On the way back it leapt a few meters away, panting like the air was something fun. Jumping and snapping at blackflies.

Suddenly it stopped, sniffing the air. Olof noticed movement on the other side of the house. The car that had been parked there during the day was gone, and now there were other people peering through the trees. He saw a bicycle catch the light.

"What do you want?"

Olof took a few steps towards them, making sounds that would frighten them away. He heard rustling among the trees, scrambling up ahead.

His heart was racing, his body temperature rising.

"Get out of here!" He raised his arms and took another couple of steps. You had to show you were willing to fight, that was what he had learned in the place he was sent, you had to get bigger and heavier if you wanted to be left in peace. His body had grown and grown until he filled every room, until the others no longer dared enter.

The staff at the juvenile detention centers were bound by confidentiality, but that didn't help him. The other boys always knew he had killed. He told them himself, whenever anyone messed with him. It had been a long time since he was last beaten up.

As the little brats scrambled out of the forest with their bikes, he saw there were three of them. Small and scrawny, barely even teenagers, they disappeared in a flash.

Olof headed inside and locked the door behind him. Heard a screech from the gulls on the roof. He had discovered that they had a nest in the chimney, and for a while he had considered lighting a fire. Not because he needed the heat, but to get rid of the birds—it was a pain if they returned year after year, he remembered his father saying that—but he didn't have the energy. A memory of him secretly, without his father's knowledge, balling up sheets of newspaper between the firewood, in order to start a fire. A grown man didn't need any paper to help him.

He didn't turn on any of the lights in the house. Had drawn the curtains on the ground floor where he was sitting, eating straight from a plastic tub of meatballs and mash. There was no silence in this house. Branches hitting it, something creaking. Maybe the wind had picked up outside. A mouse scrambled inside the walls, scurrying away. A man could die, but his voice remained. Footsteps stomping across the floor upstairs. Thud, thud on the ceiling above.

Olof realized he was sitting in the same place he had back then, at the very edge of the sofa. His mother had been beside him, at a slight distance so that her body didn't touch his. She seemed to have shrunk, as though he had outgrown her, Dad in the armchair and Ingela on Mum's other side, close to her. No one looked at Olof. His body filled the entire room. They stared at the floor, out of the window. He stared at the floor and at his hands, his disgusting hands.

As far as he could remember, no one had said a word.

Then the footsteps on the stairs as the police officers came back down, one of them holding a plastic bag. There was something soft inside it, something yellow.

They had been rummaging around in the boxes beneath his bed. The policeman placed the bag on the table. Yellow as a dandelion, like the sun, dazzling. Everyone's eyes suddenly knew where to turn. Landing like flies on the bag.

Can you tell us what this is, Olof?

How did this end up under your bed?

He couldn't say it, not while they were all looking at him, though they were pretending to look elsewhere. What that scent had done to him. Her perfume, or maybe it was her deodorant or her hair, her body that smelled so strong.

It's a cardigan, Olof.

He didn't know whose voice it was. As he looked up, he met his father's eye. He didn't recognize it.

She was wearing one just like this when she disappeared.

The clouds had drifted by without spilling any rain, and the air was hot, dry, and dusty as the coldblood trotters warmed up at the start line.

"So this is where everyone is," August said, his eyes on the numbers on the digital screens. Fräcke Prins was the overwhelming favorite, with odds of 11:1, though a win by Axel Sigfrid would bring in 780 times as much. August had been quick to volunteer when he heard they needed someone else to join her at the harness racing track.

"This is the cold blood criteria," said Eira. "It's one of the most important events of the season, after the V75."

"Is it OK if I put a twenty on?"

She gave him a look.

"Just kidding," said August.

The racetrack at Dannero hadn't been the same since the old restaurant burned down. The new buildings were bright and airy, and lacked the weary, social democratic *folkhem* feeling of the past. Her family had occasionally come there together, for the midnight race in particular—the biggest party of the summer. Eira remembered the drunk spectators and the unbearable excitement of being given ten kronor to bet on the horses, she and Magnus. Not to mention crawling around among the adults' feet, searching for betting slips people might have dropped in their drunken state. She could still remember the rush of dreams within reach, the idea that anyone could become rich in the blink of an eye.

The new restaurant and VIP lounge were packed, and the space outside soon filled up. That was where Sven Hagström used to stand, according to Karin Backe. So close that you could feel the breeze as the pack charged by, the thundering of the hooves, the intense, heady scent of the horses. Eira caught snatches of conversation from the people around her. Older men in caps and fleece jackets, despite it being twenty-five degrees, standing close, speaking softly. She overheard a tip from someone with a contact in the stables: Byske Philip had run well in training, but Eldborken wasn't expected to have a particularly good season after his injury the previous winter.

The loudspeakers barked faster and faster as Eldborken took a surprise lead, passing Byske Philip and crossing the line with odds that made someone cry out.

After the winner had been handed his bouquet and completed a lap of honor, she felt her phone buzz. The track's managing director, most likely; he had been unreachable earlier, but would be by the cashiers' desks in two minutes, behind the hot dog stand.

"There's a lot to do on a day like this," he explained, wiping the sweat from his brow. He had rolled up his shirtsleeves and could give them three minutes, at most, between sponsors.

The name Sven Hagström was not one he knew, "but there are a lot of people you recognize without knowing them by name."

Eira showed him the photograph taken roughly thirty meters from where they were then standing.

"Yeah, OK," said the managing director. "I know him. He's usually with the group over there, they've been regulars since before I arrived, mostly bet small sums." He pointed to a scattered cluster of older men standing close to the fence. Another two sitting on a bench might be part of the group too, he said. "Has he done something?"

"We need to talk to people who knew him."

"Knew?" The man's eyes wandered, darting between the two officers and out across the spectators' area, pausing on the screens where the odds for the next race had just flashed up. "Does that mean it was him who . . . ? Oh, man. Talk to the old boys over there. Hacke's one of the veterans, and there's a guy called Kurt Ullberg, from Prästmon. He used to keep horses . . . I don't know the others . . . Don't think I can help you any more than that, I'm afraid."

He was already dashing off as they thanked him.

The race was underway. Eira went to buy a couple of coffees in paper cups. Once Järvsö Johanna had come in as the fastest mare, they walked over to the men. The small group between the benches was both elated and depressed; one of them had won, another lost. There was no need for the photograph. Of course they bloody knew Sven, knew what had happened to him.

"Didn't even have any money in the house," said the man known as Hacke, his face full of graying beard. "Sven went all in on the V75 at the end of May, and I don't remember him having much luck since. Often happens in phases, that kind of thing."

"You sure he didn't do it himself?" asked a man called Gustav something. Eira narrowed down his accent to somewhere inland, and she gestured for August to make a note of his name. It would be difficult to keep their attention once the next odds came up. Not because the men didn't care—they were all emotionally, angrily engaged, gathering closer and closer around the officers—but because it was in their muscle memory to turn towards the sound of approaching hooves.

"Why would anyone want to hurt him?"

"There was nothing wrong with the bloke."

"Bit quiet and grumpy, but who isn't with age? You can see the way the country's going yourself."

"You going to catch the bastard, then? Or is Sven just going to end up in a filing cabinet somewhere? It's a bloody outrage that the hospitals are being moved to the coast. He might have made it otherwise."

"He was dead when they found him."

"Yeah, but still." Gustav leaned in closer, and Eira resisted the urge to back away from the stench of alcohol and poor personal hygiene. "He probably should've got some help back then. You know, with all that." Gustav was holding a plastic glass of beer in one hand, a half-eaten hot dog in the other. He waved the sausage

towards his head to clarify what he thought Sven Hagström should
have been given help with.

"What do you mean?"

He bit off a chunk of hot dog and gave her an inquisitive, possibly
intrusive glance. There was a fine line between the two.

"You got kids?"

"Not yet."

"You want the best for them," the man continued. "You'll see that
one day. And if they fall, you have to stay strong. If you can't handle
that, if they fall between your hands, if your own child hits rock
bottom, this is all you've got to turn to." The beer slopped over the
edge of his glass as he gestured. "Who are you if you can't even save
your own kid?"

"He was an alcoholic?"

"He got into some heavy stuff."

"Sven Hagström?"

"No, no, are you crazy? My lad. He's not with us anymore. I
reckon that's why I could see it in him. In Svenne, I mean. The emptiness it leaves behind."

"Did you ever talk about it?"

"I don't know if you could call it talking, he always avoided the
subject, the way people do when it's too painful." Gustav whipped
around as the speaker called the start and the horses set off, hooves
drumming the ground, breathless. The crowd was entranced by the
possibility that Hallsta Bamse would take the lead with the incredible odds of 639:1. Eira didn't notice that August Engelhardt was
standing right behind her, hadn't seen him in a while.

"You're going to want to hear this," he said.

"Hold on."

On the final bend, Hallsta Bamse faltered under the pressure and
began to gallop, the voice over the loudspeaker reaching a falsetto as
Förtrollad took a clear lead. The sensation they had all been hoping
for, dreading, failed to pass, and a movement rippled through the
spectators, a collective exhalation.

"Guess where it seems like a rapist has been hiding out." August was standing so close to her ear that he brushed up against it, she felt the heat of his breath.

"Where?"

He nodded over to the group of men. "I followed one of them inside to collect his winnings after the last race. A thousand, in fact. Got to hear a few things."

"Tell me."

August Engelhardt seemed almost unbearably cocky as he smiled. *This might be his first-ever breakthrough at work*, Eira thought, glancing at her watch. No one would be leaving for a while yet.

"I'll treat you to something in the restaurant," she said.

"Fried meat and potatoes?"

"I'm sure they've got a few lettuce leaves, too."

The vegetarian revolution hadn't quite reached Norrland's racetracks, so August ordered a bland mixed salad and a cheese sandwich, Eira meatballs with mash and lingonberry sauce.

They managed to find the table with the worst views out onto the track, the only one still free. August leaned forward to overpower the clatter of cutlery and the murmur of voices, the irritating music played before the start of each race—a poor cover of the seventies hit "Popcorn."

The man August had followed to collect his winnings was Kurt Ullberg, the same one who had once owned horses himself. August read from his somewhat messy notes.

"Sometime in spring, early May he thought it was, he heard from a cousin whose brother-in-law lives next door to this woman, or maybe it was the neighbor who was his brother-in-law . . . She'd recognized the man in Nylands Järn, that's an ironmonger's . . ."

"I know it's an ironmonger's."

"There was something about the way he spoke, his voice, even though it was forty years since she'd last heard it."

"Recognized who?"

He flicked through his pad. "Adam Vide."

Eira racked her memory, but she couldn't remember the name from the investigation or anywhere else.

"Though apparently he doesn't call himself that anymore," August continued. "Ullberg says that people have always taken refuge in the forests around here—American deserters from the Vietnam War, people escaping urban development, women fleeing their abusive husbands."

"Welcome to the edge of the wilderness," said Eira. "What does this have to do with our case?"

August Engelhardt wiped salad dressing from the corner of his mouth and finished off his Ramlösa water.

"This Adam Vide guy lives in Kungsgården now," he said. "That's why Ullberg told Sven Hagström. He thought he, if anyone, should know. And I quote: 'After all that business with his boy, the shame. That he wasn't the only one.'"

"What kind of rape are we talking about?"

"A gang rape somewhere in upper Norrland, a really brutal case apparently."

The cramped room, the humidity and the heat of all the people, the noisy atmosphere—it was too much for her to be able to think clearly. They were back outside before she managed to grasp the key questions.

"Does Ullberg know what this man calls himself now?"

"Nope, unfortunately. His cousin or his cousin's brother-in-law didn't want to share the name in case the woman was wrong, or maybe they just didn't know."

The last race of the day was over, but the old men were still hanging around by the track. Even from a distance, Eira could see that their plastic cups were full.

"But I do have her name," August continued. "She lives in Prästmon, and I've got Ullberg's number in case we need anything else from him."

"Good work," said Eira.

He smiled, fishing a scrap of paper from his back pocket. "Can I go and collect my winnings now?"

Eira never usually went for a beer with her colleagues after work. She usually drove straight home to Lunde to make sure her mother ate dinner, to make sure everything was OK.

In the Swedish language, going for a beer always meant at least three or four.

It meant a taxi home, almost ten kilometers away.

Despite all that, it was Eira who suggested it. There was something desolate about August Engelhardt's tone once they had recapped the key information from the racetrack. On the way out, he had asked whether she could recommend any good TV shows, though he already seemed to have seen most of them.

"What else is there to do in Kramfors in the evenings?"

"Have you been to Kramm yet?" Eira asked, immediately regretting her words. It wasn't her responsibility if he felt lonely.

"Sounds exciting," said August.

"Just you wait."

A few of the letters in the neon sign above the Hotel Kramm had gone out. Eira had spent plenty of drunken nights there in the distant past. One or two crazy one-night stands, too. Bodies without clear faces.

August returned from the bar with two bottles of High Coast beer.

"So what do you think about this rapist thing? Could it be something?"

"Talking about the case at the pub—you really think that's a good idea?"

"We were talking in the restaurant."

"But that was you bringing me up to speed. Besides, there was no one listening."

They both glanced around the bar. Wall-to-wall carpet and upholstered seats, a group of local women in their forties, a couple of gloomy businessmen.

August swigged from his bottle. "What's it like, living in the same place all your life? Where everyone knows you."

He leaned back, his eyes glittering. Eira felt the first rush of the alcohol, the heightened presence of the moment. There was no risk. He was too young, and he had a girlfriend, he'd told her.

"I lived in Stockholm for a few years," said Eira. "I always thought I'd move away from here as soon as it was up to me."

"But then love got in the way, right?"

"In a sense." She peered out through the window, at the tarmac and the parked cars. It was her mother who had got in the way, but that felt far too heavy a topic of conversation, far too personal. Her illness, the responsibility, the fear of being in the wrong place; that was why she had moved back the previous year. Surely that belonged under the heading of love too.

He clinked his bottle against her glass.

"Eira," he said. "That's a nice name. Unusual."

"Not in Ådalen." She waited to see whether there was any reaction. There wasn't. "The girl who died after being hit by a ricocheting military bullet in nineteen thirty-one. Eira Söderberg. I'm named after her."

"Aha. Cool."

Eira still wasn't sure he knew what she was talking about, so she ignored the fact that she didn't want to be the type of person who told stories at every turn. The shots in Ådalen were general knowledge, after all. Eira Söderberg was only twenty when she died. She wasn't even part of the demonstration, just standing to one side, watching the protesters, when she was hit by the bullet. It was a moment that had fundamentally changed Sweden. Never again would the military be brought in to deal with civilians; what would go on to become the Swedish model began right there. Peace among workers and owners, the land of compromise.

Eira knocked back the last of her beer.

"Well, cheers to that," said August, getting up to buy them another round.

Three beers later, possibly four, she was standing in front of the hotel, dialing the number for Kramfors Taxis. August had gone to the bathroom. The neon sign on the roof blinked on the metal of the cars. She heard him come out behind her and turned around, and suddenly he was far too close. Somehow she ended up in his arms, pressed up against his mouth. It came out of nowhere, she hadn't seen it coming.

"What are you doing?" she mumbled.

She couldn't understand. Her tongue was already deeply involved, but he was too young, too handsome. *I'm starved*, she thought, *it's been too long*.

"We have to work together," she said. Her words came as they gasped for air.

"Could you just be quiet?"

"You said you had a girlfriend."

"It's not that kind of relationship."

The taxi never had time to arrive, Eira forgot she had even called it. His temporary apartment was too far away; heading back into the hotel reception was far easier. She let him book the room in his name, paying with his card, "the winnings from Dannero," they laughed as he pushed her up against the wall of the lift, against the buttons, making the damned thing stop on the wrong floor. The night porter was from Syria, one of those who had stayed behind after the latest wave of refugees. He had no idea who she was, wouldn't spread any gossip.

It's just one night, she thought as August fumbled, dropping the key card. *If that. It's nothing*.

It was quarter past four in the morning, and the sun hit her square in the face. August was asleep on his front beside her, arms outstretched like some kind of Jesus figure.

She quietly got dressed, quietly tiptoed out. There was no sign of the night porter. Kramfors was sleeping soundly, but the central taxi office in Umeå, or possibly Bangalore, was open.

Twenty minutes later, she was in a car on the way to Lunde, filled with a growing sense of panic over what she might come home to.

The yellow house was still standing as it always had. The door wasn't open. Her mother hadn't wandered out and fallen into the river. There was no hint of smoke in the air, no one lying on the floor with a broken hip.

Eira had managed to arrange brief but regular visits from a carer during the day. They warmed food, checked in on her mother, and administered medicine, even helping out with her shower twice a week. If Eira ever needed to be away from home for longer, she could always call a neighbor or one of the few friends her mother had left. The number was growing smaller and smaller. If they hadn't moved away for work, they had been swept up in the great grandmother migration—women whose children had stayed put in the big city, who had followed them there in order to be closer to their grandkids.

She found her mother in her bedroom, on top of the bed. Kerstin had fallen asleep in her clothes, the reading light still on, glasses askew on her face. Her book had fallen to the floor, *The Lover* by Marguerite Duras. The pages were stained and the glue had started to crumble on the spine.

A couple of lines caught Eira's eye. The passage was about love. Not just that, she realized as she kept reading. The couple in question had just had sex. It was clear that it was the woman's first time, that she had known she would enjoy making love; or was it the man who thought he knew her? The bookmark fell out as she closed the book, and Eira pushed it back in at the wrong place. She felt a childish sense of shame at having discovered her mother reading something erotic.

It struck her, perhaps because the evidence of a lover was still so fresh in her own body that a forensic technician could have easily secured it, that she knew nothing about her mother's love life over the past nineteen years. Nor before that. Her parents had come to a kind of strained agreement to get divorced, and her father had remarried barely a year later, leading her to suspect that he had been the reason. But what if it actually had been the other way around?

She left the book on the bedside table and promised herself she would read it someday. It would be something to talk about— possibly even every morning, since Kerstin seemed to forget what she was reading. Eira wondered whether she still found the same joy in the language and the stories, or whether she simply read in bed because it was what she had always done.

She went through to the bathroom and took a shower. Her body felt both present and absent, stinging in certain places. She brushed her teeth three times, but the taste refused to subside.

Of drunkenness, of him, of everything.

The meeting had already started by the time she arrived, slightly late. Eira discreetly popped a piece of chewing gum into her mouth and held her breath as she greeted her colleagues.

She still hadn't quite managed to come to grips with exactly who was involved in the investigation. In the past they had always worked in more coherent teams, but these days people drifted in and out depending on what was needed and who brought them in from elsewhere. Everything was flexible, in motion. In a way, it resembled the wider changes in society; a group was now a fluid concept.

Information spread among large numbers of people, and the knowledge base grew and grew, but the connections became increasingly difficult to grasp. Eira didn't know which of them would still be around the next day, which she might never see again.

"But let's say you found your father dead, brutally murdered," said Silje Andersson, an investigator whose voice Eira had only ever heard via internet link from Sundsvall, "or drove the knife into him yourself. Why would you hang around in the house? What kind of person would want to be there?"

"The guy from *Psycho*?" suggested Bosse Ring. He was someone Eira had met on a number of occasions, a veteran with thirty-two years of service beneath his belt, a military career before that. Crooked nose like an old boxer, thin glasses.

Voices were deceptive. They typically had video functionality in their meetings, but few actually bothered to switch their webcams on. Judging by Silje Andersson's deep, slightly husky voice, Eira had expected a middle-aged woman who dyed her gray hair and needed reading glasses, not a busty, platinum blond beauty who probably had the criminals voluntarily following her to the station. It bothered her that she noticed that kind of thing.

"Actually, what was the story there?" Bosse Ring continued. "He didn't kill his mum, did he?"

"Who?" asked GG, glancing up from his computer.

"The guy in *Psycho*. He just hid her in the attic and used her rocking chair, didn't he?"

"I found a few reports about Olof Hagström, by the way," said Silje. "One from an institution he was sent to when he was younger. He hit some of the other boys on a few occasions, no serious injuries. From there he seems to have ended up in a foster home in Upplands Bro. No final grades from school, various jobs over the years, including at a timber yard in the same area. Different temporary addresses, but no criminal record."

"Maybe he just never got caught?" said Bosse Ring.

"But I'm wondering about the method," Silje continued. "A knife wound like that doesn't require a lot of force, but it does take some skill. It suggests self-confidence, an iciness. A nervous attacker would have kept on stabbing to make sure the man was definitely dead. And if they wanted revenge or were emotionally wounded somehow, personally involved, they would've taken out their rage on him."

Eira pictured the pale body and swallowed her nausea.

"His GP called back," she spoke up. "He confirmed a broken femur four years ago, after Sven Hagström fell from a stepladder. The shower seat was only ever supposed to be a temporary loan, but no one seems to have asked for it back."

"Please promise you'll shoot me the day I have to sit down in the shower," said Bosse Ring.

Eira sipped the coffee she had managed to pick up en route. It tasted awful paired with the minty gum. GG turned to her. She thought he looked tired, his eyes red, as though he hadn't managed to get much sleep.

"We were talking about the information you got from the races earlier. What do you make of it?"

"Not sure," said Eira, embarrassed to have arrived late. "The source seemed credible, but it's third- or fourth-hand information."

"Thinking freely for a moment here, could it have been Sven Hagström that the woman saw in the ironmonger's? Who used to call himself . . . what was it?"

"Adam Vide."

"There's nothing in Sven Hagström's past to suggest he ever changed his name," said Silje Andersson.

"That could've been what he called himself when he was picking up women," said Bosse Ring. "People can call themselves whatever they want out there. A friend of mine asked what tricks we have for finding out who someone really is; he was chatting to some woman who called herself Big Tits."

"A friend?" Silje said softly. "You know that means the same thing on social media as it does on the psychiatrist's couch, don't you? No one ever really asks on behalf of a friend."

"Silje, you go with Eira," said GG. "Pay the woman a visit, find out whether there's anything in this. Talk to the others in the chain of gossip if you need to."

He and Bosse Ring would be checking in on the building site, putting a little pressure on them. The Lithuanian builders who were busy renovating an old school into a B&B insisted that they started work at six every morning.

"We'll find out if that holds water. Some information about unpaid taxes and wage dumping has come to light, and that usually makes people talk."

They also planned to bring in a few characters with shady histories from the area, names from a list Eira had produced.

"Those men have all been either convicted of assault or tried for it at some point," she said, "but none of them have ever been suspected of murder or manslaughter."

"There's a first time for everything," said GG. "And if nothing else, I'm sure they're sitting on information of some kind. They snap up any gossip about what people have stashed away in their cabins, who's on holiday; they're always out and about at uncomfortable hours."

"Sven Hagström rarely traveled anywhere," said Silje. "His passport expired at the end of the last century."

"Maybe they'll confess to something else," said GG.

We're going down a dead-end alley here, thought Eira. *No one actually thinks it will lead anywhere; we're just doing it because we have to, pretending to be hopeful.*

"Has anyone considered whether this might actually be about money?" asked Silje, reeling off a few facts about the victim's finances. A meager pension after a lifetime of seasonal work in the forestry industry, a house with a ratable value of 19,000, savings of 13,700 kronor. "For his own funeral, I bet. He was part of the generation that doesn't want to be a burden."

"We'll look into everything," GG told her in a somewhat sharper tone. "Which means we're not ruling out anything until it can be completely ruled out. With every day that passes, another old person grows more anxious. Someone will start locking their door. Someone else will write that the police aren't doing their job."

It was two weeks to the day, almost the hour, since someone had driven a knife into Sven Hagström's abdomen, severing an artery.

They still didn't have a murder weapon, no key witnesses.

Did he really need to remind them of that?

Eira swigged from the bottle of cola she had bought to help with the nausea and slowed down as they drove through Bollstabruk, past the sad, boarded-up shops of the shrinking sawmill town.

Conversations with a new colleague were always the same, practically following a template. *How long have you been on the force, how did you end up here?* The answers were the only thing that differed slightly, but then again Silje Andersson wasn't exactly fresh out of the police academy.

"I actually wanted to be a geologist," she said. "All the other girls were into horses and dogs and boy bands, but I was obsessed with rocks. My therapist said it's linked to my childhood."

Rocks were something constant in a world that seemed so unreliable. They took thousands of years to be worn down and transformed. The information made Eira see her colleague in a different light. Silje had also completed half a psychology degree before deciding to become a police officer.

They fell silent as the news bulletin began on the radio.

The murder had slipped from the local headlines a few days back, and the focus now was on the revelation that rich Stockholm councils had secretly been sending welfare recipients to poorer regions in Norrland. Organizing leases wherever there were empty apartments, paying their train fares and one month's rent before washing their hands of them. The Kramfors authorities had discovered what was going on only when the new arrivals showed up at the welfare office.

"So how do you like working with GG?" asked Silje.

"He's OK, I guess," said Eira. "Experienced."

"Why do you think he put the two of us on this?"

"Seems pretty logical—we're going to talk to a woman about a sexual assault."

Eira was just grateful she didn't have to hunt down any local addicts who were guaranteed to tell her to say hi to Magnus, but she didn't mention that. Nor did she mention that the hill they had just passed was the infamous Bålberget, where more women had been beheaded and burnt as witches than anywhere else in the country. Over the course of one June day in the late seventeenth century, one in four women in the parish had been executed.

"Or maybe it's because his girlfriend doesn't like him being alone with me," said Silje, casting a glance at Eira. "So watch yourself."

"What do you mean?"

"He's pretty tasty, don't you think? GG has a bit of a reputation, but maybe it hasn't reached this far north yet?"

"I try to avoid having affairs with people at work," Eira told her, turning off towards the woman's address in Prästmon. "And with men who are already spoken for," she added. It was only afterwards, following a moment of silence, that she realized just how quick and easy it was to become a hypocrite.

"No, of course," Silje said with a smile. "That's what we all say, until it happens."

The woman's name was Elsebeth Franck. She was in her early fifties, but as she sat down and Silje asked her to tell them what happened, it was like she became sixteen again. She clamped her hands between her thighs, pushed back a nonexistent fringe, and seemed much slighter than she had a moment earlier.

"Why do you want to know about that?"

Her husband squeezed her hand.

"Has he done it again?" she asked. "Is that why?"

"It would be great," said Silje, "if you could just tell us what happened."

Their house, which her husband had inherited from his parents, had been tastefully renovated. Perhaps it stood on foundations from the seventeenth century. Maybe one of the witches had lived in it then. It had oiled floorboards and an enormous wood-burning stove, pale lilac curtains blowing softly in the breeze. On the expanse of lawn outside, two small robotic lawn mowers whizzed about, plowing away any unevenness. Elsebeth was wearing a pair of wide-legged trousers and a matching top, both from an expensive Swedish brand. They spent their winters in Gothenburg, her husband explained, but his wife was from even farther north.

"Jävredal, if you've heard of it."

Between Skellefteå and Piteå, on the border between the two most northerly counties, that was where the community Elsebeth Franck would never again set foot lay.

"At first I wasn't sure," she said. "I heard a man's voice behind me, and it was like my body knew before I even had time to process it. I started shaking, can you believe that?" She glanced outside, pausing, forcing back the tears or whatever else she didn't want to come out.

The sky had darkened to the northwest, a storm on its way down from the mountains.

"You think you can forget. You don't think about it for so long, then you meet a wonderful man, get married and start a family, you have a good life, and you start to think that maybe it's gone for good, that things disappear, but they don't. They never do."

"Take all the time you need," said Silje.

"As if I need any of this. Do you really think that?"

Elsebeth Franck studied the detective.

"You remind me of her, do you know that? She was so blond, so confident and beautiful; I can look at old photographs of myself and think I was pretty cute too, but I never stood a chance around her. I don't think someone like you could understand what that was like."

"What do you mean?"

"Being rejected. Always being rejected. But I still wanted to be around her more than anyone else. Why do we do that?"

"Sunlight," said Eira. "We want to bask in it."

Elsebeth Franck nodded slowly, but continued to study Silje, so closely that it was almost like she was trying to spot something beneath her skin.

"Could you tell us what happened that day in Nylands Järn?" Eira asked.

"I wish I'd gone instead," said her husband. "But she insisted. It was for my sixtieth birthday."

Elsebeth had gone into Nyland to buy the last few bits and pieces for his party and to collect the wine they had ordered. The ironmonger also functioned as a pickup point for the state-run off-license in town.

"I was trying to find the right light bulbs—it's not so easy anymore, the wattages are all different from the ones we're used to—and as I was standing there, I heard his voice behind me. Over by the drills. There must have been something inside me that recognized it immediately, because I stopped and listened, even though I was in a hurry; I had so much to do at home. The man was talking to a member of staff, they seemed to agree that one of the brands was better than the others, but he couldn't decide, and then I heard him say those words and it was like a jolt shot through me."

Her husband had moved his hand to her back, rubbing it gently.

"I remember exactly what he said, slipping back into the old melody, the dialect from up north. All I could see was the back of his head over the shelves, but I knew. It just came out. 'Adam Vide,' I said, and he turned around. No one else in the shop, just him. Those eyes. They were the same. He looked away and put down the drill, then hurried off towards the till and the door, but I'm sure of it. I'd heard him say the exact same thing before."

"What did he say?"

Elsebeth asked her husband to go and make some coffee. Once he had left the room, she continued, speaking quickly, her voice low.

"'She's the best of 'em.' He said the exact same thing that night, only then he was talking about 'the blonde one, the pretty one,' not a drill. That's what he was like, Adam Vide, though I didn't know his name at the time, it was only during the trial . . . We were at the gas station, eating burgers, and I'd had my eye on him . . . There was a whole group of them, and I thought he was handsome but not *too* handsome, if you know what I mean, and I got it into my head that he was interested, that he was looking at me; I thought he had such nice eyes, blue with a hint of green, like the sea on holiday. But it was Anette he wanted, of course it was, it was always Anette. I heard him when I passed on my way to the toilet. 'You can hit on the other one if you want,' he said to his friends—meaning me, clearly—but they could forget about the pretty one."

Elsebeth had spent a long time in the toilet that evening, and by the time she emerged, Anette was already giggling away on Adam Vide's lap. She was drunk, they all were, they'd been to the drag races, the biggest party of the year in Jävredal, and the boys weren't local, people came from all around for it. Anette shouted for Elsebeth to join them as they staggered out to the cars, the boys had more to drink in their tents down by the lake, said, "Come on, don't be so boring."

"The last thing I saw was her squeezing in between two of them in the front of a Cadillac with flames on the sides. She had her legs over Adam Vide's, and his hands were all over her, his were already under her dress, she was swigging from a bottle, singing along with some song that was thundering out across the car park. Moonshine, they said at the trial. I didn't want any. I'd slept with a few boys I didn't really like in the past, just so I didn't seem boring. I sometimes pretended to fall in love with them, because that made it feel a bit better."

She straightened up as her husband came back into the room, reaching out to lovingly and protectively stroke his cheek.

"It might be best if I talk to them on my own," she said.

"You know you don't have anything to be ashamed of, don't you? You know I'm here."

"I know."

A kiss on the forehead, and he withdrew to another part of the house.

"He doesn't know everything," Elsebeth explained. "It's not true that I haven't thought about it since. It's there all the time. I should have dragged her out of that car, I knew it didn't feel right, but I was so angry with her that I didn't do a thing; I can see her now, arms waving in the air as they drove away, but what did I do? Cried and kicked the ground as I walked two kilometers home through the woods, I felt so sorry for myself."

She got the call from Anette's mother late the next afternoon, after someone found her in the tent and raised the alarm.

Seven young men had taken part in the rape, the youngest just sixteen years old. He was the one who had brought the whole thing to a close by shoving his entire hand inside her, tearing the walls of her vagina in the process. By the time Elsebeth found out what had happened, Anette was in surgery. She had split, right through to her abdomen.

"I attended a bit of the first trial, but I couldn't handle any more than that. I switched to another school farther south so I wouldn't bump into them on the street once they were released. They only got a year. I have no idea what she's up to now, whether she's even alive. Whether she could have kids. Maybe that's the real reason I left: so I wouldn't have to see Anette anymore. I've occasionally looked for her on Facebook, trying to find out whether she's OK, whether she managed to make a life for herself, but I've never found her. I guess she probably changed her name too."

"Your husband is right," said Silje. "It wasn't your fault. It's the perpetrators who should be ashamed."

The woman turned away. Eira got the sense that she used the expensive clothes as a costume: slightly anonymous, appropriate in every context.

"Seeing him trying to decide between drills as though nothing had happened . . . Afterwards, I found myself thinking that I'd had all kinds of heavy objects around me, dangerous things. I could've hit him on the head with a spade or a brush cutter, anything, but I did nothing, I just stood there and watched him leave."

The three women jumped as a flash of lightning lit up the sky outside. The storm clouds were the same shade of bluish black as bruised skin after a serious assault, but the rain still hadn't started falling. Elsebeth Franck got up to close the window, and paused.

The clap of thunder came ten seconds later, meaning the storm was around three kilometers away.

"I haven't been to Nyland since," said Elsebeth. "I'd rather go to Sollefteå, even though it's much farther away. My husband and I often take the canoes out on the river, but now I tell him not downstream, not that way."

"How do you know that this man lives in Kungsgården?"

"Someone spoke to him on his way out. I was hiding behind the shelves, but I could still hear them: 'How are things in Kungsgården? You got fiber broadband there yet?' They didn't. Have fiber, I mean. He complained about how long it was taking."

It was only once the man had left the shop that she dared go over to the till. She had to say something. Wasn't that Adam Vide? she asked.

No, that's not his name.

"You didn't ask who he was?"

"No, I didn't. I couldn't."

Silje asked her to describe the man. Tall, taller than average, probably somewhere around six two, in fairly good shape for someone pushing sixty, a fact that angered Elsebeth. She would rather have stood face-to-face with a cripple, anything that suggested he wasn't just living his life. He still had a full head of hair, too, though it was now gray.

Eira exchanged a glance with the investigator. That ruled out Sven Hagström. He was over seventy, and much shorter.

"It's been a long time," said Silje.

"Thirty-eight years in two weeks." Elsebeth Franck studied each of them in turn. "It was the way he moved, too. And his voice. Why else would he have turned around when I said that name? He didn't even buy the drill, the one he thought was *so* good-looking."

She had paid for her light bulbs that day, but forgot all about the wine—her husband had to go back and collect it later. That was why she ultimately had to tell him what happened, later that afternoon, just before their guests arrived. He could see straight through her, the family's collective memory, their project manager, usually so on top of everything. Elsebeth had tried to act like her usual self—they were having a party, after all—but she managed to burn the pies and drop a glass, breaking down in tears over it.

It was the first her husband had ever heard about what happened that summer in Jävredal.

"I keep looking for a sign that something has changed in him, but it hasn't. Can you believe that? That he still loves me? Sometimes it makes me so angry. I feel like he must be stupid if he hasn't managed to grasp the full scope of who I am. He loves someone he thinks he understands, but who isn't me."

Towards the end of the party, once only a few of their closest friends were left, he had wanted Elsebeth to tell them, so they would understand why the atmosphere was so strange. They were among friends, after all. Relatives, people who loved her. He thought it would do her good.

To finally rid herself of it, to be free.

She let him talk, on condition that they didn't tell anyone else.

Elsebeth had gone to bed.

"But I suppose someone must have blabbed anyway, and that person must've told someone else. No one can keep another person's secret."

The storm was getting closer. Her husband came downstairs and pulled out the plugs so that it wouldn't trip the TV box or anything.

"I'm only talking about this today," said Elsebeth, "because it seems like you want to get him for something."

Her husband took up a protective position behind her as they said their goodbyes in the hallway.

"I really hope this is important," he said.

"We don't know," said Eira. "This tip came up as part of an investigation into something else; we're just exploring every angle."

"A rape?"

"A murder. It might be important, but it might not be linked."

Elsebeth Franck's hand was cold and limp as she said goodbye.

"Now I'm never going to think about it again."

The court transcripts were waiting for her, unread, in a thick envelope. Eira had left the station early in order to drive over to Härnösand to collect them. Cases from the eighties hadn't been digitized yet, and Piteå District Court had long since closed down. It had taken the woman at the National Archive quite some time to find them.

Then dinner got in the way.

"You were supposed to leave," Kerstin muttered. She had paused with the cheese slicer in her hand as they cleared the table.

"What do you mean?"

"You were supposed to make something of yourself. Yet here you are, treading water."

"Maybe I like my job," said Eira. "It's practical for me to stay here."

"But you're so talented."

"I'll take that," Eira told her, putting the cheese slicer into the dishwasher. People had been telling her these things for as long as she could remember, talking about all the possibilities that lay open to her thanks to those who had come before, telling her she could be whatever she wanted to be.

A sense that her life had begun long before she was even born.

Like the trees, the undergrowth.

Being a police officer was a disappointment, verging on a betrayal. For much of the older generation, uniforms still brought back memories of the military, of 1931.

When she could study humanities, the natural sciences, become

anything; when those who had come before had built this society for
her, one in which the children and grandchildren of sawmill workers
had the opportunity to study. To devote themselves to the literature
at the top of the food chain, from the trees that had been sawed and
cultivated, all the way up. And yet Eira had wanted to do something
concrete, something physical and definite. To escape the books, the
pompous texts. To be on the right side, so as not to slip over to the
wrong one.

"Just be happy I'm not on drugs!" Eira had once shouted when
her choice of career came crashing down like a bomb in the family.
Shattering, dividing.

She chose a random episode of *Shetland* on SVT Play and set
down a cup of tea in front of her mother. She doubted Kerstin could
really follow what was happening on-screen, but at least she enjoyed
watching the handsome policeman, so melancholy yet pleasant.

The smell of smoke drifted in from the northwest, across the river.
The local radio bulletin reported that the lightning had caused
fires in Marieberg and up by Saltsjön. The ground was dry, stoking
everyone's fears again. They all remembered the fires the previous
summer; they had destroyed large swathes of forest, forcing people
to flee their homes.

Eira sat down at the kitchen table with the verdict from Piteå
District Court.

It was thick, unusually exhaustive. The archivist in Härnösand
had remarked on just how comprehensive it was, claimed never to
have seen anything like it.

"It's incredibly detailed," she had said, repeating herself so many
times that Eira realized she must have been shocked by what she had
read.

The trial took place in November 1981.

Seven young men faced charges. Adam Vide was the first to have
assaulted the complainant, Anette Lidman. According to some of
the others, he had instigated the entire thing, undressing her in his
tent.

Off with her knickers, up with her dress.

As far as Adam Vide could recall, she had taken off her clothes herself, entirely voluntarily. He thought she was into it; she was already wet when he felt her up in the car, and she followed him to his tent. Surely that was proof that she wanted it?

What else was he supposed to think?

Others testified that Anette was inebriated to the point of blackout when they reached the campsite, that she couldn't even walk unaided.

In the early eighties, DNA technology had not yet become a key part of criminal investigations. As a result, though a substantial amount of semen was found when Anette Lidman was examined, it was impossible to say exactly who had ejaculated into her.

Adam Vide had been too drunk, he claimed. Couldn't get an erection, so he just climbed on top and rubbed against her, trying to make it work. Then he had left her there, needed to throw up, had to get out.

Outside the tent, he bumped into a guy he didn't know. He didn't know why, but he had told him there was a horny girl in his tent, that the bloke should get acquainted with her.

Or maybe he had said, "You should fuck her."

This was where the various testimonies diverged.

Adam Vide went off to get even more intoxicated elsewhere, but the young man had taken his advice and crawled into the tent, as had a number of his friends. No one had protested or told them to stop. In fact, they took it in turns, cheering their friends on—even patting one of them on the backside while he was humping her.

One after another. Page after page detailing each of the rapes. How was it possible that not a single one of them had reacted and said stop, prevented it from going on? Maybe they had wanted to, but kept quiet anyway.

One said she had thrust back, another that she was unconscious. It remained unclear who had ripped off her dress. The last of them, the sixteen-year-old, the youngest of the bunch, was told to use his fingers when he failed to get an erection. And so he did, until he realized his hand was bloody.

Adam Vide had first returned to his tent the next morning, find-ing Anette Lidman lying naked inside. She didn't reply when he asked how she was, so he left.

When someone finally raised the alarm and Anette was taken to hospital, she was still unconscious. With a blood alcohol level of 0.4 percent.

She had no idea what had happened to her.

Adam Vide and five of the others were sentenced to one year in prison for sexual abuse. In the eyes of the law, it wasn't rape, because the girl hadn't put up any resistance. The youngest was also con-victed of aggravated assault and handed over to social services.

Eira got up and boiled more water for tea.

Something was niggling away at the back of her mind, a detail from a legal course she had once taken. The law had been tightened following a heated debate around this very subject, and wasn't it in the early nineties? She googled around a little and found a par-liamentary text in which the assault in Jävredal was mentioned in connection with the proposed bill. These days, the seven rapists would hardly have got away with only a year in prison.

She sat back down to the part she had been waiting for with near unbearable patience, like a child who slowly learns not to sneak a glimpse at her Christmas presents.

Eira returned to the transcript itself, to the details of each of the accused. Names were easy enough to change in Sweden, but a per-son's ID number followed him from cradle to grave—assuming nothing particularly out of the ordinary happened, in which case the state might permit someone to be freed from his past.

That hardly applied to a man convicted of sexual abuse.

The full-time investigators were the only ones with official laptops they could take home. Eira couldn't access the various registers and databases unless she went to the station, but there were several public access sites that enabled a search of ID numbers. She wouldn't be able to get at the last four digits that way, but that didn't matter too much.

She entered Adam Vide's ID number. Born August 1959. It was

almost his birthday, in fact; *Happy birthday, dear Adam*, she thought as she typed in Nyland—the postal address covering Kungsgården and the surrounding area.

One hit.

Jesus Christ, she thought, doing a lap of the kitchen and sitting down again, staring at the name that was flickering on the screen.

Erik Tryggve Nydalen.

How could she have missed it? It was right there in the transcripts, in the box containing the accused's full name.

ADAM Erik Tryggve Vide.

He had ditched the "Adam" and taken his wife's surname when they got married. Not exactly the most advanced of disguises.

But what did this mean?

She thought back to how Tryggve Nydalen had greeted them with a firm handshake in the yard. He was certainly tall, with plenty of hair, but were his eyes blue? Eira suspected she would make a terrible witness if she was ever put on the spot. Whenever she met another person's eye, she was usually focused on trying to see what was going on behind it.

Tryggve Nydalen had come across as the levelheaded member of his agitated, at times almost hysterical family, the most reasonable one.

Eira realized that she could no longer hear the TV; the episode of *Shetland* had finished. Kerstin peered up as Eira came in. She had dozed off, was confused.

"Oh, hello, is that you?"

Undressing, nightgown, brushing her teeth. There was something Eira enjoyed about the routine. A serenity, a minor victory. They had survived another day.

As her mother got into bed with her book, the same one as the day before, Eira drew up a timeline on the back of a flyer.

The month of May, a brief spring that passed in a flash between the ice melting and summer. It had only just begun when Sven Hagström heard the gossip about a sex offender living in his immediate surroundings.

The month of May. That was also when he had made contact with
the library. Eira may have been bad with eye colors, but dates were
one thing she could remember. On the fourteenth and sixteenth
of May, the murder-victim-to-be had called for help searching for
something in the newspapers from up north. Old papers, from the
eighties.

She made a note to call the other librarian, she might know more.
Eira pulled a cardigan over her shoulders and went outside. The
smoke from the fires had formed a thick, yellowish haze that obscured the forests on the other side of the river.

There had been a call to the police, too. On 3 June. Perhaps Sven
had intended to file a complaint, or inquire about something, shout
at someone, only to change his mind and hang up.

Perhaps he didn't trust the police.

The old man wasn't exactly a pro at gathering information—he
owned neither a computer nor a mobile phone. On the other hand,
it had taken Eira roughly sixty seconds to link Adam Vide to Tryggve Nydalen. Didn't that mean there was a chance that even Sven
Hagström, who had several weeks, a month, oceans of time on his
hands, had somehow managed to do the same?

Late spring, Karin Backe had said. That was when she'd last seen
her old odd-job lover. That must mean the end of May. He had
been standing by the shore, looking up towards his house on the
other side of the bay. And he had been crying, the man who never
spoke about his feelings. Something about double truths, whether
two truths could exist simultaneously.

She could wait until the next day, of course. As soon as the archive opened, she could request the investigation from over twenty
years ago, one that hadn't yet been digitized, that had never reached
trial and therefore remained sealed, buried under decades of other
crimes.

Instead she brought up a number, one she had saved in her phone
but hadn't called in a long time.

Seven rings, then she heard his voice, raspy and familiar.

"Sorry, did I wake you?"

"No, no, good grief, I was practicing my salsa footwork," said Eilert Granlund.

"Congratulations," said Eira. "Sounds like you're really enjoying life."

"Enormously," her old colleague replied, yawning loudly. "So I hope whatever you're bothering me with is interesting."

"Sven Hagström," she said. "I guess you're still reading the paper, even though you said you were going to stop?"

"I listen to the radio," said Eilert. "Was almost surprised he was still alive. What a bloody business with his son. Hard to believe a man could ever get over something like that."

"A question came up during the investigation," said Eira. "If it's OK that I'm bothering you?"

"So you're an investigator now, are you?" He congratulated her on her progress, which she found touching. Eira occasionally missed his slightly bullish way of sharing his knowledge, the depth of experience carved into his body. "The crooks must be quivering in their boots," he shouted, so loud that she had to hold the phone away from her ear.

Eira tried to come up with a funny response, something to match the banter, but all she could find was a stupid feeling of wanting to cry. Maybe it was just the tension that had been weighing on her for the past week. None of the investigators from Violent Crimes had questioned her competence. She was the only one who did so; she always was.

"Anyway, what a bloody thing that was," Eilert said with a cough. Eira remembered the smoke from his cigarillos and hoped it wasn't lung cancer she could hear.

Her old colleague had said he was looking forward to retirement, to being able to sleep whenever he wanted, without being woken up by some damned alarm. To teaching the grandkids the names of the birds, all that stuff, but Eira thought she could hear a hint of doubt. Now she felt guilty for not having called sooner. Strange how people you once saw every day could so quickly drift out of focus.

"You were involved in the investigation back then, weren't you?"

she asked. "Do you remember interviewing someone called Tryggve Nydalen?"

"We interviewed a lot of people, asked them what they'd seen and heard, but it was over twenty years ago now. You'll have to excuse me if I can't remember them all off the top of my head."

"He had a prison sentence for sexual abuse in his baggage—by the legal standards of the time. I've read the court transcripts. The girl was unconscious, her vaginal wall split, seven guys; once you've read something like that, you don't forget it."

"Christ. No, I don't remember that, us interviewing anyone . . . I think I do remember the case, though. Up north somewhere? Led to a change in law, if it's the one I'm thinking of. Are you sure?"

"Pretty much."

There was a pause on the other end of the line.

"What you need to understand is that the investigation into Lina Stavred's death wasn't your typical murder case," he eventually said. "We had no body, no crime scene. For the first few days, it was a missing-person case. It wasn't until we received information pointing to Olof Hagström that it became a murder investigation, and the evidence was overwhelming. What we had to do was get a confession, bring things to a close. I was there when we told the girl's parents, so you can be sure I remember that . . . What exactly are you hoping to find here?"

"I don't know," said Eira. "His name just cropped up in this investigation . . ."

She suddenly regretted calling him, heard her own words as though they were echoing back across the river from Eilert Granlund's cottage.

She heard that they sounded like suspicion.

"It's probably nothing," she said. "Sorry for bothering you so late."

"No problem," he said cheerily, though a faltering note had appeared in his voice, the same way it did when he spoke about retirement or the birds. "You can call me anytime, you know that."

The rumble reached him through his dreams, shaking him back to life. His head had slumped forward onto his chest. In front of him, the door to the porch was wide open, and the air was thick with smoke. The lightning must have struck somewhere nearby.

Olof had dragged the sofa over so that he could watch the lightning as it crossed the wide sky above the river. Waiting for the rain that never came.

A lightning headache rose up from the base of his skull, pulsing through his head. That was what his mother had called them, Olof remembered. Her joints had always ached too, whenever it rained. She was like a human weather report. Sunshine was the only thing that didn't hurt.

He peered around for the dog, thought it might have been sleeping in a corner somewhere. Unless it had snuck out. It had been sitting in his lap when the thunder was at its loudest, trembling and whimpering, but Olof had stroked its back.

Thunder had never scared him. He enjoyed the spectacle of the lightning crossing the sky, counting "one pilsner, two pilsner . . ." to determine the number of seconds separating the flash from the rumble, gauging the distance. His father had taught him that a second was longer than you thought. That was why you had to say "pilsner," so you didn't count too quickly. Because it sounded funny, too. And if you divided the total by three, that gave you the distance in kilometers. It was magical, as though he could control the supernatural power of the storm. Then there was the excitement as it drew closer. They used to sit together, measuring and counting—was the storm over Prästmon now, or was it closer to Nyland?—until the sky lit up and a sudden clap made the windows rattle. Olof always waited for that moment, then cried out when it came.

But everything was quiet then. The rumble in his dreams was clearly just that, a memory of the thunder within him. Where the hell was the dog?

He got up at last, his body protesting. This constant wandering back and forth that made up earthly life. He didn't know where these words were coming from, creeping up on him. Earthly life, lightning headaches, counting in pilsners; no one spoke like that anymore.

Olof went out onto the porch and peed between the spindles in the railing. The clouds were still heavy, the haze of smoke making the night dark, as though late summer was already on its way. To-morrow, he thought, once the bottles of beer he had found in the basement—and knocked back with three jars of canned hot dogs as the lightning tore across the heavens—had left his system, he would drive away. Towards the sunset, he thought, like a goddamn cowboy, though of course the sun barely went down, and he had nowhere to go.

This week at the latest, his landlord had said in the message she'd left on his voicemail. That was when his things had to be gone. *I don't want any trouble with the police.*

They had been over there, asking questions about him, waving a sheet of paper that gave them the right to snoop through his things.

The boss had called again too, screaming down the line. Claim-ing Olof had stolen the car, saying he'd report him if he didn't bring it down now, the day before yesterday, a few days ago. Though in his next message he said he never wanted to see him again. The police must have been there, too.

Olof called for the dog again. He couldn't hear any barking, no paws in the grass, no growling to let him know it was up to no good. Just a lorry in the distance. Was that a faint crunch? It sounded like footsteps on gravel, around the other side of the house. Could be the foxes, or it could also be the dog, which hadn't worked out who its master was yet.

He went back inside. The curtains were drawn at the front of the house, so he couldn't see whether there was anyone outside. Right then, the window exploded. Shattered glass flew through the air, the curtains rose and fell, almost in slow motion, as something dropped to the floor by his feet—a rock? There was another loud crash, in the kitchen this time, and he saw a flash of light. Flames surged through the doorway. In his confusion, Olof searched for something to douse the fire. A blanket, his father's old jacket. It was everywhere, in the hallway mirror, in the windowpanes, he no longer knew where the flames were. All around him, surrounding him, licking at his legs.

He stumbled out through the porch door, down the narrow staircase, fell headlong into the grass. Another window shattered. The fire was chasing him. He slid down the steep slope and got back onto his feet, wearing only socks, a pair of thick old socks he'd found in the house and which smelled like his father. He stumbled over fallen trees and got mud on his face, in his mouth, spitting and hitting his cheeks to get rid of it, the awful taste of earth.

It was like he could feel her shadow as she stood over him, blocking the light; she was the trees and the clouds and the sky that was falling in.

You disgusting bastard, what did you think? That I'd kiss someone like you? Your mouth stinks; do you even brush your teeth?

He isn't ready, just standing there, trying to caress her, hand up underneath, her breasts, her soft breasts, he can still feel one of them between his fingers, its softness. She shoves him so hard that he ends up on the ground, in the mud beneath the tangle of nettles, and he tries to get up again, he grabs her, but it's just her cardigan, which comes off, and she kicks him again and again, shouting things, making him scramble to get away, cowering with his hands over his head, and then she is on top of him with a fistful of soil, she holds back one of his arms and forces the earth into his mouth, using the fabric of her dress to pull some of the nettles down, rubbing them in his face. Kiss this, you fucking freak.

Olof heard the roar of the flames behind him, engines revving and screeching, and knew he had to keep going, to get away. The forest creaked and hissed that someone was after him. It grew increasingly dense among the trunks, trails he could no longer see.

He never had learned how to find his way in the forest. Whether the anthills were on the north side of trees or the south, what everything was called; he couldn't understand why the trees needed so many names, the lichens and mosses, the ferns that were a thousand years old, who the hell cared? He could no longer see the ground for everything growing and tearing at his socks, the twigs whipping his face and the remnants of dead trees using their branches like spears against him. The forest meant red ants all over his legs whenever they went bilberry picking, mushrooms that all looked like they were poisonous, a sinkhole that could open up and suck you down into the ground; you would vanish and the moss would grow over you.

He had once seen a film about a man who had been completely overgrown, not a single part of him visible, though his voice was still audible through the thick, fibrous layers of moss.

Olof thought he could make out a trail between two trees, but when he reached it, it vanished and he stepped in the shit of some kind of animal, a huge pile of it, it couldn't be a bear, could it? He reeled around and became aware of something hiding.

Lina's mean laugh has faded, she is gone now. Her cardigan is all that is left, lying in the dirt. Olof's wounds are stinging and burning; he'll have to clean them if he wants to avoid getting blood poisoning. He sits down on a rock to wait for as long as he can, but as the light starts to fade the mosquitoes arrive. Mosquito season has been bad that year, and the forest is full of saplings, it's close to the water, the little bastards like that; he can't take any more bites, any more itching. He assumes the other guys have probably headed off by now. He won't have to face them. The forest isn't quite as wild or thick over in Marieberg, but it still confuses and tricks him, it looks identical yet different every way he turns, leading him in circles, every time he thinks he has found a new trail, he is back on the same one.

The road is quiet, just the occasional car passing by. He rubs his palms against his trouser legs and notices a rip in one knee.

Twigs snapped wherever he put his feet, as though the trees were growing in all directions, overturned with roots straining upwards. They hit him in the face, but he no longer felt any pain, couldn't see his feet, which had now lost both socks; he was thinking about snakes, about everything crawling among the dead trees, the way his father had broken one of them in two and showed him that it was teeming with larva and disgusting bugs inside. Here, you see, there's life in things that are dead, that's the cycle of nature.

They're still standing by the road, the whole gang. Waiting for him or for something to happen, just standing there with their mopeds, doing nothing the way you do at that age, when you're at that point, once you've grown out of playing but don't know what is going to happen next.

The silence is thanks to the magazine they are huddled around, one of Ricken's porno mags, of course. Olof just wants to go home, but one of them spots him before he has a chance.

Hey, mummy's boy Olle, you took your time, you run into a bear in there or what?

So he shoves the cardigan beneath his sweater and walks over to them, what else can he do? Muddy and dirty, his face burning, scalding hot.

Look at him, man. Fuck me, you two must've been rolling about.

Haha, look at his pants, did you get her on her knees, you bastard?

He feels a thump on his back. He sees their wide eyes.

Oh shit, says Ricken, is that a hickey?

And Olof grins and stands tall. He is damn close to being the tallest, though he is younger than every one of them.

Yeah, damn, he manages to reply. Trying to wipe the dirt from around his mouth, though that makes his face sting even more.

Man, Lina was great. Fuck me, she was great.

The ground gave way beneath his feet. Suddenly there was nothing there. Olof groped for something to hang on to, but all he found was a thick root that broke away, making him fall headlong, hitting his head on something sharp that jabbed him close to his eye. The forest crashed in on top of him. Something heavy on his head, and then there was no more air.

Just the taste of earth again.

The black roll blinds were down, meaning she couldn't tell whether it was morning or still night. Nature itself seemed just as confused: eternal light outside, compact darkness where she lay.

Eira groped for her phone on the nightstand, knocked it to the floor. The screen lit up with a name.

"Sorry for waking you."

That voice. There was no escaping what it did to her.

"What's going on?"

"Do you believe in divine justice?" asked August. "A vengeful God?"

He sounded excited, slightly short of breath, as though he were out running. So this was why she hadn't seen any sign of him the day before: he was working nights. In her last memory he was still naked, stretched out in a room at the Hotel Kramm.

"Did you really wake me at three in the morning to discuss religion?" Eira kicked back the covers. It was far too warm.

"There were a few lightning strikes last night," he said.

"Yeah, I heard on the radio," she said. "Up by Saltsjön and somewhere in Marieberg. Where do you need me?"

"Not just there." She heard him inhale, the wind crackling down the line. A roaring sound somewhere in the distance. "I'm standing outside Sven Hagström's place," he said. "Or what's left of it."

"What?"

"We've got the fire under control now, I just thought you might want to know."

Eira tugged at the blind, letting the sunlight flood into the room. She snatched up her clothes from the chair. It wasn't until she had made a thermos of coffee, saving Kerstin from having to mess about with the electricity, and was driving over the Sandö Bridge, that she remembered the dream his call had interrupted.

It was a nightmare she had been having since she was a girl, about logs that turn out to be dead bodies floating downriver. Frothing, furious water tossing them around. She wades out and tries to grab clothing, a hand, but loses her footing and is dragged beneath the surface; she swims among the dead.

Maybe it first started after Lina, or possibly earlier. Log driving was already a thing of the past by the time Eira was born, but there was still plenty of sunken timber in the river, logs trapped in the mud and at the shoreline. They could break free during the spring floods and knock a child unconscious. That was why you were never allowed to swim alone.

The nightmares might have worsened after she heard the story about the Sandö Bridge collapsing. When she learned that bodies really had been carried away by the current. In 1939, there had been plans to build a bridge to replace the last ferry crossing the great rivers, finally linking the two halves of the country together—from the southern tip to Haparanda in the far north. The world's biggest and most modern arch bridge would begin in Lunde and climb fifty meters into the air over Sandö and Svanö in a huge arch, the likes of which had never been seen, stretching all the way to the far shore. But on the afternoon of the last day of August, the bridge had collapsed. A twenty-meter wave rose up above Sandö as the steel and concrete plummeted into the water below. Eighteen people died. World War II broke out the very next day, drowning out all news of the catastrophe in the press. But for those living in the area, the image of bodies being tossed like dolls through the air endured, as though in double exposure, around the bridge that was eventually raised.

The smoke was visible from miles away. Eira pulled up on the grass behind the letter boxes to leave the road clear for the emergency vehicles and walked the rest of the way on foot.

The scorched spruces were the first thing she saw. She pulled her sweater up over her mouth against the smoke. Some of the walls were still standing, but the roof had caved in. The blackened chimney stack rose up into the air, ash falling like a dull gray rain. She saw the warped, charred, and melted remains of objects no one would ever point to and say, "I remember."

Even the outhouse had been ravaged.

The Pontiac was still parked outside.

August came towards her.

"Was he inside?" she asked.

"They don't know. The whole place had gone up by the time the fire service got here. They had their hands full over by Saltsjön, so they could only spare one engine. No way they could get inside. He might not have woken up in time."

They didn't look at each other, their faces turned to the sooty black remains of the house. It was still burning in places, the firemen working to put out the last of the flames, which kept dying down and popping up elsewhere.

"No," said Eira.

"No what?"

"I don't believe in God or revenge. I don't think the lightning chooses where to strike. This place is on high ground. There were some old TV antennas on the roof."

She fought back the urge to lean against his chest.

"They'll go in as soon as they can," said August. "And then we'll know."

It would be hours until most people in the area woke up, so Eira drove back to Lunde to get changed.

Kerstin was awake and had already brought in the newspaper. "Uff, what a stink. Where have you been?"

When Eira told her about the fires, she saw her mother's gaze wandering, searching for a solid footing.

"You shouldn't stay out all night."

"I'm a police officer, Mum. I'm not fifteen anymore."

"No, I know that."

Eira popped some bread into the toaster and wondered whether she really did know. Her mother turned her attention to the obituaries, mumbling quietly to herself. "Oh, not her, not him. Oh, that's too sad." She had brought in the post, too. It didn't seem to have been done the day before. That was something Kerstin Sjödin could still manage, so Eira left it to her, didn't want to take the little jobs away. There was a bill, a letter from the bank, a statement of pension benefits. As she opened the envelopes and put the important things in a safe place, a thought came to her.

Perhaps a person didn't need either a phone or a computer, or even to know what googling meant.

"Sven Hagström could have gone through his neighbors' post," she told Bosse Ring a few hours later, as they drove back to Kungs-gården.

When the clock struck seven, she had called GG to tell him every-thing she had found out about Tryggve Nydalen. About the convic-tion for sexual abuse that actually seemed more like a gang rape, his attempts to erase his identity.

"Let's bring him in for questioning," GG had said, heading off in a patrol car the minute he arrived in Kramfors.

It was left to Eira and Bosse Ring to deal with the family. That was where they were on their way now, to a home that had been torn apart by the decision to take one of their number away in a police car that morning, where the stench of the previous night's fire left a sense of catastrophe in the air.

Eira turned off by the back road, involving a short climb through the rough terrain. The fire service had blocked off the other driveway.

"The letter boxes are all in a row," she continued. "He only had to steal a bill from the Nydalens' box—some kind of formal letter including all his names—and he would have known that Tryggve was also called Adam. He might even have opened one and seen his ID number."

"But there must be at least twenty houses around here," Bosse Ring said once they found the trail and were making their way up the hill. "Are you saying the old man really checked every one?"

"Maybe he'd had his suspicions about who it was from the mo-ment he heard the gossip at the races. A man around the right age, originally from the area around the Pite River valley . . ." Eira hadn't noticed a northern accent when she spoke to Tryggve Nydalen, but he could have been making an effort. It had likely been much stronger when he first moved south thirty years earlier, and clearly it still came out from time to time, as it had in the ironmonger's.

"And if he confronted Nydalen," Bosse filled in. "If he reminded him of what happened back then . . . Well, you've got to wonder what that would do to a man who's managed to hide who he really is for almost forty years."

They reached the crown of the wooded hill. The homestead seemed quiet. There was no sign of anyone.

Eira noticed a few plastic toys floating in the paddling pool, saw that one of the two cars was gone.

"I wonder if his wife knew," she said.

"People always know," her colleague replied. "Even if you don't know you know."

Mejan Nydalen looked tired, one of the buttons over her stomach gaping open. She had applied mascara and filled in her brows, but seemed not to have noticed the button.

A woman trying to hold it together, thought Eira, closing the door to the kitchen. Patrik Nydalen's agitated voice was still faintly audible. He was in the living room with Bosse Ring. The two officers had split up so that the Nydalens couldn't alter their stories, influence the other to keep quiet, or change their version of events. A glance might be enough, a sigh, a breath. Breaking the ties of loyalty was the biggest challenge when it came to families. They were deep rooted and unpredictable even for those involved, who could simultaneously love and hate one another, feel a desire to protect while also being willing to betray.

Sofi Nydalen was no longer in the house. She had left with her children that morning, shortly after the police turned up.

"Where did she go?" asked Eira.

"Back home, to Stockholm." Mejan looked away, seemed to be

studying one of the cabinet doors, hand-carved in pine. They were sitting at the kitchen table, a thermos of coffee in front of them. The woman didn't seem to have any intention of producing a second cup for Eira. "It's probably just as well," she said. "You bundle the kids' grandfather into a police car, right in front of them, and refuse to say why."

"What do you know about your husband's past?" asked Eira. "Back up north, before he moved down here?"

"Tryggve and I have no secrets from each other."

"Does the name Jävredal mean anything to you?"

"So that's what this is about."

"What do you mean?"

"You want to know about that business with the girl up there," said Mejan. "It was almost forty years ago, but in your databases a person is never free. You see it written down and think you know who a man is."

"Was Tryggve keen to keep it a secret?" asked Eira. The fact that his wife knew about the assault only increased her curiosity. For a person to live with that kind of knowledge, to love.

"Is your friend with the crooked nose telling Patrik all this stuff now?" Mejan got up and took a few steps towards the door before turning back, as though she was considering marching out there. "I'm sorry, but he does look like a bit of a gangster."

"So Patrik didn't know about any of this?"

"What do you think?"

"I'm asking you."

Mejan continued her pacing, five steps forward before she had to turn back in the cramped space, ducking beneath a beam.

"Patrik loves his kids more than anything else, and now his wife has taken them away. Sofi comes from a different world, I don't know what it's like. Somewhere where family doesn't come first, where it's more about yourself and what feels comfortable. Patrik decided to stay because he doesn't want to leave me on my own. He's loyal, both to me and his father."

"How long have you known?"

"I don't know why you're dragging up all that old business. Tryggve served his time."

"I'd appreciate it if you would answer my questions."

Mejan paused, stiff and facing away from Eira, staring at an embroidered picture of wild pansies, the provincial flower, on the wall. Her hair had grayed elegantly, the way some women manage.

"He invited me for a picnic," she said. "Six months after we first met, by Akershus Fortress in Oslo. You can see right across the water from there. I almost thought he was going to propose, he seemed so tense and wanted it to be so nice, with wine and everything. And then he broke up with me. Said he was taking a job on one of the oil rigs, that it wouldn't work with him being away so much. Of course it will, I told him, it'll be fine, I'll wait for you. You have no idea how handsome he was back then, but he was also so cautious."

Mejan turned around and looked Eira straight in the eye, unyielding.

"We've never had any secrets from each other. If anyone knows what kind of man he is, it's me."

Everyone has their secrets, thought Eira, particularly those who are constantly claiming not to have any.

"At first, I thought I must be the problem," Mejan continued. "I never seriously thought I could be with someone so handsome, but it wasn't about me, he told me that over and over again. I asked what the hell it was then, refused to give in, and eventually he told me the whole story. He thought I wouldn't want him if I knew. That was how it was, that was why he wanted to run off to the middle of the North Sea."

"But you did?"

"I was pregnant," said Mejan. "I hadn't dared tell him yet, was scared he wouldn't want the baby, but I had no choice. 'I can't be anyone's father,' Tryggve told me. I started crying then, and I'm not the kind of person who cries easily. I said, 'Of course you can, you'll be the most wonderful father,' and then I suggested we get married, so he wouldn't have any more doubts."

"What did he tell you?"

"It seems like you already know."

"I've read the court's version."

Mejan's version wasn't quite the same. Eira wondered whether it was Tryggve's interpretation or whether she had reframed things herself in an attempt to make them easier to live with.

"He treated a girl horribly once," she said. "But Tryggve never meant to hurt her, he thought the girl was into it. He was drunk, of course."

"Was that how he described it?"

Mejan sat down again, at the very end of the daybed, as far away from Eira as she could get.

"He was a different person back then," she said. "The court ruling and the time he spent in prison made him understand—he even changed his name to become someone else. I called him Adam for a while in the beginning, but I always liked Tryggve better. He barely even dared touch me when we first met. But you don't want a man to fumble gently, do you? I had to tell him I wasn't made of glass, that's how scared he was."

"Of you?"

"Of himself."

"Does anyone else in the area know about this?"

Was that a shiver? Had her muscles tensed slightly? Eira wasn't sure. The pause lasted no more than a second, but she still took it as hesitation.

"I haven't told anyone, and I can't imagine Tryggve has either. There was no reason to. We're just living our life. It's a good life."

Her anxious eyes sought out the door. They could no longer hear Patrik's voice. Bosse Ring must have managed to get him to calm down.

"Was it important to Tryggve that no one found out about the assault?"

"Yes, if that's what you insist on calling it. I'm sure you know how people like to gossip and judge. Tryggve was an immature boy back then, he had no experience of women. We've never had any problems with our sex life, if that's what you think."

Various details from the trial transcripts seemed to have settled like a filter over Eira's eyes: seven men, a vaginal wall splitting. Ask open questions, she reminded herself, listen carefully. Make the woman talk. That was the key.

"How do you think Patrik would have reacted if he found out about this from someone else? Or your daughter-in-law, your daughter?"

"Why, have you called her as well?"

"Not yet."

Mejan looked away, mumbled something.

"Could you repeat that, and speak up for the tape?" Eira asked.

The woman got up and turned on the tap. Drank a glass of water. Eira tried to read her movements. Nervous, angry, shocked—or all three. She tried to work out what a more experienced interviewer would ask next. Her eyes were aching. The smell of smoke was still lingering like a bitter taste in her mouth; it was on her clothes, everywhere. She had forgotten how little she had slept.

"Sven Hagström," she eventually said.

"Yes?"

"Did Tryggve mention talking to him? During May or June, let's say."

"Maybe, I don't know. Didn't you ask about that already?" Mejan seemed to be thinking, trying to remember what had been said. "It would be about the road or the broadband if anything. The kind of thing neighbors talk about."

"We think Sven Hagström might have heard about the assault."

"So that's why you came up here, turning everything upside down . . . ?" Without warning, Mejan got to her feet. The cup rattled as she gripped the table. "Tryggve works for the council. He looks after their finances. You lot are out of your bloody minds."

"Did Sven Hagström threaten to tell anyone else?"

"I have no idea."

"Could you tell me what you were doing that morning?"

"Like we haven't already done that, over and over again." Mejan picked up her cup. The coffee she still hadn't touched sloshed over the side. She tipped it into the sink. "I think Tryggve was cleaning the drain in the bathroom. Chopping wood, that kind of thing. Everything has to be just so for Patrik and his family. Tip-top. Sofi can be a bit particular—more than a bit, actually. She wants every-thing a certain way, even though it's our house she's visiting."

"Did you actually see your husband doing those chores?"

"I was back and forth between the two buildings all morning, pottering about in the kitchen. I would have noticed if he was gone."

The sound made them both react: footsteps in the hallway, a voice. Through the window Eira saw Bosse Ring step out into the yard. Patrik slammed the door behind him. Mejan flinched, as though the sound was a physical blow. What had she said last time? That they wanted to create their own little space on earth?

Bosse Ring was getting into the car as Eira came out, and he waved in a way that made her hurry over.

"How did it go?" she asked.

"It wasn't the lightning that started the fire at Hagström's place."

The charred black ruins were a stark contrast to the beauty of summer all around them, the sunlight glittering on the river. A reminder that nothing lasts forever.

The fire was completely extinguished. By a stroke of luck it had spread only to the trees closest to the property, singeing the dry lawn. The forensic technicians moved slowly through the burnt-out home, carefully picking among the remains of a life.

"Have you found him?" asked Eira.

The crime scene investigator who came to meet them was called Costel. She had forgotten his surname, but remembered that it meant "forest" in Romanian. He came from Transylvania and had once told her that the two landscapes, with their peaks and valleys, were related.

"There's no one inside," he said.

"Are you sure?"

"Nothing bigger than a wood mouse."

He turned to the devastation, they all did. Walls that had collapsed into heaps of jet-black lumber. The sky overhead was blue and indifferent. Costel was one of the technicians who had worked the scene after the murder. Ardelean, that was it, his surname that meant "forest." Eira had seen his name in the report.

"It helps," he continued, "that I know what it looked like before."

They were still in the process of mapping the fire's progression, establishing how and where it had started, its furious route through the property. He talked about the shards of glass they had found inside, scattered across the floor in such a way that suggested the windows had been smashed from the outside. There were also a couple of broken bottles and a rock that hardly had any place in the middle of a living room.

Bosse Ring stepped to one side to call the regional command center and request details of when the call had come in and who had raised the alarm. Eira heard barking, but she didn't immediately react. A few curious onlookers had gathered nearby, beyond the cordon. Dogs were always barking, everywhere. But then she realized how close it was, and spotted the creature. Tied to a tree not far from the house, the same shaggy black dog as before. It was whimpering and chewing on the rope, spinning around.

"So the dog made it out," she said.

"A neighbor found it deeper in the forest," said Costel. "A bit farther down the hill. It was all tangled up in a rope, tied to a tree. Someone will have to take it away."

"Do we have any idea where Olof Hagström is?"

"He's not answering his phone, it's switched off. And both cars are still here. His father had an old Toyota in the garage. Not much of it left now."

Eira took a few steps in an attempt to think, a semicircle around the house. To the rear, the plastic roof over the porch had fallen in and melted onto the blackened wood and ash.

There was one possible explanation: that Olof had done it. Led the dog to safety and then set his childhood home alight.

The shadow of a cloud drifted slowly over the ground.

"Are we going to look for him then?" Eira asked once she had rejoined the others. Bosse Ring told her they were waiting for more people.

"And there's a dog handler coming down from Sollefteå. They'll be here in half an hour."

"Do we have to wait?"

The forest didn't put up any resistance. Eira ducked beneath low-hanging branches and jumped over fallen trees without a second thought. Behind her, Bosse Ring swore to himself, stumbling and getting caught on branches, the kind of thing that happens when a person grows up on city streets, away from the mountains, on flat ground with views for miles. She assumed he had, anyway. Her colleague never revealed a thing about himself. Unlike many of the others, he didn't spend his time talking about where he was from or how things were at home. Eira found that quite refreshing after GG's slightly overfamiliar baby chat.

The lead pulled tight as Rabble darted beneath a spruce. Elk droppings. The dog was a useless tracker, kept running around in circles. Maybe he was still looking for the old man. Bringing it along might not have been the best idea.

Maybe the pooch thought it was all just a game.

A phone started ringing behind her, and Bosse stopped to take the call, seemingly unable to talk and navigate the terrain at the same time. Eira peered between the trees. Trying to spot any broken branches, trampled moss, that kind of thing. She wished she knew how to read the forest better. She recognized the plants but got their names confused; she saw the age of the different trees and noticed the parasites clinging to them, but was ignorant of the connections in that ingenious ecosystem. At some point, while she was still fairly young, the forest trails had ceased to be hers. Pointing out edible plants and studying the insects' lives had been replaced by things you could do at home, like baking and crafting. Her father had continued taking Magnus into the forest, because he was older and had to learn how to hunt and handle a chainsaw.

In fairy tales, the boys went out into the forest and learned to be men. But the girls who did the same were either kidnapped by trolls or eaten by wolves.

"Hold on, they're here now," Bosse Ring groaned behind her. "They've got proper dogs. We'll be more use back at the station."

You might be, thought Eira. She had just spotted a couple of broken branches, an opening right in front of them. It was obvious that someone or something had passed through. An elk, Olof Hagström. She took another few steps and spotted a sock on the ground, half hidden by a few dead twigs, a fallen spruce. She handed the lead to Bosse and broke off a branch, carefully picked up the knitted item. It looked to be well over a size forty and had a hole in the heel, but otherwise it wasn't overly dirty.

"This can't have been here long."

"He ran out without shoes?"

Her colleague took care of the find while Eira kept looking, slowly moving forward, crouching down. She was thinking about Olof Hagström's build and any possible routes he might have taken. Moving was much easier without the unruly dog. She zigzagged between trees, no longer caring whether her colleague could keep up. In the distance, she could hear barking and voices, the sounds echoing between ravines and hollows. Troll country, that was what she had called this type of landscape when she was younger, rocks carved by the inland ice, embraced by ancient trees. She followed the trail of destruction left by the previous spring's storms, cutting between fallen trunks and avoiding the open pits left behind wherever the trees had fallen with their roots intact.

She heard twigs snapping, the sound of quick footsteps nearby.

Then a bark and a shout.

"Over here!"

The dog patrol had approached from another direction, and Eira didn't spot the man until she was almost on top of him. He was crouching down, bent over at the foot of a tree. His dog was sitting patiently a few meters away, panting, its tongue lolling.

"I've called for a helicopter and whatever the hell else they can get out here."

Eira tried to make sense of what she was seeing. A leg, a bare foot sticking up out of the ground. Dark with mud, possibly also blood. The earth all around it had been disturbed, as though someone had been digging and then refilled the hole. The other officer, whose name she hadn't caught, was gripping the sturdy ankle, feeling for a pulse. The tree almost seemed to be growing over the body, like whoever it was had burrowed beneath it or been buried there, roots snaking around their foot as though . . .

"This can't be happening," said Eira.

"What?"

"An uprooting. Everyone knows not to climb into the pits. The tree can spring upright again, closing the hole. It's the kind of thing people say to scare children. I didn't think it ever actually happened."

"He's alive," said her colleague. "He's got a fucking pulse."

"That's impossible."

The man got to his feet and gripped the trunk, trying to shift it.

"Some air must be getting in if he's still breathing—between the roots, through the soil . . . what the hell do I know. We have to get this off him."

They both put everything they had into pulling the trunk backwards. The tree had been lopped in places, its thickest branches gone, but still it resisted, wouldn't budge, as though its roots had dug deep into the earth once again.

"How is this possible? It was on its side not long ago."

"I think it creates suction, a kind of vacuum."

Eira dropped to her knees and started clawing at the ground. Judging by the angle of his foot, she realized he must be lying head down. Somewhere beside her, her colleague's phone rang; he was busy digging from the other side.

"What are they saying?"

"They can't bring the loader out. Some kind of ban . . . Fire risk. They can't use any of the forestry machinery, even the slightest spark could set . . ."

"Tell them to bring the bloody fire service along, then."

She reached something soft. A hand. It was completely limp, but Eira gripped it anyway. It was warm. Big and soft. His pulse was quick and weak, but it was there. Eira felt the watch around his wrist, managed to dig out more earth.

A watch with an inbuilt compass and a barometer.

"It's him," she said. "That's his watch."

They kept digging, fistful after fistful of earth, until they heard the sound of rotor blades in the distance and the air ambulance swept overhead.

As afternoon moved imperceptibly towards evening, Eira was alone in the office overlooking the railway tracks. She still had dirt beneath her nails.

They had managed to bring out a small skidder after all, and had dragged the tree away. Olof Hagström was now at the university hospital in Umeå. He still hadn't woken up. The doctors said he had a contusion on his skull and some bleeding on the brain, they were preparing him for the operating room. He had other injuries, too—broken ribs and blood in both lungs—and the medics couldn't say whether or not he would pull through.

The murder case had forked off in several new directions, and resources had been redirected to the arson attack.

Eira had been working for almost twelve hours straight, not including her visit to the crime scene early that morning, but someone needed to summarize the material, to find any contradictions, and GG had left it to her—or had she offered? Either way. She was surrounded by their voices, the printouts from the interviews.

Three people, one family.

Like a fracture developing, cleaving one rock mass from another.

Patrik's voice in her ears.

"You're wrong, you've got him mixed up with someone else. My dad would never do something like that. You're so fucking wrong. Seriously, what are you lot even doing? What kind of backwards officers do you have working up here? I get it. You're the people they scraped off the bottom of the barrel, the ones who couldn't find posts anywhere else. Who the fuck is Adam Vide?"

The crash of something being slammed down or breaking.

Bosse Ring's calm, methodical voice stood in sharp contrast to Patrik's outburst. He sounded warm and friendly, almost fatherly—something she had never heard from him before.

"Did you notice anything unusual when you came to stay this time? What was the mood like in the house? Have you ever seen your father resort to violence?"

Patrik's voice was incredibly strained, an octave higher than when Eira had heard him speaking earlier. He swore that everything had been the same as ever. Just a few niggles between Sofi and his mother, over the kids' clothing or something.

"I honestly don't remember what Dad was doing. He usually makes himself scarce when that happens. But we had a beer together on the porch later. The kind of thing you do when you've just killed your neighbor, don't you think? This is insane. What you're claiming right now, it's insane."

A longer silence. This was where her colleague had allowed Patrik to read what his father had been convicted of.

Another clatter, from a chair tipping over as he got to his feet.

"Are you telling my mum about this right now? How the hell is she supposed to live with this?"

It sounded like the words were being forced out of him, one drop at a time, like someone wringing out a near-dry rag.

"The people who did that . . . what it says there . . . They should've been locked up for good, people like that shouldn't be allowed to go free, they should've thrown away the key . . ."

Another pause, possibly following the realization that he would never have been born if that had happened.

"Jesus Christ, what a bastard. The thought of him with Mum . . . I can't believe I never saw it. A person can't change that much, it's impossible; you are who you are. So are you telling me he killed that old bloke because of this . . . ?"

The creaking of Patrik's footsteps as he paced back and forth across the wooden floor, the thick boards.

Mejan's statement was still fresh in Eira's mind. She had forgiven and reconciled, swore her husband was a different man now. Eira found herself thinking about the esteemed poet whose husband had become infamous for being unable to keep his hands to himself before ultimately being convicted of rape; she had strenuously defended him and accused the eighteen women who testified against him of being liars.

She batted that thought away. This was something else. Every case was unique, every person had to be heard individually. Every truth set against another.

"And to think I've been bringing my kids up here." That was the last thing Patrik said before the conversation ended. "Never again, I'll tell you that. Never again."

Eira turned her attention to the transcript of the interview with Tryggve Nydalen that was spread out on the desk in front of her. She had already listened to the whole thing, but seeing it on paper gave her a different kind of overview. The long pauses were gone, and she could skip over the endless sections in which he tried to explain what had happened almost forty years earlier. The parts where he broke down repeatedly, blaming himself for what he had put his family through, for his son finding out this way. He had been afraid for so long, then the day finally came, in the ironmonger's, when someone had called him by his old name and he had fled. And yet: there had been moments when he had longed for that very thing. These days he had to drive twenty kilometers to Kramfors if he needed so much as a screw. He should never have had children, things would have been far better that way.

But he hadn't killed Sven Hagström.

"That's not who I am. I could never. I completely understand why you think I did, and I'm sorry. Sorry. I didn't mean to hurt her."

With that, he was back in Jävredal again.

Tryggve Nydalen came across as honest, but he was also a little too . . . Eira couldn't quite put her finger on it. A little too eager, prepared? And was Mejan really as comfortable with her husband's past as she claimed, or was she a classic case of an abused woman denying and defending?

Then there was Patrik's rage. Where did that come from? Hadn't it been there the very first time she met him, the morning they were called out to Sven Hagström's place, when he was irritated with the speed of the police? Had he wanted to frame Olof Hagström, did he suspect his father, did he know more than he was letting on?

Eira got up and filled her mug at the coffee machine. It was too late in the day for caffeine, but she already knew she wouldn't be able to sleep.

Tryggve Nydalen had been in custody since lunchtime. That gave them three days. Or more like two and a half now.

She splashed her face with cold water before sitting down again.

GG hadn't given her this task for her psychological analysis, she didn't imagine that for a moment.

The fact that Tryggve's fingerprints were a match was the main reason the prosecutor had been able to request that he remain in custody. His thumb and index finger prints—fairly fresh—had been found in the house, in the kitchen and on a doorframe in the hallway.

Eira needed to find similarly concrete evidence. The kind of thing it was difficult to lie your way out of.

She noticed the small contradictions between Tryggve's statements and his wife's, about what he had been doing that morning. Cleaning the drain or tightening the leg on the bed. It could easily be the kind of thing a person forgot or mixed up, of course. Both had claimed he was chopping wood. That was something you could hear across a yard, but perhaps Mejan hadn't actually been able to see what he was doing indoors, and was choosing to protect him.

And if she was lying about a detail like that, other details fell down.

The forest road, she thought. Tryggve said he had visited Hagström to talk about the road. Eira found the name of a council worker who dealt with that kind of thing, and thought they should probably ask the other neighbors about it.

The murder weapon. They had seized a hunting knife, safely locked away alongside two guns in the cabinet. Finding Hagström's

DNA was probably too much to hope for, but the members of a hunting party were close, they saw different sides of people. Tryggve had bought the knife two years earlier but perhaps he had another, an older one. Was it the kind of thing people threw away?

"Looks like you've had a rough day."

Eira spun around in her chair. August was standing in the doorway, his fringe slightly messy, wearing jeans and a cornflower blue shirt. A damn nice color.

"How does a beer at Kramm sound?"

She realized she was still wearing the clothes she'd had on in the forest, dirt and needles clinging to her sweater, and became aware of a taste in her mouth that could be bad breath.

"I have to go over the interviews," she said, running a hand through her hair. Her fingers got caught on a tangled twig.

"All night?"

"If that's how long it takes."

"OK. Another day, then?"

Her shadow stretched out across the floor in the slanting evening light. If she raised her hand, it would touch his leg. She had to reply, to say something breezy and not too keen, nothing that made it sound like she thought there was anything going on between them—which she didn't, of course. But before she managed to utter a word, her phone rang.

Unknown number. A man who sounded relieved to have got hold of her.

Eira was already on her way out through the door, and had to run back to grab her keys, before she managed to put his name to the face of a neighbor who lived by the river, near the old customs house.

"It was my wife who spotted her, she was wandering around one of the houses near us, the blue one with the white corners, in her dressing gown . . ."

She thought she could make out the scent of August already. Almost a month away, but late summer was approaching, minute by minute. The darkness always came as a surprise, so suddenly. And then it was autumn.

Eira was sitting on the porch, wrapped in a blanket. It wasn't at all cold, but the things she was thinking about were. Frost, the winter chill. If Kerstin went wandering in her slippers then, in the kind of darkness where no friendly neighbors would spot a pink silk dressing gown fluttering between the houses . . .

They had been sitting in the kitchen when Eira got home, chatting over a cup of tea. Kerstin had insisted, the neighbors told her. The worst of her confusion had passed, but they didn't know how long she had been out, or why.

"It's a difficult decision," the woman, Inez, had said as they were leaving, patting Eira's hand. "To take away from a person like that."

Once Kerstin had fallen asleep, Eira was far too worked up to go to bed herself. She was so tired her body was aching, anxious that the number of hours until she had to get up again was getting smaller and smaller.

This couldn't go on. How long had she known that, yet been unable to bring herself to make any changes? Kerstin always said no. She wasn't going anywhere. This was her home, end of discussion; she knew where everything was, and it wasn't expensive to live there. As the need for her to move grew, the thought of it became increasingly frightening.

Her stubbornness more unyielding.

Other days, she said "but I'm just a burden," and Eira had to reas-
sure her that she wasn't at all, until the discussion came to a standstill again.

A difficult decision, to take away from a person like that. Eira
peered out into the night. Making decisions on behalf of her mother,
against her will, taking that right away from her. Every fiber of her
being screamed that it was wrong, yet it was also where every logical
thought led her.

And if she made that decision and it didn't work out?

She felt like curling up in the blanket, wished it were an embrace.
Someone who could hold her, give her advice, or at least have an
opinion on the matter.

Eira reached for her phone, didn't even need to scroll to find his
name. It was right at the very top, despite the fact that she hadn't
called him in so long. It was late, it was night, but since when had
that mattered to Magnus?

She's your mum too, she thought. *You can't leave me all on my own
in this.*

There was a click, and then she heard a tinny voice in her ear.

"This number is no longer in use."

GG didn't seem to have slept particularly well either, his eyebrows grayer than usual, his skin dull. Eira decided not to mention the stain on his shirt. She didn't want to know what he got up to at night.

"We're not going to give them a telling-off," he said once they were sitting in the car. "We're not angry with these local patrols for taking over twenty-four hours to get in touch."

Eira could have taken the quicker route via the Sandö Bridge, gaining a few minutes, but they weren't in a hurry—they were simply going for coffee and a chat with a couple of people who collaborated with the police—so she chose to drive upstream instead. She took the Hammar Bridge over the river, meaning she didn't have to go back the same way she had just come. The local patrol was made up of volunteers who drove around the area at night, keeping an eye out for anything unusual but not getting involved themselves. Eira had interrupted a break-in thanks to them, caught car thieves.

"We wouldn't stand a chance without their eyes and ears, not over these distances," GG continued. "But there's always the question of what we notice, what we actually see while observing something."

They pulled up outside a brick house. A few gnomes and elves in the garden, a small sculpture of a deer.

Flourishing, well tended, touching in the obvious care paid to it.

There are people who really choose to live here, thought Eira. *Of all the places on earth. People who don't just end up here by chance, who happen to be born here or wind up staying put for various reasons.*

Two young boys stood to attention in the hallway, solemnly greeting the officers before their father sent them off to do something else.

Coffee, always more coffee.

"We didn't think anything of it at the time," said Erik Ollikainen, pushing a pouch of snus tobacco beneath his lip. He was around thirty, with the beginnings of a paunch, and was wearing a T-shirt printed with an ad for a plumber. "I mean, it wasn't anything out of the ordinary."

"Anything unusual, that's what we look out for, things that catch our eye, if you get what I mean," his older neighbor filled in. His name was Börje Stål. He lived on the other side of the road, he said, pointing over there, in the white house on the edge of the forest. The two men had set out together that night. "So you'll have to pin the blame on the both of us."

The terrible thunderstorm had trumped anything else that night, what with the lack of rain. A sign, perhaps, that the weather was changing.

Ominous.

"We're lucky to live this high up, in any case," said Ollikainen. "With the sea levels rising."

The two men had raised the alarm about the lightning strike up by Saltsjön, seen the smoke above the trees. They'd had their hands full for a few hours after that, waiting for the fire engines and directing them down the right narrow forest roads. Sometime around midnight, once they had done their usual loop of the community, they had headed back up there again and saw that the fire was under control. Then they pulled over to the side of the road to drink coffee from their thermoses; they needed the energy boost for the last few hours. They shared some food and had music on the radio. It felt like a moment of calm after the violent outburst of the storm. That was when the roads got a bit livelier again.

"We recognized the vehicles. These lads drive around most evenings and sometimes during the night. We did the same when I was that age, from the day you got your first EPA tractor—you know the type, the reconfigured pickups you're allowed to drive from fifteen."

"It's not something we ever report," the older man added. "We didn't even pay them any notice."

"So what made you change your minds?"

"When we heard what happened, we thought, you know . . . We work with the police. We don't want anyone to claim we're not doing that. Even if it's nothing. That's how it's meant to work. We report things, you decide what measures to take—that's what we've been told over and over again."

"What did you see?"

The two men exchanged a glance. One nodded to the other, who continued: "There were three vehicles. One Volvo and two EPA tractors. They were heading towards Kungsgården. Or in that direction anyway. Could've been going to Sollefteå too, of course, or over the Hammar Bridge towards Nyland, we have no idea."

"When was this?"

"Just after midnight. We didn't write it up in the logbook, like I said, but we were scanning for radio stations at the time. We always listen to that P3 radio show until midnight, so it must've been after that."

"I said that those lads could do with jobs to get up for in the morning, remember?"

"You chat about all sorts when you're out there like that."

"Did you get the registration numbers for these vehicles?"

"No need," said Ollikainen.

They knew their names, where they lived. One of them was the grandson of Börje Stål's cousin. He said that with his eyes lowered towards his coffee cup, slowly stirring the liquid.

"They're not bad boys, they just carry on a bit. Like all kids when they've got nothing else to do. They don't have a bad bone in them."

His neighbor looked up but didn't speak. A long silence followed. There was more, that was obvious, hesitation and anguish, waiting to see who would speak first.

Erik Ollikainen hooked the tobacco from beneath his lip and crushed it between his fingers.

"And then they came back," he said quietly, lowering the pouch to his saucer. "At a hell of a pace, way faster than permitted for those reconfigured cars, but that's nothing new. People are always changing parts, souping up the engines, no one says a word."

"How much time do you think had passed?"

"Half an hour. Or more. Maybe less. God knows. You get tired by the small hours, start feeling a bit sluggish."

"We were just about to do one last lap," said Börje Stål, "when we saw the smoke and the flames over in Kungsgården. Called 112 straightaway, but someone else had already raised the alarm."

"That damned weather, what a bloody night." Erik Ollikainen turned the snus box between his fingers. "You sure it wasn't just the lightning?"

Eira would always associate the feeling of having saved up for her first EPA tractor with freedom. It was a converted Volvo Amazon with the back seats removed, and it wasn't officially allowed to go any faster than thirty kilometers an hour. Still, it looked just like a real car, and the main thing was that it allowed her to drive before she turned eighteen. The government had tried to introduce a ban during the seventies, but the public outcry in the provinces meant that the EPA tractors had been saved.

One of them was parked on the driveway where they pulled up, a Mercedes with a flatbed where the rear seats had once been, lacquered black and red.

The parents were on annual leave, already up and about, busy renovating the roof. That was fortunate, because their son was a minor, just sixteen years of age.

It took half an hour for his father to wake him and for him to get dressed.

Baggy jeans and an oversized T-shirt, still half asleep. A cup of warm chocolate milk.

"They're talking to a lot of people," said his mother, buttering two slices of bread for her son. "That doesn't mean they're accusing you of anything."

"Just tell them the truth," said his father.

The boy's name was Andreas, and he already had a record for a couple of petty thefts, a few notifications of concern to his name. Eira had managed to check the database while they were waiting for their colleagues, who were now paying a visit to one of the other boys.

"We were just driving around," said Andreas.

"Driving where?"

"On the roads, where else?"

GG brought up a map on his iPad and placed it on the table in front of the boy.

"Can you point out exactly where you went?"

"I don't bloody know."

This continued for some time, until Andreas's father ran out of patience and barked at his son: "Just tell the truth, for once in your damn life."

"I told you, I can't remember."

"Your clothes stunk of smoke in the morning."

"Yeah, so? Maybe we had a barbecue."

"You think I can't tell the difference? Do you think I'm stupid?" The man took a step forward, like he was going to shake his son, but his wife grabbed his arm.

"They're always driving around," she said. "There's not much else to do round here. Especially in the summer, when there's no school."

"As if they do any different in the winter," his father muttered. "Up all night, sleeping all day. What exactly do you get up to? You and Robban and the Torstenssons?"

"What d'you mean, get up to?"

"It would be better if you let us ask the questions," said GG.

"I've seen the kind of stuff you look up when you borrow my computer. All kinds of filth and muck, that's what."

"Please, stop," said his wife. "That's got nothing to do with any of this."

Another fifteen minutes passed. GG had asked Eira to leave the room with the father, and she returned just in time to hear the boy crack. A whisper, directed towards the table.

"Someone had to get rid of him."

"Who?"

"That dirty old perve." The boy raised his chin, looking the detective straight in the eye. "You lot clearly can't manage it. We have to do things ourselves round here."

"Are you talking about Olof Hagström?"

"He'll never do that stuff again. Not to any of our girls, anyway." Andreas unhappily sought out his mother's gaze. "Someone had to bloody do something. You're blind, the lot of you. Can't you see what they go through?"

For once, Eira left the station at a normal time that afternoon. No one noticed her leaving; they were all working flat out on the latest task: mapping the four boys' movements and lives.

In addition to the sixteen-year-old she and GG had brought in, there was another boy the same age—the driver of the other EPA tractor—plus his thirteen-year-old brother and an eighteen-year-old who had borrowed his mother's car that evening.

The heavy mood followed her out. Three teenagers in custody, plus a fourth who wasn't even fifteen. That wasn't what you hoped for from a day's work. The last thing she had done before leaving was to check the boys' search histories on the computers they had seized. The images of brutal pornography lingered in her mind.

"They claim they wanted to protect the girls," Silje had said over her shoulder, "but then they go and watch this crap, about how to best rape someone. How does that make sense?"

It doesn't, Eira thought as she walked through a cluster of redbrick apartment buildings on the edge of the town center. *People don't make sense.*

She tried to take in the everyday life all around her, everything that was healthy and alive. The flowers in the yards. The children playing in a sprinkler.

The woman whose name was on the rental agreement wasn't someone she knew, but this was the last address at which her brother had been registered. She hadn't managed to track down a new phone contract for him.

Eira rang the buzzer and was let inside.

The woman's name was Alice, a midforties beauty who opened the door in a thin summer dress.

"No, Magnus doesn't live here anymore. We broke up in spring."

Eira peered down the hallway behind her. There were traces of preteen children, rucksacks and sports shoes. The apartment smelled clean.

"But I told him he could stay registered here," Alice continued. "Until he finds something permanent. So you don't have his number?"

"Not the latest one."

Alice pointed to a small stack of envelopes on the chest of drawers in the hallway.

"He comes by to pick up his post sometimes."

Eira resisted the urge to grab them. Unpaid bills, final demands, threats of canceled subscriptions. Guaranteed to be the kind of thing that got worse the longer they went unopened. "Do you have kids?" she asked.

"Oh yes, two boys and a little girl. They're at their dad's."

Eira breathed a sigh of relief. They weren't her brother's, at least. The two he rarely saw were more than enough. Alice gave her a warm, slightly uncertain smile.

"Don't you want to come in? Magnus has told me so much about you."

"Thanks, but I really need to track him down."

"It's so interesting that you work for the police. You're so brave."

She wants to talk about him, Eira thought, *that's why. She's happy he still comes over, even if it is just to pick up his mail.*

"You might find him at Ricken's place." Alice grabbed a flyer and wrote a mobile number on the edge. "That's what Magnus told me, anyway. That he'd be staying with him for a while. You know him, don't you? Rickard?"

"Yeah, of course I know Ricken," said Eira, trying to sound unperturbed. "Is he still in Strinne?"

She pictured the small house with its asbestos cement tiles. A recreation room in the basement, with low sofas and pine panels. Eira always glanced over whenever she drove past—for professional reasons, and possibly others. She knew he was still there.

"Yeah, he and Magnus have been friends for forever," said Alice. "They call each other bro and that kind of thing." Her fingers wandered up to her upper arm, an unconscious movement that made Eira notice her tattoo. No flowers or hearts, just his name. A pretty, slightly ornate style in which one of the lines from the "M" continued in a loop around the rest of the letters.

"Love comes and goes, but friendship endures. Isn't that what they say?"

Eira parked up behind the rusty shell of a Volvo Amazon.

There were wrecked cars all over the property, some that had sunk so deep into the ground that they looked like they might have taken root there. Hops vines crept through the windows of an old Ford. A few of the cars looked like they might still run if someone fixed them up very soon, but Eira doubted that would happen. The wrecks were a statement, a sign that whoever lived there was the master of his own territory.

The municipal commissioner in Kramfors had tried to start a debate about the many junked cars in Norrland, hoping to convince Parliament to reintroduce the scrappage fund that made it worth hauling them to a scrapyard rather than dumping them at random, to allow the local authorities to issue fines. He had spoken about the degeneration of the landscape.

Rickard Strindlund probably had a different name for it. Power, perhaps. He did whatever he wanted there, and didn't give a damn about what anyone else considered beautiful or ugly, lawful or not. Those who entered had only themselves to blame.

Eira immediately recognized his sluggish gait, his long stride, swaying slightly like reeds in the breeze. That smile, charming as ever.

"Hey, Eira. It's been a while."

Ricken paused a few meters away. Pushed back his hair, squinted in the sun.

"Heard you were back. You here on cop business or did you just come to say hi?"

"I need to find Magnus," she said. "Completely personal."

"OK."

He jerked his head back to indicate that she should follow him. Ricken's name had been on the list of known petty criminals in the area, the ones GG had brought in for questioning. His record was certainly long enough—theft, drugs, an old assault charge from a Midsummer party in Norrfällsviken. She hadn't been able to avoid including him.

Ricken paused by the corner of the house. "How's it going with the murder of that old bloke in Kungsgården?" he asked. "You got anyone for it yet?"

"Not yet."

"Damn, sick bastard. Going after a lonely old man like that. If I knew who it was, I'd beat the shit out of him and serve him up on a silver plate. That's what I told your pals."

I know, thought Eira. *I know what you said.*

She was walking behind him again, his wiry body, the same tight jeans as ever, that unshakable confidence. She'd had to read through his interview. If Ricken was involved, that would complicate things. A relationship was a relationship, even if it was years ago, an eternity since he was the one she dreamed about, since she finally grew up.

The first was always the first, nothing could change that.

"We have a suspect," she said, though she knew she shouldn't say a thing. "It's just a matter of time now."

"Oh shit. Who is it?"

"I'm obviously not going to tell you." A small shift of power. Insignificant, but still. She was no longer seventeen and head-over-heels in love; she was a police officer. An investigator. With the Violent Crimes Unit.

"No, right, I know," said Ricken.

Magnus was sprawled in a rickety garden chair at the rear of the house. He reached out and grabbed her hand, but didn't get up for a hug.

"How's Mum doing?"

"Not great."

"Has something happened?"

Magnus was wearing a pair of denim cutoffs and a vest. He was tanned, his fair hair down to his shoulders. There was an open can of beer in the grass by his side. Eira didn't say a word about it, nor about the tang of marijuana she thought she could smell. Maybe it was just what she expected, or the memory of a scent. He hadn't been on the list. The most recent thing Eira had found was an assault from five years earlier, an ordinary fight. It hadn't led to a conviction, so it wasn't exactly misconduct for her to leave him out.

"She's getting worse and worse all the time," she said. "You know that. People don't recover from dementia."

She sat down in one of the old-fashioned sun loungers, the kind she had loved as a child. A piece of striped fabric on a wooden frame that could be slotted lower and lower. It was impossible to sit up straight in them.

"She seemed OK when I was there," said Magnus.

"And when was that?"

"I don't know, maybe a week ago? We had coffee."

"She didn't mention it."

"Or two. Weeks. It's summer, kind of hard to keep track." Magnus reached for his beer and took a couple of swigs, lit a cigarette. "You on holiday now, or what?"

"I'm working. Not right this second, but otherwise."

"Lucky for us." He laughed. Eira had always loved his laugh. It was so big, it spread right across the room. When Magnus laughed, so did everyone else. "What the hell though, sis. It's July, are they really driving you that hard?"

"I like my job," said Eira.

He raised an eyebrow. She expected a cutting remark or a lecture about how the cops spent their time chasing small-time crooks while the real criminals went free, the financial sharks and the corrupt politicians who let them wreak havoc, but he didn't have time. Rickard shouted through the kitchen window, asking if she wanted coffee or anything. Eira said yes to coffee, asked for some water, too.

"I'm driving," she added, as though she had to explain why she wasn't drinking beer on a summer's day when everyone else was taking it easy. Excusing herself for being so boring and conscientious all the time.

"Mum makes an effort when you're there," she said. "Can't you see that? She doesn't want you to notice anything."

"So what do you want me to do about that? I can't exactly rock up there and say 'Hey Mum, you're sicker than you think you are.' That'd be lousy."

Bees buzzed around them, happy in Ricken's overgrown garden. He had a full-blown wildflower meadow sloping down towards Strinnefjärden, a narrow channel of the river snaking between two hamlets.

Eira told Magnus that Kerstin had wandered off. About the bad days when she didn't know where she was, the dangers filling an average home. She told him all of this.

Magnus tapped the ash into his can; the cigarette burnt out and hissed as he dropped it inside. He leaned back again, either nonchalant or relaxed, and looked up at the sky. Clouds drifting slowly overhead, silvery streaks.

"I don't get why you moved home," he said. "Mum doesn't either. Says you're constantly watching over her like she can't take care of herself."

"She can't take care of herself."

"You should've stayed in Stockholm, that's what Mum thinks. You were supposed to make something of yourself. You were so good at school."

"Stop. You're not listening."

"I'm listening."

"You're the one she asks after. All the time." Eira regretted sitting down where she had, wanted to stand up, move closer to her brother, get through to him, possibly take his hand, pinch him and make him wake up, knock him to the ground and wrestle in the grass, tickling him or whatever else they hadn't done in twenty years. But instead she just slumped ever deeper. "How often do you even go over there? Once a month?"

"You can't force her to move, not against her will."

"We," said Eira. "The two of us need to deal with this together. She can't make that kind of decision anymore."

"A person's life is their own business," said Magnus. "Right down to the last fucking second. No one has the right to take that away from them."

"She wets herself sometimes. She panics when she doesn't know where she is."

"Maybe she doesn't want to hang out with a bunch of old fogeys, watching sing-along shows on TV. What happens if it's awful there, if we've already sold the house and can't do anything about it? Christ, haven't you read about what goes on in places like that? How they lock them up and leave them in shitty nappies, how they're not allowed out."

"That was somewhere else, not here. It doesn't have to be like that."

"And you can guarantee that, can you?"

"She likes those sing-along shows. We watch them every Tuesday."

"Seriously?"

Ricken came out with a chipped mug of coffee for her, interrupting their conversation. He had forgotten the water.

"I heard you guys picked up a bunch of people in Bjärtrå this morning," he said, tossing a new beer to Magnus and opening one himself. "I heard you were there."

"Don't bring that up now," said Magnus. "You know Eira can't talk cop stuff."

Ricken sat down in the grass. The insects seemed to hush, and everything went quiet. Eira saw a rowing boat glide out into the bay. Her brother had never found out about their relationship, the whole thing had played out in secret.

"I'm sure you lot have already made your minds up," Ricken continued, ignoring Magnus. "Once a person's done one thing, that means they must be guilty of another. That's the way you think."

"You don't need to tell her how she thinks," said Magnus.

"Those idiots have been bragging all over the place about burning down that house, so I know you'll get them for it, they're too dumb to keep their mouths shut, but they weren't trying to kill him. I know the dad of two them. They're just little brats."

"If you really have something to tell me," said Eira, "then it'd be better if I came back with a colleague. Either that or you should call the station."

"We haven't forgotten what Olof did to Lina Stavred," said Ricken. "So if a couple of little kids want to save Ådalen from the guy, I don't have anything against it. But fair is fair."

"Cut it out." Magnus threw the half-empty can at him. It missed his friend's head but showered him with beer all the same. "When she's sitting here, Eira isn't a cop; she's my sister."

Ricken threw the can back at him, missing too. Fooled about trying to lick the beer off himself.

Eira laughed. She liked that Magnus was taking her side and emphasizing that she was his sister, that Ricken wanted to tell her something. The whole thing made her feel warm inside, made her long to share a beer with them and remember the old times, to laugh at stupid jokes and lean back in the rickety damned chair that almost collapsed when she finally managed to get up.

"OK, I have to go," she said, lowering her cup to the grass. It tipped over, and the dregs of the coffee spilled out onto her shoe.

"I'll look in on Mum tomorrow," Magnus called after her. "Or the day after. I swear, I'll do better."

Let's go over everything we've got," said GG, standing with his back to the window, the sky and the coastal city. The buildings behind him had eight, nine stories, stepped blocks of flats climbing up the hillside.

For some reason their meeting was in Sundsvall that day. GG hadn't explained why and Eira hadn't asked.

She just got in her car and drove down.

"Everything we've got on what?" asked Bosse Ring. "Are you talking about the murder or the arson and attempted murder?"

"All of it. Every bloody case that so much as mentions the name Hagström. We should probably put our hands together and pray we're not dealing with two murders soon."

"Is it looking bad?" Silje Andersson looked up from her laptop.

"What?"

"Olof Hagström's condition."

"No change there. He's still hooked up to tubes and machines, the whole shebang. One of our colleagues in Umeå swung by this morning."

"What are they saying?"

"Want me to translate?"

"From doctor's speak? Please."

Olof Hagström was sedated and on a respirator following his operation. The bleed in the membranes surrounding his brain had clotted slightly during his time in the forest, but they had managed to remove the worst of it, ditto the blood in his lungs. They had also discovered a small hemorrhage in his liver. The doctors couldn't say how serious the damage would be. Nor whether he would wake up.

"The boys deny chasing him into the forest," GG continued. "They claim they got scared when the fire took hold. They saw him run out of the house and then they cleared off."

"But they did take care of the dog," said Bosse Ring. "Don't forget that."

The dog had come bounding out of nowhere. It went crazy when it saw the fire, but two of the boys had managed to catch it. One had wounds on his arm, bite marks, and had pulled back the dressing to show them—not without a certain amount of pride.

"'We couldn't just let it run off,'" Bosse Ring read from the interview transcript. "'It could've been run over or something.'"

"How considerate," said Silje.

One of the boys had made an anonymous call to the emergency services when he got home. He hadn't told his friends. When it came to which of them had thrown the burning bottles through the windows, their stories diverged wildly. Other than the thirteen-year-old, who claimed it was him, the others all blamed one another.

"He's probably been watching YouTube videos about how real gangster kids behave," said Silje. "Taking the blame to keep his older friends out of prison."

"Maybe he wants to impress his brother," Eira mumbled.

She had been to the station in Sundsvall many times before, but never in this role, as part of the team. As she stepped into the building, she had a vision of herself staying there. Applying for a position with Violent Crimes. It was only an hour away by car, easily commutable until she sorted things out with her mother.

"Or maybe it really was him," said Bosse Ring.

Sighs took hold throughout the room, the weight of four teenagers who had strayed so far over the line.

"But they could be telling the truth about the attack in the forest," GG continued, nodding to the crime scene technician he had asked to join the meeting.

It was a relief not to have to search for the test results on their computers. To be able to look one another in the eye over the table. That didn't happen too often.

"An unusual crime scene, I must say," Costel Ardelean spoke up as he connected his laptop to the system. "You learn something new every day."

Images of the fallen tree filled the screen on the wall. They had called out a forest ranger to inspect the uprooting late the night before. Nature's recovery: in the absence of branches, the power of gravity. Costel explained that the thickest branches had been sawn off, as had the crown. Someone had been collecting wood, doing the same to several other trees that had toppled during the powerful spring storms. It meant the equilibrium had been upset, enabling the fallen tree to spring upright again, helped along by the weight of Olof Hagström when he stumbled.

Parts of the tree had now been dug up and sent off for further analysis.

"Apparently it's happened before," said Costel. "At least one known fatality, in Blekinge in 2013. It's especially dangerous once the last of the ground frost has thawed and the spring rain loosens the earth."

"You'd have to be bloody mad to get out in nature," said Bosse Ring.

"Was it the tree that caused his head injury?" asked GG, accidentally kicking Eira beneath the table. She pulled her feet towards her. GG didn't seem to notice.

"It's possible," said Costel. "According to the medical examiner, the wound was caused by a powerful blow with a heavy branch. Traces of blood suggest it could've been the root plate. They found bark in the wound, too."

In the brief silence that followed, Eira found herself thinking about what Ricken had said about the fire and the teenage boys. The physical evidence seemed to confirm their version of events. That meant she didn't need to bring it up; she could keep the messy parts of her life separate from her professional life, where everything was clear and pure.

She leaned back and stretched out her legs, making sure to check that no one else's feet were in the way.

"In any case," said GG, "there's not much more we can do now but wait. On the test results, on Olof waking up—if he wakes up. The kids have already confessed; they were there, they'll be charged with arson regardless."

"Confusing business, this," said Costel Ardelean. "Two different investigations at the same crime scene, but both so different. Father and son. One house, one ruin."

"No doubt," said GG.

With that, they turned their attention to the murder.

They had twenty-four hours until the prosecutor would have to request that Tryggve Nydalen be remanded in custody if they wanted to hold him any longer.

"Which means driving to Härnösand and going through the whole security rigmarole, taking off our belts and emptying all the coins out of our pockets the minute we want to ask a question."

"Who has coins in their pockets these days?" asked Silje.

That was assuming they even had enough to remand him in custody.

The crime scene had burnt to the ground. They had fingerprints proving he had been in the house, but not when. The medical examiners had said all there was to say, and had released Sven Hagström's body.

Tryggve Nydalen was still maintaining his innocence. He may well be a bad person, but he hadn't had any quarrels with his neighbor.

"OK, so what have we got? First and foremost, a possible motive. Sven Hagström found out that his neighbor was a convicted sex offender and Nydalen felt like he had to silence him."

"Do we know that Sven actually threatened him?" asked Silje. She hadn't had time to go through all the material yet. "I can't see anything confirming that here."

"All we know for sure," said GG, turning to Eira, "is that Sven knew there was a sex offender in the area and that he was trying to find out more. But did he manage it?"

"It's definitely possible," said Eira. "He read articles about the assault, he seems to have been searching. His ex claims that he'd changed."

She knew how flimsy it sounded. The whole thing had seemed so solid a few days earlier, but was it really? Or was it nothing but a pattern she was trying to conjure up, the kind of images you see when you think you can glimpse the truth?

No, Sven Hagström had known. It was too much to be a sheer coincidence.

"There's something else I want to show you," said Costel Ardelean.

He pressed a couple of buttons, and the image of the uprooting was replaced by one of a hunting knife. The knife that had been seized from the suspect's gun cabinet. Its measurements corresponded with the wound, as did the shape of the blade. The technician talked at length about the model, the handle—made from curly birch and oak, with leather elements—and the sharpened, gently curved blade. Above all, he talked about the traces of dried blood they had found between the blade and the handle, barely visible to the naked eye. The location was one in which evidence might be preserved, even if you cleaned the knife.

"The DNA analysis isn't finished yet, but what we can say is that the blood isn't human."

"Is it elk?" asked GG, rocking back in his chair. "Or has he felled a bear? Don't tell me you've managed to date it back to September last year?" That was when elk hunting season got underway in that part of the country, an occasion more important than Christmas to many people.

"We'll know soon."

"And is it possible that these traces of . . . nonhuman blood could still be there even if you've used the knife since, and cleaned it thoroughly?"

"It depends what you mean by thoroughly."

"Why would someone lock the murder weapon in their own gun cabinet?" asked Silje.

"So no one notices it's missing," said Bosse. "Round here, a person without a hunting knife is more suspicious than one with."

The room fell silent. Someone ate the last of the cheese sandwiches. The phrase "murder weapon" had gained particular significance in the Swedish language since the murder of Olof Palme. The ongoing investigation, stretching across decades. Every single police officer, and the majority of ordinary citizens, knew that the murder could have been solved if they had just managed to find the murder weapon. It was a lingering trauma, proof that Sweden had changed. A country where you could get away with shooting the prime minister, where security no longer really existed.

"So what did he do with the knife?" asked GG. "Did he throw it in the river? Bury it?"

"If we hadn't caught those kids," said Bosse Ring, "I would've said that Nydalen started the fire to get rid of the evidence. It bothers me that it burnt down *that* night, just before we arrested him."

"Maybe he knew one of them? Have we checked where they got the idea?"

"Facebook, they said."

"Worth looking into?"

"That kind of thinking is everywhere out there. People have been getting worked up on various threads ever since we released Olof Hagström."

"Who knew we were on to Nydalen?"

GG turned to Eira. She thought for a moment, feeling a deep sense of unease. Had she blabbed to someone? No, she couldn't remember doing anything like that. The only person she had mentioned the name to was her old colleague, who was hunkered down in his cabin, pretending to enjoy his retirement.

"It's a pretty long way down to the river," she eventually said. "I doubt he would've chosen to dump the knife there."

"It's a bloody thicket," Bosse Ring agreed. "And he was in a hurry—a weekday morning, he could've bumped into anyone. Plus his wife was at home. She's still backing him to the hilt, by the way."

"Their accounts of what they were doing that morning differ slightly," said Eira. "But they were also in separate buildings. Tryggve could easily have snuck off for a while and come back without her noticing—assuming he didn't walk right past the bakehouse."

"Can we see a map?" asked GG.

Someone found one and brought it up on the big screen. The image kept jumping around, taking them up to Jämtland for a moment before zooming in on the area around Kungsgården.

Eira compared the map with her memories of the terrain. The Nydalen homestead was slightly higher than the Hagström house, and there was little other than forest in between. Spruce trees, the odd pine, quite a few aspen. Bilberry and lingonberry bushes. It was rocky in places, the earth couldn't be particularly deep. Other than the road, which it seemed logical to rule out, there was a snowmobile trail, plus a couple of half-overgrown paths that weren't visible in the satellite images.

"OK," said GG. "I'll try to get as many people as I can on a forest stroll with metal detectors."

Bosse Ring would be joining Eira in Kramfors, but they drove north in separate cars. It meant she could stop off in Lunde on the way. Take something out of the freezer for dinner, enabling her to work late.

There was a bunch of roses on the table. A supermarket bouquet, with the cellophane still around them.

"Have you had a visitor, Mum?"

Kerstin's face lit up.

"Magnus was here. He's doing so well, starting a new job and everything. I told him he'd have to bring the little ones over someday." Her eyes drifted to the framed photographs on the walls, the grandchildren. The pictures had been taken at nursery, back when the boys still lived in Kramfors, before his ex-girlfriend got a job in Gothenburg and moved away.

There were a couple of more recent shots on the fridge; perhaps the kids' mother had sent them.

Eira picked up the roses and unwrapped the cellophane, pulled off a few withered petals. Magnus had kept his word, at least. He had looked in on his mother.

She found a dish of lasagna and defrosted it in the microwave. Rejected a call from someone she didn't know and sat down for a moment. Maybe their living situation wasn't so pressing after all, maybe they could make it work a while longer, if they did it together.

"Have you seen the lovely flowers Magnus brought?"

Kerstin straightened them in the vase and repeated herself several times during the brief period they were sitting down, before Eira had to get going. As she got into the car she realized it had been a long time since she had last seen her mother look so happy.

She was in the middle of the Sandö Bridge when her phone rang again, Bosse Ring this time. He was already in Kungsgården, where they had arranged to meet. To "go another round with the wife," as GG had put it.

To convince Mejan Nydalen to take them through what had happened that morning, minute by minute, in the hope that they might spot the cracks in her stubborn defense of her husband.

"I'll be there in fifteen minutes," said Eira, stepping on the accelerator.

"Don't worry," he said. "There's no one home. I managed to get hold of the son on the phone, she's gone to visit a cousin in Örnsköldsvik."

"Should we drive up there?"

He hesitated for a moment before answering.

"I said we just wanted a chat, in my usual friendly way. We're not chasing her; we can do it tomorrow morning."

Eira turned off by a disused campsite, pulling over to think about where she would be most useful. She could drive back to the station and sit down at a computer with access to the full investigation— or was there anyone she should talk to?

The little wooden cabins were lopsided, their yellow paint peeling. Several had actually collapsed. The place had the charm of a bygone era, early sixties in all likelihood, back when people used to tour campsites—despite their less-than-appealing location at the foot of a concrete bridge, tucked among the exits of the former E4 highway.

She checked her mobile, saw the two calls she had missed while she was talking to her mother about how pretty the roses were.

One was from August, the other from a number she didn't recognize.

She called it.

"Rolle here."

Hagström's old workmate from the timber yard, Rolle Mattsson from Sandslån.

"Have you caught the bastard yet?" he asked. "Heard the house burnt down, too. Sven must be turning in his grave, poor sod. It was his parents' place, you know, he took over after them. Not that he's been buried yet. You know he wasn't a religious bloke, don't you?"

"It'll probably be a while before any funeral," said Eira. "Is that why you called?"

"Not at all. You were trying to get hold of the chair of the local hunting party, but he had a stroke back in May. His wife asked me to get in touch with you, in case it was urgent. Usually is when the police come calling."

"Are you a member of the same hunting group?"

"It'll probably be me who ends up taking over. If it turns out it's a bad stroke, that is."

Eira opened the car door and climbed out. The grass in the campsite had been cut recently. The owners often took care of that kind of thing even if they neglected the buildings. Letting the grass go wild was seen as the final step, the death blow.

"I had a few general questions," she began. "About the equipment you use in the hunt."

"Go for it."

"The knives, for example."

"Yes?"

They hadn't released any details about the murder weapon, but as ever there were likely people who knew, rumors swirling. And if not then, he certainly knew now.

"Does everyone have roughly the same kind of knife?" Eira knew how stupid the question sounded, but he said yes, that most people stuck to a handful of manufacturers, typically the ones available from the local ironmonger.

"And let's say your knife starts to get a little blunt, do you buy a new, identical one?"

"No, for God's sake, I sharpen it."

"Yourself?"

"Either that or I take it to Harry at Nylands Järn."

Of course.

"And everyone involved in the hunt uses their own knife, is that how it works?" Another particularly dumb question. It went without saying. You didn't need to have grown up in the forests to know that, but Eira got away with it purely because she was a woman.

"Yes, yes," he replied, still patient. "You don't want to be stuck there in the woods, unable to gut an elk. You need to be able to skin it. Some people like having one knife for that and another for small game, plus one for cutting sausages by the fire later, but I always say there's no need; it's not the tools that make a hunter."

"So you need to be good with a knife?"

"As important as being able to shoot. Out of respect for the animal. You can't be fumbling about, making mistakes."

"Is Tryggve Nydalen a member of your hunting group?"

A few seconds' pause. He had been referred to as "a fifty-nine-year-old man" in the press, but he also had a custody hearing the next day, and his name would hardly remain a secret for long. Assuming it hadn't already leaked.

Assuming he was remanded in custody.

"Yes, yes," said Rolle Mattsson. "They both are."

"Both?"

"Yeah, him and the wife."

"Mejan?"

"Don't sound so surprised. We let women in too. There was a bit of resistance at first, obviously, but it's like I always say: They can be a pretty good shot if you just get them to shut up for long enough."

He chuckled at his own joke. Eira breathed in, could smell grass. The breeze was soft and mild, but it still made her shiver.

"Do you remember," she continued, "whether either of them took down an elk last autumn?"

"Naw," he said. "I'm not sure. We've got a logbook, of course, but it's over at Sune's place—he's the one who had the stroke. Hang on though . . . I'm wondering whether Mejan didn't bring one down then. There are still a few people who think the hunt is no place for a woman, so there's always a bit of muttering whenever they get outdone by one, but was it last autumn or the one before? No, I don't know off the top of my head . . ."

Eira thanked him for getting in touch and called GG.

"They've got two hunting knives," she said, telling him—possibly a little too excitedly—about the hunting group and the various knives and what it takes to skin an elk. "So it could have been Mejan's in the cabinet."

"We've got him," said GG.

He stopped her before she had time to hang up.

"I hope you'll consider it," he said. "Next time we've got a position open."

It was his day off, but August was waiting for her in the lunchroom. He wolfed down the last of his shop-bought wild mushroom soup, direct from the carton, and got up.

"Come with me," he said.

Though it disrupted the air-conditioning, someone had opened the window. Eira felt warm. There had been a few too many days of simply bumping into each other in the corridor, in a doorway, without mentioning what had happened.

"I've spent a while looking at this," August explained, opening his computer, his own personal laptop. "In the evenings, I mean. Outside of working hours."

Eira watched as the screen lit up. It was one of the many Facebook threads calling for someone to cut off Olof Hagström's dick, the ones August had already showed her a long time ago—was it one week or two? Time felt like it had split into different orbits; it had been an eternity since she'd left him in bed in the Hotel Kramm.

Shove a baseball bat up his arse. Chase him out of the country.

The same comments that had popped up on the timelines of the teenagers suspected of arson, on their phones and their computers.

"Do you really not have anything better to do?" she asked.

"I'm open to suggestions," he replied with a smirk.

Eira kept her eyes on the screen. The threads had updated since she last looked. People were now talking about Olof Hagström's house burning down, too. Cheering and sharing enthusiastic little thumbs-up.

Pity he didn't go up in flames too, one person wrote.

He will if he shows his face again.

She shuddered as she saw an image of the gutted house. It must have been taken fairly early, because there was a fire engine parked outside. The flames hadn't been completely extinguished, and the cordon was still up.

"I think I've found the source," said August.

He enlarged a photograph on the screen. An image of a smiling Sofi Nydalen, blond hair blowing in the breeze, with her husband and children. It looked like they were in a boat.

"Are you serious?"

"There could be other people, on other forums, but she's definitely one of them."

August showed Eira the time and date of her first post. The evening after Olof Hagström was released. Sofi Nydalen had uploaded a photograph in which he was nothing but a shadow in a window.

"I was wondering how it could have happened so quickly," said August. "How there could be so much detailed information—his name, his past crime, his exact address."

He kept talking as Eira took the mouse and scrolled through the thread the young Mrs. Nydalen had created, saw it grow increasingly hateful and crude.

"I borrowed an account to trace it back," he said.

"Your girlfriend's?"

"Mmm."

"She must really trust you."

"I told her she might've been breaking the law by sharing this stuff and that it would be in her best interests to help the police. If not me, then an investigator from Violent Crimes."

He wasn't facing Eira, but she could still feel his smile. In slight profile, though all she could really see was the back of his neck. The soft down where his hair was growing out caught the light.

"And they're not the kind of people you want to mess with," he added.

August had followed the shares back and forth, through the labyrinth of new threads that had popped up. Eira saw comments flicker

by, taken out of context, occasionally pausing when he wanted
to make a point about something or simply change position. He
stopped on one comment that actually disagreed with the others.

You're such sheep, all running in the same direction, it read.

What about a bit of critical thinking?

*Have none of you read The Scapegoat? No, sorry, thought not. Do
you even know how to read, you fucking retards?*

Those words were followed by a long line of attacks on the person
who had dared question the others.

August leaned back, looking out at the sky through the open
window.

"Do you know how many people disagree with the majority view
here?" he asked. "Not that I've counted or read everything, but I'd
guess it's less than one percent. What does that say about human-
ity?"

"It doesn't really tell us much about what people think," said Eira.
"People share things with others who agree with them. They get rid
of anyone who doesn't have the same views from their feeds. They
don't have the energy, so they step back, give up, block the people
they don't like—assuming they haven't been blocked first. You just
don't see them anymore."

August put a hand on the back of her seat.

"Well, I hope Sofi Nydalen gets done for this," he said.

"And here we were thinking she left because of the kids," said
Eira, conscious that his hand was somewhere behind her. "But she
must've been scared after the fire, maybe she realized what she'd
started."

"It should be incitement at the very least."

"Along with thousands of others, in that case."

"I helped bring in one of the kids who started the fire," August
continued. "There's no way they would've come up with the idea on
their own—they weren't even born when that girl was murdered.
They live in their gaming world. If something's not online, it doesn't
exist."

Eira wasn't sure she should sit so close to him for much longer. It woke the fantasies she only ever let loose late at night, before she fell asleep. Sometimes she woke up to them, too.

"I'll raise this with GG," she said, still thinking about getting up. "The social media experts in Sundsvall might already be on it, I don't actually know."

"Defamation then?"

"That would require Olof Hagström to wake up, get out of bed, and report her."

"Shit," said August.

"Thank you."

"What for?"

"For caring. Even if it is a bit dubious, professionally speaking."

"What is?"

"Using your girlfriend's account."

She dared meet his smile only for a brief moment.

They found the bin bag later that evening. At eleven minutes to ten, as the clouds began to turn pink. Buried ten centimeters deep beside a couple of large rocks that looked like something out of a fairy tale.

A flat stone resting on top of a round one, almost like a hat. Both were overgrown with white moss. The anthill nearby was teeming, the air swarming with blackflies.

The bilberries were almost ripe.

"You have no idea of the junk people dump in these woods," said one of the men who had joined the search; Eira thought his name was Jonas.

He was one of two police cadets who had driven up from Sundsvall. They were joined by a young police assistant working overtime, not August, and a woman detective from the area whom Eira knew slightly. Several members of the local patrol had also joined in, though they had now been asked to leave.

They didn't want anyone stomping around unnecessarily.

The cadet pointed to the glade by the snowmobile trail where they had gathered all their finds. Pieces of rusty agricultural machinery. Bike wheels. Two broken rakes and the chain from a chainsaw, crooked reinforcement rods, an old lawn mower. There was even a deer skull, a pile of old bottles, and the corpse of a soccer ball, completely deflated.

The black rubbish bag was still lying where they had found it. One of them had carefully poked it open with a stick, revealing its contents.

Something black or possibly navy blue, made of thick fabric. A piece of clothing of some kind. Could be a pair of overalls.

A yellow rubber glove.

"We don't know if there's a second glove," said the cadet. "We didn't want to rummage around too much."

"Good work," said Eira. She was the first of the murder investigators on the scene. Bosse Ring had already opened a bottle of plonk in his hotel room, but he would be on his way as soon as he could get hold of a cab.

"It had been covered over with branches and last year's leaves," said the cadet. "Pretty sloppily done, but enough to hide the fact that someone had been digging."

Eira crouched down and gently prodded the plastic bag with a stick, opening it wider.

A handle made from different layers of wood. Curly birch and oak, she thought, with leather elements. The blade had a gentle curve, all the better for skinning an elk.

She stood up.

"OK," she said. "Cordon off the area."

The forest around them was fairly dense. Several of the spruce trees looked like they were dying, the lowest branches dry and covered in gray lichen. Eira took a few steps to one side and saw the red timber, a window with a painted white frame.

They were no more than twenty meters from the bakehouse.

All knives look the same." Mejan Nydalen was sitting perfectly still in the interview room, eyes steady on the printed image on the table. "It could be anyone's."

"It's identical to the knife we found in your gun cabinet. The brand is Helle, made in Holmedal. Did you buy them at the same time?"

"How am I supposed to remember that? We've had a lot of hunting knives."

"Do you recognize this?" asked Eira, placing another picture on the table. The clothing they had found in the forest.

"Overalls," said Mejan.

"Does your husband own anything like this?"

"I don't know if they're exactly like that, but he's got something similar for painting and DIY and that kind of thing, of course he does."

"And where does he usually keep them?"

She scratched her head. "Oh, let me think. In the shed, maybe?"

The overalls were a common make, available from DIY stores and online, possibly at Nylands Järn, too; they had someone checking now. Size large. They were well worn. Flecks of paint. Flecks of something else too, perhaps.

Eira pushed an image of the rubber gloves towards Mejan.

"We found all of this behind the bakehouse. Eighteen meters from it. You said you were there that morning. Are you sure you didn't see anyone in the forest?"

"I was so busy with everything. Do you mean there was someone there?"

Bosse Ring leaned forward over the table. He had been sitting quietly so far. It had been his idea for Eira to start the interview. He thought it might be easier for Mejan to open up to another woman, to lower her guard. Eira had her doubts. She often found that men had a fairly naive attitude towards women, thought they were made of softer stuff.

Mejan Nydalen's voice was steady; she didn't hesitate as she took them through their preparations ahead of the grandchildren's arrival again. There was actually a note of criticism in her voice, as though she didn't think they really understood just how much work there was to do.

Eira thought she recognized something in her, something of the women around her while she was growing up—her grandmother and mother, various old ladies with stern voices and knowledge that couldn't be questioned.

No, she had never seen anyone digging in the forest.

"You think she's lying?" Bosse Ring asked once they were back on the top floor of the police station. Through the window they watched Mejan climb into her car and reverse out of the parking bay.

"She's lying," said Eira. "She just might not realize that she's lying."

How much shit can there be in one family?" GG asked when he learned who was behind the agitation against Olof Hagström.

"Go to Stockholm," he said a little later. "Let dear Sofi know that we know. Show her the wreck of the house—why not show her a picture of the poor bastard's foot sticking out from under the tree, too. So it's etched on the inside of her skull the next time she even thinks about sharing her every thought on Facebook. Let Sofi Nydalen know that we're watching her, that we'll see if she posts as much as a picture of her dinner. And get it all on tape."

GG himself planned to have a chat with the prosecutor, once the custody hearing was over and they had time.

"Hey," he added, "be nice. I want to know what's hiding in this family, what they whisper about in the bedroom."

Eira closed her eyes as the train pulled out of Kramfors, let herself drift away. There was something about the movement of the train, about being between one place and another, powerless to influence anything. She hadn't had to clash swords with the home help or call a neighbor; Magnus had replied to her message. He would look in on their mother, maybe even stay over.

The scent of freedom, it was intoxicating.

Eira was in the quiet carriage, her phone switched to silent, but she felt the buzz of a text message come through. Tryggve Nydalen had been remanded in custody, GG wrote.

Her phone vibrated again just north of Gävle, with the seventh message from Sofi Nydalen.

Maybe better to meet outside somewhere instead?

Sure, Eira wrote back. **Where do you suggest?**

It was the third time she had wanted to change the location of their meeting, suggesting fear, nerves, possibly even guilt.

The original plan had been to meet at the Nydalens' house, in a residential area on the outskirts of town. Then she had wanted to meet at a popular patisserie in central Stockholm, both to save Eira the trip out on the commuter train and because they had incredible prawn sandwiches. Now she thought it would be better to meet at a waterfront café on Norr Mälarstrand, **since the weather's so nice.**

OK, see you there.

Sofi sent a thumbs-up and a smiley face in reply, as though the two women were friends planning coffee and cake together in the sun.

The train arrived on time at 2:38 p.m.

Eira had almost forgotten what it was like to be surrounded by so many people. The cacophony of sounds mixing and echoing beneath the arched roof in Stockholm Central, the aroma of sweat and freshly baked cinnamon buns, Asian noodle dishes from kiosks that had popped up since she had last been there.

She walked to the café, which was on a floating pontoon. Eira could make out at least seven languages being spoken around her as she waited. She felt the gentle rocking of the waves caused by the boats in Riddarfjärden, the anonymity of being in a place where the majority of people were simply passing through and didn't know a soul. There had been moments when she loved living in the big city, even if her rented apartment was pretty far from the center.

"Sorry I'm late," said Sofi Nydalen, arriving just as Eira had started to doubt she would ever show up. Wearing thin wide-legged trousers and a floaty blouse, both white. "I had to find somewhere to leave the kids. Patrik went back to work early. He doesn't cope well without anything to do. What you have to understand is that it's been an incredibly stressful time. I'll just have a bottle of water. Sparkling. With lemon, if possible."

A stubborn gull had landed where Eira was sitting when she returned with Sofi's water and a fourth refill of coffee for herself. Sofi ducked as it flapped over to the next table.

"The whole thing is so awful," she said. "It's like watching a film, only you're in it somehow, if you know what I mean. Patrik told me what his dad did to that girl, but he hasn't wanted to talk about it since. Tryggve has never done anything to me. No advances or anything like that. Do you really think he's guilty?"

Eira had been vague over the phone, giving the impression that she wanted to talk about the family in very general terms.

"What do you think?"

Sofi pushed back the hair that had blown into her face and shifted on the low sofa.

"It makes my skin crawl," she said. "What he did when he was younger. I keep picturing his old body—he walks about in nothing but his underwear sometimes. How can you let someone take you in like that? It really could be anyone." She gestured discreetly to the people around them, slumped on the other sofas. Eira thought she could see several couples who weren't quite couples; the way they were talking seemed a little too strained, and they were smiling a little too often, aware of themselves in the way only people on a first date are.

Sofi Nydalen had always thought of her father-in-law as kind, if a little evasive. Not someone you could really get close to. He wasn't particularly open, but she had just assumed that that was what men from Norrland were like.

"It was harder with Mejan, I was almost scared of her at first. She can be really bossy. In the end I got Patrik to say that we needed the house to ourselves, otherwise I wouldn't come. There are more exciting things to do on holiday, you know? I guess it's the classic mother- and daughter-in-law thing. Like I'm not good enough because I don't scrub the floors with soap or make soup from goutweed and nettles. If you google those things, it says they're weeds—makes you wonder how healthy they really are."

Sofi glanced down at the phone on the table, voice recorder running. Eira couldn't tell whether she was concerned or pleased that her words were being saved. The wind was probably so loud that their conversation would be barely audible.

"And then there's the fact I'm from Stockholm, that I've got a good job and earn decent money, all that stuff. You start to wonder if she's got a slight inferiority complex or something, but it's actually the other way around—she's the one who looks down on me. She assumes I think I'm remarkable or something. Isn't that just another kind of racism?"

Eira didn't reply. She had taken out her iPad, switched it on, and brought up the right page, all without Sofi Nydalen noticing a thing.

"It's happened again," she read aloud. "The police have let yet another sexual predator go. He's raped and murdered once, and now he's back on the streets again."

"What?"

"Did you write this?"

"God, I can't remember."

Eira placed the iPad in front of her, a screenshot of Sofi's own Facebook page with the very first post she made.

The flighty side of her seemed to disappear. "Have you been on my private Facebook account?"

"Your page is public."

"You've got no right to do that."

"What you wrote has been shared over two thousand times. One of the people it reached was my colleague, via his girlfriend. In what way do you think that's private?"

Sofi Nydalen gazed out across Riddarfjärden, towards Södermalm and its jagged cliffs rising up on the other side of the water. She put on her sunglasses, which had been perched on top of her head. Her profile wasn't protected in any way. Anyone who viewed it could see what she wrote, presumably because she also used it to advertise the interior design company where she worked—perhaps she had even been told to. There were plenty of companies that required their employees to use their private social media accounts to boost the brand.

"I have the right to write whatever I want," she said. "We have freedom of speech in this country."

"What did you think when the house burnt down?"

"It was horrible when I smelled the smoke. I was worried the fire would spread."

"You weren't concerned that someone might have burnt to death in there?"

"Do you have children?"

"That's irrelevant."

Sofi Nydalen lifted her sunglasses and studied Eira's reaction. "Thought not," she said. "If you did, you'd understand. It's a parent's job to protect their kids."

"In what way was Olof Hagström threatening your children?"

"You were there that morning, when he was arrested. And then you let him go without even telling us. You didn't stop to think how that would feel."

"I understand that you might have found it unpleasant," said Eira, remembering what GG had said about being nice.

"Unpleasant?" Sofi Nydalen swung her foot at the gull, which was still hopping around in its hunt for crumbs. It flapped away and turned its attention elsewhere. "He raped and murdered a girl—or one that we know about, anyway. I thought I was going to die when I saw him in the house where the old man had just died. I asked Patrik to do something about it, to tell him he couldn't stay there, but Patrik said there was nothing we could do, that it's his house. Private property. He said he'd come with me if I wanted to go swimming or anywhere else, but that kind of thing drives me crazy, having to take my husband with me just to go out. It's like living in Afghanistan or something. Why should a person like that be allowed to move freely and not me?"

"We've caught the people who burnt down the house," said Eira. "They'd read the threads you started."

"Are you saying it's my fault?"

"No," she said with some effort. "But I thought you should know. In case it comes up in court."

"I just wrote the truth. Is that a crime? I told it like it is—no one's going to protect us if we don't do it ourselves."

"Olof Hagström is in a coma," said Eira. "The doctors don't know if he'll make it."

"If I'd known you were going to start accusing me of things, I never would have come to meet you. I didn't even tell Patrik. He thinks you lot are harassing us. You should be offering us support right now."

"I'm not accusing you of anything. I'm just asking questions."

Sofi Nydalen glanced at her watch. A big rose gold thing. "I'm sorry, but I have to go and pick up the kids now."

The hotel Eira had booked was in the old town. Her room was spartan and minimal, the kind of place permitted under police budget rules. The only window looked out onto a dark alleyway, but the recess itself was so deep that there was room for her to sit in it. The warm, damp air seeped into the room, the murmur of the hordes of tourists. Eira scrolled through the numbers of the three or four friends she could call; maybe they could meet for a drink and a debrief on how their love lives and careers and everything else was going. For some reason the prospect made her feel more weary than excited. They had drifted apart since she'd moved back home, and she still hadn't been in touch with any of her old friends there, which meant that her social life was stuck in a kind of limbo between then and now.

Wasn't there something about the phrase itself that felt a bit much like hard work? "Social life" sounded like something that wasn't quite a life, something that had to be constructed, built up, worked on.

She peeled off her sweaty shirt and lay down on the bed instead, opened the dating app on her phone. The system automatically searched for singles in a specific radius—the very reason Eira had quickly turned it off after she moved back home. Within the space of just a few hours, three old acquaintances from school had popped up on there, along with a suspect she had helped arrest and the man who serviced the computers at the station.

From time to time, when she found herself in Umeå or Stockholm, she would reactivate the app and anonymously swipe through the pictures of men her age—plus or minus five years. She might meet up with someone who didn't need to know she was a police officer.

For one night only, so she didn't have time to confuse her feelings for love.

Twenty or so faces flashed by. A few looked nice. Two got in touch, but she chose not to reply.

Instead she dialed the number for Olof Hagström's sister.

Ingela Berg Haider answered on the second ring. "I'm in a meeting," she whispered.

"Maybe you could call me back?"

"No, just hang on a second." The sounds in the background changed as the woman stepped out, away from the others, closed a door.

"I saw that you had someone in custody," she said. "Did he do it?"

"He hasn't been charged yet," said Eira. "The investigation is still ongoing. That's all I can say."

"So why did you ring, if you can't tell me anything?"

There was no good way to say what she had to say, nothing gentle or dignified enough.

"The medical examiner released your father's body yesterday."

"What does that mean? Do I have to pick it up? Him. I can't."

"No, no, I just meant that they've finished their investigation. So the family can start planning the funeral."

"Family? What do you mean family?" Ingela Berg Haider had raised her voice; Eira could hear her stress levels rocketing. "I don't even know what kind of funeral he wanted. I don't think he went to church, he wasn't religious . . . And who's even going to come?"

"There's no rush," said Eira. "If you get in touch with a funeral director they can help you with everything."

Ingela didn't seem to be listening.

"Olof's landlady has been calling me practically every day, too. Saying she'll take his stuff to the dump if I don't go and pick it up, that she'll send me the bill. Where am I supposed to put it? I don't even have a bloody car. And imagine if he wakes up and all his things are gone—who do you think he'll blame then?"

Ingela's breathing was rapid. She was probably pacing back and forth in the corridor. Soft carpets. Eira couldn't hear any footsteps.

"I don't get why Olof didn't just clear off. Why did he stay there, in a place where everyone hates him?"

"We were planning to go over and interview him again, but we didn't have time. I don't know why he stayed."

"You keep being drawn back," said Ingela. "You try to leave, but it's impossible. You move five hundred kilometers away and make a life for yourself—a good life. I've got a job, a kid; everything just *works*. I took my mum's maiden name, that's the Berg, married a Haider, erased all that crap. Just like that. Or so I thought. But here I am with a funeral to plan and a burnt-out house. My brother's in a coma in Umeå and everyone keeps pestering me, the insurance company wants paperwork and his things are going to be taken to the dump, and I can't believe my dad is actually dead, it just won't sink in. I hardly ever thought about him while he was still alive."

Eira closed the app as it flashed up with another match.

"I'm in Stockholm," she said. "I can rent a car, drive you out there."

Ingela Berg Haider was waiting in the car park outside the Sveriges Television building. Eira never would have recognized her if they hadn't arranged to meet, yet there was definitely still something of the seventeen-year-old she had spied on as a child in there.

Her hair was dyed black and cut in a short, blunt style. She was wearing a man's jacket, cinched in at the waist with an orange belt, and had a pair of small guitar earrings hanging from her ears.

"I still don't know where I'm going to put everything," she told Eira. "We live in a flat, we have two square meters of space in the storeroom. I don't have room for all this."

"We'll take a look," said Eira, typing Olof Hagström's address—

or former address—into the GPS in the rental car. "We'll make an assessment. Maybe we'll be able to persuade the landlady to take it easy."

"I haven't seen him since he was fourteen. Most people don't even know I have a brother."

They pulled out onto Valhallavägen and drove towards the motorway heading north, inching forward in the busy rush-hour traffic. The radio had been pretuned to a station playing bluegrass from the American South. Before she left the hotel, Eira had splashed her face and pulled on the same shirt as earlier. She had forgotten all about any possible dates.

The traffic came to a standstill just after Norrtull. The sun set faster here, farther south, glittering on the endless line of cars. Eira told Ingela about Olof's condition, what the doctors had said, the uncertainty. They had managed to remove the blood from his lungs and around his liver, but he still wasn't reacting to pain.

They crept forward at a snail's pace.

"What does Olof actually do?" asked Ingela. "Or what did he do, before all this?"

"For work, you mean?"

"I don't know anything about him. Dad declined all contact, but Mum started writing to him once they got divorced. Olof never replied. I dug out his address when she was ill, but he didn't reply then either. Didn't even come to her funeral."

"He picks up cars from the countryside," said Eira. "A dealer finds them online and sells them on for a profit in the city. All off the books, of course—Olof doesn't seem to have had a regular job."

They had managed to get hold of the dealer from his call list. He had been furious at first, demanding that they return his car, but once he'd realized it was connected to a murder inquiry he had changed his tune and denied all knowledge of a Pontiac Firebird.

"What's he like?" asked Ingela.

"Olof?"

"Yeah, you met him, didn't you? Before the other stuff happened."

"Hard to say. It was a pretty intense situation." Eira tried to recall the impression he had made on her when she first walked up to the car outside Hagström's house that morning, but all she could remember was the unease. The knowledge of what he had done.

And then, by the river, once they had caught up with him: the strange stillness.

"Reserved," she said. "I had the feeling I wasn't really getting through to him. Confused, but that's not exactly surprising. I think he was scared." She thought of his huge body, but struggled to find the right words to describe it. "He mentioned a boat that used to be kept on the shore."

"I remember it. I remember that boat." Ingela peered out through the window as the enormous oaks in the royal park slowly sailed by. For a moment or two she didn't speak. The screeching of fiddles was replaced by a peaceful tune, a clear voice singing about going down to the river to pray.

"We used to go rowing, just the two of us, in the shallows along the shore. Looking for beavers or just paddling about. The trees grew right out into the water there. I remember all that, but I can't remember what he looked like when we were young. Isn't that weird?"

The traffic had finally started to move, and they passed the streamlined blocks of the social housing estate, the green expanse of the Järvafältet nature reserve.

"It's like all that's left in me is a kind of presence. A sense that my brother was there, and then he wasn't. I'm screaming at him, but I only remember that internally, I don't actually see him. 'You sick fuck, freak, don't touch me,' that kind of thing; how the hell was I meant to deal with it? I was only seventeen. I didn't understand a thing. Everyone stared at me at school, wanted to know if he'd ever tried it on with me. I remember Dad dragging everything out of his room, getting rid of all his stuff. Everything that was him. I don't know how much time had passed by then. I can't get the pieces to fit."

She trailed off. The roads ahead cleared out as they approached Upplands Bro.

"What do you mean, you can't get the pieces to fit?" asked Eira.

"It was all such a mess, everything. I couldn't handle it. Had to change school, moved around."

The address took them to the edge of the suburbs, past an industrial area and down a winding road towards Lake Mälaren, through what had once been a farming district.

They pulled up outside a large red-painted villa with an outhouse and an apple tree in the garden. The woman who came to meet them was in her fifties, wearing a pair of dungarees and a vest, her hair tied back. She smiled and pulled off her gardening gloves.

They introduced themselves, said they had come to look through Olof's things.

Her smile faded. "The police said they were done here. We rented out a room, that's all. Helped a person with a place to live. I realize now that we should have done a more thorough background check, but you want to trust people, you know?"

She had already emptied the room, but Ingela asked to see it anyway. The woman—Yvonne—reluctantly fetched the key and followed them in. The room was in an outbuilding, down a slope, hidden behind bushes and trees. The landlords couldn't see it from the main house, and didn't keep track of whether their tenant was home or not, as they had already told the other officers.

"We're not control freaks, we live out here for the peace and quiet."

Aside from a few cans of paint, a stool, and some protective paper on the floor, the outbuilding was empty. Fifteen square meters at most, a simple pantry kitchen with a hot plate in one corner. The only running water was in the shower, crammed into a box room in the porch.

"We'll have to deep-clean the place before we can let it out again. I had no idea what kind of state it was in. And the stench! The sprays we had to use shouldn't even be legal."

His things were beneath a tarpaulin outside.

"Is it OK if I leave you to it?" The woman strode away.

Ingela tore back the plastic sheet.

Olof didn't have much furniture. A huge mattress, but no bed-frame or headboard. A mattress topper and bedding, rolled up. A tired old armchair, a table and two chairs, a Yamaha stereo, complete with enormous speakers, all in a heap. Eira counted seven cardboard boxes and three bin bags.

"Guess it'll all have to go to the tip," said Ingela.

"We have space for the stereo," said Eira. "And a few other boxes."

She peered into the bin bag closest to her. Musty smells. Towels, clothes. All just tossed inside. She should have hired a bigger car, she thought. Pleading with the landlady no longer felt like a good idea. One heavy rain shower and everything would be damp, go moldy; there would be nothing left.

Ingela slumped down onto one of the chairs.

"I thought he was such a loser. I hated him for banging on the bathroom door while I was in there, for going into my room and stealing my things, the kind of crap siblings fight about all the time. I didn't even believe what I heard, but I told on him anyway."

She pulled a box towards her and folded back the lid, took out a pan. A handful of ladles and cutlery, a letter. Ingela turned over the envelope.

"From Mum," she said. There were more letters; she soon had an entire stack in her hands. "Look, he opened them. Olof must have read them, but he never replied. Why not?" Her voice broke as she picked up a thick white envelope. "I recognize this one. It's the invitation to Mum's funeral."

Ingela turned away. Eira didn't know what to say. She peered into the box that was closest to her. A pack of quick-cook macaroni, jars of hot dogs.

"What didn't you believe?" she eventually asked.

"What?"

"You said before that you didn't believe what you heard, but you told on him anyway."

"That Olof followed Lina into the woods." Ingela put the letters in a neat pile beside her, then pulled out a tissue and blew her nose. "My little brother. He was still into model-making kits. Planes. I mean, his room sometimes stunk of something other than sweat—he was fourteen, and he'd had a huge growth spurt that year—but still . . . I thought they were talking crap, that they were lying, so I don't know why I told Mum. I was just so angry with him—or more with Mum and Dad. They were always having a go at me about what I got up to, even though I was three years older, but they let Olof stay out however late he wanted with those older boys. He probably stole cigarettes and beers for them or whatever else it took to hang out with Ricken and Tore and that lot."

"Rickard Strindlund?"

"Was that his name? I can't remember all of them, it's so long ago now, but I do remember how annoyed I was that Olof was hanging out with them. Guys my own age, and a few were really cute too, the kind you could imagine being with . . . But everything about him annoyed me back then, I was so caught up in myself and thought I . . ."

Ingela peered down at the pile of letters on the ground.

"Everyone said it was him. And he confessed, right? So it must've been him?"

The first train of the morning pulled into Kramfors just before lunch. Eira found a scene of calm at the police station. Empty offices and stuffy air, no word about what might be expected of her during the rest of the day.

In the lunchroom she found a local investigator who had been on the force for an eternity. The woman never seemed to need to take any leave. There were rumors that Anja Larionova had married a Russian a few years earlier, hence the name, but she didn't wear a wedding ring and no one knew where the Russian had gone. Some of the others whispered that she had just tried to make it look like she was married.

"How's the investigation going, then?" Anja asked, in the same tone she might use to remark on the weather.

"Good," said Eira. "Not much to do right now. We're waiting on the reports from forensics."

"On the things you found in the forest?"

"Mmm. And you?"

"More summer visitors on their way in," Anja replied with a deep sigh. "They're coming to look at the pictures of the stolen goods we found in Lo. They'll spot their things and I'll have to explain that they won't necessarily get them back. I had a couple in yesterday who'd had a pair of folding Japanese screens with a cherry blossom pattern on them stolen. You can guarantee there's only one pair of those in the whole of Ångermanland, so it was tricky to make them understand why we couldn't just go and seize them."

"No other distinguishing features to prove the screens were theirs?"

"Nope. A bit of cherry blossom doesn't warrant a raid."

Eira rinsed out her mug and said goodbye. She sent a message to GG, asking him to call her whenever he had a moment. The morning meeting had been canceled because he was at the custodial prison in Härnösand, and the others were likely busy with other things. He called her back half an hour later, from the car on the way to Sundsvall.

"Nydalen's keeping mum," he told her. "Hasn't said a word since we showed him the pictures of the things we found buried in the forest."

"Is there anything particular you want me to do?"

"We're still waiting on the forensic reports, but they probably won't come in before tomorrow—at the earliest. Are we behind on any reports?"

"I was wondering if I should take a look at the old preliminary investigation," said Eira. "To make sure Nydalen's name doesn't crop up anywhere."

"Just don't kick up a load of old dust," said GG. He sounded slightly absentminded, as though his thoughts were already elsewhere. "And for God's sake don't let any reporters cotton on to what you're doing. They get a hard-on from old cases; they think it'll win them an award or something."

It took Eira almost three hours to track down the old preliminary investigation, buried deep in the archives. The caretaker who was temping over the summer carried the boxes from the lift for her.

According to the paperwork, no one had accessed the material since it was archived in 1996. A handful of journalists had requested it over the years, but they had been refused every time.

It ran to many thousands of pages, mostly printed transcripts from the interviews. Boxes full of videotapes, blocky VHS cassettes bearing witness to another era.

A dead beetle dropped into Eira's lap as she lifted the folders from a box.

That smile. So bright, forever frozen in what would be the enduring image of Lina.

The background was bluish and artificial, a school photograph, the one that had popped up everywhere that summer. Her hair in soft waves over her shoulders; long, medium blond, almost certainly curled ahead of the shoot. The papers had also published a few more relaxed images, private family photographs and snaps they had either begged or bought from friends, but the picture that fell out of the preliminary investigation was the familiar one: Lina Stavred with her head turned half towards the camera, smiling.

Taken a few months before the end of term in her first year of senior high school.

Now comes the time for flowers.

For joy, for beauty great.

Like every other child in Sweden, she must have sung that old hymn, about the gentle sun's warmth coaxing fresh growth from everything that was dead.

As soon as she approaches, reborn life lies ahead.

Eira was almost trembling as she opened the files, her heart pounding. She was assisting in a murder inquiry, she was the nine-year-old creeping along the beaches, looking for evidence.

The files smelled dry, like old paper.

She barely even noticed the afternoon pass, the daylight growing cooler outside. She was working in a different era now. Days that dragged on. That went round in circles, always returning to the same point.

The third of July, a warm summer night. It had been sunny, the air almost breathless, the night Lina Stavred disappeared.

No one had noticed until the next day. It was the summer holiday, after all, and Lina had said she was staying over at a friend's. She wasn't reported missing until late in the evening on the fourth.

The tips had quickly come flooding in. Eira skimmed through a number of pages, days in which the police had bounced around like balls in a pinball machine, looking into reports that Lina had been seen here and there. One person claimed she was with the "tree huggers" in the collective up by Näsåker, another that they had seen her among the prostitutes on Malmskillnadsgatan in Stockholm, in a boat on the river, on the sea, outside a pub in Härnösand and at a party at the foot of Skuleberget; one man even claimed to have had sex with her in his dreams, and wanted to report himself. On top of that, there were countless tips about suspicious men in the area, various foreigners in particular—people from Russia and Lithuania and Yugoslavia, "Though you're meant to say Serbia now, aren't you? Or Bosnia, I don't bloody know where they're from, it's all the same to me." Neighbors who had been seen naked in their own homes and young men roaming around, up to no good.

In the end she found Tryggve Nydalen's name in connection with the door knocking. The police had spoken to the people living in the surrounding communities, trawling the houses for anyone who might have seen something.

A brief note, that was all.

Family dinner at home. Confirmed by wife and sister-in-law. Evening of July 3: fishing trip on the river with his six-year-old son and nephew. No sightings.

That was all.

Eira could have put the folder down at that point. Packed it back into the boxes with all the others.

Let the dust settle again, for good.

But now that she had everything in front of her?

She would never get the chance to look through these files again. However popular it was out there for cold cases to be brought back to life, it wasn't something the police really spent much time on. Particularly not when they were solved, archived, and marked confidential.

The tip about Olof Hagström had come in on the morning of the sixth of July. "It's probably nothing, but you know, you want to . . ."

Eira stared at the name for a moment. Gunnel Hagström.

His own mother had made the call.

"It seems like a few people saw the girl go into the woods there, or that's what they're saying. I hadn't heard about it myself, but the teenagers are all saying that Olof . . . Well, that he . . . I didn't want you to hear it from someone else, for you to think . . ."

Eira tried to picture the house in Kungsgården as it might have looked back then, with a tidy hallway and flowers in the kitchen window, thin summer curtains. When it was still home to a whole family. Ingela had come back and blabbed about what she had heard, what the older boys were saying about Olof. About Lina. About what they had done in the woods—or what he claimed to have done.

Gunnel Hagström had waited until morning. Gone to sleep, or not—likely suffered through a terrible night—before getting up and calling the police.

Because she believed it? Or because she didn't know what to think?

The person who took her call had reacted like any semiattentive police officer would. Whenever they appealed to the public for information, there were always plenty of fools calling up. The craziest were often the most insistent.

More often than not, doubt hid a truth.

The first conversation with the family had taken place around two hours later. The questions were broadly the same ones Eira would have asked, the answers brief. Olof didn't say much.

OH: *No.*
OH: *Who said that?*
OH: *Don't know.*
OH: *No.*

He answered most of their questions with silence.
Then his father spoke up:

SH: *Just tell the truth so we can get this cleared up. The police have better things to be doing.*

It was a strange feeling to see Sven Hagström rise from the dead—
or his words, at least. In black on white, or black on slightly yellow.

SH: *Just tell the truth now, lad.*

Then, to the police:

SH: *That's what I've raised both my kids to do. To stick to the truth.*

Eira wondered whether Ingela had been interviewed in the same
room, whether Olof knew where the information had come from,
whether he knew it was his mother who had called it in.

The police had returned the next day, with a decision from the
prosecutor. They had taken his fingerprints and searched the house.

Eira scanned through the report. She could imagine the silence
in Olof's boyhood room as they pulled out the box from beneath
his bed. The room was on the second floor. She had never been
up there herself, but she knew from the description that it was the
narrow box room beneath the sloping roof often found in that type
of house.

According to the report, the box was full to bursting.

Comic books. Sweet wrappers. Rotting banana skins. A plane
with a broken wing.

A yellow cardigan.

Eira had a handful of memories of the TV news from those days.
Her mother hadn't been able to keep her away from it, however
hard she tried.

A breakthrough, that was what they had called it. She remembered that because she hadn't known what the word meant. She had
thought it was something to do with broken bones, and felt stupid in
front of her mother's friend, who was staying with them at the time.

The two women had glanced at one another and considered their
words in front of her, but in the end her mother had explained that
it meant they had found the person who . . . "That we'll know what
happened to Lina soon, sweetie."

They still hadn't come out and said that she was dead, but no child could have failed to notice the whispering. The voices that lowered the minute you came close. Forced reassurances that "there's nothing to worry about, but no, you can't go out on your own."

Perhaps that was the night when they found Lina's cardigan.

When the investigation entered a new phase.

Eira flicked through to the interviews that had started the very next day. She realized she had hundreds of pages ahead of her. Week after week of questioning.

EG: *Could you tell us what happened when you followed Lina into the forest?*

OH: *[No answer]*

EG: *Why did you follow her into the forest? Did you like Lina? Look at the photograph. She was pretty, wasn't she?*

OH: *[Shakes his head]*

EG: *You'll have to speak up for the tape. Look me in the eye when we talk, Olof. Look at me.*

OH: *Mmm.*

EG: that was Eilert Granlund, her old colleague. Eira hadn't realized he had been so deeply involved, that he had occasionally led the interrogation. Page after page—hours of interviews, day after day for over a month. She dipped into the transcripts here and there, read another segment, saw another interview leader she didn't know enter the scene, a woman this time. Eira tried to picture Olof Hagström sitting in front of her, the fourteen-year-old boy— what could have been hiding behind "no answer" and "shakes his head"?

The sound of a door closing made her jump. She had the investigation piled up all around her, almost like a wall, and hadn't noticed anyone coming and going. That evening's patrol was based in Sollefteå, which meant there were no officers on duty in Kramfors. The building was quiet. For a while she thought she must be the only one left, but then she heard something bang, someone swear. It was the temp caretaker, busy emptying the coffee machine. The red light on it had been blinking all day, telling them to change the filter or whatever it was.

"This really isn't my job," he muttered. "But there'll be no decent coffee for people in the morning otherwise."

"Do you know where I can find a VHS player?" asked Eira.

The fourteen-year-old slumped forward, burying his head in his hands.

An arm reached into the frame, a body leaning in front of the camera and pulling his hands away.

"I'd like to see your face while we're talking, Olof."

It was the woman interview leader again. Eira had looked her up online and found an old article about her. She came from down south and was often called in as an expert in interviewing children. By that point it had been over a week since Olof Hagström became the primary focus of the investigation.

"We have five people who claim you were covered in mud and dirt when you came back out of the woods. How does that fit with you not doing anything?"

"I fell over."

"Were you trying to grab Lina?"

Silence.

"You're a boy, Olof. Becoming a man. There's nothing unusual about that. Maybe there are things happening to your body that you don't quite understand. Take another look at the photograph for me. Isn't she beautiful? Did you think Lina was beautiful?"

Olof looked away. Repeatedly rubbed his neck. Eira struggled to see his features in the grown man she had met. His eyes, possibly. The boy sitting alone on a vinyl sofa in a bare interview room was tall and thin, and had an awkwardness when he moved, as though his body had grown too quickly. He had broad shoulders, but was a long way off the bulky frame he had since developed.

After almost three hours in a cramped cupboard where the air had quickly become bone dry, Eira realized she would never manage to go through everything.

The first week alone involved around twenty hours of interviews. A few quick calculations told her that she was looking at around one hundred hours of footage in total. Eira rifled through the VHS tapes. Several were marked WALK-THROUGH.

There was a reason investigators weren't keen to reopen old cases.

There had to be clear grounds, new evidence. The police couldn't simply take it upon themselves to reexamine a closed case; that was what investigative journalists did, as they had with Swedish alleged serial killer Thomas Quick.

Quick had confessed to over thirty murders and been convicted of eight. Despite walk-throughs of the murder scenes, he couldn't lead the police to a single body. The only forensic evidence was a fragment of bone belonging to a girl—though it was later found to be plastic. The entire case was built on therapy sessions intended to bring out repressed memories of murders he didn't even know he had committed.

"Olof, look at me," the woman insisted. She wasn't visible on-screen herself. "What did Lina do when you grabbed her? Did she scream? Is that why you wanted to shut her up?"

Eira switched off the VHS player. She needed to eat something, she realized. To call her mother and try to make sure everything was OK. Kerstin told her she had eaten a few sandwiches, had a glass of wine, and was about to go to bed, but Eira was willing to believe her only once she had repeated the same information twice.

She found a few crispbreads in one of the cupboards in the lunchroom, some cheese and butter belonging to someone else. People had only themselves to blame if they didn't label their food.

Then she called August.

"Why exactly do you want us to go through this?" Her colleague had come in willingly, but he had also grown impatient after just thirty minutes.

Because no one told me a thing when I was younger, she thought. Eira explained that she needed another pair of eyes, that there were certain things that raised doubts. That she had only that evening and night, then the boxes of videotapes would be taken back to the archives and she would be in the patrol car again, driving mile after mile around the area.

She didn't say that she liked having him there with her, in a room no more than a few square meters in size.

"There he is again, without either of his parents," Eira said as she fast-forwarded through the footage. "Did you notice that? He's underage, and he's all alone."

"That's just how it was back then."

August had swung one leg up onto the table, and his foot was bobbing up and down in front of the steady footage of the boy on the vinyl sofa. Hour after hour, always the same angle. Eira flicked through the transcripts in an attempt to skip to the sections where something happened. They had passed over a whole stack of tapes and were now on to the third week of interviews.

"Hold on," said Eira. "There's something here, he actually starts talking now."

Olof looked down at the floor, his face almost entirely hidden in his hands.

"That's not how it was," he said.

"What do you mean?"

"It wasn't like I told them."

"Are you talking about your friends now? The boys waiting by the road?"

The woman interviewer seemed to be sitting off to one side; Olof briefly glanced over to her.

"She pushed me and I fell."

"Now what are you saying?"

"The ground was dirty. All kinds of muck."

"Lina, who weighed somewhere around fifty kilos?"

"Mmm." Eyes fixed on the floor again.

"Why didn't you mention any of this before?"

"Because . . . because . . . She's a girl. It's just, I wasn't expecting it. That must've been why I fell. I'm strong."

"We know you are, Olof. We know you're strong."

"And then she grabbed some nettles, like this." He demonstrated for them, rubbing around his mouth, across his face, using both hands. "And shoved soil in my mouth, said it was my fault she was dirty, that I'd ruined everything."

"Was that why you lost your temper?"

"No. No."

"Look at me now, Olof."

He shook his head, didn't look up.

"What did he just say?" asked August.

Eira rewound the tape and turned up the volume to hear what the fourteen-year-old had mumbled.

"She walked away," he said. "I was the only one on the ground."

"Is that what you did to her face? Is that what you're saying?"

"No. It was her."

"But this doesn't match what you told your friends. Which is the truth, Olof?"

"What the hell was I supposed to say?"

"Now I don't know what to think. First you say you didn't do anything to Lina, and now you're claiming she's the one who did something to you. How are we supposed to know which is true?"

"It's true."

"Which part? I'm confused now, Olof." The woman leaned in, half into shot. "There can only be one truth. Were you lying to your friends when you came out of the woods?"

"Can we stop now?"

"No, Olof, we have to keep going a little longer. We have to keep going until you tell us the truth. You understand that, don't you? That we can't stop until you tell us what you did to Lina."

This was followed by a section in which the fourteen-year-old repeatedly asked to stop. Then he asked for his mother to join them.

"Your mum is sitting outside."

"I want her to come in."

"We've decided she shouldn't be in here right now. But she wants you to tell the truth too. She and your dad both do."

Eira's palm felt hot as August took the remote control from her hand.

"What's going on here?" he asked, pausing the video. "Is he lying again, or is he telling the truth?"

"I don't know."

They sat quietly for a moment. Eira flicked through the summary, trying to make sense of the timeline and events.

"The interviews went on for several weeks after this, then he confessed everything. He supposedly pointed out the place where he threw her body into the river. I remember the picture of the sallow branch—they showed it on TV. The one he used to strangle her. I remember my mum started crying with relief when they announced that they'd solved the murder. I didn't understand what was going on, I'd always thought people only cried when they were sad."

Eira rummaged through the tapes again, looking for the last few, each marked with a date in late August.

The labels read WALK-THROUGH 3.

Shaky handheld footage, a group of people moving slowly through the forest.

The fourteen-year-old was in the middle, taking slightly awkward steps. One of the officers had a hand on his back, but it was impossible to tell whether the gesture was protective or urging—or both. *Trust us, you're safe here, we're leading you to the precipice.* When the officer turned around, Eira recognized her old colleague, a much younger version.

It was slightly breezy, making the microphone crackle.

"What did you use to kill her? Can you remember, Olof? What made her stop breathing? Can you show us?"

Another person stepped into the shot, holding a large doll. It was the same size as a human body. Arms hanging limply, possibly made from some kind of fabric, with no facial features whatsoever.

"Was this where she was lying when you had sex with her? Like this?"

The doll was pushed around on the ground. Olof shook his head.

"You said earlier that you tried to have sex with her. That you were lying on the ground. Could you show us how you were both lying?"

He eventually pointed. There was a rock, a fallen tree blocking the trail. There was an infinite slowness to everything happening. Eira rewound the tape and watched several sections again, parts where they thought they had missed something. When Olof said he had used a sallow branch just like that to strangle her, did he even say that was how she died?

"No, Olof, we can't go yet."

"I need a piss."

"We can go once we have a clear understanding of what happened. You said something about soil and nettles in your mouth, did you suffocate her using soil?"

"No, no."

"Can you see anything else around here that you used? Was it a branch, or something you'd brought with you? A belt? We need you to remember now, Olof. I know it's in here." The interview leader's hand on his forehead. "I need you to be brave and remember now, buddy."

Eira stopped the tape.

"They're putting words into his mouth," she said.

"They're trying to access his memories," said August. "Stuff he's shelved somehow. It happens sometimes when a person goes through something really traumatic."

"Repressed memories, you mean? It's been repeatedly proved that they don't exist. People remember the terrible things that happen to them; it's the ordinary stuff they forget. The things they don't even notice. No one forgot being in Auschwitz, for example."

"This is from, like, twenty years ago," said August. "And by the way, it's not that clear cut. A friend of mine did a course in forensic psychology at Stockholm University. The tutor had been involved in several cases like this and had gone through therapy himself—stuff came back to him, abuse and that kind of thing. He was convinced it was real."

"We're police officers," said Eira. "It's not our job to believe things that don't exist."

"So using your imagination's banned?" That smile of his, teasing, irritating.

"Mmm," she managed to mutter. "At work."

It was almost two in the morning but Eira was no longer tired. She fast-forwarded through the footage. On that day in late August 1996, it was now afternoon. The walk-through with the suspect had been going on for almost two hours.

Olof had picked up something from the ground, tossed it away, picked up something else, a branch.

"Was it one of those?"

"Maybe."

"Can you show me what you did with it?"

Olof bent the branch, making it into a loop.

"The sallow branch," said Eira.

"Can I go home now?" asked Olof.

"You've been very good," said the interview leader. "Now I just want you to show me how you carried her out of here. Could you show me, using the doll? Did you carry her like this, in your arms? Or was it like this?"

The footage ended as Olof swung the doll up over his shoulder and the image started to flicker. Eira changed the tape.

"They seemed completely sure it was him," she said. "Everyone knew it. I remember that so clearly. I've known it all my life." She felt an urge to take August's hand—it was so close to hers, draped nonchalantly over the armrest.

The footage started again, a different setting this time. There was the river, a beach. Sand, or possibly mud.

The interview leader's voice sounded a little hoarse.

"Did you put her down here? Was this where she dropped her keys? Or was it you who dropped her things here? What happened to the rucksack she was wearing? Did you throw it into the water? Could you show us where you threw it in?"

Past a metal shed, still clutching the doll, its arms swinging as though they were pounding his back, to the very edge of the jetty.

That was somewhere no child was allowed to play. The water was thirty meters deep, they said; huge ships had docked there during the sawmill era. And yet it wasn't even the deepest point of the river. Slightly farther out, there was a dizzying drop to one hundred meters depth, hidden beneath the deceptively glittering surface. Anyone could disappear for good there.

"Was this where you threw her in? Or was it farther down?"

"No, no."

"So it was here? Could you show us what you did?"

Olof tossed the doll away.

"Is that how you threw her? Did Lina fall into the water then? Was she already dead when you threw her into the water?"

"She wasn't," the boy whimpered, hunched over on the jetty, eyes fixed on the concrete. "She wasn't dead."

The interview leader crouched down beside him. She adjusted something in her ear and glanced up. Despair on her face, exhaustion. Eira saw her eyes seeking out someone behind the camera. *She's getting help with these questions*, she thought.

The crackling of wind in a microphone.

"Was she still alive when you threw her in?"

GG arrived at the station in Kramfors just after lunch. Striding down the corridor with his phone clamped to his ear.

Eira waited until he had finished the call before stepping into the room and placing the summary of the preliminary investigation on his desk.

"I'm not sure he did it," she said.

"What?" GG looked down at the folder in confusion.

"Olof Hagström." Eira had managed to get only a few hours' sleep, but she had dreamed about the interrogation room with the vinyl sofa, she had teetered on the edge of the jetty in Marieberg. The limp, faceless doll had also made an appearance.

"Aha," said GG. "OK, got you."

He picked up the folder by its corner, just enough to be able to read the writing on the cover. The case. The year.

"He didn't confess to anything the police hadn't already said to him," Eira continued. "They interviewed him for hours without his parents present." She had gone through what she wanted to say in her head, rewording it. Over and over again. Speaking up like this went against everything she had been taught growing up; you were supposed to be humble, and you definitely weren't meant to act like you thought you knew better than all those who had come before you. It was about loyalty and disloyalty, and it felt like a vague knot in her gut. "The interviewers put words into his mouth. They told Olof he couldn't go home until he pointed out where he'd thrown her into the water, until he showed them how he killed her."

GG stroked his bristly chin.

"Weren't you just checking to see whether Nydalen's name came up?"

"It's in there," said Eira. "In the notes from the door knocking."

She told him what she had found, that the Nydalens had relatives over that evening, that Tryggve had taken the kids out fishing.

"But they didn't ask any follow-up questions, they just noted down what he said."

"It wasn't him," said GG.

"I'm not saying it was, but don't you think it would be worth asking those questions? They didn't know he was a convicted sex offender, and his family are the only ones who gave him an alibi. There are huge gaps in the investigation."

"Tryggve Nydalen is innocent. He didn't kill Sven Hagström."

"What?"

"The overalls aren't his. We got the results a few hours ago. He never had those rubber gloves on. The blood is Sven Hagström's, loads of it, but there's not a single molecule that points to Tryggve Nydalen. That said, the overalls are covered in someone else's prints and DNA, the gloves too . . ."

"Whose?"

"They're not in the database."

Eira slumped into one of the armchairs in the corner of the room. The sky had clouded over outside. Rain, maybe they would finally get a little rain.

She forced herself to focus on the current investigation, away from the past.

The murder of Sven Hagström. It had all seemed so clear cut, the motive so strong. A man who hid his identity, whose life would fall apart if people found out who he was, the group assault in his past.

The knife, identical to the other one.

"Is his wife in the database?" she asked.

"Not yet."

"One of the knives is hers."

"I know."

Eira thought about Mejan Nydalen, the powerful yet compliant sides of her, the desire to take charge and smooth over. She thought about their marriage, how intertwined they were, like a fortress against the world around them; she thought about the shame. The wife of a rapist, who had known and yet kept quiet.

"Mejan had just as much to lose. She's been protecting his secret just as much as he has."

"The thought did occur to me," said GG. "We've got a car heading over there now."

Eira couldn't think of anything else to say, and was making her way out of the room when he called her back.

"Don't forget this," he said, holding out the folder. He held on to it for a second too long after she gripped it.

"Do you feel responsible?" he asked.

"For what?"

"Olof Hagström. Could we have prevented what happened? Should we have warned him? We knew people were getting riled up online; you're the one who told me about it."

Eira looked down at the document in her hand.

"We were in the middle of a murder investigation," she said.

"Well, if we missed anything," said GG, "it's on me."

It had been only a month since they were last done, but Mejan had cleaned all the windows. There were always fly droppings and seed casings getting caught in the breeze and sticking to the glass.

She had also dusted and scrubbed the floors, naturally. Paying particular attention to the kitchen and living room, plus the bedroom she had shared with her husband for almost thirty years.

Tryggve's snoring, which sometimes kept her awake. The bright, shimmering nights in spring and the dark quiet of autumn, the pale winter moonlight reflected in the snow.

All those nights.

The hours that made them up.

She had washed the bedding and stretched the sheets as best she could on her own, trapping one end in a drawer. After all, Tryggve wasn't there to help her like usual, pulling the sheet taut and then folding it in the middle, walking towards each other and continuing the fold, meaning the sheet was a neat little parcel as they came together—just as she had been taught by her grandmother, with whom she had occasionally gone to stay when things got difficult at home.

It started with a fleck of dirt in one corner, she had been told, and quickly went downhill from there.

A dust bunny, a stain, an unmade bed or one that simply looked messy, with the duvet thrown on top, as Patrik had in his teens.

As Tryggve had when they first met. Mejan remembered his room in Norway, the place where they first slept together, clothes ending up in a pile on the floor, dirty dishes for her to wash.

Tryggve had very little idea about what went on in other people's heads. He didn't know a thing about jealousy or what happens when a petty old bastard sets his mind on something.

Sometimes she wondered whether he even knew his own son.

Tell Patrik? Was he out of his mind?

Their son, their beautiful boy, who carried so much anger inside him. "I hate that fucking bastard," he had shouted across the yard before he left.

"That's no way to talk about your father!" Mejan had snapped back.

"You knew. How could you sleep in the same bed as him, how could you . . ."

His voice left deep wounds.

You have no idea how handsome he was, she had wanted to say, to stroke her son's hair and explain. *Who else would have stuck with me all these years, been there for me while I was pregnant, once you arrived? What do you know about not having anyone at all?*

Perhaps it was only a matter of hours now, or would she have another day? Mejan knew roughly how long those kinds of analyses could take—she read thrillers and watched crime dramas like everyone else, and had planned her activities accordingly.

She divided the cinnamon buns into bags. Loaded servings of lasagna into the freezer. Broccoli soup, sausages and mash; Wiener schnitzel with sauce, peas and potatoes. All portioned out into decent meals. The potatoes would turn floury and dry in the freezer, but Tryggve would still appreciate having everything ready for him when he got home. Mejan labeled every plastic dish and freezer bag.

He would be able to survive on what she had prepared for a few weeks. Would have to go to the supermarket in Nyland only to buy any extra fresh produce he needed.

Their daughter would probably arrive by then.

Jenny, who had been in Australia for so long, who almost never got in touch. That was no place to live, not with all the fires everywhere. And now that her father would be all on his own, surely it was high time she came home?

You're going to hear things about both me and your dad, Mejan
wrote.

Don't judge him. He hasn't been a bad father.
Do you remember when he built you a doll's house?

Her letter grew long, asking Jenny to think things through and
understand, telling her it was time to think of someone other than
herself.

At the end of the day, family is all we really have.

Mejan had also started several letters to Tryggve, but that proved
trickier. She balled up each sheet of paper after just a few lines, burning them in the fireplace and then allowing it to go out, so that there
weren't any embers.

In the end, she just wrote him a brief note.

There's food in the freezer.
Hugs and kisses,
Mejan

By the time the patrol car pulled up in the yard, she was sitting
on the porch with a thermos of coffee. She had saved two of the cinnamon buns for herself. Mejan was dressed the way she had decided
to dress. Simply and respectably, yet still suitably elegant in a pair
of black trousers and a rust-colored pussy bow blouse—something
that had largely hung in her wardrobe since she found it on sale in
Kramfors.

What looked good in the shop often felt a bit much at home.

She had been sitting outside for an hour or two, despite the stiff
breeze and the biting rain blowing into the open porch.

They had talked about having it glazed, possibly that autumn.

She wondered whether Tryggve would bother now, or whether
he would simply give up and let the house fall into disrepair, like so

many others in the area. Decaying in plain sight. For some reason she found herself thinking about the house where Lina Stavred once lived, just a few kilometers away. No one had moved in since the family left. A few of the windows were broken and the chimney had started to collapse; the entire facade looked frightful. Mejan understood that the family had suffered terribly, but still.

She brushed a couple of crumbs from her lap before getting to her feet. Everything was so visible against the black fabric.

"Marianne Nydalen?"

Two officers in uniform cut across the lawn.

"Yes, that's me."

"We need to ask you to come with us to Kramfors."

Mejan was already on her way down the steps. She didn't want them traipsing up there with muddy shoes. One of the officers moved to take hold of her arm.

"I can walk on my own, thank you."

As though from a distance, she heard them saying something about the prosecutor and fingerprints and DNA, that she wasn't under arrest, she was simply being taken in for questioning. Beyond that, she heard the breeze in the trees and felt the rain on her face. It all felt so fresh.

Eira would sort through the folders and put everything in the right order, that was all. Make sure the old case files were lugged back down to the archive, where they probably belonged.

"Beyond all reasonable doubt," as they would have said if it had ever gone to court.

There had been seven police officers at the core of the Lina Stavred investigation. Several of them were the most experienced on the force, and they had been backed up by forensics and psychologists and God knows what else.

Eira was only thirty-two. She had been a police assistant for almost six years and an investigator for just over two weeks, so who was she kidding?

The videotapes wouldn't fit back into their box, and Eira had to repack them to get them inside.

GG hadn't exactly been explicit about what he wanted her to do, but his hints were more than enough. An unwillingness to listen. A suspicion that she was digging into Olof Hagström's past because she felt guilty.

He was right. Olof Hagström was the ghost of her childhood. That feeling had been there when she first walked over to him in the car, when she caught up with him in the forest, sat in a cramped interrogation room with him; it was in the smell of his sweat.

It wasn't just unease, it was stronger than that. It was disgust and contempt and a kind of curiosity that made her stray beyond the strictly professional.

Interviews. Witness statements. Crime scene investigation.

She just needed to sort through it all first.

Some of the material had been mixed up when she found it. The least she could do was leave it in a better order. That was why, although it took time, she checked every cover page—even on the stacks of paper she hadn't read. Dates and contents, names and personal details.

She flicked through them fairly quickly, but still managed to catch some of the detail in passing—the fact that a significant number of the addresses were in Marieberg, for example. They must have interviewed everyone living in the area around the crime scene. Many of the witnesses had been born around 1980, making them roughly the same age as Lina at the time, sixteen or seventeen. Her friends and schoolmates.

One of the birth dates stopped her in her tracks. The familiar structure, the order of the digits.

And then the name.

Everything seemed to go silent around her, assuming there had even been any sound.

It wasn't strange, she told herself. A girl had gone missing, and the police wanted to talk to as many people as possible. They had been at the same school in Kramfors; what choice did they have?

There were no other names, he wasn't part of the group of schoolmates interviewed in case they knew her, in case they had seen anything and so on.

It was just him. Alone, for page after page.

INTERVIEW WITH MAGNUS SJÖDIN

EG: *When did you last talk to Lina Stavred?*
MS: *I don't know where she is, I've told you.*
EG: *Just answer the question.*
MS: *A week ago, maybe.*
EG: *It's important you try to be precise.*
MS: *I told you, we broke up. We're not going out anymore.*
EG: *How did you feel when she broke up with you?*

MS: *How would you feel?*
EG: *I think I'd be pretty upset. Angry, even. That I'd struggle to accept it.*
MS: *It just ended.*
EG: *We've spoken to Lina's friends. They say you have very strong feelings for her, but that she doesn't feel the same way.*
MS: *They don't know how I feel.*
EG: *Did you want her back?*
MS: *I've told you, I don't know where she is.*

Eira couldn't remember how her brother sounded when he was seventeen; the voice in her head belonged to the grown-up Magnus, the one she had spoken to a few days earlier. Eilert's creaky voice came through loud and clear.

EG: *Where were you on the evening of July third?*
MS: *I was at home.*
EG: *What time was it when you got home?*
MS: *Maybe around nine or so.*
EG: *Was anyone else there? Anyone who can confirm that?*

Kerstin had the radio on when Eira got home. It felt like she had just stepped onto a stage set. The house where she grew up, her family, everything she thought she knew, the security and strength.

She drank a glass of water and turned down the volume.

"Just turn it off," said Kerstin. "It's all doom and gloom anyway. You don't want a coffee?"

"Sure."

The thermos from that morning was empty. Eira spilled the ground coffee as she went to fill the percolator.

"I'll clean that up," said her mother. "You sit, you've been working all day."

"Thanks."

"And I've got plenty of sandwiches, too."

Eira sat down, searching for somewhere to start. Magnus, Lina, Lina, Magnus, the evening of July 3, 1996. Kerstin took over. Making coffee still came naturally to her, though she did sometimes make mistakes: miscalculating, adding the wrong amount.

"Do you remember the summer when Lina Stavred went missing?"

"Uff, yes. When was it again? It must've been nineteen—"

"Ninety-six. They interviewed Magnus about it, several times."

"Is that so?"

Eira caught a hint of something in her mother's voice. A way of avoiding the subject, withdrawing, that wasn't down to her usual forgetfulness.

"You must remember that, Mum? Them taking Magnus in for questioning? Why didn't you tell me Lina was his girlfriend?"

"Ah, well . . . Was she?"

Dementia, the doctors at the hospital had told her, didn't mean that everything would vanish. The memories were still there, they were just harder to grasp. As a family member, Eira could help by keeping them alive—though they probably meant by playing old songs and looking through photo albums rather than this.

"Lina broke up with Magnus a week before she went missing," Eira continued. "They interviewed you too. Right here. You must've sat in the kitchen? Where was I? You confirmed that Magnus was at home on the night she disappeared."

Kerstin had paused with the cheese in her hand, as though she couldn't quite remember what it was for.

"But Magnus was never at home in the evening," Eira went on. "The two of you were always fighting about it. So why that particular night, when his girlfriend was murdered?"

Perhaps it was Kerstin's illness making her gaze slip away. "It was a boy who did it, what was his name . . ."

"Olof Hagström."

"Yes, that was it . . ."

"Did you both go to Lina's funeral, too?" It struck Eira that she didn't know whether there had been one. Her body had never been

found, after all. A fragment of a memory came back to her, TV footage of a ceremony. "How could you keep quiet about something like
this all these years?"

A clumsy hand reached out, veined and slightly wrinkled, stroked
her hair.

"Oh, love . . . You were so young."

Eira brushed off her hand, as irritated by her mother's touch as
she had been in her teens. Her tone, her manner, at once tender and
strained; not even five terms at police college could overcome that.
Whatever you do or don't remember, she thought, *there's something
you're trying to protect me from.*

S he's confessed."

The call was from GG. He was in the car on the way up from Sundsvall. Eira could hear Springsteen singing in the background.

Mejan Nydalen had been prepared to confess during the very first interview, and they had had to stop her while they waited for the lawyer. No one should confess to premeditated murder without legal representation.

"We're on the home straight now," said GG. "We're on the home bloody straight."

Eira was in the stairwell at the police station when he called, climbing the stairs two at a time. She sat down at a free computer and logged in using the password she had been given when she joined the investigation group.

INTERVIEW WITH MARIANNE NYDALEN

MN: *I protected my family. That's what I did. Someone had to put up a fight. I suppose you could say I'm the stronger of the two of us.*

Eira had spoken to the woman often enough to be able to clearly hear her voice, at once warm and stern.

MN: *But my husband had nothing to do with this. It was me, I did it on my own. You should leave him in peace now. He's suffered enough.*

MN: *The only thing I regret is letting Tryggve sit in custody for so long. I honestly never thought you'd keep an innocent man locked up; I spent every waking hour waiting for him to come home. Would you tell him that, please?*

There was a sense of calm to the entire confession. The woman took her time without ever falling silent or trying to wriggle out of anything. Suspects usually wanted to get away from the interrogation room as fast as they could, but Mejan actually seemed pleased to be able to speak at last.

Tryggve had come home visibly shaken one day in late April. That was the start of the nightmare, hearing a woman say his real name at the ironmonger in Nyland.

No, not real, that wasn't quite right.

His old name.

Adam Vide had left their lives years ago. He was a nonexisting person. The name he had taken, that was who he was now.

Mejan had told him it was probably nothing to worry about, but deep down she knew that they had to expect the worst.

Like dark clouds gathering over the mountains, like cancer after feeling that first lump.

The kind of gossip that petered out and died a natural death simply didn't exist, and never had. She had grown up with it, knew what it was like to be seen as someone inferior.

It was barely a month or so before her husband came home agitated again, early one morning when Mejan had only just had her coffee.

Tryggve had heard terrible things when he went down to the letter box. From Sven Hagström of all people.

"Your missus know what you got up to in the past? That the kind of thing you tell the wife?"

Tryggve had tried to ignore him, but that was probably the wrong approach.

Things only got worse.

"I never would've believed you were such a filthy perve, Nydalen. I wonder what people would think if they found out? What does your remarkable son make of all this? And his Stockholm girl? You have told the lad, haven't you? Does he know what a dirty dog his old man is?"

Tryggve had probably tried talking to him, being friendly and everything else, but it didn't stop. Hagström just got bolder and bolder. Stood outside, staring at their house. He even threw it right in Mejan's face one day when she went out to weed the nettles between the red currant bushes.

"Has he done it to you too? What about your daughter? Is that why she cleared off to Australia?"

The summer holidays were fast approaching. The lilacs bloomed far too early that spring. Patrik and the children would soon be there. Tryggve withdrew cash, several thousand, and went over to convince Hagström to keep quiet.

"Nope, you won't get away with it that easily. Right is right, even is even. People like you think you can buy everything. Well, try to buy your family back—just you try it once they've gone."

I'll have to tell Patrik, that was what Tryggve had said that day. *He needs to hear it from his dad, not from someone else.*

Mejan convinced him to wait until Patrik had arrived, to do it face-to-face. She knew she would have to solve the problem before then.

But she had put it off, day after day.

Hoping, as people do, for a miracle.

A heart attack or something.

Yet Sven Hagström just kept on living. Spewing his bile.

In the days leading up to Patrik's arrival, she had got up at night and snuck over there. Stood outside, gazing at the calm, quiet house, thinking about how it might play out. How everything would fall apart if she couldn't find the nerve. She simply had to find the strength to do what she had to do.

She took the knife with her on the last night, walked right up to the house and tried the door. It was locked. The dog started barking, so she hurried away and didn't sleep another wink.

She knew that Hagström went out to fetch the paper every morning.

Surely no one locked the door after that, particularly not during the summer when you'd soon be out and about again.

She took out a piece of meat meant for a stew. There wasn't a dog on earth that could resist a titbit like that.

Mejan had dragged Tryggve out of bed early that morning, reminding him just how much there was to do. She came up with the bed leg and the drain to keep him busy inside while she snuck off.

She peered in through the window when she got to Hagström's house, but she couldn't see him. What she did see was the steam on the bathroom window. She forced herself to move closer, heard the water in the pipes. The dog managed to yelp once before she served it a nice piece of elk, just tossed the lump of meat into the kitchen and that was that.

Mejan knew how to handle a hunting knife. It felt like an extension of her hand. You couldn't hesitate when you drove it into flesh, living or dead.

It was all very quick.

Did he cry out?

She couldn't say. Probably not. His jaw had certainly dropped, typical of a bad man who didn't think anything bad could happen to him, who thought he was master of everything and could treat other people however he liked.

"No doubts there, right?"

Eira was dragged back to the present, to the office, the sun high in the sky outside. GG was standing in the doorway behind her with a mug of coffee in one hand, a smile on his face.

"Good work," he said. "It was great to have you on board, but I'm afraid I've had a nudge from your boss; they want you back."

"Right now?"

"I couldn't argue to keep you on, unfortunately, but I told him to try to cope until Monday, so you can have a few days off at least."

"OK."

Eira closed the document, the case that looked to have been solved. Mejan's confession didn't leave any obvious question marks. It was clear and meticulous down to the very last detail, and even explained the issue of the keys. She had taken Sven's key from the inside of the door when she left, locked it from the outside, and then dropped it into a hole beneath the porch. It struck Eira that they wouldn't find it there.

In the ashes, perhaps.

It had been a long time since she had last had several days off in a row.

"Thanks," she said. "It's been rewarding to work with you."

"Glad to hear it," said GG. "But you'll have to hold off with the goodbyes."

They were going to take one last trip out to Kungsgården first.

Tryggve Nydalen was sitting in a garden chair at the end of the old barn. There was an ax lying on the ground by the chopping block, and the air smelled like freshly cut wood.

He had been questioned briefly before leaving custody, but hadn't said much. Things might be different now that he was at home, with a little distance from his wife's confession.

"I was about to stack the wood," he said. "But then I found myself wondering what the point was."

"Shall we sit here?" asked Eira.

Tryggve shrugged and nodded to the veranda, but didn't get up. She assumed that meant they could fetch a chair each.

GG explained that their conversation was being recorded, and placed his mobile phone in the grass.

Did Tryggve know about his wife's plans in advance? Did they come up with it together?

"I would've rather taken the gun out," Tryggve Nydalen replied, "and turned it on myself."

The thought had been there, yes, it had definitely crossed his mind. That Mejan . . .

But he never would have thought . . .

It was only when they put the photographs of the hunting knife and overalls down in front of him that he realized.

Really understood.

"It's my fault," he said, his gaze fixed somewhere around the tree-tops. "If I hadn't done what I did, the bloke would still be alive. What business did Hagström have getting mixed up in my life? It was an injustice, that's what he said when I went over there to plead and beg, that one person could suffer so much when another got away with it. But I didn't get away with anything. I served my time."

He blew his nose between his fingers, wiped his hand on his trousers.

"I should never have done any of this," he said.

"What do you mean?"

Tryggve gestured to the yard. The well-tended house, the abandoned trampoline. The grandchildren's toys piled neatly in the sand-pit, the deflated swan-shaped paddling pool.

"Family, the whole lot. I never asked for any of it, I was ready to head off to the oil rigs. It would've been an adventure. No one cares where you're from out there on the North Sea, but she started crying, got in the way when I tried to leave. So I told her everything. About Jävredal, all of it. Any woman with an ounce of sense would've run a mile, not teamed up with me like she thought she could save me from myself. And she was pregnant, too. Didn't even want to talk about an abortion. Said she didn't know what she'd do if I left."

"Has she ever shown any violent tendencies before?"

"You won't make me say a bad word about Mejan. I'd rather go back to prison."

Eira felt a sting of pain on her shoulder and swatted away a horse-fly. They had arrived en masse with the high summer. She saw a fat one land on Tryggve's forearm, and another on his bare wrist, but he didn't seem to notice the pain when they bit.

He had thought Mejan seemed like her usual self that day. Around lunch, she had come into the bathroom where Tryggve was clean-ing the drain. It wasn't clogged, but she had been nagging him about it, and over the years he had learned it was easiest just to do what she wanted.

"Seems very quiet over at Hagström's place," she had said. "Wonder if he's gone away. Or if he's in hospital or something. No need for you to tell Patrik about all that stuff now."

When Sven Hagström was eventually found dead, Tryggve had convinced himself it was all just a coincidence. He didn't believe in God. It was more like his lottery numbers had finally come up.

Like everyone else, he thought it must have been the son.

When suspicions turned to him, it was what it was. He knew he would end up in the spotlight as soon as people found out who he was.

"That was why I kept quiet back then, too," he said. "You lot would've hauled me in otherwise."

"What do you mean?"

"When that girl went missing," he said. "They would've trawled through my past, and that would've been it. Mejan agreed. She said, 'They'll run you through their databases and all that business will come up, they'll pin the blame on you. They'll arrest you, Tryggve, and what'll happen to me then? To the kids?'"

Eira felt a chill as he spoke, creeping up her spine, as though the summer was suddenly over.

"Which girl are you talking about?"

But Tryggve didn't seem to hear her, barely seemed to notice that she was leaning in to him.

"So it was a relief," he continued, "when they narrowed in on the Hagström lad. He was a bit sneaky, after all. We always suspected he was the one who let the kids' rabbits out. But it wasn't him."

"Who let the rabbits out?" said GG.

"Who killed her. And now he's as good as dead himself . . ." Tryggve Nydalen wiped the sweat from his forehead with his hand, leaving a dark streak of dirt on his skin. He had probably been digging or doing some other work, fixing the woodwork on the house or pottering around in the yard, the kind of thing people did in the summer.

"What exactly did you keep quiet about back then?" Eira asked softly.

"I saw her."

His eyes wandered slowly over the yard, lingering on every building as though he was taking in the scene for the last time, like he
was saying goodbye. GG kept quiet. Eira could hear his breathing.
He was paying attention, but he likely also knew that this was her
home turf.

"Are you talking about Lina Stavred?"

"Mmm. We were out on the river."

"On July 3, 1996?"

He nodded.

"You told the police you were out fishing . . ." Eira kept her voice
calm, though her heart was galloping in her chest. "With Patrik. He
must've been six at the time?"

"And his cousin, who's a year younger. It was late for them to be
up, I remember that because Mejan's sister started complaining when
we got home, she's so overprotective. Questions everything you do."

Tryggve turned to look at the house again, as though he were
seeking his wife's permission to talk.

"But that just made it more exciting for the boys, they were hanging over the gunwale, waiting for something to tug on the float.
They probably didn't even notice the other boat passing."

"The other boat?"

A rowing boat, that was why it approached so quietly. Tryggve
hadn't spotted it until they were right alongside them. He was pre-
occupied, of course, with the two unruly young boys in his boat,
noses practically touching the water though they didn't know how
to swim.

"They?" asked Eira.

"Yeah, Patrik's cousin was with us too."

"I mean in the other boat. You said 'they' rowed by."

"Ah, yes, two girls," said Tryggve. "One of them was her, the
blond. I didn't have a clue who she was at the time, but when I saw
her in the paper later . . . It was definitely her. Leaning back in the
stern, sprawled out with her legs up and her skirt all . . . The kind
of girl that catches your eye. Even if she was young. I mean, it was a
long time ago . . ."

He ran a hand through his hair and looked down at the ground, mumbled something inaudible, apologetic.

"And the other one?" asked Eira.

"Ah, well, she was darker. Long hair sort of hanging over her face as she rowed, like this." Tryggve moved his hands around his own face to show what he meant. "And she wasn't much of a rower either—the oars kept splashing on the surface. She wasn't dressed as . . . well, she wasn't as undressed, I suppose. But my eyes were on the other one, and I never saw anything about the dark-haired girl in the paper, so I don't know who she was."

"Could you be more precise about the time?"

"Quarter past ten."

"And you know that exactly?" GG interjected. "Even though it was over twenty years ago?"

"After they rowed off, I remember thinking that we should probably head home before the old crones got upset and picked a fight, so I checked the time on my watch."

"Do you remember anything else about what she was wearing, the blond?" Eira couldn't bring herself to say Lina's name. It would be like taking his words as the truth. And yet . . . The story seemed so reluctant to come out, he both wanted and didn't want to say any more. That suggested it might be true to him, though it still seemed unlikely.

"Just a vest and a skirt," he said. "Or maybe it was a dress. Either way, her shoulders were bare, with those thin shoulder straps."

"No cardigan? It must've been quite chilly by that time."

"Nope."

"No, it wasn't chilly, or no, she wasn't wearing a cardigan?"

"She wasn't wearing a cardigan, I just told you."

Tryggve seemed annoyed to be questioned. Eira noticed GG glance over to her. *He doesn't know*, she thought. The papers had all reported on what Lina Stavred was wearing the night she went missing. The description issued by the police had mentioned the yellow cardigan. This was before they found it under Olof Hagström's bed.

"I don't suppose you remember whether she had a bag with her too?"

"I couldn't just keep staring at her . . . But I think she did. She had it down here . . ." Another gesture, between his legs. *So that was where he had been looking,* thought Eira, *while the two young boys watched for fish.* "She reached into it and lit a cigarette just as the boat passed, and then I could only see her back."

He made a spiral motion in the air and breathed in, the smoke that hung over the river all those years ago.

"I was surprised when I saw her in the paper later, but like I said . . ."

"Whereabouts on the river were you?"

"By Köja, just drifting slowly with the current . . ."

Eira fished out her phone and brought up a map, handed it to him. Tryggve used two fingers to zoom in. She leaned closer.

"Just west of the island there," he said, turning it so she could see. "You don't want to go too far out with two little monsters in the boat. Just there, right before the inlet."

Eira dropped a pin on the map and took a screenshot of the image, though she knew she would never forget the location he had pointed out. The narrow bay cut in behind the island like an appendix. Strinnefjärden.

"You didn't say a word about any of this twenty-three years ago," said GG, leaning back in his chair. "Even though the search for Lina Stavred went on for days, and even though your closest neighbor's son was accused of her murder. Why should we believe you now?"

"Believe what you want."

"And why today, right after we released you, while your wife is sitting in custody . . . ? What do you stand to gain from this?"

"I need to go," said Tryggve. He got up, supporting himself against the back of his chair. His legs seemed stiff, his back crooked, as though old age had suddenly caught up with him. "So could you leave me in peace now? Or do you want to stay and watch me take a shit?"

Lorries. A caravan, a tractor with machinery in tow and cars bobbing in and out of the lane while they waited to overtake.

"He's trying to mess with us," GG said as they got stuck at the fork in the road. "A girl in a boat on the river? What does that even mean?"

Eira switched off the engine. It was too stressful to watch for a gap in the traffic while her mind was racing.

"The missing-person report said Lina was wearing a dress and a yellow cardigan," she said. "If he's making the whole thing up, why wouldn't he just say that? If he's going off what he read in the paper?"

"Maybe he forgot," said GG. "It was an eternity ago."

"So why bring up Lina's case at all?"

"He wants to make himself look like the good guy. Nydalen has to live with everyone knowing what he did—and what his wife did—for the rest of his life. Where's he meant to hide now?"

"The timeline was vague . . ." Eira was lost in several trains of thought, comparing Tryggve's words with what she remembered from the preliminary report. "It was entirely based on witness statements from a group of teenagers who saw Olof follow Lina into the woods. They didn't care what time it was; they didn't have anywhere to be. It doesn't even get dark at midnight in early July."

"I was on the force back then," said GG. "But I was working down in Gothenburg. I only followed the case from a distance."

"They found her things down by the beach, pretty close to the jetty where he supposedly dumped her body."

"And how far is that, in relation to this fishing spot?"

"Two kilometers upstream, maybe more like three. Don't ask me how long that takes to row."

Another caravan passed.

"And from here, by car?"

"Ten minutes, max."

They parked the car in an overgrown field, wandered through the near-desolate landscape. The sawmill in Marieberg had been in operation for one hundred years before it closed down in the early seventies. Several of the buildings were still standing. The timber warehouse was the most striking: a corrugated metal behemoth almost two hundred meters in length. A group of enthusiasts had attempted to make the old wood-drying building into an artists' studio a few years back, but it soon transpired that the dioxin levels in the ground were far too high to be safe.

The poison, the same substance used by the United States in World War II and later on the forests of Vietnam under the name Agent Orange, originated from an American chemical weapons factory. Between the wars, it had been used to keep mold and pests away from the timber in Swedish sawmills.

The end of the quay still looked the same as it had in the videotape, the one filmed on a shaky handheld camera when Olof Hagström was brought to the area. The concrete had started to crack, weeds poking through.

GG peered over the edge. "Thirty meters, did you say?"

"Down to one hundred meters a bit farther out. And with the currents and the fact that it's not too far to the coast . . ."

Clouds had gathered overhead, the water darkening, and the wind had picked up. The surface of the river rippled, small waves with white crests breaking in the distance.

Eira looked around. The spot where they were standing was obscured by the huge shed, but still—the fact that there wasn't a single eyewitness to the murder itself?

On a warm summer's evening?

"Was this where they found her things?"

GG pointed to a scrap of beach nearby, some twenty or so meters away. They climbed down from the quay.

"Keys and a makeup brush," said Eira. "That was all."

A few meters of sand among clusters of reeds. Sharp, rotting wooden posts stood in the water, the remains of an old steamboat quay. Just twenty years earlier the small headland behind them had been densely wooded, but the vegetation had since been cut back, leaving the view clear. There were three small boats moored to the rocks, bobbing gently with the movements of the river.

"What was the weather like that day?" asked GG.

"Nice. Warm. She went out late in just a thin cardigan."

"We had a cabin by the sea," said GG. "And if there's one thing people kept an eye on, it was the boats that came and went. Two girls in a rowing boat on the river, past ten in the evening? Someone else must have seen them."

Eira thought about the small communities dotted like pearls along the riverbank: Marieberg, Nyhamn, Köja. Virtually every house had a veranda that stretched down to the water and the evening sun, each one bigger than the last; this was the sunny side of the river.

"Maybe they did," said Eira, trying to remember everything she had skim-read, the tips that had been phoned in, the door knocking, everything that was done while the case was still being treated as a disappearance. "I seem to remember someone claiming to have seen her in a boat, but people said they'd seen her all over the place—in forest collectives, at campsites, across half the country . . ."

"Missing-people cases." GG sighed.

"And then they got hold of Olof Hagström."

"So it was never followed up?"

"It's possible," said Eira. "I didn't go through everything."

GG scanned the river. The line of trees on the other shore seemed a long way away, like a watercolor foreground with the mountains beyond.

"It could have been another day," he said. "Or another girl. Ny-dalen was talking about bare shoulders and what she had between her legs, but did he actually see her face? And even if we assume that he wants to tell the truth now, it could be that his memories have since changed."

A dog appeared, making its way between them. Its owner came strolling after it, shouting hello from a distance. Eira called back. She didn't recognize the man. He threw a stick, let the dog swim. From the beach, the ground sloped up towards the forest. It was steeper than she had imagined, a longer walk.

"The dogs followed the scent from over there," she said, pointing out the direction as she remembered it from a map in the prelimi-nary investigation, the crosses and lines.

"Nothing beats a walk in the woods," said GG.

Eira took the lead through the wild grass and relics from the golden years of the sawmill. They clambered over broken steps lead-ing nowhere and through the foundations of a house, past a couple of brick buildings belonging to the mill. She remembered them be-ing pointed out to her once, years ago, by her father or her grandfa-ther. There was the forge and the workers' bathhouse, so small that it could surely fit only a few tubs, the machine hall that still seemed to be in use somehow—there were a couple of threadbare armchairs outside, a new-looking barbecue. The building known as the Strong-hold loomed overhead, as white and stately as a manor house, albeit fairly down at heel. It was from there that the bosses and officials from the sawmill had reigned, watching the ships come and go.

The views from the top of the hill were magnificent.

The place had changed hands a few times over the years, its incredi-ble views luring in newcomers with business plans and dreams of new lives. They renovated one room, possibly even two, and found them-selves with fourteen still to go. The large wooden houses of the Ådalen Valley didn't really lend themselves to harmony. Marriages crumbled and budgets followed suit, or maybe it was the other way around.

"Did anyone live here back then?" asked GG.

"I don't know," said Eira. "No one seems to have seen anything if they did. From the moment Lina entered the forest to Olof reemerg-ing on his own."

The spruce trees took over.

Nature vanquished all evidence, the moss thick and shimmering green. Eira spent a while calculating steps and distances, imagining the weight of a body, before eventually giving up. It was pointless trying to guess which towering spruce Olof had caught up with Lina Stavred behind, which glade.

"So this is where they last saw her?"

They had reached the road. The patch of gravel outside the old co-op was overgrown with grass. But someone seemed to be living there now, at least during the summer months. There were curtains in the windows, plastic chairs against the gable end, a trike that had toppled over.

"There was a group of five boys hanging out here that night, with Olof," said Eira. "They all gave roughly the same version of events."

"Did they know her?"

"They knew who she was."

Eira could just picture them now, leaning over their mopeds or motorbikes, cigarettes and beers in hand. Just like the groups of boys she had seen at every crossroads, outside every petrol station growing up.

Bored, waiting for something to happen, on the lookout. She could almost hear their wolf whistles as Lina appeared. Was that why she had turned off into the forest?

Ricken must have known more about her than he had let on in his police interviews—weren't he and Magnus already best friends then? They always had been, thick as thieves, blood brothers, for as long as she could remember.

"Were there any other suspects?" GG asked as they turned to walk away, along the edge of the ditch, round the curve, and back to the car.

Eira looked down at the tarmac. She could hear his footsteps, her own, out of sync. The road was full of potholes and cracks, damage caused by the ground frost.

"I don't know. Like I said, I haven't gone through everything."

The old preliminary investigation could wait. It wasn't exactly going to gather much more dust overnight.

"We're not going to move heaven and earth," GG had told her as they made their way back to the car, "but I want to know if there's anything concrete in this boat thing."

He cut across the tarmac to his car, heading back to Sundsvall. Eira paused with her keys in her hand, watching him go. Something in his tone told her he was taking this seriously; he sounded dogged, possibly resigned. He had probably thought he was done with Kramfors now, that he could spend the rest of the summer making babies.

Eira set off, back over to the sunny side of the river. Ricken was busy digging in the garden as she pulled up among the wrecked cars.

"Magnus isn't here," he said.

"Where is he?"

"You tried ringing him?"

"He never picks up," said Eira. That wasn't quite true. She hadn't even tried to get hold of him, because she didn't want to talk over the phone. She needed to see her brother's reaction when she brought up Lina's name.

"He's got a girl over by the coast somewhere," said Ricken, brushing the soil from his hands; he had been digging without gloves. Eira had never thought of him as a gardener, but she could actually see some beautiful roses. There were even a few potato plants sticking out of the earth.

"Where by the coast?"

"Not sure. Nordingrå maybe. Loads of shit-hot girls over there, if you ask me. The place has been crawling with Stockholmers since it became a World Heritage site."

"Why didn't you mention that you were one of the last people to see Lina Stavred?"

Ricken looked up at the sky, among the crowns of the trees. Following a plane making its way south.

"You were just a kid back then, sweetie."

"I mean later, when we . . ." She felt like grabbing him, shaking him, taking hold of his evasiveness and gripping it tight, but she had tried that before. "You were the ones who put the police on to Olof's scent. You were heroes, I don't get why you never bragged about it."

He shoved his hands into the pockets of his shorts, a pair of cutoff jeans.

"If you're going to have a go at me," he said, "I'm going to need a cup of java first."

Eira sat down in a vinyl car seat leaning against the wall of the house, one of many assorted bits of furniture scattered around the yard. This was probably Ricken's idea of freedom, she thought, always being able to choose a different place to sit. As she listened to him rattling around behind the mosquito net over the open kitchen window, she realized that he might well have talked about Lina back then. It wasn't the summer warmth making her face hot, it was embarrassment. Ricken just hadn't talked to *her*. She had blown up their brief love affair into something far bigger than it was. A few months, in secret—almost a year if she included their trysts once it was over—that had come to define the concept of love. Its brokenness and heat, its forbidden nature.

Opening yourself up the way you don't to anyone else.

"It wasn't something I wanted to think about," Ricken told her when he came back out, handing her a chipped mug of coffee. "It was horrible, like being in the middle of a horror film." He sat down in the grass, as he had the last time she was there. "That's why I didn't want to talk to you about it."

"So it didn't have anything to do with Magnus?"

"How d'you mean?" Ricken watched a couple of small white but-
terflies dance across the grass.

"I just found out my own brother was seeing Lina Stavred," said
Eira. "Twenty-three years later. In an old preliminary investigation,
because I happen to be in the police."

"Ah, OK. But it was over between them when it happened . . ."

The coffee was sweet. Did he really think she still took sugar
like she had back then, a hundred years ago, when she had to add
spoonful after spoonful just to be able to bear the taste, to grow up
faster?

"I don't know the stats off the top of my head," said Eira. "But
one of the most dangerous things a woman can do is break up with
a man who still wants her, who's angry to have lost his power."

"What the hell are you suggesting?"

"Nothing," she said. "But that's clearly what the detectives thought
at first, until you and your friends pointed out Olof Hagström. Did
you do it to protect Magnus?"

"There were five of us who saw them," he said. "It wasn't just me."

"I read who was there, Ricken. The others were at least a year
younger than you . . ."

"What is this, a fucking interrogation? Shouldn't you read me my
rights?"

Ricken got up, or rather leapt to his feet, and started walking
barefoot towards the river. Tense shoulders, nervousness, wiry muscles beneath tanned skin.

Eira put down her cup.

She had lost her virginity in an abandoned oil cistern. There had
been a time when she thought that was something remarkable,
something utterly unique, shameful, and incredibly arousing—
particularly as she wasn't allowed to tell anyone about it.

He forbade her.

One afternoon many years ago, in early spring, she was sixteen at
the time. Ricken had pulled up in their yard, the crunch of brakes

on gravel. He was twenty-four. How long had she secretly been in love with him? Two years, three? Long before she understood what things really meant.

Magnus wasn't home, probably with a girl or at some temp job. Eira didn't care which, because Ricken hung around and she got to try out the lines she had been practicing beneath the covers in her room.

"I can come with you instead."

"Where?"

"Somewhere I've never been before."

His arm resting in the open window, cigarette in his hand. She did the same, blew the smoke outside.

The two enormous oil cisterns were on one of the islands in the shadow of the Sandö Bridge, nestled between the overgrown trees. Rusty metal. The last remnants of the sulfite factory that had been torn down during the seventies. Ricken knew which door to take.

An empty cistern, fifty or one hundred meters of enclosed space over their heads. The place was full of junk, bottles, and a sleeping bag, a sleeping mat. They ran around, through the echoes of each other's voices, shouting and singing, until eventually she let herself fall and dragged him down with her.

"Magnus is going to kill me," he mumbled during their very first kiss, but they had kept going, despite the floor being filthy and hard.

The echo of the sounds he'd made was still inside her. She had kept quiet, trying not to embarrass herself, too scared to say that it was her first time.

He probably knew.

"You're not going to say anything about this, are you?" he asked as he dropped her off afterwards, down by the road in case Magnus was already home. "He needs to hear it from me. He'll kill me otherwise. You promise?"

It felt strange to place a hand on his shoulder. His sun-warmed skin. So long ago now. Ricken flinched at her touch.

"I just want to know," said Eira.

The lawn sloped sharply towards the edge of the river. He had a small jetty, with a wooden rowing boat.

"Once they closed the case," he said, "it was like we never talked about Lina again. Magnus couldn't handle it. It was forbidden territory, a minefield, if you know what I mean. And I couldn't talk to you about it—that would've been like betraying him . . ."

"I understand." Their friendship came before all else, she knew that. Always had.

"He was at my place whenever he wasn't at the station, couldn't stop shaking. He thought they were going to frame him."

"Was he really in love with her?"

Ricken nodded. "Lina wasn't as innocent as she looked in the pictures, she really messed with his feelings, broke up with him and then wanted to keep seeing him anyway. That whole game, you know? Magnus was a complete wreck when it turned out she was dead, he cleared off and didn't say where he was going, didn't even tell your mum. I don't know where he slept."

Eira tried to remember, but all she could recall was a general sense of anxiety for Magnus, shouting and screaming at home. Though that could have been any year back then.

Drugs being found, skipping school, money disappearing.

"A new witness has come forward," she said softly. "Someone who claims to have seen Lina later that evening, in a boat on the river."

Ricken turned around, his eyes boring into her, green shifting to brown, a color she could never forget.

"That's impossible," he said.

"Is it?"

"Olof confessed."

"Over a month later," said Eira. "After the interviewers fed him every last detail from their own theories."

"What are you getting at?"

"When the police search started, you didn't get in touch to say you'd seen her straightaway. Why did you wait until they were tipped off?"

Ricken slumped down to the grass.

"Because that's what I decided," he said. "And I told the others to keep their mouths shut, otherwise we'd all be in trouble. I was terrified of what they might tell the cops. We'd been smoking up there, and I was the one who got the hash. I sold it by the joint to anyone who couldn't afford any more. I was an idiot back then."

"You've always been an idiot."

A crooked smile. "I know. And I let them look at my porno mags, too."

"I can just picture it."

"But then, once I realized she was missing and they took Magnus in for questioning, I started talking anyway. Not that I called the cops or anything, certain people wouldn't have liked that . . ."

"The people you bought the hash from?"

"Mmm. But I talked to some friends anyway, and that obviously got back to the cops somehow."

"Because you wanted to draw their attention to someone else?"

"Not just that."

Eira sat down beside him. She wanted to talk about something else, about the weather or how his parents were doing, she wanted the silence to last, for the questions to be forgotten, as though she had never asked them. Her thoughts drifted to Ingela, Olof's sister, who had snapped up the rumor and taken it home with her, set everything in motion.

"It obviously wasn't Magnus," said Ricken. "I never thought it was. You get that, right? But he was a complete mess—first Lina was gone, then the cops came after him. I guess I thought they might as well question someone else instead."

"A fourteen-year-old?"

Eira glanced at her old boyfriend, at his familiar profile. It had become more accentuated over time, more finely tuned. His jaw was tense, his hands clutching the grass. Even after all these years, she still thought she could tell what he was thinking, as though the boundaries between two people didn't exist. No skin, no secrets. As though it was her job to carry his pain, his love, his inability, whatever the hell it was.

"We made Olof do it," said Ricken, his voice muted. "That's another reason I didn't want anyone to talk to the cops. I was the one who was always coming up with stuff to do, the others just did what I did."

"What do you mean?"

"I was taunting him, and the others joined in—all, 'Come on, aren't you gonna follow her? Have you ever fucked anyone? Do you even know what to do with a girl?' The kind of meaningless stuff we used to say. I was pissed off with Lina, too. Said some horrible stuff about her. But then he actually did it, he followed her into the forest. I never thought Olof would try it on, he wasn't the type . . . I didn't believe it when he came back out either, even though he was dirty, his face all red. I knew what Lina was like, so goddamn self-centered, she would never . . ."

"So what type was Olof?"

"Insecure and cocky. Big for his age, but immature. Not that I really knew him, but . . ."

"I read parts of your interview. You didn't seem to have any doubts back then."

"I guess it was all that stuff . . . with Magnus . . . The cops were all over him . . ."

"So you sounded more sure than you were?"

"I just said what we saw. And no matter what Olof did or didn't do, I knew Magnus was innocent."

"Because?"

"Because he was at home."

"Was he?"

"Come on, he's your brother. I've known him all my life."

Eira looked out at the water, the steady flow of the current. *It's always someone's brother*, she thought, though she couldn't bring herself to say it. That would mean following the thought to its conclusion, getting into an argument. Ricken would defend Magnus until the last, she knew that; he had broken up with her to avoid ruining their friendship, or at least that was what he had told her at the time. Maybe he just hadn't loved her, but still. Their brotherhood came first.

"If this witness is telling the truth," she said softly. "If he saw what he thinks he saw, that means Lina was alive when Olof came out of the woods."

"So where's she supposed to have gone?"

"Out in a boat," said Eira. "Two girls rowed past this witness over by Köja, in towards the island, where they turned off."

"This way?" said Ricken. "Into the bay?"

The very same one they were looking out at then. Strinnefjärden was its name, at least if you lived on this side of the water. Eira had heard that those on the other side called it Lockneviken. It was all a matter of perspective.

"Where were they going?" asked Eira. "What was out here twenty-three years ago?"

"Nothing. Houses. That's pretty much it." Ricken squinted across the river, as though he might spot something else. "You might come out here to visit someone, I don't know what other reason you could have."

Eira moved closer to the water's edge and heard him follow her. Soft footsteps in the grass.

"What's on the other side?" she asked.

"Farmers," Ricken said to the back of her head. "A few nice old places from the sawmill years, the manor in Lockne. Horse paddocks. I don't know whether there are any horses now, but there might've been back then."

"And there?"

Eira pointed to a cluster of poles sticking up out of the water. The beach was overgrown, the trees spilling out into the river. There was a beaver's dam, a sliver of roof visible beyond the greenery. Farther back, the landscape rose steeply, dramatic rocks rising up out of the water.

"Lorelei," said Ricken.

"What?"

"People call it the Lorelei rock." His eyes were fixed in the distance, on the steep gray slope. "You know, after the woman who sat on top of a huge rock by the Rhine, singing and combing her golden hair. She bewitched the sailors, made them forget to keep watch for dangerous reefs."

"I mean there," said Eira. "By the old quay."

"Ah, the mill," said Ricken. "Some of it's still there, but it's been falling apart for decades; that place shut down back in the forties."

Eira thought about the places he had taken her. The oil cistern wasn't the only one. They had gone to empty houses and the abandoned ruins of factories, the kind of thing Ådalen was full of. Places where no one would see them. She would never be able to find her way back to most of them, had been focused on everything other than the geography.

"Did you and I ever go over there?" she asked.

"Nah, damn, must've missed that one." He was laughing, she was sure of that. Or smiling at the very least. "But it's not too late."

She gently stroked his arm before she left.

"Thanks for telling me."

There were seven tips about a boat on the river. Several could be dismissed out of hand, but three were a fit for both the time and the location.

Just outside Nyhamn, an elderly couple who were sitting on their veranda. They had almost certainly passed away. Nyhamn was midway between Marieberg and Strinnefjärden. They thought it had been around ten o'clock, just after the late shipping news on the radio.

Over by Köja, a few teenagers who were drinking beer on a jetty. They weren't sure of the time. Only one of them actually remembered the boat, she had waved because she thought it was someone she knew inside, but she had been mistaken.

The third tip came from a fisherman who had been somewhere downstream of Litanön and thought he saw someone row into Strinnefjärden. It caught his eye because the person was so terrible at rowing; he'd probably reacted more to the sound of the oars than anything. He didn't have his glasses with him in the boat—could fish perfectly well without them—and couldn't be sure whether it was the girl or not, but he had heard laughter carrying across the water, and it was from a young lady.

All of the witnesses had been contacted, their statements taken down, but Eira couldn't find any further action after that.

Sheer routine.

"There was one more thing," she said.

"What?"

GG seemed annoyed, replying curtly to everything she said. They were no longer a team, to the extent they ever had been. It had been days since she last saw Bosse Ring. He was probably on another case, or possibly on leave. Silje Andersson, too. Still, Mejan Nydalen had confessed and been remanded in custody, the forensic evidence was solid, so why else would GG have driven the one hundred kilometers to Kramfors?

For coffee?

He knows, thought Eira. *He either feels or suspects that there really is something in this.* For the first time, she saw something of herself in him. A stubbornness, something niggling away inside.

"It was more a complaint than a real tip," she continued. "But no one seems to have looked into it or even called back. There wasn't anything to directly connect it to Lina."

"But?"

"A widow, in Lockne. She said she was calling for the third time."

Eira read aloud from the transcript of her phone call. They had taken such care with that kind of thing twenty-three years ago, making sure nothing fell between the cracks. Everything had been documented and filed away. She felt an urge to slip into the woman's Ångermanland accent, a blending of several old dialects you rarely heard anymore; she associated them with her grandparents, with a bygone world. Instead, she translated for GG:

"There are people in the sawmill again. God knows what they're up to, but the police haven't been over yet."

"Sorry, but where are you talking about?"

"Over here, in Lockne. The door's wide open, so anyone and their mother can walk straight in. Doesn't feel good not knowing what kind of folk are running around. And now with everything with that girl. Nasty business."

"Have you seen her?"

"Don't dare go down there with those types hanging about."

The person who took the call then said "if this isn't about the missing girl, Lina Stavred, I'd advise you to call on a different line . . ." and the woman launched into a general rant about the authorities turning their backs on the community just because it wasn't on the coast.

GG had taken a seat and was drumming his pen on the edge of the desk.

"I'm not quite sure I follow," he said. "How is this interesting?"

Eira put down her iPad and brought up a map.

"It's just a thought," she said. "But if you look at the area here . . ." The narrow inlet was five kilometers long, like a tributary with no destination. She pointed out the old sawmill in Lockne, halfway in.

"Why would they row up here?" she asked. "If they were going to visit someone, shouldn't that person have come forward . . . ?" Neither vocalized the thought that followed, but she could see it in his eyes: unless that person was the killer.

"Who could the other person in the boat have been?" GG asked instead. "Surely they can't have failed to notice another missing girl?"

Eira enlarged the satellite image. Blurry greenery and spots that could be roofs were all that was visible of the area beyond the poles in the water by Lockne.

"When I was younger, we used to go out to places like this. All a bit out of the way, somewhere where you could feel free."

"What did her parents say? Where did they think she was?"

"Lina had told them she was staying over at a friend's, but she never showed up. She must have had a reason to walk all the way over to Marieberg—I mean, it's a few kilometers away."

"To meet boys?"

"Then why wouldn't she just stay by the road where the whole gang was hanging out?"

"What did the police make of it?"

"They lost all interest in where she was going the minute they turned their attention to Olof Hagström. It wasn't important anymore."

GG spun around in his chair, eyes panning out across the flat roofs of central Kramfors, a prolonged silence.

"I spoke to a doctor in Umeå yesterday," he said. "He's got a lung infection and a fever, but it's going down. His pupils react, he responds to touch."

"Do they think he'll wake up?"

"They're like us—they try not to second-guess."

Eira waited out yet another silence.

"There's a moment," she eventually said. "In the interviews with Olof Hagström."

"Mmm?"

"Do you have time? It'll only take a few minutes."

"What's this about?"

"I'd like you to see it for yourself."

GG got up with a certain listlessness, filled his mug with coffee on the way. He grabbed a handful of jelly sweets from a plastic tub, the kind parents buy from children collecting for a school trip. There was a whole stack of them in the cupboard.

They squeezed into the cramped TV room. Eira had watched the video again, and had fast-forwarded to the right place.

The image appeared on the screen: Olof on the vinyl sofa, his eyes on the floor.

"It wasn't like I told them . . . She pushed me and I fell . . . The ground was dirty. All kinds of muck."

"Why didn't you mention any of this before?"

"Because . . . because . . . She's a girl. It's just, I wasn't expecting it. That must've been why I fell . . ."

GG munched on sweet after sweet as the disjointed story rolled towards its end. They heard the interviewer's increasingly forceful exhortations that Olof should stop lying, the part where he asked for his mother.

Eira hit STOP.

"What if he's telling the truth?" she said, ignoring the familiar deep-seated urge to keep quiet. "If Lina left on her own, then Nydalen's statement could be true. Maybe there was someone waiting for her down by the river. Why else would she take that path?"

"Play it again."

Eira rewound the tape, knew the time stamps by heart now.

"And then she grabbed some nettles, like this . . . And shoved soil in my mouth, said it was my fault she was dirty, that I'd ruined everything."

GG took the remote control from her hand, pressed PAUSE.

"Is that a common reaction to being raped?"

"What?"

"Worrying about being dirty—in the literal sense, I mean."

Before the segment had finished again, GG was on his feet. Pacing back and forth in the corridor outside. Eira let the video keep rolling. None of the boys she had known growing up would have told his friends if he had been pushed over and humiliated by a girl. Who wouldn't have said what Olof was reported to have said: *"Man, Lina was great. Fuck me, she was great"*?

From the corridor outside, she heard snatches of a telephone conversation every time GG came closer or raised his voice.

"I'm not saying we should reopen the investigation, but if mistakes were made . . . No, I can't do that, he's in a coma as you know . . . Yes, I'm aware that it was over twenty years ago, but before some reporter from Sveriges Television catches wind of this . . . No, we don't let the media steer us, that's not what I'm saying, but if there's a new witness statement surely we should take the initiative and put a few people on it, just to take a closer look at the area . . . ?"

The man who had taken it upon himself to show her the way pushed back the branches ahead of him. There was something special about the light filtering through the birch trees that had been left to grow in peace on the old industrial land, something magical. They waded through the ferns.

"You need to know where you're going if you want to find your way," he said.

They were almost on top of the old sawmill in Lockne when it emerged from the dense greenery ahead of them, great chunks of crumbling plaster, bricks, and cracked mortar. The forensic technicians had been working for twelve hours now, and still hadn't reported a single find.

Eira stepped over a pile of broken bricks. The door was hanging at a forty-five-degree angle. Where there had once been windows, there were now nothing but gaping holes. A technician was moving methodically inside, carefully lifting scrap metal, sweeping away mortar. A rusty oven of some kind, fallen beams. You could see straight through the building; half the wall to the rear had collapsed.

The forest was making its way inside.

"This was the boiler house and the forge," said the older man. He had been standing by the side of the road when Eira climbed out of the car, and had volunteered to join her, had noticed the activity in the area. "Used to be full of Norwegian refugees, they worked here during the war. Have you ever heard of Georg Scherman, the foreman who shot live rounds in the courthouse in Sollefteå? People had been cheating him out of money and the entire thing was about to go down the drain. This was before the big sawmill boom in the early twentieth century; it was like the Wild West round here . . ."

Eira watched the technicians' glove-clad movements, studying the objects they picked up, old tools and levers, a rusty chain.

Twenty thousand men had worked in the forestry industry in its heyday, and there had been sixty sawmills in the valley. The only one still in operation—in Bollstabruk—now produced more than those sixty mills combined, with fewer than three hundred employees.

Those who didn't know better called the area sparsely populated, rural, but the truth was that the Ådalen river valley was, at heart, an industrial area. And though the industries were long gone, they still lingered, like phantom pains.

Scattered stories from someone who had heard it from someone else. A slow recovery, nature eating its way in.

The man was still behind Eira, peering over her shoulder. He had fallen quiet when she failed to respond to his knowledge of former sawmill bosses.

"Do you get a lot of kids hanging around here?" she asked.

"Not these days. They've probably got better things to do. Netflix and that kind of thing, I suppose, the few still living in the area."

"Were you here in the midnineties?"

"Oh yes," he said. "Arrived in the seventies, from Arboga. It wasn't anywhere near as dilapidated back then, of course—I think the walls were still intact, but I'm not sure. You stop paying any notice once you've seen it a few times; you look past it all. But this place has never drawn a lot of visitors, it's so inaccessible, barely even visible from the road—or the river, for that matter."

The forensic technician spotted them and came over with a brick in one hand. They introduced themselves through the empty window.

"What a place," he said. "Strange that people haven't made off with everything. It's like an archaeological dig, except everything's already lying out in the open."

It was OK for her to come in, there was hardly likely to be any evidence that the local wildlife and the weather hadn't already destroyed. Eira thanked her guide and was just about to climb the half-meter to the door where the steps had rotted away when her phone rang.

A prepaid number she knew by heart.

She pushed through a tangle of nettles and sat down on the stone foundation of something long gone.

"What are you lot up to?" asked Magnus.

"Why don't you ever pick up?" She had tried to call him several times. It irritated her when he made himself unreachable.

"Sorry for not constantly being on my phone," he said. "What did you want?"

"To talk."

"About something that happened twenty-three years ago?"

He knows, thought Eira. *He picks up when his friend calls. It's me he doesn't want to speak to.*

"Why didn't you ever mention that Lina Stavred was your girl-friend?"

"I heard you were sniffing about in that," said Magnus. "What's the point?"

The wind whispered in the trees, a cuckoo calling in the distance. If only it was possible to isolate the sounds of the forest from those of her body, her pulse, the beat of her heart, it would have been idyllic.

"I'd rather not do this over the phone," said Eira.

Barely fifty meters from the old forge was a yellow wooden house dating back to the sawmill's heyday. It looked like it had once been a manager's villa.

That was where the old widow once lived, the one who had called in the complaints. One of her daughters had since taken over the family home, and offered Eira a glass of rhubarb juice in the garden.

"I remember it very well," she said. "Mum wanted me to come up here virtually every five minutes—I was living down in Härnösand at the time. She was so shaken up by what happened."

Ingamaj was long dead, of course. She was already over eighty when Lina Stavred vanished.

"Why are you getting in touch now? Mum said no one even bothered to call her back, that no one wanted to listen to an old woman."

Eira considered her words. There wasn't a person in Lockne who didn't already know that the police were sniffing about the old mill, but they hardly had any reason to link that to Lina's disappearance.

"We've received a new tip," she said. "So we're also going through a number of old ones. It doesn't necessarily have anything to do with this, but I'd appreciate it if you didn't mention this to anyone. It'll just make our work harder."

"No, no, of course," said the woman, pouring more juice. It was made according to her mother's recipe, and her grandmother's before her.

She remembered parts of what Ingamaj had talked about, back in the nineties.

That there were some teenagers hanging around in the old forge. She had noticed the smell first, when they lit a fire. The ground was so dry at the time, there was a real risk of it spreading.

Ingamaj had walked to the edge of the property and shouted at them, but they just laughed. She had later seen one of them washing in the river, when she went down there to rinse her rag rugs—something she insisted on doing despite having had a washing machine for decades.

He looked like a bum.

"Mum's words, obviously."

Unless she was mistaken, someone else had also pulled up on a motorcycle.

"This is more than your mother said over the phone," said Eira.

"I guess she was nervous about speaking to the police. And she assumed someone would come out here to listen to what she had to say."

"And you're sure about the date, that it was around the time Lina Stavred went missing?"

The woman thought for a moment.

"Maybe not sure," she said. "I know she mentioned it then, of course—I had to leave the kids to drive up here and stay over, so it was definitely something. I offered to go and have a look the next day. She didn't want me to, but I went over anyway, in the middle of the day. I didn't see anything. Maybe it was just that everything she was worried about came flooding out, you know how it can be. Something happened then, but other aspects might've been ten years old."

Eira reminded her not to mention their conversation to anyone else, and praised the rhubarb juice before she left.

The landscape became increasingly spectacular as she approached the High Coast. The road wound between soft hills and sheer rock faces rising increasingly sharply above her, lakes and bays, the flat water reflecting the dark forests and the bright sky.

It was like something out of a fairy tale, something enchanted; that was the type of word it conjured up.

Eira had no trouble finding the right address, a farmstead just south of Nordingrå.

FLEA MARKET—GALLERY—COFFEE, read the hand-painted sign. There were several cars parked on the driveway, though not like at Ricken's place, far from it. These cars were all gleaming, Audis and BMWs. One had German plates, another Norwegian. Tourists making their way through the World Heritage region.

The woman Magnus was currently staying with held out a cool hand. Marina Arnesdotter. She was older than him, somewhere around fifty, and sold her own ceramics from the barn. Fortunately she was busy with customers.

"But take some lime pie in with you," she said, serving two slices onto a plate from the table outside the gallery. "It's so nice that you've come to visit."

The word "nice" clung to Eira like a cruel irony as she knocked on the door. Magnus answered, but he didn't welcome her in, just turned and walked through to the kitchen.

His hair was shorter than it had been the last time she'd seen him.

Even during his worst periods, his hair had always looked good. He never had to pay to have it cut.

"Have you been together long?" Eira asked once she had taken a seat, attempting to start somewhere less painful.

Magnus shrugged, his back to her. "It's nothing serious."

"She seems nice. Older than you."

"Marina's great. She leaves me be, doesn't nag all the time."

"I've got a meeting with the support officer next week."

"OK." Magnus irritably shook a tin of coffee, searching the cupboards for more and closing the doors a little too hard. Eira felt herself flinch inside; it was second nature for sounds like that to leave her uneasy. A sign of arguments brewing. Her brother shouting and screaming, lashing out. At the doors and walls, not his family. Mum crying as the door slammed shut. The sound of his engine, his motorcycle on the gravel, the silence once he was gone.

"What was she like?" said Eira.

"She was asleep last time I went over," said Magnus. "But everything seemed fine."

"Come off it, you know who I mean. Lina Stavred. How do you think it felt to find out that she was your girlfriend from the preliminary report?"

"You were still playing with dolls back then."

"I used to pretend that they'd died," said Eira. "I threw my Barbie into the river and watched the current carry her away."

"What do you want to know?"

"Why didn't you ever say anything?"

Magnus leaned back against the kitchen counter. Ran a hand through his hair, the way he always had.

"What was I supposed to say? I was just a fucking kid back then, I thought she was the love of my life, that the two of us were, like . . ."

He was near a breaking point, Eira had sensed that the moment she stepped inside, a looming eruption, like when the birds fall silent ahead of a thunderstorm, the harsh sun warning of rain. Another person wouldn't have noticed, all the small signs: the anxious hands, the tense jaw, eyes locked onto the window without really taking anything in.

"Ricken called to say you'd been over," he said. "So you talk to him about me now, do you? Behind my back."

"I was looking for you."

"Say what you wanted to say, then."

"It's to do with Lina's case," she began. "There are things in the old investigation that . . ." Eira ate a spoonful of lime pie, weighing one thing against another, his anger against being honest, the truth against a longing to avoid a fight. Arnesdotter knew how to bake, she had to give her that. "It might have been another perpetrator."

"What the fuck." Magnus didn't move, which was almost worse than him hitting something. *He already knows*, she thought, *he's not surprised. But why is he pretending this is news to him?* "So the cops are coming for me again, are they? You recording this conversation?"

"No, I'm not."

"And how am I meant to know that?"

Eira pulled out her phone and pushed it across the table.

"They haven't officially reopened the case," she said. "But there's a chance they will."

"Why aren't you saying 'we'? You're one of them, aren't you?"

"This kind of thing is down to the prosecutor, you know that."

"So are you going to interview Marina too? Since you're here. Want me to call her through? Maybe you want to ask if I'm violent, if I've ever hurt her? They went on and on for days, can you imagine that? In and out of the station in Kramfors. You have no idea what it—"

"Were you really at home that night, like you said?"

"Ask Mum."

"You know I can't do that."

"She's not as confused as you think. She remembers the boys' birthdays and name days, she sends them presents and checks in." His eyes drifted to the fridge, where a picture of his two sons was held in place by a couple of heart-shaped magnets. The same photo as at home. "Maybe you're actually making everything worse by taking charge of things she should be able to manage herself."

"What does that have to do with any of this?"

"It's to do with you, the way you are, the way you always have to butt in to other people's lives."

"I don't do it because I enjoy it. This is about a murder case that ended up on my desk, and then I find out the two of you have been lying to me all these years—or withholding important information, at the very least."

"You really do sound like a cop now."

Eira wanted to get up, but she remained sitting. She felt like she had been backed into a corner, despite the sense of lightness and space in the bright country kitchen where everything was painted white, from the floorboards to the exposed beams on the ceiling. The age of the wood shone through in a rustic, countrified way.

"You don't know what it was like," said Magnus. "Or what you're dredging up by going around, talking about Lina."

"Would it be better if I hadn't said anything?"

"The cops brought me in. Did you know that was the first time? I'd barely even nicked a bit of chocolate before that."

"So it's their fault you went off the rails? Are you saying they shouldn't have bothered investigating the murder of a sixteen-year-old girl? That they shouldn't have asked her boyfriend questions . . . ?"

"Do you think I had something to do with it?"

"No, of course not, but . . ."

"If it was serious, they would've sent a real cop. But you just can't stay away, can you?"

Eira heard a door open in the hallway. Magnus didn't seem to realize that his girlfriend had come in.

"It was exactly the same with Dad," he continued. "You just had to go over there and sort through his stuff after he died, even though he had a new wife. Even though he left us."

"She couldn't do it," said Eira. "It was a mess, she was grieving. Someone had to . . ."

"Weren't you?" asked Magnus. "Weren't you grieving?"

"Surely this has nothing to do with Lina Stavred's murder?"

"No, but it says plenty about you."

Eira lost her footing. That was what Magnus always did to her: warped her perspective, made her feel stupid. It struck her that she hadn't seen any interviews with their father. He must have been out on the road at the time, like always, driving the lorry somewhere in upper Norrland, or down towards the continent.

"Oops, sorry, I've barged into something here."

Marina Arnesdotter appeared in the doorway, accompanied by the scent of laundered linens and fresh thyme. She was holding a bunch of herbs in one hand. Eira realized she must have been eavesdropping, and was ashamed of what she might have heard. Right then she saw her brother's face transform, from hypertense anger, threatening to explode, to a smile that could have convinced any woman to ask him to move in with her.

"It's OK," he said, reaching out for his girlfriend, pulling her close. "Eira was just leaving. She's got a lot on with work."

"Oh, that's a shame—now that I finally get the chance to meet some of Magnus's family. You'll have to stay overnight next time, so we can have a glass of wine together."

She laughed into his hair.

Eira got up and cleared away her plate.

"Thanks for the lime pie," she said. "It was really tasty."

Eira had only just shouted that she was home when her phone rang.

"Hello there," Bosse Ring yelled. "We need you to come out to . . . what's it called . . . Lockne?"

"Have they found something?"

"The boss says you're the best person to decide that."

"Is GG there?"

"Nope, he's off, doctor's appointment."

"Give me half an hour," said Eira.

She felt guilty about neglecting her mother again, but Kerstin seemed to be in a good mood. Hopefully this would be one of the things she forgot. Eira heated some shop-bought hash, cracked two eggs, and served the yolks in half shells, because it looked nice.

"What day is it today?" Kerstin grabbed the newspaper. "Wednesday, aha—not much on TV then."

"That's a few days old," said Eira, noticing the headline on the front page: "Charged with Kungsgården Murder." An image of a woman with a jacket pulled over her head. Mejan had managed to completely obscure her face. "Today's Friday," she added.

"Well, that's much better."

Her mother studied the egg yolk for a moment before tipping it into the hash. Eira ate quickly, questions swirling around her head. About that night, where her father had been, about why Magnus had spiraled out of control, but she managed to keep them to herself, couldn't handle never being given any answers. No need to ruin dinner.

Kerstin waved dismissively when she excused herself.

"Are you off to meet anyone nice?"

"No, sadly not. It's just work."

"You shouldn't leave it too long, you know. You'll shrivel up."

"Thanks, Mum, that's encouraging."

The world was bathed in soft blue tones as she drove over the Sandö Bridge, the mountains and river blending with the colors of the sky in the pale sunset.

The area around the old sawmill was now brightly lit. Eira heard voices from the large space inside the forge. Bosse Ring saw her coming and called her over.

The room was bare, emptied of whatever machine parts had been left behind. There was a staircase leading to nowhere. Eira said hello to the forensic technician, the same man she had met that morning. He excused himself and stepped outside. The cables from the generator were snaking down towards the river; she had already noticed the bright lights beyond the trees.

"You know this case better than most," said Bosse Ring. "Does any of this say anything to you?"

They had heaped up the bricks and mortar on the floor, spread out a plastic sheet. Eira walked slowly along the line of objects. Unidentifiable garments, a glove, a sleeping bag, and a broken shoe. Three condoms, beer cans.

She paused by one of the pieces of fabric. It was scrunched up and filthy, likely faded by the passage of time, but she could still make out the pale blue color.

"Lina was wearing a dress when she disappeared," said Eira. "It had thin shoulder straps, according to Nydalen."

Bosse Ring grabbed a stick and poked at the material.

Shoulder straps.

The hum of the generator was the only sound they could hear.

"So what do we do now?" asked Eira. "Do we show it to the witnesses or wait for DNA?"

"Do her parents still live in the area?"

"They moved to Finland."

"Understandable."

"Neither of them knew what their daughter was wearing, she'd snuck out."

"And the others who saw her?"

"Five teenage boys," said Eira, trying to remember their various statements. "There were different claims about the color of her dress, but several of them thought it was blue."

The bright light made the details seem sharp, the air hot.

"Where was it found?" she asked.

"Don't know, I've only been here a few hours."

Eira took a turn through the rest of the finds. The shoe looked to be bigger than size 40. She knew very little about how long a condom took to disintegrate.

"Looks like a Pripps Blå from the ancient past," Bosse Ring said as he studied the beer cans. He crouched down and poked at one of them with a stick, trying to make out the best-before date.

Hearing a voice behind her, Eira jumped.

"Come with me. We've got something."

The lights were blinding. Movement in the doorway, a shape against the gloom outside.

"Down by the beach," the technician clarified.

He strode off before they had time to get outside. Another set of broken steps, a pile of spongy planks.

The footpath down to the river was now well trodden. Birches bowed towards the water, the spotlights painting their trunks unnaturally white.

They were standing at the water's edge, hunched over and crouching, partly in the river: three people in full protective gear. Lockne was another area where high levels of dioxin had been found. The poison wasn't too dangerous while it was trapped in the ground, but that changed once you started digging.

Eira followed her colleague as he drew closer.

A tangle of wood was visible just beneath the surface. A few sticks and planks sticking up into the air. Likely the remains of the jetty that had once stood there. Farther out in the river, the pilings that had supported it still rose up out of the water. It looked like a sparse fence.

"We found it right here," said one of the technicians, Shirin ben Hassen, who was leading the search. She pointed to an area where the bank met the water, sloping sharply downwards. Earth and more old wood. Blue clay, so common along the riverbanks. Eira had played in it as a child, painting her face blue to scare anyone walking by.

"We wouldn't have spotted it if the water wasn't so low," said Shirin.

The lack of snow over the previous winter meant that the mountain rivers were shallower than usual, revealing things that were typically hidden. They had to take half a step into the water to see. One of the technicians was already up to his knees. The spotlights were casting shadows from the birches nearby.

It was a hand.

Wedged into the riverbank, partly above the surface.

The bones of a hand.

"There's more there," said Shirin, pointing down into the water.

Slightly murky, difficult to see; golden brown sediment mixing with the clear river water.

"A thigh bone," Eira heard a voice beside her say. "Likely a thigh bone."

He was floating, as though through water, drifting upwards. Had no idea where he was coming from, or where he was going, and he didn't know how he could be breathing if it really was water.

There were voices, but he couldn't reach them. Floating far away from him, up above, like birds in the sky, crossing overhead, like the cuckoo on the other side of the river, calling out.

There was a name.

Olof.

In the distance, where there was nothing.

Olof.

The jazz club was in the very heart of Sundsvall, on a tree-lined boulevard that suggested that, in its heyday, the city had once dreamed of becoming another Paris.

The walls were lined with photographs of jazz legends, footage of a fire burning on a TV screen. Eira immediately recognized the woman sitting at the bar, a half-empty glass of beer in front of her.

Unni, twenty years later, but with the same cropped hair, still dyed red. Wearing a pair of tight jeans and multiple necklaces. Before she met a jazz musician and moved to Sundsvall, she was always over at their house, one of Kerstin's many friends who had scattered in the wind. Eira remembered their voices drifting through the wall.

She had to be well over seventy now.

"God, you're all grown up! Let's have a look at you. Such a pretty girl now!"

Unni protested when Eira tried to order a nonalcoholic beer—she could stay the night, couldn't she? She'd always have a place for Kerstin's daughter to sleep.

"Funny you got in touch today of all days," she said. "Have you seen the news? Looks like they've found that girl who went missing in Marieberg. I was staying with you when all that happened, do you remember?"

News of the discovery in Lockne was already out; it had broken on the local radio that morning, and by afternoon the speculation was rife. It didn't take long. The dust had been stirred up recently, ever since the murder of Sven Hagström, and the journalists quickly put two and two together.

*The question on everyone's lips: Is the body that of missing Lina
Stavred, who vanished one July day twenty-three years ago . . . ?*

"Yeah, I remember," said Eira. She sipped her beer, dark and bitter. "That's actually why I wanted to talk to you."

"And here's me thinking it must be something to do with Kerstin." Unni clutched her chest, breathed a sigh of relief. "I didn't
dare ask over the phone; I was sure you were going to say something
about cancer or death."

Eira quickly told her about the dementia.

"I'll be damned," said Unni. "That has to be the worst—
disappearing though you're still here."

"I don't know why the two of you lost touch."

"It happens sometimes." Unni watched as a couple of musicians
stepped onto the stage, tuned their instruments. Turning up amps,
testing the strings on a double bass.

"We don't know whether it's Lina Stavred's body yet," said Eira.
"It's all just media speculation. That kind of thing takes time to
determine—especially if it's been underwater for years. At this stage
they often don't even know if the body is historic or recent; they
haven't found all the pieces yet . . ."

Unni stared at her for a few seconds, then laughed. "My God, I
forget you're a police officer now. To me you'll always be that little
girl with pigtails and dungarees. I remember how you used to try
to hide behind the sofa to eavesdrop on us while we were drinking
wine."

"I'm not here on police business."

"Ah, good. Then you'll have another."

Unni waved to the bartender, gesturing for two more IPAs without even asking. Eira felt a sudden urge to knock it back in one go.

"You know Magnus and Lina Stavred were dating," she said.

"Uff, yes, it's awful when it's so close to home. Kerstin was pet-
rified. Your brother ran off and got drunk instead of talking about
it, kept everything inside, you know? Boys." Unni drank a little too
quickly, her gaze wandering. Following the musicians as they got ready
onstage, reacting to every new customer who came into the bar.

"I miss her so much sometimes," she continued. "We lost touch after I met Benke and fell head over heels in love. Maybe you remember him? Played bass like a god. Probably still does. Kerstin was honest with me, told me he was no good. I was angry that she couldn't just be happy for me, but she was right. It lasted seven years and he definitely wasn't good for me, but I'd do it again in a flash."

"I was wondering what you remember from those days," said Eira. "When they were looking for Lina and you came to stay with us . . ."

"Everything, I think. You don't tend to forget the things that scare you most—I can still remember the nightmares I had as a girl." Unni pulled out a lipstick and found her reflection in the glass on one of the frames on the wall, her face blending with Louis Armstrong's. "I lived on my own over in Paradise, you know? One of the workers' blocks in Marieberg. And then I heard that was where Lina went missing. Not even a kilometer away."

"Do you remember what you were doing that evening?"

"I went down to the sauna. Swam naked in the river. This was earlier in the evening mind you, but I couldn't stop thinking that it could've been me. Before they found out who he was, obviously. A fourteen-year-old would hardly have tried anything with me."

Unni rubbed her lips together, pouted, and smiled.

"And Mum," said Eira. "Did she tell you what she was doing?"

"Yes . . . I think so . . . She was at home, wasn't she?"

Her eyes were wandering again. The musicians had started playing, quiet, traditional jazz. The murmur in the bar died down, everyone focused on the stage.

"And Magnus?"

Unni raised a finger to her lips, gestured to the musicians. Eira lowered her voice.

"Mum has always taken his side, no matter what he's done. She still does. Even at his worst, it was never Magnus's fault. If he'd said he was ill or feeling down or something, I might have believed it, but my brother was never just at home. And don't tell me I was too young—I know. I know that I missed him all the time."

A trumpet solo came and went.

"Let's go further back so we're not disturbing anyone." Unni carried the glasses to the other end of the room, out of sight of the stage. Eira grabbed a glass of water from the bar on the way.

They sat down in a couple of low leather armchairs.

"I promised her," said Unni. "I swore I'd never tell either of you."

"It was a murder inquiry," said Eira.

"But they caught him, the boy who did it. You have no idea how relieved Kerstin was when she found out. I remember her crying for days."

"I thought she was upset."

"You don't know how much pressure she was under."

"I meet plenty of people who lie to the police," said Eira. "They always think they've got a good reason."

"I don't want to say that Kerstin lied," said Unni. "She just didn't know what to tell them when they asked."

"Was Magnus at home or wasn't he?"

"Shh."

Eira hadn't noticed that she had raised her voice. A few members of the audience hushed her, several glancing angrily in her direction.

Unni leaned in.

"Kerstin didn't know. She just repeated what Magnus had told them, to avoid any more questions."

"You've lost me now."

"She wasn't at home the night Lina Stavred went missing. Once you'd gone to sleep, around nine I suppose, she snuck out. She was gone a few hours. She couldn't exactly tell anyone—well, except me, but this was afterwards."

"Snuck out where?"

Unni closed her eyes as though she were enjoying the music, but she was also fidgeting nervously with her bracelets, several on each arm.

"You mustn't judge your mum too harshly."

"I really need to know."

"OK."

The crowd clapped, the musicians announced an interval. A deep woman's voice drifted from the speakers, a familiar song about lonely lovers meeting under a blue moon.

Unni reached for the second glass, which Eira still hadn't touched.

"Your dad was almost never home," she said. "Veine was constantly out on the road. Things weren't great between your parents, hadn't been for years."

"What are you trying to say?"

"Please, just let me talk."

It had been going on for some time, several months if Unni remembered correctly. In secret, of course; they were both married. It was possible that Unni was the only person Kerstin dared confide in.

They lived in such a small community that something as simple as a wink could spark gossip, and even worse than that: meetings late at night, a walk along the river, a car ride under the pretense of buying milk, a windbreak somewhere in the forest . . .

This time it was Eira who closed her eyes, blocking out the world for at least a few seconds. Her brother could have been anywhere that evening. Her mother had lied to the police. She had snuck out while Eira slept.

"Who was he?"

"Does the name Lars-Åke mean anything to you?"

Eira shook her head.

"He lived nearby," said Unni. "I never met him, but she pointed out his house once, down towards the river, by the beach near the old customs house, you know, where some of the events happened in 1931 . . ."

"Do you remember if it was blue?"

"What?"

"The house, was it blue with white corners?"

Unni nodded and Eira saw it clearly, as though caught in a camera flash: the empty house where a couple of neighbors had found her mother one night in the recent past.

A confused old woman losing her way? Not quite. She had just forgotten that her lover no longer lived there.

"When I moved in with you back then," Unni continued, "Kerstin was beside herself with worry. It was only once they caught the boy who did it that she broke down, told me she hadn't been honest with the police. She was ashamed, of course she was—for leaving you alone, too. But you were sleeping, and it's not like you were a baby. If she'd changed her story, things would've been even worse for Magnus. If he said he was at home, she believed him, she had to. And in the end it made no difference: they caught the person who did it."

Unni tensed and straightened up.

"Why exactly are you asking about all this?"

Eira chose not to drive straight home that evening, and continued into Kramfors. Parked up in her usual spot outside the police station.

It was only a short walk from there, along the edge of the small river. Hällgumsgatan wasn't exactly idyllic, but it was somewhere you could find an empty apartment ready to move into the very next day. Kramfors's own version of a social housing program had been planned during the sixties, back when the authorities were confident the area would continue to need large numbers of workers. Until the very recent past, when the borders closed, the three-story blocks had been used to house asylum seekers. The local restaurant, Träffen, still served ćevapčići following the previous wave of refugees.

Now every other window was dark and empty again, without any flowers on the balconies.

Eira didn't send a message to see whether he was still awake until she was already outside his door, once it felt too late to change her mind.

August came down to let her in, barefoot.

"Sorry for bothering you so late," she said.

"You're not," he said. "I was actually thinking about calling you . . ."

"Were you?"

Eira didn't give him time to answer. He was wearing nothing but an open shirt and a pair of boxers, and she peeled off his shirt the minute they stepped into his flat. They got no farther than the hallway, a suitably placed chest of drawers. Her arms got tangled up in his as they tried to pull off her clothes. The newly fledged police assistant may have tried to say something, but she kissed away the damn words, she ate him up.

Take my thoughts away, take me away.

It was only later that he managed to speak, as they lay sprawled in his hot, sparsely furnished room, still sticky—they had done it again in his bed. He had an Ikea sofa, a TV; it was an apartment for people on the run, passing through. Anonymous, with no memories.

Eira would have preferred to lie in silence. Staring up at the ceiling, exhausted, her mind blank.

"I thought you didn't want to do this anymore," August said with a laugh.

"Do you always know what you want?"

"Absolutely."

He laughed again. Eira threw back the duvet. It was too hot. Thanks to the sixties' vogue for light and air, the buildings were set back from one another, meaning she could stand naked by the open balcony door on the third floor without anyone seeing her.

No one but him, the boy from Stockholm, who couldn't understand the most basic things about silence.

"I was thinking about calling you tonight, like I said, but then it got late and I thought you might want . . ."

"We don't have to talk about it," said Eira.

"OK. Sure."

Mirrored in the glass, she saw him sit up on the edge of the bed, pull a sheet around his shoulders. The air outside felt slightly raw, almost chilly. She liked it. The feeling of moisture on her skin.

"I just thought you might want to know . . ." he continued.

"Why do we always have to know? Can't things just *be* sometimes?"

"Sorry," he said. "You're right. I need to learn not to take my work home with me—and into the bedroom at that, it's pretty messed up. Your approach is far better. Switching off. It's healthy."

Eira turned around. "What are you talking about?"

"The body, obviously," said August. "The one you found in Lockne.

I heard just before I left, and then I thought about you. I don't know how involved you are now—they said you'd be back with us next week, which is good. For me, I mean."

"Is that what you were trying to tell me?" Eira felt like an idiot. She was an idiot. Thinking he wanted to call her to . . . "What did you hear?"

"That it's not her, the body they found."

"What?"

"It's not Lina Stavred."

Eira stared at August. Tried to understand.

"But they can't have the DNA results already, it's only been one day . . ."

"They found the skull."

The skull. The simplest way to determine the sex of a skeleton. The eye sockets, the jaw, the curve of the back of the head . . . Eira suddenly felt so defenseless. Like one of those dreams in which she accidentally went to school naked. She grabbed the blanket from the floor and wrapped it around herself.

"Is it a man?" she asked.

August nodded.

"And the timeframe?"

"The timeframe?"

"Yeah, is the body recent or . . ."

"I don't know anything about that."

It struck Eira that she had two missed calls. Unknown number. She had forgotten to switch her phone off silent after the jazz club, and had only realized as she was standing outside, sending a text with a pounding heart. Which pocket was her phone in, trousers or jacket? She rummaged through the clothes scattered across the floor.

August's voice behind her:

"But they were talking about opening a preliminary investigation, so I guess that means it's not from the Middle Ages."

Many of the 220 bones that make up an adult skeleton were still missing, but the man had at least begun to take shape.

Whoever he was.

The cooling unit made the air inside the old engine room almost icily cold. The various objects were gone from the floor—the dress, the beer cans, and everything else that had been sent off for analysis—and the bones had been laid out in their place. The cold air was to preserve them while they waited for specialist transportation. The blue clay had been rinsed off, revealing a white substance on some of the bones.

"Corpse wax," Shirin ben Hassen explained, adding another piece to the puzzle of the man's left leg. "It could have something to do with the blue clay. I've seen it before, when we recovered the crew of the DC-3. You know, the one shot down off the coast of Gotland during the Cold War; they found it fifteen years ago. They had been embedded in blue clay, too."

It was Shirin who had tried to reach Eira the night before, wanting to talk to someone with knowledge of the case. GG had given her Eira's number. He was busy elsewhere, apparently, though he had now sent a message to say that he was on his way from Sundsvall.

Shirin had been ankle deep in the blue clay since seven o'clock that morning, and didn't have much time for people who would rather spend their weekends watching TV or sleeping in. Not when it looked like the guy's head had been caved in.

"You can tell that already?" asked Eira.

When it came to analyzing skeletal remains, it often took half an eternity to determine the cause of death—assuming anyone ever managed. Shirin pulled out an iPad and showed Eira a photograph of the man's skull, which had already been sent off to the lab.

"You see this?"

She scrolled slowly through a series of images taken from different angles. Sure enough, the skull had a number of typical male characteristics. Square eye sockets, a powerful jaw. The forehead more sloping than a woman's.

"Someone gave him a pretty nasty bash," she said, enlarging the image. Small indentations in the bone, a nick.

"Could that have happened afterwards, in the water?"

"Lucky for this guy it was me they sent." Shirin's fingers brushed across the screen, almost like she was stroking it. "Often when they recover the body, there isn't anyone with osteological expertise present—even though we do try to demand it. It can take weeks to find something like this otherwise."

Yes, the injuries had arisen prior to death. They were looking at a case of serious, likely lethal violence.

Shirin pointed into the forge.

"If it happened in there," she said, "there's no shortage of iron bars and sledgehammers and other rusty objects; the place is a treasure trove for anyone wanting to cave someone's head in. With a bit of luck we'll find some DNA, but if it were me I would've tossed the murder weapon as far into the river as I could. Getting rid of a body is much trickier. Coffee?"

"Please."

There was a thermos and a few mugs on a collapsible table outside. Eira gratefully helped herself to a couple of cinnamon swirls.

The greenery round about seemed to have come alive after the rain, crawling and buzzing with life.

Shirin excused herself to go and talk to a colleague. Eira remained where she was, trying to process the fact that, despite everything, they had managed to uncover a murder. It wasn't Lina, but someone out there would soon learn what had happened to a relative—

assuming the man's family was still alive. She remembered a case in which an excavator had found human remains in a park in the Södermalm area of Stockholm. The murder investigation was eventually closed when they discovered the body had been buried in a cholera cemetery dating back to the eighteenth century.

"I know it's too early to ask," she said once the forensic technician had returned, "but can you say anything at all about the timeframe?"

Shirin pulled off her gloves and pumped herself a fresh cup of coffee.

"No earlier than April 1960," she said. "And most likely after 1974."

Eira laughed. "Are you serious?"

"Come with me."

The ground was muddy after the previous day's rain. A tent had been put up down by the edge of the river, and the area had been marked out with pegs and string, some of them in the water, forming a grid. Every discovery was given coordinates. There was a camera on a tripod, carefully documenting everything.

Eira said hello to the two technicians working inside the tent.

"We found this this morning," said Shirin.

She paused by a plastic container right by the beach. When Eira leaned in, she saw a shoe floating inside.

"We're keeping it filled with river water to maintain the same temperature until we can send it off, to prevent any decomposition from setting in. We want to know everything this little beauty can tell us."

It was a black leather boot. Laced, with a thick sole. It didn't look brand new, but nor was it especially old.

"Is that a Doc Martens?"

"Yup, the classic 1460 model. It first went on sale in April 1960, hence the name."

"Are you sure it's his?"

"Well, no one lost this by accident, that's for sure." She turned the container around so that the boot moved slightly. Eira could make out something white inside.

"That's the foot you can see. More corpse wax." Shirin took a bite of the cinnamon swirl in her hand. "And since we found it at the end of a right leg, it likely belongs to the same man."

"So why after 1974?"

"That's when Sko-Uno opened on Gamla Brogatan in Stockholm. Obviously our guy could have bought his Docs in London before then, but that doesn't seem too likely unless he was a British factory worker. The boots didn't become trendy among teenagers until the late sixties. The skinheads were first, then the neo-Nazis—they liked the steel toe caps . . ."

"A neo-Nazi?"

"Doubtful," said Shirin. "But this is all guesswork now, so don't write it up in any reports."

She pointed to the boot with a stick. "The Nazis laced their boots all the way to the top. I actually don't think they ever forgot."

Eira leaned in closer. The boot had eight eyelets on each side, but it was laced only halfway, with the top four holes empty. Even the knot had been preserved by the blue clay and whatever else was on the riverbed.

"I'd guess our guy was a grunge kid," said Shirin.

Eira laughed again. "Do you have special training in subcultures or something?"

"No, not exactly," said Shirin. "But I was a teenager in the nineties when Dr. Martens were super popular and Kurt Cobain was god. I saved my pocket money for over six months just to go to Sko-Uno and buy a pair. I would rather have died than lace them all the way up."

A cool breeze cut across the river, making the surface ripple.

"So what you're saying is that the body ended up in the water sometime between the early nineties, when grunge was big, and . . ."

"A guess, like I said."

The sound of a phone ringing interrupted them. It was GG. He was up by the road, wondering where exactly they were. Shirin took them through everything again once he arrived, and Eira listened as she watched a family of frogs cross the path.

"So he didn't drown?" asked GG.

"And bury himself under the remains of a steamboat quay?" Shirin countered.

"Was he there before it collapsed, or did someone bury him there afterwards?"

"Even without the boot, I'd say afterwards. We've sent off some requests for images of the area over the past few decades."

"Not historic, in other words," said GG.

"Not unless grunge is historic."

Just over half an hour later, GG and Eira left together. GG stuck to the edge of the trampled path, where the mud wasn't quite so sticky and deep.

"So, what should we make of all this?" he asked once they had reached the cars, pausing to light a cigarette. "Is it a coincidence we've found one body while looking for another?"

Eira didn't know what to say, but he probably wasn't expecting an answer.

"I've spoken to the prosecutor," he continued. "We're looking at a new preliminary investigation into the murder."

He exhaled the smoke in a long sigh.

"Guess I can take some time off this autumn instead. Or winter. Get away when it's really dark."

A thought came and went, wondering how it had gone with his girlfriend, having a baby, all that.

"I hope we can borrow you again," said GG. "Your local knowledge has been invaluable; you've been able to see things no one else has. Unless you're on leave, that is?"

"No . . . I don't have any time booked off before August."

Eira noticed a swarm of blackflies around his head. She could see the sign for an old school in the distance, a memory of the once lively community. She could just make out the roof of the forge building, the wound on the ridge where the tiles had come loose.

Local knowledge. That was such a superficial phrase, as thin as the new ice in November. It said nothing about the depths of the abyss, or the complications lurking beneath, in which every person was connected to another, memories tricking and deceiving. It said nothing about love.

"I can't," she said.

"Oh, OK . . ." GG seemed surprised. "I got the impression you enjoyed working with us?"

"I do," she said. "Absolutely. It's just . . ."

Words, those damned words. The feeling that she should just tell him the truth. But why bring up her brother's name, an old investigation that had long since been shelved? Did she have to mention it? This investigation was completely separate. It was about the murder of a man, not Lina; it might not even have happened during the nineties. What proof did they have of that? A shoelace?

At the same time, she saw the earlier finds. The dress that might have been Lina's. The sense that it was all too much of a coincidence.

"It just feels a bit disloyal," she eventually said. "To my colleagues in Kramfors, I mean. Before long we'll have nothing but brand-new police assistants straight out of the academy."

"I understand."

GG pinched out his cigarette, stamping on the last few flakes of ash that sailed down to the ground. He glanced back towards where the sawmill had once stood, to the newly clear sky above.

"Grunge," he said. "What else does that tell us about our man, while we wait to find out who he is?"

"That he was young?"

"I've got a pair, you know," said GG.

"Of Doc Martens?"

"Mmm. Bought them last autumn after I decided I needed to re-invent myself, but I've barely even worn them. They're stiff as hell, terrible for walking in."

"There probably weren't many older men walking about in Doc Martens back then . . ."

"Excuse me?"

"I mean grown men, in the prime of their life."

"Thank you," GG said with a smile.

Eira felt a flicker of sadness, a melancholy at no longer being able to work with him.

"Like Shirin said, they were mostly a youth culture thing, a kind of rebellion . . ." A sudden thought came to her, not because she really knew—to her, the nineties belonged to the Spice Girls—but because she did know something about longing for the kinds of things you saw only in magazines and on TV, someplace else.

"There probably weren't many kids in them either," she continued. "Not here, not in the nineties. Maybe in Härnösand they had the kind of guy who walked around in vintage coats and played in bands, but in Kramfors? In the villages round about? People didn't have that kind of money. I think a pair of Doc Martens would've stuck out."

"See, I told you," GG said with a sigh. "Local knowledge."

Not much was happening in the southern Ångermanland police district on the day Eira returned to the beat.

An assault in Bollsta, at an address familiar to the team; a break-in at the kiosk by the swimming area in Lo. The perpetrator had made off with the stock of sweets and emptied the ice cream freezer. A local tragedy, but there wasn't much for the police to do other than show the local residents' association and a handful of upset children that they were taking it seriously.

"I've got an interview next week," August announced as they drove away with the windows rolled down. "For a post with Stockholm Västerort."

"Congratulations," said Eira. "Good luck. I hope you get it, really."

"That's if I want it."

"Because it's not inner city?" She felt herself getting annoyed. Fresh out of training, but the jobs that were out there still weren't good enough for him.

"I could also stay here," said August. "If a job opens up."

"You're kidding."

August was quiet. He wasn't laughing. Sought out her free hand, grazed her thigh. That was how far they had come.

"No one *wants* to stay here," said Eira. "People stay because they've got family up here, roots, memories; because they can't do without the hunting and fishing and the river and the forest, because they've started a family and want their kids to be able to run free. But not because of a job. You could spend thirty years as a police assistant up here. Management positions only come up every fifteen years, if you want to make a career."

"Maybe I like it up here."

"You'd go crazy."

"There's a calmness up here that I've never felt anywhere else. Being so close to nature, feeling like you're really breathing clean air. And this light . . ."

"You've never been here in November. You don't know just how dark it gets then. You've never been stuck in a freezing car that won't start in January."

"Can always huddle up," he said with a laugh, squeezing her thigh.

"And what would your girlfriend make of that?"

"I told you, we don't own each other."

Eira turned on the radio to avoid getting dragged into that discussion. They were playing a summer hit with a reggae beat from a few years earlier and August sang along, drumming his fingers in the open window.

There was nothing wrong with his voice. It was the happy-go-lucky, carefree side of him that made her uncomfortable, the way he seemed to exist entirely in the moment. Blurting out things like that, things he didn't mean anything by.

She slowed down and turned off onto a narrow track that rose sharply over a ridge.

"Aren't we meant to be heading back to Kramfors?" he asked.

"Yeah," said Eira. "But this won't take long, it's not a big detour."

On the other side of the ridge, a lush valley took over. Eira had always liked that it reminded her of an alpine landscape, with rolling meadows and grazing cows, scattered farms.

A straight gravel track led up to a house at the edge of the wood. The lawn was neat, but otherwise the place bore every sign of having been abandoned. With a fence that was bowing in several places, paint that had been worn down by the elements. She thought she could see a birds' nest in the chimney pot.

"Are you buying a house?" asked August. "Or do you just want to make out?"

Eira turned off the engine and climbed out of the car.

"Honestly," he said, standing behind her as he surveyed the decay. "Doesn't it need a bit much work?"

"This is where she lived," said Eira.

August was quiet for a moment, a fact she appreciated. It was a place that demanded reverence, to bow down to the sorrow it bore.

Either that or he was simply slow.

"Lina, you mean?"

"Mmm."

"Hasn't anyone else lived here since?"

"They moved to Finland pretty soon after, wound everything up. Her dad worked with agricultural machinery and I think her mum was a teacher."

She saw the curtains still hanging in the windows. That wasn't unusual. People didn't always know whether they would be coming back.

"Once a year had passed, they asked for her to be declared dead—as soon as they could, in other words, considering there was no body."

August walked along the fence, pushed open the gate. The hinges creaked softly.

"How could anyone just leave a house like this?" he asked. "It's the value they're destroying."

"I guess they didn't really think about that."

"I don't just mean this cottage, everywhere. Why don't people buy them up—OK, not this one, but all the others—and renovate them, sell them to people from Stockholm or Germany? You could do good business like that."

"If you renovate somewhere up here," said Eira, feeling irritated that he had called it a cottage when it was actually a fairly grand Ångermanland-style building over two floors, "then it's because the house needs it, or because you want to make things nice round about. You'll never get your money back. It costs far more to renovate than you can squeeze out of the property market."

"That's just because people haven't discovered the area yet. Once they see how beautiful it is . . ."

She felt his breath on her neck, his arms around her waist.

"My, my, what's going on here?"

Eira struggled out of August's embrace and turned around. An elderly woman in shorts and a sun hat was standing on the gravel track, clutching a lead in one hand. Her dog was likely running loose somewhere nearby.

"For all this business to be dredged up again," she said.

They moved closer and introduced themselves. There was something about the woman's surname that sounded familiar. Nyberg was fairly common, but still.

"There have been journalists snooping about out here too, filming things, ever since you found that body in Lockne. But it wasn't Lina, was it? They said on the news that it was a man, do you know who . . . ?"

"Not yet," said Eira.

The woman squinted in the sun. "So what are you doing here, at the Stavreds' place? Surely there's nothing left to see here. The police asked around back then, they investigated all sorts. They were good people who just wanted to pay their way."

She turned towards the house, perhaps more than to Eira, as though the Stavreds were still present and could hear her words.

"Did you know them?"

"Yes, oh yes, of course. I live just over there." She pointed to a red semidetached house no more than two hundred meters away. "The girls were always out playing when they were little—and after that, too. Once they found other games to play, I suppose you could say."

Nyberg, Nyberg . . . Names and statements from the witness interviews tumbled through Eira's head. Neighbors, friends.

"What's your daughter's name?"

"Elvira, though people have always called her Elvis. Why do you want to know?"

"I think I recognize the name."

"Yes, she's got the nail salon in Kramfors, maybe you've met her there? Though she's called Sjögren now, that's her married name . . ."

The woman glanced at Eira's nails. They certainly didn't look like they regularly saw the inside of a salon. Unpainted, cut short.

"Do you really have to bother her with all that stuff again? You have no idea how long it took for Elvis to dare to think to the future again. Years and years. She and Lina had known each other all their lives. I held that girl in my arms myself. He's the one who did it, Hagström's lad, it was solved, it's just the papers speculating like usual, isn't it?"

The woman was anxious, that much was clear. Perhaps not even she fully believed what she was saying.

"Who cuts the grass?" asked August.

"If you let the forest take over, that's it. At least this way people can see that there's someone here from time to time. That's not a crime, is it?"

They had made it only a few kilometers when Eira's phone pinged with a message.

Where are you?

She pulled over to the side of the road. It was from GG. She wrote back to say that they were in Bjärtrå, on their way in.

Got time to swing by Kungsgården?

Eira's pulse picked up. No new alerts had come in from the command center in Umeå, so an afternoon coffee at the station was virtually all that was beckoning.

OK, why? she wrote, waiting for a horse box to pass before she pulled back out onto the road. She drove slowly, clutching her phone to the wheel, saw a new message come in.

Ask Nydalen if this could have been the person he saw.

Ping. Ping.

A face appeared on her screen.

Long, dark hair. Narrow face, softish features. Eyes staring, like the majority of people in a passport photograph. The young man looked to be in his twenties.

"What's this about?" August asked, for the second or third time.

"Looks like they've identified the body in Lockne."

"Oh shit."

Her phone beeped again with two other images. The same face, slightly younger in one of the shots; the same long hair, but in a green-and-white Hammarby football jersey this time. A Stockholm team. As Eira pulled into the Nydalens' yard, she realized she had been right: he was from elsewhere.

There were two cars parked outside the garage, one gleaming and new, from a rental company. A young woman came out onto the porch. She was wearing a pair of rolled-up jeans, and put down a black rubbish bag.

"That's our daughter Jenny, she came home," Tryggve explained as he walked towards them, hesitant, suspicious. "From Australia. Do you really have to cause a fuss with her too?"

"I just wanted to ask you to take a look at a couple of pictures," said Eira.

"Will this never end?"

Eira brought up the first image and held out her phone.

"Could this be the person you saw on the river the night Lina Stavred went missing?"

Tryggve patted his pockets and excused himself, heading into the house to fetch his glasses. The young woman slammed the lid of the bin and came towards them, stopping at a safe distance. She looked younger than her twenty-seven years.

"What do you want?" she asked, shoving her hands into her pockets, defiantly hunching her shoulders.

"It's to do with another case."

"Right."

Jenny lingered, as though she was expecting questions.

"It must've come as a real shock to you," said Eira, hearing just how pathetic the words sounded. What were you supposed to say to someone whose mother had confessed to murder? Who had just found out that her father wasn't who she thought he was?

"I came back to go through my stuff," she said. "I only took a backpack when I left. I thought there might be something from my childhood that I wanted to keep, before Dad sells up, but what would that be? Memories of what?"

"Is he going to sell?"

"He can do what he wants as far as I'm concerned." She looked over to the house. Her father had just reemerged, glasses in one hand. "Looks nice on the outside, huh?" she said. "God, they worked so hard on the house and the garden, trying to make everything perfect."

Eira wanted to ask more, but that wasn't why they were there. She was no longer investigating the murder of Sven Hagström. Not everything could be explained. They had the confession, the murder weapon, and a motive. The evidence against Mejan was strong; there was no reason for the police to delve into her psyche or her background. That was the defense team's problem now, if they chose to pursue that angle. Or the court's, once it handed down its verdict.

Jenny turned and walked away as her father approached, kicking a football into one of the lovingly planned flower beds. She turned her head as they passed.

Tryggve watched his daughter for a moment before putting on his glasses and taking Eira's phone.

"Who is this?" he asked, studying the image.

"You said the person rowing the boat had dark hair hanging over their face . . . ?"

"Yes . . . I remember the hair, it was down to her shoulders like that, and I remember she was a useless rower. Women in boats, you know?" He laughed, hoping for August to join in, then lowered his eyes when he got no response.

"But you think it could've been him?" he asked.

"What do you think?"

"I don't know." He paused on the photograph with the football shirt. "He does look a bit like a girl. Skinny, not much of a bloke . . ."

"I know it must be hard to tell this long after the event," said Eira.

Tryggve handed back her phone.

"Yeah," he said, his intonation betraying his northern roots. Eira found herself wondering if that was where he would go now, whether those towns and villages had the ability to forget. "It could've been someone else, but it also could've been him."

It was thanks to his teeth that they had been able to identify him so quickly.

Kenneth Emanuel Isaksson.

"We found him in the missing-persons database," said Silje, who was temporarily back in Kramfors. She turned her laptop for Eira to see.

Born 1976 in Hägersten Parish, Stockholm. Kenneth had just turned twenty when he was reported missing in early June 1996.

Eira counted forward and back. That was less than a month before Lina vanished, not even four weeks—twenty-six days, to be precise.

"He ran away from the Hassela Collective in northern Hälsingland," said Silje.

"Is that place still open?" Eira recalled a treatment home for young addicts 150 or so kilometers south, on the other side of the county line.

"There's something else there now, but back when our guy was there, their comradely support in the spirit of Marxism was still in full swing."

"I remember the place was pretty controversial."

"Collective child-rearing," said Silje. "They achieved quite a lot, but they also got a load of criticism—for encouraging the kids to inform on one another, among other things."

Silje scrolled through the material, a summary of the police investigation into Kenneth Isaksson's disappearance in 1996.

"They thought he'd run off to Stockholm. He'd done it a few

times before, but the police always found him in the city in one or the other usual places."

"Have you managed to speak to any of his relatives?"

"His dad is dead and his mum broke off all contact with him the year before he vanished. Kenneth stole pretty much everything he could sell from their house."

"So what was he doing in Ådalen?"

"Hiding? Maybe he didn't want to get caught again. Or reported."

"He could've been making his way somewhere else," said Eira. "To Norway or Finland . . . He could get hold of drugs pretty much anywhere."

"The people at Hassela said he'd been clean for a while."

"And no one knew where he was going?"

"Apparently not," said Silje. "I guess he'd kept his mouth shut around his friends this time."

Eira read through the relatively short text again.

"If it was him out on the river with Lina Stavred," she said, "then it can't have been the first time they met. She hardly walked down to the river on a whim; they must have agreed to meet."

"Hmm," said Silje. "Some would say it's too early to be drawing conclusions like that."

Eira turned back to the image of Kenneth Isaksson. His messy hair, the elusive look in his eyes.

"If you were sixteen or seventeen," she said, "would you have been into this guy?"

Silje looked into the boy's piercing eyes.

"I would have liked the fact he was on the run, or maybe it would've scared me. God knows which would've won out. I guess I'd have thought he looked like a rock star."

"Lina walked all the way down to Marieberg," said Eira. "That's over a kilometer from her house, almost two. She was dressed up, didn't want to get dirty . . ." Eira was now back in the woods, among the nettles, on the trail leading down to the water. She pictured the boy in the boat. Where had he got hold of it? Stolen, of course.

Dozens of rowing boats could go missing in a single season. The beach, that was where the last sign of Lina had been found.

"The makeup brush," she said.

"What?"

"It was found in the sand. Lina put on makeup before he arrived."

The air was thick with acetone and perfume. Calling it a salon was probably a bit of a stretch—it was in the basement of an ordinary residential building—but Elvira Sjögren had done her very best to make it look like one.

Posters of French landscapes on the walls, mirrors with golden frames, candles on every free surface. Sandalwood and rosemary.

"My God, woman," she said, studying Eira's hands. "When did you last have your nails done?"

"I just want something simple," said Eira.

"You don't want to treat yourself? I think you deserve it."

The woman known as Elvis dug out some boxes of artificial nails painted in every color under the sun, long and pointed, rounded and shapely, as Eira debated how honest to be. As a police officer, she was walking a fine line—assuming she hadn't already crossed it—but no one could hold it against her for wanting to look nice.

She pointed to a near-white shade with a hint of pearlescent shimmer.

"And we'll build them up a bit, too," said Elvis, gently rubbing Eira's fingers between her own.

"Not too much," said Eira. "Having long nails is no good in my job." That wasn't strictly true; plenty of her fellow officers wore bright pink fake nails to compensate for the masculine uniform.

"God, that's a shame, what do you do?"

"Police."

"Ooh, that sounds exciting, you must see so much."

"Just keep it very simple, like I said," Eira told her. Elvira gave her a sad smile, as though she pitied her for not thinking she was worthy of more.

She was led over to a chair, and Elvira started filing and moisturizing, talking about different ways to strengthen her nails or build them up using some kind of gel-like material.

"I think I recognize you," Eira said after a round of chitchat about the weather and holidays. "Weren't you friends with Lina, the girl who went missing?"

"I was. She was my best friend."

Forty minutes, Eira thought. That was how long it would take to do ten nails. Thirty-five to go.

"It must've been awful—for you too, I mean."

Elvis adjusted the bright lamp above the table.

"You just want to forget, but you can't. The whole thing actually came up again recently, when the papers started saying they might have found her body . . . You start thinking, OK, so there'll be a funeral. They only had a memorial back then, but it was still nice, they played her favorite music and talked about what a great person she was and could have been . . ."

Working on Eira's nails, the woman had no choice but to look down, though perhaps she would have avoided making eye contact anyway. There was a certain weightlessness to words that weren't deeply rooted.

"I didn't know her myself," said Eira. "I was too young. But my brother did. They were dating, actually."

The tool in Elvis's hand slipped, something sharp hitting the cuticle. She looked up.

"Sjödin! God, that never even occurred to me. Are you Magnus's sister? Of course you bloody are, I knew his little sister was in the police now."

The air suddenly felt slightly easier to breathe, despite the candles, as Elvis dropped the usual salon chat about what a woman was worth, what she should treat herself to.

Eira dodged a few questions about Magnus, about how he was these days, what he was up to, who he was seeing.

"What was she really like, Lina?"

"What has Magnus said?"

"Nothing," said Eira. "You know what brothers are like."

"He probably just wanted to forget too." Elvis put down the nail file. Picked up one of the small bottles she had brought over and applied a neat layer of undercoat, holding Eira's hand steady. "People only ever talked about how nice and beautiful she was. You couldn't disagree with them—you'd look like a terrible person."

"Do you remember Ricken?"

"Of course I do."

"He said that Lina was just messing with Magnus."

"She was the worst," said Elvis. "Sorry, I'd never say that to anyone else, but you are his sister, you might as well know. Lina broke up with him and then took him back, she was seeing other people but claimed she still had feelings for him—you know how it is, the person who's in love practically loses their mind. You don't think you can live without them in the end."

She pushed Eira's hand beneath a heat lamp and left it to rest there for a while.

"I was actually kind of into Magnus myself," she said. Her cheeks flushed slightly, or maybe it was just the heat of the lamp. "Not that I told the police or anything, they probably would've thought I killed her in some fit of jealousy. But I never stood a chance against Lina, not in anything. I sort of started seeing him after she disappeared, I guess it was a comfort thing, or I don't know . . . I couldn't be like her. Magnus changed too, I noticed that. He was always pretty lively before, I'm sure you know. Someone who slaloms through life, this way and that; the type of person everyone loves because he's so handsome and nice. And kind too, I always thought he was kind, but then . . . Sorry to have to say this, but he wasn't so kind to me. Told me to stop being so clingy when I just wanted to hang out . . . Well, you know. When you get too keen. I thought he was sad and that I was the only person there for him, that he needed to be comforted. Love, you know? Ugh, God, sorry, I forgot . . ."

Elvis turned off the lamp and got to work on the next coat. Some of the varnish ended up on Eira's skin, but she wiped it away. Did the same thing again.

"So he's OK these days?" she asked, voice hesitant.

"Magnus? Yeah, yeah, he's got a girlfriend over by the coast."

"I hope she's good to him."

"I think she is."

"He could be jealous, too," Elvis continued. "Not with me, but with Lina. Properly green with envy, you know? To the extent that he would spend half the night standing outside her house just to see whether she brought anyone else home. I lived really close by. I used to hear him pull up on his motorbike."

"Was he right? Do you know whether Lina was seeing anyone else?"

"She'd kill me if I told you."

Eira smiled. "Well, she can hardly do that now."

"No, but . . . All that stuff about how bloody saintly she was, that's still there. You don't talk crap about the dead, you know? You're supposed to rise above all that. Start sobbing and going on about how she was the most amazing friend ever."

"But . . . ?"

"She could be so mean. One minute she wanted me to come over because I was her best friend in the whole world, and then she'd call me a retard—all because I wasn't as smart as her. Just because she read these fancy books, French authors and that kind of thing, books you could barely even understand. I'm sure she just pretended to read them, as though anyone actually cared." Elvis looked up again. "I would never use that word, 'retard,' I mean. But that's what people said back then. You wouldn't do it now. Or no one with any sense would, anyway. It's a handicap—though you're not meant to say that either. I should know, I work as a care assistant too. 'Functional diversity,' that's the term. Still, that's what Lina called people when she thought they were being idiots. And I just kept on hanging out with her."

Elvis reached away from the table and grabbed some paper from a holder, blew her nose. She wiped her hands on a wet wipe.

"You should try a bit more color, if you ask me."

"Maybe next time."

Eira studied her as she screwed the lids back onto the bottles, put everything in order.

"Who was Lina seeing? The person you weren't allowed to talk about?"

"I know I should've told the police, but I was only fifteen . . . If the police had found them, Lina would've hated me forever. She'd lied to her parents and said she was hanging out with me, that's why they never asked. Lina's folks were so strict, teetotalers, they went crazy when she snuck out to go drinking and that kind of thing. One time it got so bad they said they were going to send her off to live with relatives in Finland, or to some school somewhere, with super-strict rules and curfews . . ."

"So what was Lina really doing that evening?"

"She was going to leave," said Elvis. "Clear off for good with that guy. I thought that was what she'd done, so I didn't say anything, and then all that stuff about Olof came out, about what really happened . . ."

"Who was he?"

"She never told me his name."

"Did Magnus know?"

"If I know Lina, she probably threw it right in his face. She told me that the sex was amazing, that the guys round here had no idea . . . And poor little me, the 'retard,' who had no idea about sex . . . Well, I was just thinking about Magnus, about how upset he'd be. But she was wrong, by the way. He was great in bed. Oops, sorry, you probably didn't want to know that."

"So he wasn't from round here?" said Eira.

Elvis shook her head.

"How did they meet?"

"She was hitchhiking."

"He had a car?"

"Yeah, I guess he must have, because they'd fucked in it— assuming that was true. Lina was always saying stuff like that to tease me, because I didn't have a boyfriend, and then she'd make me swear not to tell anyone. I was meant to just, like, coo over her secrets and feel jealous. She even told me he was wanted, to make it even more exciting, like he was in some American film or something. It was so typical of her, to make up something like that to make me feel stupid and inexperienced."

Eira wondered whether she would put two and two together once the picture of Kenneth Isaksson was made public. The next day or the day after, it wouldn't be long.

She pulled out her phone and opened the payment app, entered the ID number from the poster on the wall.

"I forgot to ask how much it would be," she said.

There they were, chatting about the weather. Eating individual portions of oven-baked salmon. Eira thought her mother seemed slightly skeptical, poking at her food. Salmon was supposed to come fresh from the river, caught by someone you knew, not wrapped in plastic from a farm in Norway, shipped via the local grocery store to your kitchen table.

"What did you say his name was?" Kerstin had stopped chewing.

"Lars-Åke, he lived down by the old customs house. Don't you remember him, Mum? I got the impression the two of you were pretty close."

Her gaze was distant, elsewhere, lingering for slightly too long.

"I really should scrape the paint off these windows this year."

Eira couldn't work out what her mother had forgotten and what she was running away from, or whether they were sometimes the same thing.

She walked down to the river after dinner, past the blue house where the man called Lars-Åke supposedly once lived. It was empty, though it didn't seem to have been abandoned. Perhaps they had children who couldn't agree on the inheritance. There were countless reasons why a house might be left vacant: families falling apart, people dying, memories no one wanted to touch.

Eira followed the shore, thinking back to the summer when they threw their dolls into the water there, wanting to see them float—or sink. The river grew darker and the ocean that took over to the east was infinite, though it was really just an inland sea. She wasn't used to how quiet the area had become. From time to time she could still hear the traffic roaring through the community like it had when she was younger, before the new bridge was built along the coast and the E4 was redrawn. Eight minutes had been shaved off the journey between north and south, and Lunde had ended up on a back road and withered away.

With the river so low, there were small pools of water dotted along the bank. They were all stagnant and cloudy, dragonflies dancing over the surface. Eira had caught a few once, while they were still nymphs. Three of them, in glass jars on her windowsill, with air holes poked in the lids. She had wanted to watch them develop, to see their wings take on color, emerald green and sky blue.

But when she woke the next morning the jars were gone. She found them in the grass outside. Magnus had let her nymphs go.

Never trap a living thing. If I catch you doing it again, I'll give you a smack.

Eira dialed his number again. Still no answer.

She saw one of the dragonflies dart and catch an insect midair. Back when she was younger, she had only ever found them beautiful. Enchanting. She hadn't realized they were predators.

Don't you get that they can die?

A moment later, her phone started ringing.

Magnus's number, but a woman's voice. "He's not here. I don't know where he is."

Marina Arnesdotter, the woman he was staying with. It was hard to hear what she was saying; she sounded like she was crying.

"I saw that you'd called," she said. "I've been trying to reach Magnus all day but I've just realized his phone is here. Why would he leave without his phone?"

"What happened?"

Eira sat down on a rock by one of the pools. The blackflies quickly became unbearable, the swarm following her when she got back to her feet.

Magnus had started drinking a few days earlier, got incredibly drunk. They had argued. About the alcohol at first—Marina knew he had a problem, he had never tried to hide that from her, but he had promised to stop—and then about everything else: Magnus felt like she didn't want him there anymore, that he wasn't good enough for her, and then he had started accusing her of the most insane things.

"Like what?"

"Like sleeping with other people, for example—which I'm not. Who could it even be? I spend all my time in the workshop and the gallery."

"You said a few days ago, but can you be more exact?"

"It wasn't even evening. I mean, who starts drinking in the middle of the day? And when I woke up this morning he was gone. I always get up before him."

Eira forgot all about the blackflies, barely even felt them biting. She managed to get the woman to tell her when it had started.

"But he was pretty jumpy even before that, ever since you were here actually . . ."

It could be a coincidence. The woman had probably wanted them to have a glass of wine, a cozy evening together, but Eira knew it wouldn't be cozy. Marina Arnesdotter was likely one of those people who had one glass and ended up drinking the entire bottle, but if Magnus did the same he might keep drinking for weeks. Eira tried her best to convince herself that it was the woman's fault, with her ceramic hearts and the natural wines she almost certainly drank, but there was no escaping the facts.

It had started the same day the news of the find in Lockne broke.

"I don't know what I've done wrong. Imagine if he's hurt himself . . ."

At lunchtime, on that very day. Eira could no longer feel the hand gripping her phone; it was ice cold.

"Call me the minute you hear anything."

"You too."

They were just back from a car chase that had taken them north of Sollefteå, almost all the way up to Junsele. The carjackers had driven off the road and been apprehended.

Known couriers from the criminal underworld, transporting drugs from the south of the country to the roads of Norrland, via Sundsvall. Now they were in custody, had been dropped off at the cells, and Eira was standing by the coffee machine.

"Do you have a minute?"

The voice was GG's, behind her back. Eira accidentally pressed the wrong button and a beige cappuccino the color of pale sludge started streaming into the mug instead of her usual extra-strong filter coffee.

"Absolutely," she said, turning around with a smile.

GG nodded for her to follow him, closed the door behind them.

"We've got a match on her DNA," he said.

"Lina's?"

"You were right. It was her dress. She obviously wasn't in the database, given that she disappeared before DNA analysis was really a thing, but they managed to match it to the cardigan."

Eira slumped into an armchair.

"So we're expanding the search," said GG. He was facing the window, away from her. "Bringing in more people. If she's there, we'll find her."

Eira had left her coffee at the machine, and her body was screaming for caffeine after that morning's lengthy call out. The headache started at the base of her skull, spreading upwards. A weariness in her body after the adrenaline of the chase.

"That clears Olof Hagström, in any case," she said.

"Steady on," said GG. "We still don't have a body. Theoretically, she could have dumped the dress on another occasion."

"And left there naked?"

"We found DNA from the dead man too, Kenneth Isaksson, on what looks like it might've been his sleeping bag—though some animal seems to have eaten most of it. A badger, that's what forensics thought."

"Is there anything linking him to Lina?"

"Yup. Both their DNA on the remains of a rucksack."

"So they were there together." Eira saw the same image in her mind again, of Lina walking into the woods. Summer dress, yellow cardigan, a small rucksack. The kind she used to carry to school, though that wasn't where she was going. It was like a film clip playing on repeat.

"The old forge is obviously full of DNA," GG continued. "God knows if they haven't also found the DNA of whoever used to make tools or whatever they did there."

He took a seat in the armchair opposite her.

"But they also got a hit on someone else," he said. "From a condom, of all places. There were a couple of them there."

"Yeah, I saw," said Eira, recalling the objects on the floor as she noticed the shift in his tone.

"One Magnus Erik Veine Sjödin."

The Erik was after their grandfather, Veine after their dad; names that had been passed down through the generations, so you knew where you came from and where you belonged.

"That's my brother," she said. "My older brother."

The air in the room was as stuffy as ever. No, worse than usual. Suffocating.

"I know," said GG. "His name came up immediately because we already had him on file. Nothing serious, but a few thefts, an assault . . ."

"OK."

"There were traces of Lina Stavred there, too. On the same object."

Eira felt herself falling, through the armchair and down to the ground floor. She saw herself running away.

They had been to the forge in Lockne, she thought. *They had sex. But that doesn't prove anything. All it proves is that they had sex.*

You bastard, she thought. *What the hell have you done?*

"They were dating," she said. "On and off for quite a while, but it ended before Lina disappeared." She paused, both to catch her breath and in order to speak calmly and normally. "I didn't know until I saw his name in the old preliminary investigation. I was only nine back then. No one told me anything."

"And you didn't think to mention this?"

"I did, but we weren't meant to be looking into Lina's case and there were no outstanding suspicions against him; the case was solved."

Excuses, evasion. The truth was that it had been on her mind ever since. GG studied her. *As a detective*, she thought. *He's not looking at me like a colleague right now.*

"You know you have the right not to say anything," he said. "I can get someone else to go through the material right now, if you'd prefer."

Eira tried to moisten her mouth.

"Magnus was only interviewed because of their relationship," she said. "While it was still considered a missing-person case, before anyone knew whether a crime had been committed."

"And then they narrowed in on Olof Hagström?"

"Mmm." She couldn't bear the fact that he was studying her so solemnly. "In the interviews, Magnus said he was home that night. The interview leader didn't take it any further."

"You know we have to question your brother, don't you? For the murder in Lockne."

"I understand."

What do you think? she felt like screaming. *Do I look like a complete idiot?*

"We haven't managed to find a phone contract for him," GG continued. "And we tried to track him down at the address where he's registered in Kramfors, but the woman we spoke to said he doesn't live there anymore."

"He's got another girlfriend now," said Eira, giving GG her details. "But she called me last night. He's not there either."

She mentioned Ricken's name, but they had already checked with him.

"Can you think of anywhere else?" asked GG. "Anywhere he might be?"

Eira tried to smile, but it became more of a struggle not to cry.

"Is this where I'm supposed to say that there's a secret lake? Somewhere my brother used to take me fishing?"

"For his own sake."

"Magnus was never home. He disappeared for days at a time and only occasionally showed up to sleep or to steal from the kitty. I don't know. I have no idea where he is."

Something touched his arm. There were lights, there were shadows; nothing was still.

Small dots danced in front of his eyes.

Olof wanted to scratch his arm, but he couldn't move. He wanted to tell whoever was holding his hand to go on their way. In the past he would have roared, but no sound came out.

Where am I? Can anyone tell me?

They leaned in over him. He wanted to tell them to go, to leave him in peace, but instead they gripped him and talked and said:

Olof? Can you hear me?

Olof?

Jesus Christ, it was itchy.

Eira bought a bag of sweet buns before driving over the bridge and turning off towards Klockestrand.

The summerhouse was roughly where she remembered it, just slightly farther back from the road and not quite so close to the river. She saw her former colleague come around the corner of the building.

"I'll be damned, I wasn't expecting to see you." Eilert Granlund greeted her the way people used to in the past: no unnecessary hugs, just a simple hand in the air.

Like the majority of people on that side of the river, he was overly fond of his veranda, which was well on its way to outgrowing the house itself.

"Every year I decide it could be a bit bigger," said Eilert. "You need a project, you know? To keep you from dying early."

He had a thermos of coffee ready, and Eira took the buns out of the bag. Eilert's wife came over to say hello before returning to the flower bed she was building.

"What about you, how's your project going?"

"I'm back on patrol," said Eira.

"Did it all go to pot?"

"No, no."

"But?"

"That's not what I wanted to talk to you about."

"Shoot, baby," said Eilert, tucking into one of the cinnamon buns. "But first how about a little leak about the man you found in Lockne?"

"I thought you hated the police leaking information?"

"To journalists, yes, but it's different if it's to an old fogey who doesn't talk to anyone but the snails in his garden."

Eilert's laugh was as loud and bullish as she remembered it. The corridors had been much quieter since he retired.

Eira told him about the Dr. Martens boot. That was the kind of thing he liked, details that demonstrated the skills on the force. He even demanded to listen to Nirvana to really understand what grunge was.

"If your bloke was playing this at full volume," he said, "then I can understand why someone in Lockne might have lost their patience." Another salvo of laughter.

"I've been reading the preliminary investigation into Lina's disappearance," said Eira.

"Aha, and why's that?"

Eilert Granlund stopped laughing.

"Right, right," he continued before she had time to reply. "It's to do with the murder of Hagström's old man, you called me about it, asking if that other bloke's name cropped up in the files. I've been thinking about it, whether we might have missed anything. It was such a big case, probably the biggest one I worked during my time on the force."

He rubbed his chin, shook his head, himself.

"But we solved it in the end. We did, even though it was bloody hard work. Such a young perpetrator, and the girl—having to talk to her parents . . . What you have to cling to is the knowledge that you did your job, however many sleepless nights it cost you. I don't think my wife's ever come so close to leaving me as she did then."

Everything Eira wasn't going to say was swirling round and round in her mind. About the interviews that had gone on for hours on end, the words that were put into Olof's mouth, the fact that Lina might not have been dumped in the river after all.

She wasn't there to question him, she had to remember that. She sipped her coffee and tore off pieces of cinnamon bun as he talked. Lina's parents had made a real impression on him, possibly because he saw himself in her father. Like so many others, they came from families that had been torn apart by drinking, but Stavred had chosen the life of sobriety. Both he and her mother were active in the temperance movement, and were worried about what their daughter got up to; time and time again she kept slipping through the net they had wound so tightly. Her older brothers had already moved out, so it was just Lina left, Lina and the concerns they had for her.

"You interviewed someone else . . ." said Eira.

"Yes, there were a lot, like I said. My memory never usually fails me. Crosswords, that's what the wife says, never stop doing the crossword. But I hate them, they don't go anywhere."

"Magnus Sjödin."

"I must've interviewed thousands of people over the years . . ."

"He was Lina's boyfriend. You brought him in for several interviews."

"Ah, yes, now I remember . . . Sjödin, you said? He a relative of yours?"

"My brother," said Eira. Sjödin wasn't the most unusual name in the area, so it wasn't surprising that it hadn't been his first thought.

"Ah, I had no idea." Eilert squinted towards the sun, which was still peeping up beyond the mountains. His porch had been angled so that he wouldn't miss a moment of the spectacular sunsets. A few gulls screeched as they flew overhead.

"I remember him, now that you mention it. You remember the context, the questions and answers, the faces. The impression you had of the person in the room and their relationship to the crime, the thoughts you had. It's just the names that mess around with you, slipping away as your brain gets clogged up."

"Do you remember what you thought while you were interviewing him?"

"Why are you asking about this?" Eilert squinted at her, his eyes as piercing as ever.

"There are eight years between us," said Eira. "I was too young, and then we sort of drifted apart. I need to know who my brother really is."

She desperately hoped that Magnus wouldn't be headline fodder the next day or the day after. Though if he was, she would have bigger problems than Eilert Granlund feeling like she had duped him.

"Did you ever think it was him?" she asked.

"No, we became convinced it was Olof Hagström pretty early on. There was evidence, witnesses . . . It was crystal clear."

"I mean before that, during the first few days, do you remember what you thought then?"

"Hmm. I think I'll have a whisky, that usually helps."

As he disappeared into the house Eira realized that she had noticed the smell as soon as she arrived. That he had seemed a little unsteady on his feet. She checked her phone. Three missed calls from August, no messages.

"Ah, you're driving, poor sod," Eilert told her once he returned with a glass and a bottle of single malt from the High Coast Distillery, pouring one for himself. Gripping the table as he sat down.

A soft groan, an ache he was trying to ignore.

"We focused on the boyfriend, of course we did, that's just where you look—as well as all the others, known criminals and that kind of thing . . . There was some talk among her friends about him being jealous. Lina had tried to break things off a few times, but he kept hanging on. It's a pattern we'd seen before. He had an alibi, I don't remember what it was, but it was flimsy. For a day or two the boyfriend was our prime suspect, but if you ask me . . ."

"I'm asking you."

"He didn't have it in him. That was my gut feeling. He was . . . how should I put it . . . adaptable. Some of the others thought he was lying because he was guilty, but I wasn't so sure . . . I thought it was more that he didn't want to make a mistake. Tiptoeing around, thinking for a second too long before he answered, that kind of thing. I thought maybe he was lying for someone else. We toyed with that idea for a while, that there could be someone else involved."

"Like who?"

"No one. I was wrong. Magnus Sjödin didn't know Olof Hagström, he wouldn't have risked anything for him." Eilert Granlund knocked back his second whisky, or whatever number it was, and poured another.

"Sometimes you just have to admit that you're wrong. That's a lesson too. Cheers!"

Yet another whisky disappeared.

A blood alcohol level of 0.8 per mill. Magnus Sjödin had been pulled over in a routine traffic stop just south of Härnösand.

"Was that why you tried to call me yesterday?" asked Eira.

"I thought you would want to know," said August.

She had had three missed calls from him the evening before, but Eira hadn't called back. She had assumed August wanted to meet and didn't have the energy to fix herself up, to act sexy; she had thought it would do him good to experience a bit of resistance.

That was why she had only just found out, at work, when he grabbed her by the wrist and pulled her into an empty meeting room.

"What were you doing there, south of Härnösand?" she asked.

"I did an extra shift yesterday, they needed people. We were the closest car when the call came in for help transporting the person they'd apprehended."

"How did you know he was my brother?"

"He said."

"He did?"

"Yeah, or . . . he shouted it really, that his sister was a cop."

Eira slumped into a chair. The conference table stretched out in front of her like an ocean. Someone had left a few half-empty bottles of sparkling water behind.

"I'm sorry," said August. "I didn't even realize you had a brother."

Because I didn't tell you, she thought, *because no one needs to know*.

She had spent the night awake, wondering if he was dead. Whether he had slammed into a rock face somewhere, anywhere; the whole of the Ådalen river valley was full of rock faces to smash into. Or maybe he had jumped from the High Coast Bridge or sped off the end of a jetty and was sitting in a car thirty meters below the surface, fish swimming around him.

Images like that.

No, she had thought. *Magnus would never kill himself, he loves his kids, his beautiful boys, despite being a useless father.* As though people who committed suicide didn't love their children. It was themselves they couldn't stand.

But he was alive.

Unbeknownst to her, her brother had been sitting in a cell in the county town all night. Magnus, who couldn't handle being shut in, who ran the minute a woman tried to pin him down.

Eira remembered his girlfriend in Nordingrå and sent her a quick message to say that she knew where Magnus was but that she couldn't talk now.

It struck her that there were only twenty or so kilometers between the woman's house and where he was arrested, yet he had been missing for almost forty-eight hours.

"Did Magnus say where he'd been?"

"I don't know," said August. "He was coming from the south. Said he was going home, that he didn't want to go into fucking Härnösand."

"Home? Home where?"

"Don't know."

"Did he say anything else?"

"He called us fascist pigs and stuff like that. Said he needed to talk to his sister, because she was a real cop, not an idiot like the rest of us."

Eira had to laugh. "That's my brother."

Then she had to cry. An awkward hand on the back of her neck, August pulled her in close. He smelled like hand sanitizer and soap, his hands soft, no calluses or hard skin.

"Hey," he said.

"Don't worry. I'm OK."

Eira pulled away and got up, wiped her face on her sleeve. "Isn't there anything going on here? Has the criminal world gone on holiday?"

No one was willing to admit it, but police officers wanted things to happen. They hadn't joined the force to be called out over false alarms or break-ins that had happened months earlier.

They wanted to go all in, to use their full capacity; they wanted to feel their hearts racing, adrenaline pumping—which isn't to say that they advocated crime.

It was the same as surgeons getting off on complex operations, actors on *Hamlet* and *King Lear*.

Eira took one last look at the records scattered across the floor.

"Those bastards," said the man who had just come up to his cabin for a much-anticipated break. "They've nicked my entire Bowie collection."

"You might want to consider having an alarm fitted," said Eira.

"Should that really be necessary? In the countryside?"

"Bowie's on Spotify these days," said August, a remark that made the owner of the cabin look like he wanted to kill someone.

As they drove away, they passed the road to Lockne for the third time that day. Eira felt a powerful urge to turn off.

She hadn't heard whether the technicians had found anything else.

Surely she would have heard if they had?

On the radio, if nowhere else. She had stopped August when he tried to change to a better music station, forced him to listen to the local radio all morning. The police had released Kenneth Isaksson's name and picture, that was the latest development. Eira guessed the investigators must be snowed under with tips by now, the majority of which would prove utterly worthless.

Their focus would be on Magnus. That was certainly how she would have looked at it. Someone who could be definitively linked to the crime scene, who had relations with the same woman as the victim, intimate relations; she worried they would throw everything into that line of inquiry.

The sign for Lockne disappeared behind them.

"Do you have siblings?" she asked.

"I had a sister," said August. "She committed suicide when she was nineteen."

Eira searched for something to say. She had always thought August seemed so easygoing, so irritatingly carefree.

"It's OK, you don't need to say anything." August glanced over to her. He was behind the wheel now; she had asked him to drive. "I'd had enough of psychologists before I even turned twenty."

"So she was older than you?"

"Twin."

Eira placed her hand on top of his, caressed it. The act felt awkward, more emotional than before.

"I have a brother too," he said. "He's three years younger. It's up to us to live now."

It was afternoon by the time Eira managed to bring herself to call Härnösand. She wasn't allowed to talk to Magnus, of course, but she did leave messages with at least three people—the duty officer, the custody manager, and someone else—to say that whenever Magnus Sjödin was permitted to make a call, if he was permitted, this was the number he should dial.

He would know that he wasn't alone, at the very least.

After that she went to see the local investigator, Anja Larionova, to give her yet another summerhouse break-in to add to the pile.

They had received the full list of missing items via email: Thirty-seven Bowie records, all individually named. Queen, Prince, Bruce Springsteen. A dinner service from Rörstrand, around fifty pieces. And so on.

Anja cast a quick glance at the list. "Did Bowie really record that many albums?"

"Some of them are bootlegs," said Eira. "Priceless, apparently. They'll probably sell for twenty kronor at some flea market."

"I'm flat out with all these old boats right now," said Anja, "but I'll take a look later." She was sitting with her feet on the desk, a stack of documents in her lap. Eira recognized the dusty smell.

"What boats?"

"Anything reported missing between June and the first few days of July 1996." She sounded enthusiastic. Anja Larionova was well known for loving petty crimes—no theft too small. From a human perspective, she argued, the loss of a Barbie doll could be even worse than a stolen BMW. "The hottie from Violent Crimes asked me to look into it."

"Have you found any?"

"Six. Three went missing over Midsummer weekend, but they all turned up within a few days—guess people just needed to get home from parties somehow."

"And the others?"

"Two were stolen a fair way north of Sollefteå, which might be a bit too far. Apparently the witnesses were clear that this Kenneth Isaksson guy could barely row. He was better known for stealing cars."

"If it was him Lina was hanging out with," said Eira, "then he might have picked her up in a car."

"Cars are a bit trickier—we're looking at a bigger search area, a completely different volume of thefts. He could've stolen one anywhere along the way, but he hardly rowed right up here from northern Hälsingland."

Anja Larionova used her pen to scratch her head.

"But a rowing boat did go missing from Nyland sometime during the night between the first and second of July."

"Was it ever found?"

"Just over two weeks later, below Sprängsviken. It probably drifted ashore, it hadn't been tied up."

Eira closed her eyes to get a better sense of the geography. From Nyland to Marieberg—straight across the river and with the help of the current—likely took an hour or so to row, at most. Sprängsviken was farther down, in her own neck of the woods, around ten kilometers as the crow flies.

A boat drifting downriver.

What did that mean?

"Maybe the owner just tied it badly," said Anja Larionova, "and it floated off itself."

Eira went over to her own desk and checked her emails before heading home. The owner of the summerhouse had been in touch to add another two records to the list. She felt slightly out of breath when she saw an email from GG, but it was just the charges against the boys who had set fire to Olof Hagström's house. He asked whether anyone had taken any screenshots of the hate directed at Olof online. That had fallen slightly through the cracks, and much of it had already been deleted. The IT team might be able to retrieve some of the comments, but they were currently snowed under. Eira brought up a couple of the posts on her screen and was struck, yet again, by the harsh tone. It could probably wait, she thought.

She debriefed, got changed. Bumped into August outside the changing room.

"Do you have another shift tonight?" she asked.

"Nope, not tonight."

Eira glanced around, checking none of their colleagues were within earshot.

"I'm not working tomorrow," she said quietly. "I have to go home and check on my mum for a few hours, but I could come over after that if you like?"

"That would've been great," said August. "But tonight doesn't really work."

He zipped up his windbreaker and smiled. "I've got to pick up my girlfriend from the station."

It really was high time they sorted out the garden. The flower beds and vegetable patch were Kerstin's pride and joy—on par with her book collection—yet somehow they had been neglected over the summer.

Eira knew it was entirely her fault. All it would have taken was for her to say, "Let's do a bit of work in the garden today" and Kerstin would have been out the door in a flash, remembering exactly where she had left her gardening gloves.

Taking the initiative was a complex process for the brain, one of the first things to go.

Kerstin was now on her knees, yanking goosefoot out of the potato patch, pulling up the hops snaking around the red currant bushes.

"I just don't understand how it could have spread so much, I only weeded it recently."

Eira loosened the soil, turning it over and making the worms and wood lice wriggle and scuttle in the light of day. She tried to remember the flower beds in their glory, to distinguish the weeds from whatever had simply finished blooming.

"Careful!" Kerstin shouted as Eira tugged on something with a thick stalk and dense leaves. "That's a fire lily, can't you see?"

"And this?"

"No, no, no, a daylily. I got that cutting from your granny. And be careful with the Finnish rose—it only flowers for a week, but oh, what a lovely smell."

And so on.

When her thoughts became too much, Eira started the strimmer and shut out the world with a pair of ear defenders. That meant she didn't notice someone was approaching until Kerstin straightened up and pulled off her gloves, hitting them together to get rid of the soil and raising a hand to shade her eyes.

Eira felt an immediate sense of danger, a premonition of misfortune, when she saw who it was.

Silje Andersson, strolling towards them in a white shirt. Her mouth moved, she said something. Eira turned off the strimmer and took off the ear defenders as her colleague greeted her mother.

"Sorry, I can see you've got your hands full here, but could I borrow Eira a moment?" The breezy tone only reinforced the sense that she was intruding.

"That's OK, isn't it, Mum?"

"Yes, yes, you go, I'll soldier on. You have to pull up the roots with the thistles, you know, otherwise they'll split and triple by next summer."

She seemed so happy, so comfortable and content. Eira glanced back as she made her way to the other side of the house, wanted to see her like that again.

Silje paused once they had rounded the corner of the building.

"I could have just called," she said. "But I thought it would be better to come and talk to you in person. I heard you were off duty."

"Is it about Magnus?" said Eira. "Have you questioned him?"

"The prosecutor has decided to remand him in custody."

"For drunk driving? The reading was only zero point eight, surely that should only be a fine . . . ?" She knew she had said "only" twice in quick succession, that she shouldn't play down a crime in that way; drunk driving was drunk driving, even if it wasn't serious.

"For murder," said Silje. "Or the manslaughter of Kenneth Isaksson."

Eira instinctively cast a glance over to the road. She could see a man washing his car. The people next door were oiling their garden furniture on the lawn.

She fled into the house and gestured for Silje to follow her.

Closed the door.

"There's no way," she said.

"I'm sorry."

"I knew he'd be questioned because of the DNA they found, but . . ."

Eira gripped the edge of the chest of drawers. The rest of the house was spinning, but the pale green chest of drawers and its iron hardware was steady. An heirloom from someone who had died long before she was even born.

"What does he say?" she asked.

"He denies it."

"Was it you who interviewed him?"

"GG started this morning, but then he had me take over."

"I see."

Silje Andersson, who could make a man's jaw drop just by entering a room.

"And Lina?"

"So far our suspicions only concern Kenneth Isaksson," said Silje.

"So far?"

"You know I shouldn't be talking to you about this."

"Have you found her?"

"They've expanded the search area."

The investigator was standing less than two meters away from Eira, trying to be compassionate while paying attention to her every reaction. The porch was too small for both of them.

"We'll need to talk to you too, but we can do that at the station tomorrow. I just wanted to let you know."

Silje opened her diary and started talking about penciling something in, about things like mornings and afternoons and times.

"Who is his lawyer?" asked Eira.

She wrote down a name she vaguely recognized on an envelope in the hallway.

"See you tomorrow, then," said Silje.

They always used to burn the weeds in the garden, but that was typically earlier in the spring. There was a ban on fires across the entire country right then.

Eira shoved everything they had pulled out into black rubbish bags. She had a memory of her mother cooking goosefoot from time to time, boiling it in cream and serving it with salmon.

Kerstin had fallen asleep on the sofa.

Eira turned off the TV and studied her mother's sleeping face. It had been a good day in the garden.

Her soft snoring.

When should she tell her that Magnus was in custody?

Before it appeared in the papers, before the neighbors started looking at them differently, before the news vans parked up outside the house.

Just not this night.

After three hours of trying, she eventually managed to get hold of Magnus's lawyer. Eira went upstairs to be sure her mother couldn't hear her.

"I'm so glad you called," said the lawyer, Petra Falk. "Magnus asked me to give you a ring, but I never got round to it."

Her bright voice didn't provide much comfort. Eira pictured a platinum blond with round, golden glasses; maybe their paths had crossed in court, or during an interview with a suspect.

"How is he?"

"It's been a difficult day," said Petra Falk. "But as good as we could hope for."

"I know I'm not allowed to talk to him."

"It's complicated. You have a certain amount of knowledge of the case—you know things that not even the investigators know."

"They're going to question me tomorrow."

Eira sat down on the edge of her bed. She could see the treetops outside, a sliver of reddish yellow moon. It was almost full.

"How's it looking for him?"

She heard the lawyer speak, slowly and matter-of-factly. The drunk driving was, of course, the least of his worries. The suspicion

of the murder—or manslaughter—of Kenneth Isaksson was something that had the potential to drag on. Evidentiary problems after
twenty-three years, vague circumstantial evidence and witness statements, forensic finds that left room for interpretation. Petra Falk
hoped to have the charges dropped on lack of evidence—assuming
it even got that far. Either that or to have them reduced to manslaughter.

"And Lina?"

"I'm determined to make them keep the murder of Lina Stavred
out of this. The only thing pointing to her even being there that day
is the twenty-three-year-old statement of someone who thought they
saw her in a boat. They've got nothing."

"But they found her dress," said Eira, realizing as the words left
her mouth that it was she who had led them there. It was to her
credit, but it was also her fault. "And the rucksack she had with her
when she went missing."

"I haven't seen their reports yet, but as I understand it we're looking at fragments of material that could be interpreted as a rucksack.
Seems like we've got a badger on our side there."

Eira sat quietly for a moment, trying to bring some kind of order
to the many details. The cardigan, the dress, the condom, Kenneth
Isaksson being a better lover than the others . . . It was like a sprawl-
ing root system, covered in the insects and parasites that fed off it,
such a swarm that you couldn't distinguish one from the next.

She heard the lawyer's bright voice, a torrent of words, and saw
the moon break free from the treetops and rise higher in the sky.

"If the prosecutor decides to merge this with Lina's case, I'll be
emphasizing Kenneth Isaksson's criminal past, the drugs . . . Isn't
he the more likely killer? But like I said, I doubt it'll get that far, not
unless they find her body. Even if Lina Stavred was in Lockne on
the night in question—something that hasn't by any means been
proved—there's nothing to say that she died there. She could have
drowned in the river at a later date. From the forensic evidence, she
could even have walked away."

"Without her dress?"

"I'm not being literal here," said Petra Falk. "It was just an example of a possible line of argument."

Eira didn't say what she was thinking. She was too tired, felt a powerful longing to slump back on the mattress. She couldn't cope with yet another person talking about argumentation, even if it was her job. More than anything, she just wanted to sleep.

"Was there anything specific you wanted to tell me?" she asked.

"Like I said, I'd emphasize that there are a number of plausible scenarios . . ."

"You said Magnus asked you to call me."

"Oh yes, sorry, I almost forgot."

It sounded like she was reading aloud. *Magnus wrote this himself,* thought Eira. She could just picture his scrawl on a scrap of paper.

She imagined it being unfolded.

Tell my sister I didn't do it. I didn't kill her. You don't do that kind of thing to the person you love. Tell Eira, so she understands.

Eira was rowing against the stream, fighting the power of the river. She was in a hurry now, because she had forgotten about a meeting at the station. It had already started, everyone else was there; she was the only one who was late. The oars caught in some kind of vegetation, seaweed or something, and then she saw the bodies floating around the hull and had to let go of the oars to grab them. Some of them weren't quite dead yet. One of the oars popped out, and Eira leaned over the gunwale, paddling with her hands; she had to catch it. She saw a face beneath the water, his eyes still full of life. The boat drifted on and he slipped beneath it, she could no longer see him.

Magnus.

Eira forced herself up to the surface, opened her eyes. She knew the dream so well that she recognized it for what it was even in her sleep. Still, it made her heart race.

Light spilled into the room. It was dawn, just after four o'clock. The blind was up. She had fallen asleep on top of the covers.

There were no scents in her dreams, but she still thought she could smell them, like a taste in her mouth. The slightly brackish water, the decay. She brushed her teeth and reheated an old cup of coffee.

It was just a dream. Any old amateur psychologist would have frowned and said that she felt a need to save her brother, but that wasn't the thought that lingered, or the feeling of floating freely among the dead.

It was the rowing boat, the one that had washed ashore.

She knew the movements of the river, understood the currents; five hundred cubic meters of water passed through the power stations every second, before continuing out to the Gulf of Bothnia. Was it really possible that an unmanned rowing boat could have meandered past the islands and drifted ashore in Sprängsviken, just downstream of Lunde, where she currently was? She sat still for some time, staring at the trees outside her bedroom window as her mind journeyed along the river.

A great tit flapped away as she stood up.

She got dressed and checked in on her mother, who had spent the night asleep on the sofa. Then she went out and started the car.

Lockne was quiet at that time of day. None of the crime scene technicians had arrived yet. Despite that, Eira left her car a little farther along the road, hidden behind an abandoned outbuilding. Vigilant neighbors could easily be up at five in the morning, wondering who she was.

She crossed a line as she ducked beneath the plastic cordon. This was a crime scene, one to which she didn't technically have access. The morning sun filtered among the trees, glittering in the spiderwebs and the dew. The ground had been dug up in places, and she saw heaps of earth and torn moss. Eira found herself thinking about the dioxin that must have been released into the air.

At the edge of the river, among clumps of reeds and the old pillars of the jetty, the dragonflies were hovering over the surface of the water. Emerald green, translucent wings, a breathlessness to them.

Those few short lines.

Tell my sister I didn't do it. I didn't kill her.

Magnus had begged for her understanding, that wasn't so strange, but why had he mentioned only Lina when it was Kenneth Isaksson he was accused of killing?

You don't do that kind of thing to the person you love. Tell Eira, so she understands.

Eira couldn't shake the feeling that it sounded like a riddle.

What did he want her to understand?

That he had killed Kenneth Isaksson out of love for Lina?

If Magnus had brought an iron bar crashing down onto Kenneth Isaksson's head, it would have hardly been because he thought it was fun. He had never even pulled the wings off a fly. That was what their mother had told Eira after she caught her in the act, that Magnus had certainly never done anything like that at her age.

The white morning haze was thick over the river, obscuring the beach on the other side of the bay. Eira could just see them making their way over in the boat, city boy Kenneth, who barely knew how to row, and Lina, sprawled in the stern in her thin summer dress.

If Magnus knew that the girl he loved was coming out here with someone else. If Lina had thrown that fact in his face, trying to make him jealous; if this was their secret meeting place, where she and Magnus had discarded used condoms, then that would have been a brutal provocation.

A real kick in the teeth.

If Magnus had come out here. On his motorbike, of course, the lightweight thing he had back then, the blue one. Eira remembered the vibrations, the dizzying speed from the few times he had let her ride with him. But then it had been stolen, and he had got himself another one, red this time.

They came on motorcycles, too.

That was what she had said, the old woman who lived nearby, she had talked about the damn motorcycle.

If Magnus had parked by the forge. Crept over and saw them together, through one of the many broken windows, Lina with her dress off. If he was wounded and half-mad with envy, and there were iron bars everywhere . . . Or maybe it was Kenneth who spotted him, who started a fight, and Magnus had to defend himself . . .

Eira slumped down onto a rock a few meters from the spot where they had found the first few pieces of Kenneth Isaksson's body buried beneath the blue clay.

Lina was the only one who didn't fit into the picture. It was as though she withdrew, out of sight, vanishing into thin air like the mist over the river.

Had Magnus's fury continued? Had he completely lost his mind, did it happen during the chaos of their fight?

Had he hidden a body beneath the junk in the river and then gone on to dig a grave for her?

Magnus wasn't the kind of cool, calculating person who tidied up after himself. It was Eira who had inherited those traits. He was all impulse and emotion, a leaf in the wind; Magnus was chaos.

Eira picked up a stick and threw it into the river. A few of the dragonflies careered off to one side, and the rings spread out across the surface of the water. The stick remained where it had landed on the surface, barely moving. The current didn't reach that far into the bay. A boat would hardly have drifted off on its own, not unless there was a storm blowing. It might have bobbed about by the bank, maybe even moved a short distance in the breeze, but it would've caught in the first beaver's dam.

You don't do that kind of thing to the person you love.

She heard the rustling sound of the dragonflies' wings touching. Thirty beats every second, though they looked completely motionless.

Tell Eira, so she understands.

H as Magnus ever talked to you about what happened that evening?"
"Never," said Eira.

They were in the conference room at the station in Kramfors, somewhere she had sat many times before. It was more relaxed than the interrogation rooms, according to Silje Andersson, but that just made the situation all the more confusing. Like they were there for the morning meeting, just waiting for the others to arrive.

"GG tried to get someone else in to do this," she had said. "That obviously would've been better, but with the summer holidays . . . We're just trying to get a sense of who he is, and it would be unfortunate if we didn't hear his family's side of things. I understand it might be tricky to talk to his mother?"

"You can't," said Eira. "She's not well, she doesn't know anything."

That just left her.

"Did you notice a change in Magnus after Lina Stavred's murder?"

"I thought you wanted to talk about Kenneth Isaksson?"

"OK, let's put it like this," said Silje. "Did Magnus change in early July that year?"

Eira had the right not to answer, she could choose to ignore Silje's questions if she liked. As a close relative, she wasn't obliged to give evidence. The duty to tell the truth could come into conflict with the desire to protect those closest to you, and the law made an exception for such cases. Yet she was also a police officer, and should stand up for the truth.

"Yes," she said. "Magnus went off the rails, started doing drugs, but that's hardly surprising given what happened to the girl he was in love with."

"Several people have mentioned his jealousy," said Silje. "What's your impression of that?"

"I can't answer that."

"Like I said, we're not investigating the murder of Lina Stavred, but she does play a part in this. There's no ignoring that."

"If it was a murder," said Eira.

"What do you mean?"

"You've been digging, but you still haven't found her body. Surely you have to ask why he wouldn't just hide it in the same place as Kenneth Isaksson's?"

"What do you think?"

The investigator studied her calmly. Eira had always admired Silje Andersson; her low-key intelligence also applied on an emotional level, which meant she often hit the mark.

But in that moment it seemed more frightening than anything.

Everything Eira said could be interpreted as an attempt to protect her brother. Turned on its head to show the opposite. A tentative thought they had recently been bouncing back and forth could now prove that Eira knew more than she was letting on. Uncertainty might mean she was lying, but so could being dead certain about something.

"I don't know what I think anymore," she said. "It's all just so confusing."

"I understand."

Like hell you do, thought Eira.

"Has Magnus ever mentioned the name Kenneth Isaksson?" asked Silje.

"Never."

"Did they know each other?"

"No idea. Have you found anything to suggest they did?"

"No, but it's possible they were both in a relationship with Lina. There are several pieces of evidence and witness statements suggesting that's the case, as you know."

"Do you know why Kenneth Isaksson ran away up here?"

"He wanted to get out into the wilderness." Silje leaned back with her hands behind her head, relaxed. "We spoke to a girl who lived in the same collective back then. She wanted him to get away, so she didn't snitch on him at the time. According to Kenny—that's what they called him—the wilderness was where you could find true freedom. Away from civilization, which turns free men and women into brain-dead subjects."

Silje didn't seem to react to the fact that the interview had taken a turn, that Eira was now asking the questions. Perhaps she also felt torn, or maybe it was just a tactic, to give the impression that they were equals.

"Other than this girl," she continued, "no one has a good word to say about him—not even his own mother. In and out of treatment homes from the age of fifteen, robbing and assaulting people, including his mum; drug-related crimes, a history of violence. But in this case he's the victim, and that's how we have to look at him. Well, you know all that."

"Magnus isn't a violent person," said Eira.

Silje raised an eyebrow, just a fraction, barely even noticeable. Eira might not have seen it if she hadn't been used to studying the person on the other side of the table, to trying to guess the meaning behind every reaction.

She hadn't been asked about his violence.

"He sometimes punched the wall and that kind of thing," she continued. "Or slammed the door when he stormed out, but he never hit anyone at home."

"Threats of violence are also a form of violence," said Silje.

"Have you entertained the thought that it might have been Kenneth Isaksson who killed Lina?"

Silje looked down at her iPad, searching for something.

"Magnus has a record for assault," she said. "Five years ago . . ."

"A drunken brawl," said Eira. "An ordinary fight outside Kramm." She knew how wrong it sounded, but the words just spilled out of her. Brawling didn't feature in the penal code. The term was assault, even if it was the other man who started it. Even if Magnus had received a beating himself.

Silje asked her several more questions, but looking back later Eira would barely remember any of them. What stuck with her was what she had said herself. You didn't expose those closest to you like that. Telling an outsider that Magnus was actually a sensitive soul, weak, that he had never quite managed to make sense of life.

She wanted to give a truthful picture of who he was, beyond the police reports and rumors and problems, and she knew he would hate her for it if he ever found out.

"Are we almost done here?" she asked. "I told GG I would send him some files . . ."

"Absolutely," said Silje. "I won't bother you anymore."

"It's OK."

Out of sheer habit and aching fatigue, Eira headed straight for the coffee machine, but she turned around when she saw a couple of colleagues chatting next to it.

August was one of them.

She wished she could put on her uniform, making everything feel clear, but she wasn't working, was free to go home.

It wasn't OK. She had failed both to protect her brother and to give a stable impression, to keep her professional life separate from her private life the way everyone said you had to.

She had never understood how. You took all your personal qualities to work with you, and the work followed you home. It was still the same brain, it kept ticking over; sleep knew no such boundaries.

She wondered whether August was able to keep his professional life separate from his private life.

When he came home to his girlfriend.

She wondered whether he had driven her around the area, possibly stopping off at the monument in Lunde, googling the shooting in Ådalen in 1931.

Johanna, that was her name. Eira studied her profile picture on the page she had saved. She seemed chilly, with long glossy hair and white teeth.

An agent for a line of skincare products.

August's girlfriend had been one of the first people to share the hate-filled posts about Olof Hagström, number three in the chain that started with Sofi Nydalen. Maybe the two women used the same skincare line.

Hated the same things.

Eira was meant only to be gathering the material she had and sending it over to GG, but she found herself getting sucked into the thread again. This Johanna wasn't just cool and beautiful, there was another side to her, one that shouted about cutting the dicks off men like that. *Yet again we see a rapist walk free while no one listens to the girls.* She supported the idea of publishing their names and pictures online, locking them up for life, and even gave a thumbs-up to the prospect of their being gang-raped in prison.

Eira wondered how August dealt with that side of her, though they likely didn't talk about the rule of law in the bedroom. As she read on, more comments emerged, each one sharper than the last, as though it was spotlit.

You're such sheep . . . Have none of you read The Scapegoat? No, sorry, thought not.

Do you even know how to read, you fucking retards?

Eira recognized that post. She and August had noticed it because it stood out, didn't follow the current in the same direction as the others.

There were likely thousands of people who used that phrase— people who refused to stop using offensive language.

Simone, that was the poster's name.

Eira scanned through the rest of the thread to see if she popped up anywhere else. She did, on one occasion.

He was such a loser, he really only had himself to blame.

She read the two posts over and over again, until she thought she could almost hear the girl's voice. She couldn't see her face. Simone had Daphne Duck as her profile picture. It wasn't uncommon for people to use strange images like that on Facebook; not all people wanted to show their real face.

He was such a loser.

That made it sound like the poster had known Olof Hagström back in the day. Plenty of people had, of course. Scores of classmates. It simply suggested that Simone came from the area.

You're such sheep . . . Have none of you read The Scapegoat?

Something else Elvis had said came back to her: that Lina read fancy French books, or pretended to—whichever it was. Eira brought up an online bookshop and searched for the title. Found a couple of thrillers and a book by a writer with a French-sounding name.

Expulsion and victims are a way of stabilizing society, in which violence is channeled through sacred rituals . . .

Eira returned to the thread. Aside from one man who thought political action was required to transform the justice system rather than hanging people out to dry, Simone seemed to be the only person going against the flow.

Do you even know how to read, you fucking retards?

Eira couldn't make sense of her argument. Was she defending Olof Hagström? It sounded like Simone thought she was smarter than everyone else, that she knew something no one else knew.

Since it was only a screenshot, she couldn't click through to her page, so Eira logged in to her own account instead—a profile without a photograph that she only ever used for work. August's girlfriend's page was private. Eira searched for Simone and found herself staring at a list of countless users, clicking through thirty or so of them until she spotted the picture of Daphne Duck.

Private.

She got up, opened the window for some fresh air. Looked out over the rooftops, to the mountains in the distance, the expanse of sky.

Air, reality, balance.

A boat coming ashore by Sprängsviken. Kenneth Isaksson, who wanted to live free in the wilderness. Lina, who wanted to get away.

Freedom.

To leave and never return.

She shut down her computer and went through to Anja Larionova's office.

"Do you still have those old reports to hand?"

The local investigator took off her glasses, letting them swing from the cord around her neck.

"If you mean the stolen boats from 1996, then yes."

"Do you think you could check whether anyone reported a motorcycle missing in July that year?"

Anja Larionova studied her closely. Her icy blue eyes matched her hair perfectly, not faltering at anything. Eira steeled herself, determined not to explain. Doing so would force her colleague to say no—unless she was willing to cross the line herself.

"A whole month of motorcycles, in the middle of the summer?" said Anja. "Come on."

"A blue one," said Eira. "Lightweight. A Suzuki." She debated whether or not to mention the owner, but decided it would be simpler not to.

"Sure," said Anja Larionova.

"Thanks."

Eira then tracked down August. He was sitting alone in the lunchroom with a buffet salad from the supermarket.

"Oh, hey, I thought you were off today." He smiled, still fiddling with his phone, then looked down at the plastic tub again. Eira had experienced this before: a slight shift, once the breeziness was gone.

"I need to talk to your girlfriend," she said.

The name of the café had changed since Eira had last been there, though on the other hand she didn't go out for coffee in central Kramfors particularly often. It had been taken over by a Thai woman who had moved to the area for love.

Johanna was shorter than Eira had imagined. Cuter, and not quite so chilly.

If anything, she was chirpy.

"It's great to meet you, August has told me so much about you. It's so beautiful round here." Johanna glanced out of the window, across the square in the very heart of Kramfors. It was a textbook example of the kind of Swedish town center that had sprung up following the wave of demolitions in the sixties. "Well, maybe not right here . . ."

Eira wondered what August had said about her, about them, but had no intention of finding out.

"Do you know what this is about?" she asked instead.

"Look, I'm really sorry I shared all that stuff, but there's so much activity across my feeds that I don't always have time to think first."

"I'm not accusing you of anything," said Eira.

"No, why would you?" The green smoothie Johanna had ordered arrived. It reminded Eira of water that had been standing for a little too long in a shallow brook. "Everyone's got the right to an opinion, don't they?"

Eira took a bite of her Kramfors cake, chocolate with glazed frosting.

"It's to do with one of your friends," she explained.

"On Facebook? It's just . . . I've got a load of friends on there that I don't actually know; I use my profile for marketing quite a lot." Johanna took unusually small sips of her drink, like she was simply wetting her lips. "I work in skincare," she added, "but I'm sure August must have told you that. I do the marketing for a brand. It's not mine, but I'm their agent in Sweden. You have to let me do an analysis of your skin type."

"Maybe later."

Eira had asked August whether his girlfriend knew they were having sex. "Yeah, yeah, of course," he had replied, as though it were a stupid question, a nonissue.

"It's about a girl called Simone," she continued. "I need to get hold of her."

"OK . . ." Johanna picked up her phone, which had been buzzing on the table. "God, I've got so many followers, I can't remember all of them. What did you say she was called?"

Eira repeated the name.

"Yeah, here she is, she doesn't even have a profile picture. Why do people do that—are they ashamed of the way they look? I think it's all so superficial, this obsession with looks on social media; surely the main thing is that you feel good on the inside, that's real beauty. Hold on, let me check our mutual friends, that might jog my memory . . ."

Eira excused herself and went to the toilet. She splashed her face with cold water afterwards, in an attempt to keep her mind clear. She really didn't have anything against the concept of free love, it was a beautiful thought, but she just couldn't understand what August saw in Johanna that he also saw in her—two such different people. Or maybe that was the point, finding someone for the various sides of himself, because no one person could be everything.

She had never even considered that her skin might be a little dry.

"It's just come to me," Johanna yelled across half the café. "Come here, let me show you."

She moved her chair closer until their shoulders and upper arms, one knee, were touching. It was too intimate, but Eira couldn't bring herself to pull away. She became very aware of Johanna's body. There was something strangely arousing about August's absence between them, allowing them to get so close.

She swallowed and leaned in over the phone as Johanna tried to show her how her network overlapped with Simone's.

"She was dating a guy I know from my last job. We met in the restaurant he owns, sometime last spring."

"And then you became friends?"

"Well, friends and friends," said Johanna. "Since I'm self-employed I have to do a lot of networking, and she's not exactly the youngest, she's at the age where it starts getting really urgent."

"And when is that?"

"How old are you?"

"Thirty-two."

"Aha, OK, well Simone is probably a bit older, somewhere around forty. I'd have a better idea if I'd analyzed her skin. That's how you can really tell a person's age."

She smiled at Eira and gently stroked two fingers down her cheek.

"You've got really great skin, for your age."

The minute Olof closed his eyes, images from the house came flooding back to him. The flames and the smoke. It felt like so long ago, yet also so recent. Sometimes he saw his family there, when he closed his eyes, and then he saw his father in the bathroom.

The branches hitting his face as he ran.

"I didn't have any shoes on," he said. "I ran out of the house in my socks. Then I don't know."

"It's OK," said the physiotherapist who was sitting on the edge of his bed. She was massaging his hand, encouraging him to move his fingers, and spoke in a soft voice. "You don't need to put pressure on yourself."

Olof had said that he didn't want to talk to anyone, but then the physiotherapist had come into his room.

He thought she was pretty.

"Your memory will come back little by little," she said. "It's OK. You're getting better every day."

Every stupid little thing he remembered made her happy. If he bent a finger or wiggled his toes, his big fat toes that peeped out whenever she folded back the blanket. She was always saying that things were getting better, but Olof knew she was wrong.

Things would get worse, because if they got better like she said they would discharge him, and then he would no longer be tucked up in a bed with fresh sheets every five minutes, eating good food—double portions if he wanted them—and gazing out at the sky. His room at the university hospital in Umeå was so high up that the sky was all he could see. Clouds sailing by, the occasional flock of birds, turning sharply as one. He tried to work out which of the birds was in charge, but they were gone again in the blink of an eye.

The earth, the ground, the people down below: he didn't have to see any of that.

"You've had a nasty shock," said the physiotherapist. "And you sustained some injuries, but there's nothing to say that you won't make a complete recovery and get back to your old life again."

"I don't think I can remember anything else," said Olof. "It's just black. My head hurts. I can't think anymore."

"It'll come," said the woman. "It's nothing you need to rush. I'll tell the nurse to bring you some painkillers."

She patted Olof's hand as she left. The hand he had first regained all feeling in. If he lay perfectly still he could feel her hands touching him, massaging him, for a long time after she left.

Like hell am I going to remember any more, he thought.

It was madness to catch a train to Stockholm to hunt for ghosts that probably didn't even exist, of course it was. Though on the other hand it was only a five-hour journey, a little more, providing you didn't have to wait too long between trains in Sundsvall.

Her boss had been almost worryingly understanding.

"No problem, we'll cover it, the Stockholm kid has been gagging for more shifts. Of course you can have a few days off."

Eira bought a half bottle of wine from the buffet car then returned to her seat.

Let the flat landscape rush by outside, the endless man-made forests.

She scribbled down a number of possible scenarios on the back of a flyer. Eira knew she was on the very edge of probability here, yet it all added up.

Everything that hadn't made sense fell into place.

The fact that they had never found Lina's body. The boat, which had drifted a little too far.

Magnus, who had kept quiet all these years.

He was in his second day of custody now. The prosecutor had had until the next day to decide whether to retain him or not, if their suspicions remained.

Eira had gone through every imaginable explanation, but that hadn't helped. All that remained now was the unimaginable.

Was it possible for a person to disappear, to become someone else, to live on despite being declared dead?

By the time Eira left the train at Stockholm Central, she felt slightly tipsy from the wine. But more from the thought that Lina Stavred might still be alive.

For some reason she had been expecting a grand restaurant in the inner city, the kind of place she assumed August's girlfriend would like. But instead the address led her, via the metro, to the southern suburbs.

An Italian deli with a salad bar and seven types of coffee on the menu. The owner, the man Simone had been dating, was called Ivan Wendel. He wasn't there. Eira had chosen not to get in touch in advance. According to the girl at the till, he had been off sick all week.

After waving her ID around, Eira left with his address. Two buses later, she found herself in a different suburb. Standing outside a villa with an apple tree in the garden. The man who opened the door looked to be just shy of fifty, with a shaved head and a pair of trendy glasses, wearing nothing but a pair of pajama bottoms.

"Simone?" He peered out at the road behind Eira with an anxious look on his face. "No . . . She doesn't live here anymore. What is this about?"

"Could I come in?"

"We can talk here."

Ivan Wendel remained in the doorway. Eira could make out a bright home behind him, all white walls and airy furniture.

"Do you know how I can get hold of Simone?" she asked.

"I haven't seen her in over a week." He craned his neck, trying to see over the hedge. "Has something happened?"

Eira explained that she was with the police and held up her ID. She knew she shouldn't keep waving it around while she wasn't on duty.

"I just want to talk to her," she said. "It's to do with a case involving a missing girl."

The man studied her closely. "Did Simone give the police this address? I find that hard to believe."

"What do you mean?"

"She doesn't trust the cops, doesn't trust the authorities in general. She's never had any help from them."

"Help with what?"

"The bloke she had to hide from. I told Simone she should report him, but she said she'd tried that, that the police didn't do anything. Seems like he's pretty powerful up in Norrland—that's where she's from—that he has contacts. It's a bloody outrage you lot don't do anything about people like him."

Eira looked at him, at the apple trees in the garden, the leafy villa setting.

"Where in Norrland?" she asked.

"No idea, I've never been any farther north than Uppsala. Simone didn't want to talk about it, and I guess that's understandable."

"Could we sit down on the steps a moment?" asked Eira.

"I don't understand what you want," said Ivan Wendel.

"Does the name Lina Stavred mean anything to you?"

"Lina who? I know a couple of Linas, it's a common . . ." He trailed off, staring at her. "Why are you asking me this? What does it have to do with Simone?"

Eira pulled out her phone. She didn't know whether this was something she should be doing, but at this stage she couldn't come up with a single reason not to, so she brought up the school photograph of Lina that one of the papers had recently republished.

"Do you think this could be Simone when she was younger?"

Ivan Wendel peered down at the image. Zoomed in.

"How old . . . ?"

"Sixteen."

"I don't know. They all look kind of alike at that age somehow, and I don't mean that in any chauvinist sense, I've got a grown daughter myself. Simone has blue eyes like her, but her hair's darker."

"Hair can be changed."

"But it must've been . . . How long?"

"Twenty-three years."

He handed the phone back to her. "Why are you asking me this?"

"Because this girl was assumed to have been murdered. A young man was arrested for it. And that's a bit unfortunate if it turns out she's actually still alive."

"Is this a bad joke or something?"

"Do I look like I'm joking?"

Ivan tugged at his pajama bottoms, which had slipped so low on his hips that the top of his underwear was visible. He turned and stepped into the house, leaving the door open. Eira wondered whether it was an invitation to follow him in, but he was soon back, with a pack of cigarettes in one hand. He closed the door behind him, shook out a cigarette.

"What the hell is it with women?" he muttered. "One day we're talking about getting married, and the next she's gone. Packed up all her stuff while I was out. Not a word."

"When was this?"

She knew the minute he said it. A little more than a week ago, nine or ten days, that was when they had found the remains in Lockne. The same day the news broke.

"And you haven't heard from her since?"

Ivan Wendel sat down at a safe distance.

"I haven't been able to talk to a single fucking person about any of this. I even lied to my own staff, told them I'd had some dodgy results from a medical, just to get away from it. My mind keeps racing, you know? Feels like I'm going crazy."

His first thought was that Simone's ex must have tracked her down, making her flee. But it wasn't like he could call the police; he had promised her he would never reveal anything, never tell anyone where she lived. She used a prepaid phone and couldn't even get her own credit card, always worked off the books, lived a life in the shadows—despite walking about like anyone else.

Simone wasn't even her real name.

"This has been going on for years. There were even periods where she lived on the street, as I understand it. She's a pretty broken person, though she hides it well. Maybe that's what I fell for, what was hiding underneath."

"What's her real name?"

"I don't know. Never asked either. I have to respect a woman's desire to be whoever she wants to be, you know?"

"Absolutely," said Eira.

"And what is a name anyway? It's just a label slapped on a person. She called herself Simone because that was who she wanted to be— after Simone de Beauvoir. And that's who I fell for. Didn't care what her name was before."

"Where did you meet?"

"In real life. None of that Tinder crap. She came into my deli one day, asking for a job. Told me it would have to be unofficial . . ." He glanced at Eira. "Obviously I told her we only employ people properly, on the books, but we clicked and I invited her to lunch, then we met again. She's more vulnerable than she wants to let on, I knew that right away, and then I found out just how tricky her situation was. But I can afford to support a woman, and Simone wasn't the type to have a problem with that."

He got up and walked out onto the lawn, stroked his shaved head, lit another cigarette.

"I thought we loved each other, but the minute I got serious about wanting a future with her, she cleared off." Ivan took a few steps in one direction, then turned and walked back, pacing like an animal in a cramped cage. "When she didn't answer the phone and I found out she'd canceled the prepaid card, I went to a few of the places where I knew she used to work, in town—the kind of places that hire people off the books—and I saw her. Followed her. But then she met up with some slick bastard, kissed him right there on the street. And that was that. I knew she wasn't in a ditch somewhere, that she'd just met someone else. It didn't even take her a week."

"Do you know who he was?" asked Eira.

Ivan shook his head. "I was going to follow them, but then I saw myself reflected in a shop window and realized I was turning into someone like him. Her ex. So I walked away. Haven't seen her since."

"Do you have any photos of Simone?"

"She hates having her picture taken. It's because of her fears, she's worried someone will upload it somewhere. I liked that about her, that she wasn't fixated on pictures of herself. But I still took a few, of course. In secret, when she wasn't looking."

"Would you mind showing me?" asked Eira.

Ivan Wendel had stopped his pacing and stood quietly for a moment, just looking at her.

"I don't have them anymore," he said. "My phone died. The same day she left me."

It was good to have a book in hand when you went to a restaurant alone. Certainly better than showing up and waving a police badge in a place that employed people off the books.

That was why Eira had bought one as she passed through Central Station. By chance she had spotted the very book she had promised herself she would read, her mother's favorite: *The Lover* by Marguerite Duras.

She was now sitting at a table in the window, with a view of both the restaurant and the street outside. Eira couldn't concentrate on the plot, about a girl and her significantly older lover in Saigon, and just read a little from time to time to make it look like she was enjoying herself. A passage caught her eye, describing the people strolling along the street and into the middle of the road: outside of things, alone in the crowd, without purpose or goal.

"Are you ready to order?" The waiter was a young man with long hair on one side, his head shaved on the other. "Or maybe you'd like to start with something to drink?"

Eira ordered two small plates and a glass of wine. If this didn't lead anywhere, she could have a main meal at the next place. Ivan had given her the names of three restaurants Simone had mentioned, places she had previously worked.

This one, in the Vasastan area of the city, was the one he had seen her leaving the last time he saw her, where she had kissed a man outside.

"Is Simone working tonight?" she asked the waiter when he returned with her wine.

"Who?"

"Simone, doesn't she work here? She's in her forties, blue eyes . . ."

"I'm new here, so . . ."

"Maybe you could ask?"

"Sure."

Alone in the crowd, she thought. How easy—or hard—was it to hide in a big city? To fly under the radar, never fully visible. In a country that had perhaps the most thorough system of registration in the world, where a personal ID number was everything. If you never used a debit card, never went to the bank, worked only off the books. Found men you could move in with, who were willing to look after you and pay for everything, maybe even arrange to see a doctor if you got ill.

But for twenty-three years?

Maybe she had a fake ID. Simone, who had fled the minute her boyfriend mentioned marriage, as soon as the old Lina case reared its head, who never allowed anyone to take her photograph.

Did she know that Ivan had taken her picture in secret?

Junking a mobile phone was pretty simple, all you had to do was get it wet. Eira had done it herself a few times.

"No, no one knows anyone called Simone," the waiter told her when he came back to clear the table. "Are you sure she works here?"

By the time she got to the third place, Eira switched to coffee. She couldn't face any more wine. That was fortunate, because it was a café, full of teenagers half sprawled across the sofas as the clock approached midnight.

She spent a while watching the dark-haired woman serving the overpriced grilled sandwiches. From behind she could easily have been twenty-five, but when she turned around the years were visible on her face. The dim lighting in the café made it impossible to see the color of her eyes.

"What's the girl over there called?" Eira asked when another waitress—short haired and slightly plump—squeezed between the tables, stacking the empty mugs into a wavering tower. "I think I recognize her."

"Who?"

"Over there, she's just going into the kitchen, with the dark hair."

"Ah. Kaitlin, maybe. Or Kate? I'm not sure, there are so many people working shifts here, new ones every week."

The woman wiped the table in one fluid motion, sweeping the crumbs to the floor.

"Do you know Simone?"

"Who?"

It was difficult to hear what anyone was saying over the din, the chatter of too many people who had drunk too much and wanted to avoid going home alone.

"Simone," Eira repeated. "I heard she worked here. She's a friend of a friend."

"I know who she is," said the waitress, picking up the tray. Her eyes scanned the tables nearby, looking for more dirty cups. "But I haven't seen her in a while. Want me to pass on a message if I do?"

"Sure."

Eira wrote her name and phone number on a napkin. She knew Simone was unlikely to call her, but that didn't matter. She blew her nose on the other napkin and balled it up in her pocket, saving the waitstaff from having to deal with it. *Lina*, she told herself, *is probably lying on the bottom of the river. You can't solve this on your own. Stop mixing your private life with your working life, and don't drink any more wine.* Eira got up to leave, almost treading on someone's foot. Alone in the crowd, she thought. Magnus's life was his own. He was the one who had told her to stop caring.

That last thought was painful.

"You forgot this," said the waitress, passing her the book as she turned to leave.

"Your brother has confessed."

The lawyer's feeble voice, floating somewhere in the distance.

"Hold on." Eira got up to leave the quiet carriage, where she had sat down to get some sleep. She had a splitting headache. The train was just leaving Hudiksvall.

"What exactly has he confessed to?"

"To killing Kenneth Isaksson."

Hills and green valleys swept by at increasing speed outside. The strange rocking of the high-speed train made her feel like throwing up.

"How?"

"It was a fight, out by the sawmill," said the lawyer. "He acted out of jealousy. Magnus claims there was no intent. If the court sees things our way then we can get the charges reduced to manslaughter."

Eira clung to one of the handrails by the doors to stop herself from falling as the train tilted.

"And Lina?"

"I've had no indication that they're planning to bring up that case."

Eira went into the toilet to splash her face and hold her wrists beneath the cold tap, the way she had after stealing too much booze from the drinks cabinet as a teenager. The tap wouldn't work. She walked through to the buffet car instead and bought a cola, swallowed two painkillers. Then returned to the vestibule between the two carriages and called GG.

"Thanks for interrupting me," he said. "Looks like I've got my holiday after all."

"Are you investigating the Lina case?"

"No," he said. "The prosecutor has decided not to reopen the investigation. Why?"

"I'm in Sundsvall," said Eira. "And it's a pretty long wait for the next train. Do you have time?"

The train had started to slow into the station, people lugging their bags into the passageway where she was standing.

"I have time," said GG. "Three weeks to be precise. I'd planned to be on a boat in the archipelago, but I'm not. There are people who claim Sundsvall doesn't have an archipelago. How many islands does it take, exactly?"

He lived precisely how Eira had imagined, in a grand turn-of-the-century building on the central esplanade.

"Wine?" he asked.

"I think I had enough yesterday."

GG topped up his own glass from a half-empty bottle of red and said he knew she must be finding it tough.

"We're only human," he said. "It's hard when it hits close to home, when things get personal."

"Was it you my brother confessed to?"

"No."

He insisted on going out onto the balcony, sitting down with a cigarette. Dressing for the holiday seemed to consist of undoing the top button of his shirt. Eira had never seen him without shoes on before. There was something intimate about a man in stockinged feet.

"I'm not going to lie to you, I'd like to reopen the Lina Stavred case, but the prosecutor doesn't think we have enough to go on. We've called off the search in Lockne."

"Lina didn't die there," said Eira.

"That's possible. Or maybe she did. Maybe she died in the woods in Marieberg after all, just like they thought back then."

"Do you really believe that?"

He tapped his cigarette into a flowerpot. It looked like there had once been a geranium in it, but now it was nothing but a stick with a few clumps of withered brown petals hanging from it.

"I hoped we'd be able to get to the bottom of it," he said. "I fought for it, as you know—we wouldn't have found Kenneth Isaksson otherwise. You were probably right, to a certain degree. That investigation was done in a different time. If Olof Hagström had been convicted back then, he might have been given a new hearing now, but he wasn't. The case was closed and it's going to remain closed. It would be a different story if we'd found Lina's body. Your brother might be looking at a double murder charge right now."

Eira leaned against the railing and looked down at the treetops lining the middle of the broad boulevard. She could hear a lone saxophone over the murmur of the people sitting outside the bars and cafés. The jazz club was just a few blocks away.

"If I can give you one piece of advice for the future," GG continued behind her, "it's to let a case remain closed. You can't let it keep niggling away at you. Let bygones be bygones, as they said in Vietnam."

She heard the glugging of wine as he topped up his glass.

"Did you hear that Olof Hagström has woken up?"

Eira wheeled around and stared at him. "Really?"

"Yup," said GG. "Looks like he'll make a full recovery."

"Have you spoken to him?"

"We'll be interviewing him in relation to the arson case, but they can deal with that from Umeå. There are no real question marks left there."

"He should know," said Eira.

"Know what?"

"What really happened to Lina Stavred."

GG turned his empty glass in his hands, squinting into the afternoon sun as he studied her.

"And what are you thinking now?"

"I think I'll have a glass of wine after all."

"Bring another bottle out," said GG, telling her where to find a glass. "And the corkscrew," he called after her.

The kitchen was full of dirty plates, a genuine mess that grated against the professional image she had of him. If GG were a suspect, she would have wondered why he was drinking alone on the first day of his summer holiday, thought that something didn't seem right.

Eira sat down beside him, in a cane chair that was much too low.

"Did you grow up in Sundsvall?" she asked as he opened the new bottle.

"Mostly," said GG. "When we weren't out in the archipelago during the summer. If it even exists."

She held out her glass.

"When you grow up like I did," she said, "it's all about how to get to the next town or beyond, how to get home or away. From the moment you get your first bike, to a moped or an EPA tractor, and so on. Life only starts once you get your driving license. It's all about vehicles."

"OK."

"And what I couldn't stop thinking about was how they got there and how they got away."

"Are we talking about the Lina case again now?"

"If Magnus went to Lockne that evening, he would have gone on his motorbike."

"Yeah, that's what your brother says," said GG. "He wanted to see what the two of them were up to, but when he got there Kenneth Isaksson was alone. He didn't see Lina that evening, never saw her again. Jealousy is a terrible bloody thing."

"So if Lina wasn't there, who took the motorbike and who rowed away?"

"The case is closed," said GG.

Maybe it was because her superior was in stockinged feet, or because he was tipsy and the red wine had stained his teeth, but Eira no longer felt any respect for his authority. She no longer housed any illusions of becoming part of what he was. Being a police assistant in Kramfors wasn't so bad.

For the next thirty years. Assuming they were willing to keep her.

She pulled out her phone. The email from Anja Larionova had arrived that morning, just before the train left Stockholm.

A blue Suzuki. It had been found by the freight yard, just a hundred or so meters from the train station in Härnösand on July 6, 1996. The owner: one Magnus Sjödin. "Though he didn't report it missing until two days later," according to Anja Larionova.

Eira brought up a map of the area. GG didn't argue. In fact, he leaned in close.

"The boat was found here," she said. "In Sprängsviken, which is just below Lunde, over ten kilometers away. There's no way it drifted that far on its own. And I don't think Lina rowed it there. I think she was terrible at rowing—why else would she have sat back while the kid from Stockholm made a fool of himself at the oars?"

"OK?"

"I think Magnus lent her his motorbike," Eira continued. "And he rowed the boat back himself. We live in Lunde, we grew up there. I've played by the river ever since I was a little kid who wasn't allowed to go down to the water. If he pushed the boat back out once he came ashore, that's probably where it would've ended up, in Sprängsviken. Then he gave her a few days to disappear before reporting his bike stolen."

She didn't say a word about the dragonfly nymphs, about her brother valuing freedom so highly that he let them go before they got their wings.

"So you're trying to say what, exactly . . . ?"

Eira reached for the bottle of wine, not because she wanted it but because she needed it. In order to lift the weight off herself and ignore what he thought.

"Has it ever occurred to you that Lina Stavred might actually be alive?"

"If I was investigating the case," GG said carefully, "then that might be something that crossed my mind. But like I said, I'm not."

"Just listen to me, give me a minute."

In the end, it took almost twenty. By the time she finished, she had told him all about Simone and why it had first occurred to her that she could be Lina, how much of a coincidence it would be for Eira to have stumbled over a woman who made such an effort to remain anonymous.

"Twenty-three years," said GG, looking up at the sky, at the soft white clouds. "That's a long time. Would it even be possible to live like that for twenty-three years?"

"There are plenty of people who live under the radar, we know that—people without documentation, criminals, people living under threat . . ."

"Yeah, of course, but I mean from a human point of view, knowing that you'd hurt your parents like that . . ."

"Lina was planning to run off with Kenneth Isaksson," said Eira. "Maybe she really didn't want to go home again. From what I've heard about Lina Stavred, she always put herself first. She only became the sweet girl once she went missing."

"Or maybe she always was, in her parents' eyes."

"If I'm right, there should be DNA to . . ."

"No." GG put his hand on hers, only for a brief moment. It wasn't an invitation, nothing like that; it was simply meant to keep her grounded.

Telling her to calm down.

To pull herself together.

"She was with Ivan Wendel for almost a year," said Eira. "There must be traces of her, clothes she left behind, maybe even a hairbrush . . ."

"I'm serious," said GG. "You have to drop this."

He got up and patted her on the shoulder, headed inside to the bathroom. Eira heard the spatter of liquid, realized he wasn't the kind of person who closed the door in his own home.

Then he was behind her again.

"You know there has to be a strong justification," he said. "A suspicion of wrongdoing, a decision from the prosecutor. We don't just collect DNA because we feel like it."

"I know," said Eira, getting up.

"And even if you're right," he continued, "it's not a crime to go into hiding. It's hardly illegal to live."

Eira left her half-empty glass on the table and excused herself by saying she needed to catch the next train to Kramfors.

"How's it going, by the way?" she asked as they stood in the hallway, where a couple of moving boxes were jostling for space with bin bags.

"What?"

"You talked about having kids, or not."

"Ah, no, it didn't work out in the end."

"Sorry, it's none of my business."

GG passed her the shoehorn. "You like to think you're immortal," he said. "But then a few months pass and nothing happens, and in the end you have to face up to your responsibilities. Go to the doctor, find out who the problem is with." He gestured to his tall body, making Eira think thoughts she didn't want to think. "And then she didn't feel it was so urgent anymore, finding an apartment together. It turned out she'd never deleted her Tinder account."

"You're right," said Eira. "I think I need a holiday."

GG took her hand, warm and lingering.

"I meant what I said before," he said. "In case a job opens up this autumn."

There was another woman sitting in the chair by his bed now. With two small guitars dangling from her ears.

They swung as she leaned forward.

"I didn't realize you were awake," she said. "How are you feeling?"

Olof didn't know what to tell her. He never said much to the nurses, only slightly more to the physiotherapist. It would be good to know which group this woman belonged to. The cleaners were the easiest; they didn't speak much Swedish.

"I only just got here," said the woman. "You were sleeping. They told me you're doing much better."

He thought he recognized her. There were far more people working in a hospital than he could keep track of. He hadn't spoken to so many women in years. Ever, as far as he could remember.

Olof flinched as she took his hand.

"I'm so sorry," she said. "I should have been there for you."

With those words, the memories started coming back to him. He wanted more morphine, but they had started phasing it out. A door slamming shut. Someone shouting at him.

You sick bastard. Get out of my room.

"Ingela?"

"God, it's been so long. I don't know what to . . ."

His sister started laughing. No, maybe she was crying. Both. How was he meant to deal with this? Olof pulled his hand away. He had regained a lot of movement in it by then, thanks to the exercises and the massages.

"You didn't do it, Olof. I know you didn't do anything to that girl. It wasn't you. Dad should never have sent you away. I'm sorry. Can you forgive me?"

Now that he knew she was his sister, he saw her differently. At first she had just been a woman, one who looked pretty different. Nice, somehow. Colorful glasses. He liked the little guitars. Those were fun.

And then Ingela was there, in this strange woman's face. She was barefoot and small, his big sister, bounding away from him.

Come on, Olof. Come and see what I found.

You can't catch me, you can't catch me.

He reached for a tissue from the bedside table and blew his nose. Christ, that was loud. There was half a mug of cordial on the table, and he gulped it down.

"How did you get here?" he asked.

"I took the train. We don't have a car."

"From which station?"

"Stockholm. That's where I live now. I've got a daughter. You're an uncle, Olof. Do you want to see?"

He saw a picture of a child, an image on her phone.

"Dad . . ." Olof began. He felt like he had to say it.

That word. It settled like a boulder on his chest, making it hard to breathe.

"It's lucky you showed up," said Ingela. "So you found him. Has anyone told you what actually happened?"

"It was the neighbor woman."

He had felt a sense of relief when he first found out. An emptiness. They weren't going to lock him up again.

"Do you think you can manage to talk about the funeral?"

Olof nodded, but it was Ingela who did most of the talking. About the fact that Sven had reserved a plot in the cemetery in Bjärtrå, but that he probably didn't want a priest. Olof thought about his mother's funeral, how he had decided not to go. He had read the card detailing the time and place, the instruction to wear bright clothing, and had tried to imagine what would happen if he showed up and all those strange faces turned to him, faces he might also recognize.

His sister said something about the letters she had found among his things and he felt himself growing angry that she had been there, snooping about.

"Why didn't you reply to Mum's letters?" she asked.

"I'm no good at writing," said Olof. The room fell silent.

The words inside him seemed to clump together, making it impossible for him to get them out. How he had read the letters she wrote, saying that Olof was still her son, that she was still his mother, despite what he had done.

I believe you, Olof. She hadn't written that.

"The house is gone," he eventually said. "All Sven's things burnt. Sorry."

It was easier to say his name than the word "Dad."

"Olof," said Ingela. "You don't need to apologize because a couple of idiots set fire to the house. It wasn't your fault."

"The police told me what happened. They did it because I was there."

His sister was crying now. *That won't help*, Olof wanted to tell her. *They can get to you if you cry.* He wondered whether the train to Stockholm left soon.

"I spoke to a police officer I know a little," she managed to tell him, once he had started to wonder whether he needed to pass her a tissue or something. "You've actually met her too, Eira Sjödin. I called her to ask how you were doing and she told me that you didn't kill Lina. You didn't do it, Olof."

The evil in his head came flooding back now. All the heavy things, dragging him down and making him think he would never be able to get out of bed, even though the lovely physiotherapist got him up every day, even though he had started walking to her room on his own.

"They don't have enough evidence to prove it," Ingela continued, "but Lina was alive when you walked out of the forest. It can't have been you. This officer, she wanted us both to know."

Olof turned away so that he didn't have to meet her eye. He might start crying otherwise. He stared at the button instead, the red one he was meant to press whenever he needed more medicine or to go to the toilet or something.

"The dog," he said, clearing his throat.

"What was that?"

"Sven had a dog. A black one. I don't know what breed it is."

"Did you hear what I just said?"

"Can you stop talking about that stuff?"

"But you're innocent, Olof, you should be able to claim redress or something. I work for Sveriges Television, not as a journalist or anything, but I can talk to our reporters, I'm sure someone will want to take on your case."

"Quiet," he said, pressing the alarm button.

He remembered that it had always been this way. Ingela had to make the decisions: come here, Olof; go and fetch this, don't do that.

"But . . ."

His head was falling apart. He remembered too much. He saw himself following Lina, catching up with her and killing her in the forest, or was it down by the water? There were so many different images of it in his mind, yet she was also the one who pushed him, who knocked him to the ground before walking away. Shouting at him, disappearing among the trees, gone. His memories shattered. It didn't make sense. Olof didn't know what was right, because everything was wrong; no matter what he thought or believed, someone always told him it was wrong, that it hadn't happened like that.

"You have to go there," he said.

"Where?"

"To the pound. I don't want it to be there."

"I'm sorry, Olof, but I can't look after a dog, I live in an apartment and my daughter is allergic . . ."

An assistant nurse appeared, asked what he needed. The room felt cramped with so many people in it.

"It's lovely to see you've got a visitor," she said.

"I'm in pain," he told her. "I think I need more morphine."

The nurse smiled sweetly, the way they always did, and gave him two paracetamol. As though that were enough.

"Let's check your blood pressure, too."

Ingela got up. The train was probably leaving soon.

"I'll go down to the kiosk," she said. "I can get you an ice cream or something."

"OK."

His sister paused in the doorway.

"A cone," she said. "You used to like those, didn't you?"

There was someone sitting on the porch steps when Eira got home. The car headlights briefly illuminated his face, so fleeting that she could have been mistaken.

She climbed out of the car.

"Hey, Sis."

It really was him.

"So they let you go," she said.

"Cells were full," said Magnus, pulling a face that might have been a smile. Eira wanted to stroke his hair, let him rest his head in her lap.

"Is Mum asleep?" she asked.

"You were right," said Magnus. "She thought I still worked at the sawmill in Bollsta."

"That was fifteen years ago."

"I know."

Eira went inside to get something to drink. Magnus was already nursing a beer. She would force him to stay over, couldn't let him out on the road again.

She found a bottle of raspberry soda that had been in the pantry for an eternity. Alcohol was something she could drink in other people's company, not his.

"You missed the meeting with the support officer," said Eira, taking a seat beside him on the steps. From where they were sitting they could see the gravel driveway and the withered lilacs, the rhubarb that seemed to survive everything.

"Sorry," said Magnus. "I got held up."

Eira actually managed to laugh. "It's OK, I pushed it back to next week."

Magnus took the bottle from her and prized off the cap with his lighter, passed it back.

"They didn't think I was a flight risk," he said. "Guess that's another thing. And because I confessed. The lawyer thinks I'm looking at the minimum sentence for manslaughter."

"Six years."

"I'll be out after four if I behave."

Eira swatted away the blackflies. Sipped the sweet juice. Scratched a bite. If she left it to Magnus, they could easily sit there in silence all night, for another twenty-three years.

"So what really happened that evening?" she asked. "And don't just tell me what you told the police who interviewed you, about Lina not being there when you got to Lockne."

"You're police too."

"And a little brat no one tells anything."

"I need another beer."

Eira felt his hands on her shoulders when he returned, as though he wanted to give her a massage.

"You're not miked up or anything?"

"Come off it."

Magnus sat down beside her. Rolled the cold bottle across his forehead before opening it. The cap flew away, landing somewhere.

"I'll only say this once, and only to you," he said.

Now and never again.

That evening. When he rode his motorbike over to Lockne because he knew Lina would be meeting someone there.

"She saved my life," he said.

"What do you mean?"

"Can you just shut up for once and let me talk?"

Eira covered her mouth with her hand, she shut up.

"Lina told me they were meeting there, that she was going to run away with that guy, and I was just so fucking jealous." Magnus spoke without looking at Eira. They were both staring straight ahead, past each other. "I was going to take her back with me, either that or punch the guy, I didn't know what I was doing there. Maybe I just wanted to see them so I could finally get it into my thick head that it was over, really finished, that I'd lost her for good. But then I saw them inside. She was naked, and . . . Fuck, I thought he was raping her, there were all these chains and things."

Magnus had stormed in. Wanted to grab Lina, protect her, punch the guy in the face, but suddenly the guy was on top of him, he hadn't known his full name until recently, back then he was just Kenny, that was what Lina kept screaming, so loud that it echoed around the old forge; Kenny, who went completely crazy and got Magnus in a judo grip, slamming him down to the stone floor. Next thing he knew there was a chain around his throat, and everything went black.

When Magnus finally managed to breathe again, Kenny was lying flat out on top of him like a sandbag. There was blood everywhere. And Lina . . . Lina was standing there with an iron rod in her hand.

It was only once he pushed the body off him that he realized the guy was dead.

"Just lying there, staring straight into fucking nothingness."

"So it was her," said Eira. "It wasn't you."

"I told her I'd take the blame, but Lina refused. She started screaming at me, saying her life would be over if I snitched, that they'd send her away and lock her up. She was jumpy, obviously high on something, shouting that it was all my fault, that we'd both get locked up for years and that she'd rather kill herself."

Magnus sniffed and wiped his face with the sleeve of his sweatshirt. Eira couldn't quite tell in the dim light, but she thought he might be crying.

"It was true," he said. "She never would've survived. Lina wasn't the kind of person you could lock up, she always had seven different thoughts swirling round her head, at least half of them dark; I think she drank to get away from herself. Her parents tried to keep her in, but she'd climb out through the attic if she had to. And she was so good at playing all saintly, lying about what she got up to—they definitely didn't know she was having sex, and she wore long sleeves at home so they wouldn't see her tattoo."

"What tattoo?" Eira had read through the description of Lina again before she caught the train to Stockholm. "There was nothing about a tattoo in the missing-person report."

"No, exactly. It was her parents who gave the description, and there was a lot they didn't know. I was with her when she got it."

Magnus ran a hand over his own left arm. He had filled it with a number of classic designs at some point during his twenties, the kind sailors often had.

"A heart and a couple of birds. I convinced myself it was a symbol of me, of our love. What a fucking idiot."

He kept talking, returning to that night when they had struggled to drag the body down to the river from the forge, but Eira barely heard a word he said.

She saw the heart right in front of her, on a forearm, two birds flying up towards the crook of an arm. A waitress clearing cups from a table in a Stockholm café. She had been staring right at that very tattoo and hadn't realized a thing. The woman had been slightly too plump, her hair slightly too short; she hadn't believed that that was how Lina would have chosen to look. *Want me to pass on a message?* Eira had given the waitress her name, she must have understood—if not right there and then, then later, once she looked her up, realized whose sister the woman in the café was.

"I have to go to the toilet," she said, taking her phone inside with her.

As she peed, she searched for the woman who called herself Simone, but she was no longer there.

The profile was gone.

Magnus was sitting with his head in his hands when she came back out.

"I spent so long waiting for someone to find him, for the river level to drop, for his body to float to the surface. Every day when I woke up, I was ready for it."

"You shouldn't have confessed to something you didn't do," Eira told him.

"It was all my fault—I went there looking for trouble. I should've just let them go wherever the hell they wanted to go."

"You said he was raping her."

"That's what I thought, but Lina said she wanted it, to try some rougher stuff, I don't know. The whole thing was just such a fucking mess."

Lina had changed her clothes. She had taken them over there the day before, when they were planning their escape. Then she had driven away on the motorbike. Magnus rowed the boat down to Lunde, where they had met again. He found a few more things for her to wear, and emptied the kitty.

"Mum wasn't home," he said. "And you . . . I guess you were asleep."

Lina had then climbed back onto the motorcycle. Magnus pointed to the spot where it used to stand by the garage wall. He didn't know which way she was going, where she was heading. They had agreed that she would dump the motorbike after a couple of days.

Gone forever.

Without a trace.

"How could you keep quiet when they arrested Olof Hagström?" asked Eira. "You let a fourteen-year-old take the blame."

"He was all over her in the woods. Lina told me, after we'd dragged the guy down to the river and I was busy dumping planks and other junk on top of him, crying my eyes out; she told me she'd had a really shitty day."

Magnus got up. It felt like he was trying to look at Eira, but couldn't quite manage it.

"He was never convicted though, he went free. I spent that summer blind drunk, barely knew what was happening."

"Free?"

"He never should have confessed," said Magnus.

"No, the two of you should have confessed, you and Lina."

Eira saw that his face had hardened and knew she had found his limit.

"I've confessed now," said Magnus. "I'll do my time. I'm going to hate it, but at least I'll have done it."

"That doesn't help Olof Hagström."

"If you say a word about any of this," he said. "I'll confess to killing Lina, too."

"She's alive," said Eira.

"Maybe, maybe not. I tried to convince myself that she died that night too, so hard that I almost started believing it. It made it easier to lie."

"Don't you want to know where she is?"

"I want to believe that she found the freedom she was looking for, that she found somewhere she could be at peace."

Eira thought about the woman who called herself Simone, the hairbrush in the bag in her car. It was full of dark strands of hair that could hardly have come from Ivan Wendel's shaved head. Eira had stolen it from his bathroom when she asked to use the toilet. Grabbed a silk scarf from the hallway, too. She couldn't hand them in for DNA analysis right away, but maybe at some point in the future, once everything had calmed down.

If Lina Stavred's case ever came up again.

The truth was still clawing at her, but it slowly started to settle as she breathed deeply, like the wind dying down.

They sat in silence for at least half an hour as the clouds overhead parted and the moon peeped through.

"You should find someone," said Magnus. "Someone who's good for you."

"What does that have to do with anything?"

"It's just what I think."

Eira gazed out into the night, at the sky that was slowly growing brighter somewhere behind them, over the Gulf of Bothnia. For a split second she found herself thinking about August. She couldn't quite get a grip on his face, on how he looked.

"I tried," she said. "But it probably won't come to anything."

"Then he's an idiot," said her brother, flinching at the sound of a dog barking. Loud, somewhere close by.

"Shit," said Eira, leaping up. She had forgotten about the dog. It had been locked in her car for several hours, and bounded out as she opened the door.

"Rabble!" she shouted. "Come here!"

But the dog was off, bolting away. Eira walked over to the hedge, but she couldn't see him anywhere.

"Have you got yourself a dog?" asked Magnus.

"I'm just looking after Rabble for a while. It's Sven Hagström's dog, and Olof is still in hospital. They took Rabble to the pound, but his sister called me, said she couldn't take him herself . . ."

"I didn't even know you liked dogs."

Magnus whistled. A shadow by the neighboring property yapped and came lumbering over.

Eira grabbed the dog's collar.

"Someone had to look after him."

AUTHOR'S NOTE

This novel is a work of fiction, but as ever I have borrowed from reality. A similar incident to the gang rape in Jävredal took place in Vallsberget in Piteå, in the summer of 1985. The lenient sentences handed down in that case led to a furious debate and a change in the Swedish law. Likewise, the interviews with Olof Hagström were also inspired by real investigations in which, after long interrogations, children confessed to murders they didn't commit. In Arvika in 1998, for example, two brothers were believed to be guilty of killing a four-year-old, and in Hovsjö in 2001, a twelve-year-old was accused of killing his best friend. Similar "walk-throughs" were also conducted in the case of Thomas Quick. Years later, following journalists' scrutiny of the cases, each of the accused has been freed of all suspicion.

Almost twenty years ago, my family and I bought a house in the Ådalen, a place with views stretching for miles across rivers and distant mountains—and all for the price of a pokey little closet in Stockholm. My longing to write about this landscape, in both its lightness and its melancholy, has grown stronger and stronger, but I would never have dared do it alone. So, a warm thank-you to everyone from Ådalen who has answered my strange questions, driven me around when I didn't have the energy to cycle, shared stories and tales and checked local details: Ulla-Karin Hällström Sahlén and

Jan Sahlén, Mats De Vahl, Tony Naima, Hanna Sahlén, Åsa Bergdahl, and, not least, Fredrik Högberg—without you, I never would have found my way.

Another huge thanks to Veronica Andersson with the Violent Crimes Unit in Sundsvall and to the other officers in the region. To Per Bucht, cousin and former police investigator. To Zorah Linder Ben-Salah, my fount of knowledge in all things relating to skeletal remains in blue clay, and to Peter Rönnerfalk for his medical expertise: thank you.

Any mistakes or extravagances are, of course, my own.

My warmest thanks also go to those of you who were by my side during the writing process, making the whole thing much less lonely: Boel Forsell, for your discussions about storytelling and drama; Liza Marklund, Gith Haring, Anna Zettersten, and Malin Crépin, for your sharp eyes and for reading my words, developing both me and the text; and Göran Parkrud, for your conversations about the plot, the characters, and the psychology. I love that you always push me out into much deeper water.

My publishing house, Kristoffer Lind, Kajsa Willén, and everyone else at Lind & Co: it is a constant joy to work with you. Astri von Arbin Ahlander, Kaisa Palo, and the whole gang at Ahlander Agency, I'm so happy that you have taken on my books.

Astrid, Amelie, and Matilde, most important of all. Thank you for every minute you are around me, caring and supporting; for being the wonderful people you are.

—*Tove Alsterdal*